————

"Kyria Kilian?"

Kyria. Madame. They all call me Madame now. This time, it was Elyan Greek. The day before, it had been Hortensian German, and the day before that, Common English. *So many diplomatic discussions.* So much politeness. *Because I'm a diplomat.* Jani Moragh Kilian, ex-Service, ex-fugitive, ex-human. Somewhere atop some storied mountain, gods laughed.

Jani stood straighter, relaxed her hands, breathed through her mouth until she steadied, then returned to studying the portrait. There had been something—yes—a splash of dried blood in the lower right corner, barely visible against the russets and wine reds. A round splotch, nearly a perfect circle, as though someone had stood close and flicked a droplet from the end of their finger. Not elongated, like the spray that would result from a blow or the exit wound caused by a projectile weapon. *And you know this how, Kilian? Because you're such an expert?* Well, she had been called to crime scenes in the past, though not to examine the physical evidence. Her job had been more peripheral, to uncover the paper trail, the reason for the assault.

"Kyria?"

Take this...case, for example. Service Investigative Forensics had already scanned the room. The blood spatters had been imaged, their dimensions measured, the information entered into multiple databases. Algorithms had been run, likely angles of attack determined, the scenario mapped out. The exact spot where the victim had stood as the blows had rained down. Where he had fallen, then been hoisted to his feet and dragged from the room.

————

Echoes of War

Sixth Book in the Jani Kilian Chronicles

Kristine Smith

Copyrights & Credits

Contents

Chapter One

The shuttle faded in and out of view, shades of black and grey flitting across its surface as stealth shielding fought to adjust to the blowing sand and turbulent night sky, the occasional bright burst as Helios, the smaller of Elyas' two moons, peeked through tumbling clouds. Winter storm approaching. Soon there'd be lightning, thunder, and rain.

Pauly Nikos watched from the shelter of his carefully-constructed rock cave, and tried to squelch the fear that jabbed harder than the sharp stone through his thin coverall. A hundred meters of flat between him and the shuttle, twice that distance to the next outcropping large enough to hide him. No chance, if they detected him. He could run fast, but not that fast. He'd be a target in a shooting gallery. They'd pick him off easy as you please.

The fuck are they waiting for? The shuttle had landed more than a common hour before. Then it just sat there. If they were smugglers —and who the fuck else landed a shielded craft on the Karistos flat in the middle of the night—they were dumb. Their ground team should've been waiting for them with the goods ready to load. They should've been up in the air moments after landing. But now, the sand had time to crap things up, scratch the shuttle skin beyond its ability to repair itself, work its way throughout the body. Then the rain would finish the job, warping the shielding, contaminating the bioworks. First thing you learned when you lived in Karistos. Sand and water always found a way.

Pauly dug his handheld out of his slingbag and checked the time, cupping the device in his hands so the light from the display wouldn't bounce off the rocks and betray his hiding place. Yes, this had to happen tonight, didn't it? His best night in months. Four sandies, a hen and her three eggs. Even in the dark, the hen's feathers glistened, breaking what light there was into rainbow threads. The unborn chicks' down, fine as silk, was even more valuable. It would give the light movement, a back-and-forth shimmer like a living thing. Yes, this haul would make lots of pretties for the rich bitches. The Karistos jewelers could fake them, of course, but the real feathers from real birds cost more. Real always cost more.

He looked back out at the shuttle. If they spotted him, he'd wait until they grabbed him, offer them the feathers, hope that would be enough to buy him a break. He was small for fourteen—he could still pass for ten if he kept his voice from cracking. They might rough him up a little, but even smugglers drew the line at killing kids.

Usually.

He heard the skimmer before he saw it, that whispery whine as it struggled against the wind. A small two-seater, it ran dark, the safety illumins squelched and the cabin interior hidden from view by black-tinted windows. As it slowed in approach, the shuttle finally showed signs of activity. The underside loading bay door dropped down and two figures emerged. Men, judging from their heights and builds. They stopped at the end of the ramp and waited for the skimmer to draw alongside, the gullwing doors to open, the driver and passenger to emerge.

Then it all happened, so fast. One of the shuttle men raised a shooter, fired twice. The skimmer driver collapsed; the passenger staggered, then tried to get back inside the vehicle. But before they could pull the door shut, the killer and his partner closed the distance in a few strides, yanked the door open, dragged them out. Then came a shout, cut short by the shooter crack.

The shuttle men moved quickly now. They walked around to the skimmer boot, opened the hatch, hauled out what lay inside. A wrapped bundle, body-sized and shaped. As they worked, a third man emerged from the shuttle dragging a gurney. They lifted the bundle onto it, hefted the other bodies into the skimmer, then maneuvered both up the ramp and into the cargo bay. The door closed.

Seconds later, engines hummed as the shuttle accelerated, coursed over the flat, then rose into the air.

Pauly watched it until it vanished into the clouds, waited until he felt sure it wouldn't return. Then he gathered the hen, the eggs, his snares, and jammed everything into his bag. Rocks tore his coverall, sliced into his skin, as he struggled out of his tiny cave, then ran like hell.

Chapter Two

Jani Kilian studied the framed print. It was a static image, as were all the pictures that hung on the walls of the sparsely-furnished living room. A human female from an earlier time, straight of nose and full-lipped, flowing hair the same dark copper and gold as the embroidered garment she wore, eyes the same silver grey as the armor encasing her forearms, the sword she gripped with both hands.

Joan of Arc. Jani struggled to recall details, to focus her scattered thoughts. *Rosetti.* The name of the artist. *Pre-Raphaelite.* The style, or school, or whatever the hell Niall Pierce called it. *Oh, Niall, you and your redheads.*

She took a step back, and flinched as something crunched beneath her boot heel. One of the glass shards that lay scattered across the carpet, the shattered remains of a whiskey decanter. She swallowed hard—the liquor stink still hung in the air, filled her nose, roiled her stomach. Her skin tingled, a sensation sharp as pinpricks. A few heartbeats passed before she realized she had clenched her fists.

"Kyria Kilian?"

Kyria. Madame. They all call me Madame now. This time, it was Elyan Greek. The day before, it had been Hortensian German, and the day before that, Common English. *So many diplomatic discussions.* So much politeness. *Because I'm a diplomat.* Jani Moragh Kilian, ex-Service, ex-fugitive, ex-human. Somewhere atop some storied mountain, gods laughed.

Jani stood straighter, relaxed her hands, breathed through her mouth until she steadied, then returned to studying the portrait. There had been something—yes—a splash of dried blood in the lower right corner, barely visible against the russets and wine reds. A round splotch, nearly a perfect circle, as though someone had stood close and flicked a droplet from the end of their finger. Not elongated, like the spray that would result from a blow or the exit wound caused by a projectile weapon. *And you know this how, Kilian? Because you're such an expert?* Well, she had been called to crime scenes in the past, though not to examine the physical evidence. Her job had been more peripheral, to uncover the paper trail, the reason for the assault.

"Kyria?"

Take this...case, for example. Service Investigative Forensics had already scanned the room. The blood spatters had been imaged, their dimensions measured, the information entered into multiple databases. Algorithms had been run, likely angles of attack determined, the scenario mapped out. The exact spot where the victim had stood as the blows had rained down. Where he had fallen, then been hoisted to his feet and dragged from the room.

"*Ná Kièrshia.*"

Jani blinked. "Pathenrau." She turned. "Your accent. Are you from Phillipa?"

The woman who stood in the middle of the room stared at her, then shook her head as though emerging from a daze. "If I were, what has that to do with this investigation?" Beech, her name tag read. A tall blonde, fully human, kitted out in Fort Karistos base casual tan trousers and short-sleeve shirt. The oak leaves on her collar signified

Major. The Service Investigative Bureau patches adorning her sleeves guaranteed trouble.

"Just curious. Not used to hearing that dip at the end of words. Most of the idomeni living near Karistos are Vynshà or Sìah. The Pathenrau stick closer to Shèrá since they became the ruling sect." Jani inhaled, then exhaled slowly. "I'm sorry."

"Are you sure you don't want me to summon a doctor?" Beech hesitated, then stepped closer. "There are several specialists at the base who have experience with your condition."

Jani looked down at her hands, the fingers so spindly, dark brown skin tinged with gold. *My condition.* As though she suffered from some disease. "Not necessary."

"If your old Service augmentation—"

"Not anymore." Jani tapped the side of her head. "That was rendered nonoperational some time ago. Hybrid neurotransmitters are just different enough." She smoothed a hand over the front of her overrobe. The silken cloth felt cool, the sand shade calming to the eye —she pondered the nubby weave for a few long seconds before looking up. "I'm still adjusting to physical changes. It's the idomeni reaction to stress, apparently. All fight, not much flight." She snorted. "Explains a lot."

Beech nodded, eventually. "Well, if we could return to the matter at hand?"

"Of course."

"When was the last time you spoke with Colonel Pierce?"

Jani sorted the words as she formulated her response. *Spoke with, not saw.* Because they knew about the weekly lunches, the occasional opera or play. Now they wanted to confirm whatever comport messages they had intercepted over the last few weeks. "Yesterday." She let her gaze drift around the room, from the glass strewn across the carpet to the overturned lounge chair, the couch with its dislodged cushions, the books tumbled from their shelves. The far corner, where two Service Forensics technicians stood huddled over their handhelds, their muttered conversation a whispery rise and fall.

"He confirmed our opera date for next week." She wondered whether they would miss that performance, or the one after that, then pushed the thought from her mind.

"That's all?"

As if you don't know. "Yes."

"You discussed nothing else?"

"He asked if I would still be able to attend. I said yes. He cut the comm."

"Seems a bit terse."

"We said what needed to be said."

Now came Beech's turn to look about the room. "You never discussed politics?"

"During that call, no. Sometimes, in general terms, yes. But did we discuss specifics? No."

"You never discussed, say, last week's riot—"

"It was an orderly demonstration until—"

"—in Karistos' main agora. Your hybrids caused a great deal of damage to several floors of Government Hall."

"My hybrids kept the situation from boiling over when Service Security fired tear gas into the crowd." Jani's breathing quickened as sense memory flooded back. The eye-searing burn of lachrymator and the head-splitting squeal of the emergency sirens. "Your latest batch of recruits came direct from Earth. They've no experience with human colonials, much less hybrids, and their response towards peaceful demonstration is...rigid." More words teetered on the brink of speech, so many more words, but she bit them back.

Beech entered notes into her handheld. "Did you express your displeasure to Colonel Pierce?"

"I didn't have to. He's colony-born, same as I. We've dealt with Earthbound rigidity before."

"I must remember to relay your comments to Base Command."

"They're more tempered than the ones I've already delivered personally."

Beech frowned, as though the fact that Jani could go over her head bothered her. "When was the last time you visited Colonel Pierce in this apartment?"

She states his name each time. Because they were being recorded even now. *She was supposed to inform of me that.* Maybe she assumed an ex-Service officer would know. *Or maybe she's hoping I'd forget.* "That's a matter of base record. Check the visitor's log for this building."

"This is an off-base residence. We don't monitor—"

"Yes, you do."

Beech sighed. "Humor me, Kyria."

"Last week. Wednesday."

"Planet day or Common calendar."

"Planet day." Jani walked to the nearest bookcase, one of four in the room, and the only one that hadn't been capsized. "I returned a book." She stepped over and around the strewn volumes, most made of paper, a few bound in rare leather.

"Which one?"

"The Annotated 'King Lear.'" Jani pointed to a dark green book that lay splayed on the floor. "Niall wanted me to be up to speed for the Capitol touring company performance next month." She looked back at Beech. "I assume everything's been scanned?" She waited until the woman nodded, then picked up the book. She closed it and set it on a shelf, then turned to find Beech regarding her coolly.

"I wondered what you'd be like." The woman shut down her handheld and tucked it into the holster on her belt. "The ghost of Knevçet Shèràa."

Jani rubbed her hands together as the skin prickling returned. "Is that what they're calling me now?"

"It fits. You came in the night. You killed a lot of people." Beech shrugged. "Well, idomeni. Then you vanished for so long." A curve of lip, a smile in a technical sense only. "And now, here you are."

Jani took in the examining look she had been subjected to so many times. As always, it moved from head to toe, assessing her height, her attenuated limbs, a neck just a little too long.

Then, finally, it settled on her eyes, sclera the palest green of old glass, shattered jade irises too large by half. Eyes given her long ago by someone with the best of intentions, a real-life example of that old saying about the road to Hell. *You don't like me, Major—I get that. First I was a traitor to the Service, then the Commonwealth, and finally the human race.* "And now, here I am."

Beech nodded, then gestured toward Jani's overrobe. "Didn't you used to have red bands on your sleeves?"

"Those denote a propitiator. An idomeni priest. I'm no longer training for that vocation."

"Bombed out, huh?"

Jani forced a smile. *She's baiting you, Kilian. Don't lose your temper. It's what she wants.* She counted to three, turned her back, and walked to Niall's desk, an island of old ebony in the corner farthest from the entry. Another book rested there, one of the volumes of Proust's *In Search of Lost Time*, perfectly centered in the middle of the old-fashioned brown blotter pad, a tiny speck of order amid the tumble.

Volume Five. Jani glanced at the cover, then away, Beech's gaze still resting like a weight. *The Prisoner.* She imagined Niall taking the book from its shelf and setting it in place before going to the center of the room to meet his visitors, one last message before whatever happened, happened. *Dammit.* She drummed her fingers on the desktop, then flicked the book cover open and closed once, then again. *Nothing.* No note scribbled in haste, or slip of paper tucked between the pages. *It happened too fast.* She shivered and blamed the chill of the room, as ever at war with her heat-craving hybrid system.

"Ná Kièrshia?" Beech made a show of studying her timepiece. "I just have a few more questions—"

"Major?" A SIB corporal who had been assigned to keep away the curious entered the flat, a hand hovering over her shooter holster. "We have a situation."

Shit. Jani followed Beech into the corridor just as voices sounded from the direction of the main entrance. Human for the most part, but here and there smatterings of *idomeni* languages—

—including a familiar Vynshà rumble that caused her to quicken her pace. She rounded the corner hard on Beech's heels and was treated to the sight of a quartet of Haárin males looming over a pair of Spacers First Class. The young men were on the short side and slight of build, the tops of their heads barely reaching the Haárins' shoulders. Like the corporal, they'd set their hands too close to their sidearms for comfort, their voices rising in pitch as the idomeni pressed closer, forcing them to backpedal.

"Tanz?" Beech stopped a few paces away from the burgeoning diplomatic incident.

One of the SFCs turned. "They just barged—" He stopped, took a deep breath. "They disabled the cordon field and entered the lobby and I explained that this was the site of an ongoing investigation and therefore off-limits and he—" He pointed to the tallest Haárin, a golden-skinned edifice clothed in flowing shirt and trousers in eye-watering shades of yellow and green. "—he replied that such was not his concern."

Said tallest Haárin, who answered to Dathim Naré when he was in the mood, had stilled and now stood, arms folded, gaze fixed on the wall opposite.

"Ní Dathim Naré is a security suborn of the Thalassan enclave." Jani caught Dathim's attention, then raised her left hand and made a flicking motion with her fingers, a Low Vynshà gesture that meant *slow down.* Dathim being Dathim, he might have chosen that moment to pretend ignorance of his born language, but to her relief, he simply stepped back, and gestured for his companions to do the same.

"We are here to escort ná Kièrshia." Instead of the usual idomeni rises and falls, Dathim's voice held level calmness. "Ná Feyó Tal, secular dominant of all Elyan Haárin, would speak with her."

"Ná Kièrshia is free to go, of course." Beech curved her left arm upward at waist-level, a gesture that signified acquiescence in a number of idomeni languages, both bornsect and Haárin. She followed with a tight smile that betrayed her irritation, then nodded toward Jani. "We will contact you if we have more questions."

Jani felt the major's gaze drill a hole between her shoulder blades as she followed Dathim and his cohort out a secondary exit and onto the narrow side street. Her heart quickened when she saw the size of the crowd that had gathered in the short time since her arrival. Several hundred at least—they filled the walkways, the street and the entries to businesses, and stared out from street-level windows and second floor balconies. Humans, mostly, residents of the working class neighborhood that bordered the off-base housing complex, taller Haárin scattered among them like adults herding restive children.

Voices rose when they spotted Jani and the rest, a mash of Elyan Greek, Vynshà Haárin, numerous other languages human and idomeni. As the crowd pressed closer, Dathim and the others surrounded Jani and shepherded her to the white double-length skimmer that hovered curbside—as they drew close, the rear passenger gullwing swept up. Dathim pushed Jani inside, then piled in after her along with two of his suborns as the third clambered over the divider and onto the seat next to the driver, who met Jani's eye in his rearview mirror and shook his head, white-blond hair flashing back the sunlight that filtered through the tinted security glass.

"This was dumb." Lucien Pascal muttered in his native Provincial French. "We're too exposed. We should've used the building's underground garage."

Jani struggled with her overrobe, which had twisted around her like bandaging. "It was closed off. Beech said Forensics still needed to scan it."

"Bullshit." Lucien edged the vehicle away from the curb, then stopped when a human teenaged male pounded the hood with his fists. Others followed suit, Haárin and human both, striking with their fists or slapping with open palms. The skimmer shuddered under the blows, then rocked back and forth as the crowd pressed close enough to nudge it to the middle of the street. Once there, they pushed the vehicle out ahead of them and stood back, as though they released a toy boat upon the water.

"I don't like it when they do that." Lucien's knuckles whitened as he clenched the steering wheel. "You should tell Feyó to order them to stop."

"The humans won't listen to her, so the Haárin will just start doing it again anyway." Jani waited until they cleared their informal escort and rounded the corner, then sagged back into her seat. "It's a sign of support."

"It's loud enough to mask shooter fire."

"This vehicle is proofed against small arms." Dathim sat ramrod straight, hands on knees, the top of his head grazing the cabin canopy. "It is of explosive devices you should worry, ní Lucien."

"Thank you, ní Dathim," Lucien grumbled under his breath, the off-and-on infatuation he nursed for the Haárin male apparently set in *off* mode.

Jani waited for a few silent moments to pass. "You had people in the crowd."

Lucien nodded, eventually. "Yes."

"Snipers on the rooftops. Sniffers and drones in the air."

"One sniper." Lucien's knuckles paled once more. "Pierce supplemented with his own people. He had a fully-staffed command center. The latest equipment. All that vanished when the Service pulled him off your security detail. I do what I can on my own, but I've got fewer personnel and less gear and Feyó denies all my requests for additional support."

"You can only do so much, you know." Jani stared at Lucien in the mirror until he met her eye. "I recall a professional once telling me that if someone really wants to get you, there's nothing you can do to stop them." Given that Lucien had been the professional in question, that earned her a glare of her very own.

She massaged the knot that had formed at the base of her neck. Fiddled with cuffs and hems. Then she felt the press of a stare, and looked up to find Dathim regarding her, gold eyes dull and corners of his mouth downturned, an expression as close to sadness as she had ever seen. "What?"

"Ní Tsecha once said what you say now. A season later, idomeni killed him as humans kill those they fear. In secret, from a distance." Dathim hesitated. His relationship with Tsecha had been contentious at times, but the loss of his dominant had shaken him, exposing a vein of gloomy reflection at odds with his usual brashness . "Humanish are most as idomeni, as we are most as you. The blending he foretold is an afterthought. We have always been most the same."

Unsettled quiet fell. Jani turned to the window, squinting as the reflection of the Elyan sun off the white buildings overpowered the window filters. "What does ná Feyó want to talk to me about?" *As if I don't know.*

"She did not tell me," Dathim replied, eventually.

You've learned how to lie, ní Dathim. Human and idomeni really are the same. Jani closed her eyes as the first throbs of a headache came to call, kept them closed even as recent memories replayed before her mind's eye. Tumbled furniture. A blood-spattered painting. A book, centered with care on an old-fashioned blotter, bearing a message only she would understand.

A conversation, one she and Niall had weeks earlier.

———

They had met for lunch at a new place near the agora that served a cuisine called Haárin fusion, a South Asian-Vynshà mélange which, to Jani's surprise, challenged the heat tolerance of even her hybridized palate. While she ate, Niall picked at a less combustible curry, drank water instead of his usual ale, spent long minutes staring out the window at the bustling marketplace scene beyond.

"I see faces," he said, finally. "In the street. At the theater. In meetings. From my past." He pushed away his plate, dug his nicstick case out of his shirt pocket, removed a glossy brown cylinder. "Scared the hell out of a poor woman last week. Followed her halfway across the base, into the archives building and the lift. Could've sworn we'd spent a teenaged summer boosting skimmer boards back on Victoria." He cracked the ignition tip against the edge of the table, waited for the red glow, then took a deep drag and released the smoke with a sigh.

Jani noted Niall's narrow, wolfish visage, the tanned skin dull and lined by fatigue, then checked his hands, the ragged quicks flecked with blood, and wondered when he had started biting his nails. "I gather this did not prove the case?"

Niall managed a smile, the scar that scored the left side of his face from his nose to the corner of his mouth curving upward to reveal the tip of a jagged canine. "Earth native. Elyas was her first ever colonial posting." Another pull. A stream of smoke. "Do you ever think, with all the shit you've done in your life, that something might come back to bite you?"

"It crosses my mind. Current threats concern me more, though. The deteriorating situation between Shèrá and Chicago, with us stuck in the middle. The fear that Chicago is trying to provoke a fight, and that they might just succeed." Jani pushed food around her plate as thoughts of brewing conflicts blunted her appetite. "Besides, given the life expectancy of the average low-level smuggler, I'm guessing most all the ones I tangled with are dead."

"We're still around."

"We reformed."

That earned another smile. "Yeah. Quite the model citizens, you and I."

Further attempts at conversation fizzled. Then came Niall's mumbled apology and hurried exit. Jani worried, of course—Niall Pierce gone quiet had never been a good sign—but she had grown used to his moods over the four or so years they'd known one another, his habit of feeding her the story in bits and pieces. She knew he would tell her what concerned him eventually, given a little prodding. But every time she hinted, he changed the subject.

And now he was gone.

Chapter Three

Ná Feyó Tal, secular dominant of the Elyan Haárin, sat at her worktable and perused Jani's latest report. Like a historian examining an ancient tome, she took hold of the barest edges of pages and turned them slowly as though they were aged parchment that might crumble and not idomeni-made paper that would still look fresh off the roller a thousand years hence.

Niall's description of the female dropped into Jani's head. *Painted by El Greco.* Feyó was tall, willowy, with a long, sad face, her pale gold skin smooth and unblemished despite her having reached the idomeni equivalent of late middle age. Like most Haárin, she wore her state of outcast proudly, forsaking the braided fringe of a breeding adult for a human-style waistfall of grey-streaked brown hair bound with thin cord. Today she had added earrings, short curves of silver studded with roughly-carved grey stones that bore an eerie resemblance to her cracked-glass eyes.

Jani sat across from her, perched on the edge of her seat. She did so more from necessity than nerves—the chair rocked and threatened to tip each time she moved. It was higher than Feyó's, in accordance with idomeni custom, and wobbly, forcing her to keep one foot on the floor at all times to avoid toppling over. She had seen one of Feyó's suborns carry it into the office as she waited in the anteroom, which confirmed her long-held suspicion that it had been built just for her.

I feel so special. She concentrated on the calming view through the floor-to-ceiling window. An unseasonably cool early summer had delayed the usual algae bloom, which meant the Bay of Siros appeared a deep sun-dappled blue. Lovely enough, though not as striking as the fabled amethyst that drew tourists from across the Commonwealth. *Less itchy, though.* Stunning as the color was, swimmers learned to their dismay that the underlying cause exuded a nasty skin irritant.

Speaking of irritants. Jani buried every outward sign of impatience. The current slow reading was purely for show—Feyó had already studied the report as well as the numerous follow-up analyses provided by her departmental suborns. She simply wanted to give the impression that she had not yet read it, that any communication from the hybrid enclave of Thalassa merited but a few minutes of time better spent elsewhere. Like too many idomeni dominants, she had studied humanish mannerisms and adopted the most aggravating.

I will not fidget. Jani tried to settle herself by focusing on one of the wall hangings, a woven study of tree bark that at first appeared innocuous. But upon closer examination, some of the darker whorls and patches reminded her too much of dried blood, so she resumed studying the bay. Counted the minutes she had so far been kept waiting, and pondered the odds that Niall had not yet passed through at least one GateWay but could still be imprisoned somewhere on Elyas. *I will not scream.*

Then she heard the scrape of a chair across tile, and looked up to find Feyó had pushed back from her worktable and now sat, hands folded atop the bare polished wood, and gazed in her general direction. *There had been a time when she met my eye.* But that time was long past.

"Ní Genta Res. What is he?" Feyó asked in Sìah Haárin, her born language and the official tongue of the Elyan enclave.

See pages 3, 14, and 20. "Ní Genta Res was among the first Haárin to settle in the enclave on Whalen's Planet, and he has been a member of the NorthPort Trade Board for almost twenty Common years." Jani hoped like hell that her Sìah would prove up to the task. It was close enough to Vynshà that she could usually manage, but there were differences and they mattered. "His experience in human-ish-idomeni commerce would be most helpful and is greatly to be wished."

"You have spoken with him."

"I knew him when I lived in NorthPort." Jani tried to parse her next words, but the idomeni languages didn't lend themselves to pars-ing. "I communicated with him during my time in the south, in Mete-ora, and my investigation into the smuggling operations based there."

Feyó met Jani's gaze for the barest moment. "A time spent without my sanction or the approval of the Karistos Trade Board."

Jani counted to three. Swallowed hard. "At that time such was not needed. Thalassa was its own entity. I was free to go where I needed to go and speak with whom I needed to speak." *The good old days.* Before Aden nìRau Wuntoi, Chief Oligarch of the Shèráin worldskein, ordered Jani and Feyó to work together more closely, a directive Feyó took to mean that Jani had become her suborn and thus subject to her authority. Efforts to clarify the situation had met with silence from Shèrá, which meant Wuntoi either approved or couldn't be bothered to object.

One minute passed. Another. Waiting for the underling to fill the silence—yet another of the human tactics Feyó had adopted. When it became obvious that wouldn't happen, she slowly clenched her left hand into a fist. Not as much an indication of anger as rounded shoul-ders, but headed in that direction. "Genta is Vynshà, is he not?"

Yup. Right there on page 3. Jani raised her left hand and nodded once in affirmation. "Yes, ná Feyó."

"We need no more Vynshà here." Feyó flicked a finger in the direction of Jani's report. "What else?"

Where do I bloody start? Jani held back in time, and fixed on the patterned tile floor. *Count slowly...one...* Then her inner protocol cop gave her a kick and reminded her of idomeni sightline etiquette—she jerked upright and focused on a point above Feyó's head in formal recognition of the female's dominance. "If I may, ná Feyó?" She waited until she saw the slight nod out of the corner of her eye. "Haárin enjoy the freedom they have gained from doing business with humanish, but when it comes to the concept of payment, many haven't moved past the idomeni barter system. The dock owners and traders are building up Commonwealth currency reserves they don't know what to do with, and the financial sharks smell blood." She caught the tilt of Feyó's head, a posture that signaled puzzlement. "Commonwealth financial dominants would trick them. They would pretend to help them so that they could steal their money."

"Humanish being humanish." Feyó slashed the air with her right hand, another gesture that edged into anger without quite crossing the line.

A reflexive protest sprang to Jani's lips, then stalled because really, what could she say? She gestured acceptance of the point, then paused for a beat before resuming. "I would like to go to Samvasta. Because of the huge influx of Vynshà over the last Common year, it is by far the largest Haárin colony and therefore the most vulnerable. I could speak to the Trade Board dominants, discuss ways to move forward to address this issue."

"Let our trade dominants speak to them." Feyó sat back, hands tented, fingers so long and spindly they looked like they had extra knuckles. "I most believe you should not travel for a time."

Jani sat back as well. Folded her hands in her lap. *You didn't expect her to agree, did you?* Still, she had to try. "I would like to at least see if the rumors are true that they are developing a hybrid scanpack." She reached into her belt holster and removed her own palm-sized device, the black poly case faded and scuffed from over twenty years' use. "My unit's fully human brain functions erratically at best and will only become worse as I continue to hybridize. It recognizes my touch only half the time. The hybrid trace compounds in my sweat and skin confuse it. Unless we develop a functional prototype soon, we will be unable to compose our own documents, and our systems will fall prey to rampant fraud and abuse." She quieted, and waited as Feyó continued to regard her, fingertips pressed to her chin. *Blank face. Stick to the script.* Give Feyó enough but no more. *Keep your secrets, Kilian. Forget you have secrets at all.*

After a few moments, Feyó bared her teeth. "You learned of this rumor from ní Genta. He contacted you and together you made plans to meet. Without permission. For no other reason than your need to see." Another finger flick, this one directed at Jani's scanpack. "You will use that which you have until it no longer functions. Such is the godly sanction for being that which you are."

Jani sat up straighter and raised her chin, a posture of acceptance. Bit the inside of her cheek to keep from smiling. Lucien had told her months before that Feyó monitored Thalassa's communications. Insults were a small price to pay for the chance to use it against her. *There's your bone, Feyó. Gnaw away.* Let the female believe she had learned all the secrets.

Feyó continued to watch her, then lowered her hands. "I wondered why there were so many messages from humanish dominants when I arrived this morning. Governor Markos. The Service liaison. The Deputy Exterior Minister. Before they spoke to me of Colonel Pierce, they asked if I knew where you were." The tenses, the modifying words, Feyó's posture, gestures, and voice, all grew more formal, her grey gaze sharp and hard as metal. "Markos, he told me of the colonel. Of his actions in the years before the war and during the war itself. He said that an event such as this was not to be unexpected."

Jani said nothing. Idomeni history was one of serial civil warfare; triumph in such conflicts was how the winning sect ascended to the status of *rau* and cemented its claim to power until their turn came to be challenged. But for the last twenty years, when an idomeni spoke of *the war*, they meant the most recent. The War of Vynshàrau

Ascension. The first in which humans became involved. The war that changed everything.

And yes, Niall Pierce had been very, very involved.

Do you ever think, with all the shit you've done in your life...

"What did Major—" Feyó tapped her fingers on the edge of the table. "—Beech. Major Beech. What did she want of you?"

Jani gestured uncertainty. "I believe she sought to learn whether Colonel Pierce and I spoke of matters possibly related to his disappearance."

"She asked you of the Elyan secessionist groups?"

"She didn't get the chance, and I didn't volunteer." Jani had already run through the roster of names in her head, human mostly but here and there the odd Haárin, a list that grew longer with each passing month. "There are three that are organized and well-equipped enough to manage a kidnapping of this magnitude. Colonel Pierce made it easier by choosing to live off-base."

"Why did he do so?"

Damned if I know. Jani had tried to talk Niall out of it, but he had been adamant. "He's a colonial himself. He told me he preferred living in a working class neighborhood, surrounded by people like those he grew up with."

"So he could learn their thoughts, their loyalties." Feyó's voice deepened. One more step closer to the line. "The secret ways of humanish." Another glance in Jani's direction. Lower this time, acknowledgement stripped of any regard. "I have lodged a protest with Service Base Command. There are protocols in place for such as this. Beech should not have summoned you." A pause. "And you should not have obeyed."

Jani thumbed through her usual list of excuses and justifications, then decided that given Feyó's mood, simple truth would be the best choice. "I wanted to see what happened."

"Yes, you always want to see." Feyó rose and walked to the window. "Such is why you traveled to Meteora. Why you wish to travel to Samvasta. So you can see." She pressed a hand to the glass and stared out at the bay. "NìRau Tsecha told me so much of you." Like Jani, she referred to Tsecha by his former bornsect title despite his status as Haárin. "He said you are the Kièrshia, the bringer of pain and change. That you will do that which you will do, that which you must." Her fingers curled, formed a fist. "But the fate of a humanish, a Service dominant, is not our pain to suffer. We have more than enough of our own."

Jani felt a shiver of idomeni-grade rage, and bit back a sharp protest. *Not now, dammit. Breathe.* "Niall Pierce is my friend."

"NìRau Tsecha was my friend." Feyó's voice fell nearly to a whisper, speech stripped of all gesture. "When I thought humanish killed him, I wished death upon them. When I learned that his own Vynshàrau had killed him, I wished much the same. I would have destroyed them, as we destroyed all in the past who blasphemed. Thus is godly order restored. Thus is godly order maintained." She hung her head and rounded her shoulders, outward signs of anger that grew even as her voice remained calm. "But order never can be restored now, because the Vynshà who killed nìRau Tsecha now live on Samvasta. Such was the decision you made for idomeni. Without sanction. Without right."

Jani's shoulders hunched. Her neck crackled as she struggled to regain her respectful posture, to sit up straight. At every meeting, despite the planned agenda, Feyó managed to turn the discussion to Tsecha's assassination and all that followed. "Two idomeni killed nìRau Tsecha, the one who ordered his killing and the one who carried it out. The rest were innocent."

Feyó turned, pale gold skin darkened, eyes wide and bright. "Do you believe, and truly, that on the night of Vynshàrau Ascension, nìRau Tsecha did not take up a blessed blade against the Laum? You, who studied with him? Who claimed him as friend? Do you believe that he asked them if they had conspired with humanish or not, or followed the dominants who did so, before he struck them down? Do you believe that he cared for the difference?" Her hands clenched, again and again, as though grasping for a weapon she could not reach.

"No. He honored the gods on that night. He honored Caith and Shiou, chaos and the return to order."

Jani raked through her memories for some rebuttal, some defense of her old teacher, her friend. But instead she felt her heart pound as memories flooded. Her run through the streets and alleys of the idomeni capital. The shouts and screams. The smoke and blood. The sight of Vynshàrau, some so young they needed two hands to raise their blades, striking down adult Laum who knelt to receive godly judgment. *You know the truth, Kilian. No point lying to yourself about the dead.* "I believe that at that time, he did that which he did. I believe that now, in this time, in this case, he would have seen and understood the difference."

"Do you?" Feyó's voice sharpened. "You would have convinced him?"

"I could convince him of nothing. He considered, and he chose to change his mind or not."

Brittle silence fell. Then Feyó stepped away from the window. "Hansen Wyle. He died on his way to a meeting. A meeting to bargain you away from the physicians who made you that which you are now."

Jani tensed. Feyó had never mentioned her late friend before. "A meeting he was to attend at nìRau Tsecha's request."

"Wyle died on his way to that meeting. Because of you. NìRau Tsecha strayed from his path because of you both. After Wyle died, he returned to it for a time." Feyó inscribed a symbol in the air, a protective charm. "But then he heard the mutters of demons. That you had survived the crash. That you lived. Such gave him hope, and hope made him reckless." Her voice deepened so that she sounded hoarse. "You should have died at Knevçet Shèràa. If you had, nìRau Tsecha would have remained on a godly path. He would have been made Haárin eventually, yes, because he was that which he was and such was his way. But he would have survived. Instead, he went to live with you and your hybrids. And there he died."

Jani struggled to draw breath. *I always knew she hated me.* But knowing something unspoken felt nothing like hearing the actual words. She exhaled slowly, then started to raise her right hand in question. "Ná Feyó—"

Feyó chopped the air with her left hand, a sharp gesture of denial. "No, ná Kièrshia, you will not speak now. And you will not go to Samvasta to *see*. You will not talk to NorthPort Vynshà. You will not labor to blend the godly ways of idomeni with the chaos of humanish. You have brought enough disorder, enough pain and change. You will return to Thalassa and you will remain there until I summon you again. You will maintain what little order you have." She turned back to the window. "We have finished here."

As if on cue, the entry door opened and one of Feyó's numerous clerical suborns stepped inside. "You are needed, ná Feyó, and quickly."

The male spoke so rapidly that Jani could barely understand him. A meeting with an agriculture committee, the members of which were very upset about...something. She stood, gestured farewell to Feyó's back, and started toward the door.

Then she paused. "If I had died at Knevçet Sheràa, little would have changed. John Shroud would have continued his hybridization experiments and nìRau Tsecha would have spoken of the blending as he had for years before Hansen Wyle and I arrived at the Academy. Before he had met us or even knew our names. To deny such is to deny that which he had always been and which he was until the day the assassin's weapon claimed him. He was not a youngish who could be led by the hand and it is an insult to his memory that you maintain such."

Feyó turned. This time, she met Jani's eye. "You dare—"

"Yes." Jani waited, shock giving way to fury, the blood fizzing under her skin as though ants crawled. Now would be the time. For Feyó to offer challenge. For her to accept. For the disorder of humanish and the order of idomeni to meet once again in the circle and declare themselves with blades and blood. *Not a good idea,* the human in her whispered. *Hybrids and Haárin who esteem Feyó won't understand and others will use it as a weapon.* The bornsects who sought to challenge Pathenrau for leadership of the worldskein. Humans who sought to sow discord for reasons of their own.

But instead, Feyó broke eye contact and gripped her left shoulder with her right hand, a posture of profound sadness. "He would not wish it." Her voice emerged soft and flat as a human's as she uttered the answer to the question she had not asked, the offer she had not made.

Jani forced herself to breathe, to calm. So many things she wanted to say. That she didn't want to fight. That her hybrids needed support. That there were problems developing for hybrids and Haárin that threatened their very existence. But the charge in the air, like the quiet before a storm, stopped her. "Glories of the day to you, ná Feyó." Weighty silence fell as she walked to the door, replaced by hurried discussion as the panel slid closed behind her. She caught only a single word in Low Sìah, an exhalation that sounded at first like a sigh. *Hálè.*

Follow.

Chapter Four

Jani left the building through the Haárin passage, where Dathim and one of his suborns stood waiting under the wary supervision of three members of Feyó's security staff. The pair bracketed her on the way to the skimmer, but this time Dathim herded her into the front passenger seat, lowered the gullwing, then joined his team in the back.

Lucien raised the privacy barrier, then pulled out onto the street—the skimmer shuddered as it connected with the traffic guidance track. He held up a finger for Jani to wait, then tapped out a pattern on the lighted dash. Another more gentle shaking followed, a sign that the vehicle had disconnected from the Karistos grid and that the interior was now secure. "Well?"

Jani tucked her hands in her sleeves and rubbed her goosepimpled arms. Lucien got to adjust the cabin environment to his liking since he did all the driving, one of the myriad ways they dealt with their differing physical natures. Unfortunately, his preferred temperature bordered on the idomeni definition of subarctic. "I should've died at Knevçet Shèràa. If I had, Tsecha would still be alive."

"She's still beating that drum?" Lucien's gaze alternated between the street activity and the dashboard sensors.

"She inferred it before. This is the first time she came out and said it. I didn't think it would feel worse, but I was wrong." Jani looked out the window at the passing weekday parade. "Beech had no right to summon me, and I shouldn't have gone. Markos and others called her to ask if she knew where I was. I don't know if that means they think I was involved or might know who is."

"Any questions about...shipments?"

"None."

"Really?"

"She wouldn't hold back if she suspected we were working on the hybrid 'pack. That's the last thing she wants me to have." Jani patted her balky device as though she comforted an aging pet. "She would shut us down. Send security suborns to strip the labs. We're lucky most of the research materials can be classified as medical and those needs are pretty wide-ranging. Nothing Theo and his group are working on will raise alarms."

"The decoy move worked? She is monitoring our comms?"

"Yeah, it worked. No jaunt to Samvasta to meet with ní Genta Res. I'm to go back to Thalassa and stay there."

"So she thinks she thwarted you. Odds are she won't look any further, at least for a little while. You gave up what you could afford to lose. She thinks she won." Lucien tapped a decisive drum roll on the wheel. "Breathing room."

Jani nodded, then shivered and rubbed her arms again. "Breathing room."

Lucien glanced at her sidelong, then adjusted a control on the steering column to raise the temperature. "They didn't tag you with anything. I scanned you as soon as you exited the building. You're clean."

"And they wouldn't bother anyway, because they'd know that's the first thing you'd check." Jani pointed towards the sky. "We're still being tracked." She sagged into her seat and flexed her neck. Not even noon yet, and already the tightening, the ache. "What have you heard?"

Lucien muttered under his breath as more pedestrians spilled onto the street. "General buzz is that no suspect ships docked at Elyas Station around the time Pierce disappeared. That means shit. A snatch this big, they'd have their people in place to set up the forged paperwork and phony flight plans and wave them through." He eased along until they came to an intersection. Then he turned hard to the left, cutting across the oncoming lanes and earning a warning blare from a truck laden with prefabricated vendor booths. "God, I hate Market Day."

Jani waited until he zipped up the side street and down a series of alleys. Multi-story buildings gave way to single-story houses, ordered streets to a tangle of lanes barely wide enough for their skimmer. "Even phony paperwork leaves a trail. I'm betting they used one of the private docks that no one admits exists."

"Private means Family."

"Not always. If a shipping company is strapped enough, they'll set aside a slip or two and look the other way."

"The former smuggler speaks from experience?" Lucien smiled.

Jani sighed. "You take far too much pleasure in bringing up my checkered past."

"You should know by now that it's one of the things I like most about you." Lucien exited the residential section, crossed the last road that led into Karistos, then guided the skimmer down the rocky slope to the bay. "One of Beech's crew let slip that Pierce was seen entering his building a little before twenty-three-up Common time yesterday. A neighbor said he heard noises less than an hour later. Thumps, like things falling on the floor."

"Books." Jani thought back to the single orderly spot in the room, like the eye of a storm. "I found one on his desk, centered on the blotter. The title was *The Prisoner*."

"Not much help, is it?"

"I think it means he's alive. That they weren't taking him somewhere to kill him."

Lucien pondered the point for a moment, then gave a nodding shrug that didn't appear as positive as one might wish. "Given the time the SIB arrived at the flat, that means whoever took him has had at least a six-hour head start. That's enough time to punch through the nearest GateWay and who knows where they're headed after that? The J-Loop? Pearl Way?"

"Any chance at all that he's still in Karistos?"

"What do you think?"

After a beat, Jani shook her head. As the vehicle glided over the top of the water, she checked her passenger side mirror and watched Karistos recede. *So many tall buildings.* In a city that not so long ago had consisted of scatterings of one-story cubes. The population of the Elyan capital had more than tripled in the two Common years since her arrival, with more emigres streaming in every day. Even Elyas' more isolated mountain settlements had grown. *So many strangers.* And more than a few of them up to no good. "Niall did tell me he felt breath on his neck." She fielded Lucien's puzzled look. "We had lunch a couple of weeks ago. He thought something from his past had caught up to him."

"He had good reason to be paranoid." Lucien opened the skimmer canopy, taking care to raise the vehicle high enough to avoid the spray. "His pre-war Service record makes for damned interesting reading and it doesn't even touch on what he got up to before his forced enlistment."

"But that was all over twenty years ago. Why come after him now?"

"You know the answer to that as well as I do. When it comes to the bad stuff, people have long memories."

Jani considered arguing. But despite Lucien's deficiencies with respect to the gentler aspects of human nature, he did possess a keen understanding of its dark side. *And I don't?* She'd seen it more than once during her years on the run, an act of revenge exacted with patience and planning of a military campaign. *Plant the seed, grow the tree, cut it down, make the weapons.* Instead of replying, she breathed in the warm air as it buffeted her face and soothed her tense muscles.

Then she remembered how much Niall loved the scenery she savored now, the bay and the sheer cliffs fringed with red strands of vine-like grass. The first view of Thalassa, bright white houses with their multicolor tiled roofs, sticking out from the cliff faces like dice pressed into clay. The Main House, glass-walled upper floors emerging from the rock like a vast ice-ship. As it all washed over her, fear for her friend sank its teeth and this time logic and reasoning and orders from above failed to lessen its hold.

Lucien, as usual, read her thoughts. "He's the Admiral-General's Colonel. You're what you are. You wouldn't be doing him any favors if you got involved." He stared at the side of her face. "The way things are now, Chicago versus Shèrá and colonies still muttering about secession and Thalassa in the middle of it all? His loyalty comes into question, best that happens is Mako squelches an enquiry and forces him to resign his commission. The worst? He has an accident and nobody saw a thing." When Jani refused to meet his eye, he rapped the steering wheel. "It's not doing you any good, either. You can't just take anyone as a friend anymore."

"What about you?" Jani forced herself to meet the gaze that reflected the engineered damage done to its owner, deep, rich brown that promised warmth but never quite lost its chill. Face of a fallen angel. Tall, rangy frame with just the right amount of muscle. A background in intelligence and surveillance. *Among other things.* "You're the only fully human at Thalassa and you head my security."

"I'm not Service anymore." Lucien closed the skimmer canopy as they skirted the Thalassa shoreline and began the slow float up the winding road that led into the settlement. "I'm not dancing around a Commonwealth loyalty oath every time I talk to you."

"Niall and I have a list of topics to avoid and we stick to it."

"Appearances matter and you know it."

Before Jani could respond, their ascent grew steeper. She gripped the edge of her seat as the vehicle tipped back, the gut-clenching incline combining with ruts and gaps in the skimtrack to make for an acrophobe's nightmare of a climb.

"Why don't they fix this?" Lucien struggled to level the vehicle, which shuddered uncomfortably close to the edge. "They have the equipment. You signed off on the damned invoice."

Jani glanced to her left in time to see waves crash onto the jagged rocks that lined the shore. "Keeps out the less-determined curiosity seekers."

"Then there's the concept of guardrails." After a short battle, Lucien forced the skimmer level.

"Refer to my previous statement." Jani relaxed as the vehicle's shuddering eased. The road widened, and the first houses came into view. "I want to go to the main warehouse."

Lucien huffed. "What are they going to tell you?"

"It borders the flat. If Niall was moved off-world, someone may have seen something." Jani straightened her overrobe, smoothing the wrinkles caused by the safety harness. "Any updates about—"

"The new guy?" Lucien's voice emerged rough. A warning growl. "Nothing since Dieter's update last week during which he stated that he had pushed his friend in Service Archives as far as he dared and my update two days ago that my connection in Records declined my last three calls. If you remember, this was followed by a discussion—"

"I remember."

"—about delegating. We're outsiders on various watch lists and if we push too hard we risk losing what inroads we have. You either trust us to do our jobs or you don't."

"I do." Jani removed her scanpack from its case and massaged away a smudge on the age-clouded case. "I just wish this worked properly.

"So you could do what? Run the background checks of every new arrival? That's not your job."

"I stand corrected." Jani watched the scenery for a few moments.

"François Roland, Master Sergeant Commonwealth Service last stationed on Amsun. Received a medical discharge three months ago after it became apparent during a routine physical that he had begun the hybridization process. A few scrapes. One Article 13. Beginning, middle, and end of story." She tucked her scanpack back into its case. "I used to know everyone's name without having to dig it out of a weekly update.

"That was always going to change." Lucien turned onto a level interior street, then slowed to a walking pace as Thalassans stepped out of their homes to wave or rap the skimmer hood in greeting. "And I know the main reason you want to go to the warehouse has nothing to do with Niall's disappearance."

"It's just a feeling." Jani forced a smile for her welcoming committee, but the expression faded as they left them behind and their vehicle approached a trio of linked single-story buildings located at the far end of a dusty track. As they drew closer, a Haárin male standing in one of the entries ducked inside and closed the door. "The work we're doing is too important. We can't afford to mess up." As soon as the skimmer slowed to a stop, she opened her gullwing and exited. By the time Lucien, Dathim, and the others caught up, she had already keyed in and entered the first building.

Chapter Five

The cool, still air made Jani shiver. This was the general storage wing of the warehouse, rows of open shelves that reached to the lighted ceiling filled with bins holding the various materials and components needed to keep Thalassa functioning. Foodstuffs and the more specialized medical and research supplies and equipment were stored in the interior of the building, in secured cages and controlled-environment chambers.

They stood at the far end of the main aisle, the group that organized the warehouse, filled the orders, inventoried the contents. A handful of Haárin documents technicians and a dozen or so hybrid operators, all clad in coveralls, a few with protective headgear. They looked at her the same way every warehouse worker and shipping clerk had looked at her since her Service days, gazes moving from her face to the leather holster that hung from her belt and the scanpack contained therein.

Once a documents examiner, always a documents examiner. For all the good it would do me. Jani could take it out for show if necessary. She could evaluate a relatively simple document, possibly. But the risk of a misfire was better than even, and if certain individuals in this crew knew her vaunted device malfunctioned, whatever brakes existed on their extracurricular activities would be gone. *Not that they're models of good behavior now.* She caught the odd movement of hand to belt or shoulder pocket wherein comlinks resided, signals to those busy burying things in the stacks to get a move on because *Mummy is here.* She forced a smile and raised her hands, palms facing out. "I just want to ask a few questions."

"About what?" A hulking figure shouldered out of the back row shadows to the front of the group. François Roland, the new warehouse dominant. On paper, he had seemed a perfect fit for the position.

On paper. Jani often wondered what he had gotten himself up to prior to his illness. Amsun Base had a reputation as a *loose ship*, and given the lack of strict Service form that often prevailed on colonial bases, that was saying something. She assumed garden-variety smuggling with some racketeering on the side. Not the reputation you would want to bring home to meet the family, but not the worst experience to have when trying to wrangle goods from a Commonwealth that would prefer you didn't exist. "Did anyone hear or see anything unusual overnight or this morning. Along the shore? Out on the flat?"

"No more than usual." Roland folded his arms, planted his feet wide apart. Like most who had hybridized when older, he'd retained his human body shape, squat and wide. A low form wall that blocked any outsider. "Chased off some town kids poaching sandies. Pilot lizard tripped a border alarm." Behind him, his crew remained still, silent, watchful.

"No skimmers?"

"No."

"No craft of any kind?"

"No." Roland sniffed. "Ná Kièrshia."

"Nothing on the security scans?"

"No scans. Relay malfunctioned." Roland jerked his chin towards Lucien, who stood off to one side. "We told him."

Jani forced herself to not look at her security chief, to make it seem as though she simply confirmed what he had already told her. *Why didn't you tell me, Lucien?* She counted to three, then fixed again on Roland. "What model is that unit? Eamon DeVries had the initial system installed during Thalassa's construction. Serkiss-April, designed for desert conditions."

"One of the kids swiped that relay a few months ago. We think for parts."

"Replaced with?"

A pause. "Pellikan."

Jani pretended fascination with the ceiling, then with the floor at her feet. "Pellikan is a Victorian company. They specialize in components that function in tropical conditions." One of the older ploys in a long list. Install parts guaranteed to malfunction and then pretend surprise when they do just that. Meanwhile, half the known universe wanders in and out at will. "Serkiss-April is a Karistos-based company. We can just skim across the bay and pick up what we need."

"We had the Pellikan parts in stock—"

"No, you didn't. They're not on our vendor list." Jani took one step toward the equipment-stocked shelves, then another, and felt the ramp-up in tension like an influx of chilled air. "So who did you buy them from? The Tovash group? Xeno? Brethren?" She rattled off the names from her past, names she'd hoped to never hear again.

Then she paused. Swore under her breath. "Please tell me you're not dealing with Morwenna." The sea of blank looks she received in reply told her all she needed to know. "She has Family and Cabinet Row connections. It's a known fact that when circumstances warrant, she informs NUVA-SCAN about her buyers in exchange for access to slips at Commonwealth stations and no questions asked. If you bought anything from her, Chicago knows all about it."

"Let Chicago raid us," one of the female Haárin piped. "We know how to hide what needs hiding."

"Who told you Chicago could raid us? They do that, it's an illegal incursion into an Haárin protected area and diplomatic heads explode." Jani waited. "No, they would inform Governor Markos of their findings and he would ask ná Feyó Tal what's going on and her security team would pay us a visit." She watched as gazes drifted in Roland's direction, pretty much as expected.

"We know why you're really here." Roland raised his voice to drown out the scattered mutterings. "You're searching for your Service friend who's disappeared. Why do you care so much for him, ná Kièrshia?"

All the stares now moved to Jani—she felt them like a weight. *Because he would do the same for me.* But that brand of loyalty didn't seem to be worth much anymore. "Because Service Investigative called me in because they think we're involved. Because some of you here took part in the upset at Guv Hall last week—"

"So you're checking up on us now?" came a voice from the back.

"No, ComPol is. I hear about it the same way I hear about altogether too many things lately. From people in Karistos with designators on their collars."

"They don't like us." One of the newer hybrids, a young woman named Eva, piped. "You know that, right?"

Jani shook her head. "No, I don't know that. Just this morning, the reception I received after leaving my meeting with Service Investigative was pretty much the opposite of 'don't like.'" She shoved her hands in her pockets and wandered along the shelves, stopping ever so often to check labels. "I do know that the individual who drew you into that fight last week was not Karistosian and could not be found for follow-up questioning. We're a handy group to blame and there are those who would be happy to shovel it our way." With every step she took towards the rear of the warehouse, she felt the charge in the air grow.

"What's back there that you don't want me to see?" Jani held up a hand to silence the imaginary replies. "Let me guess. They started you small. Handheld weapons. A few long shooters. A lot of nasty things happen on the flat, they said. It's just self-protection." She leaned against a rack and met the gazes, some of which turned away.

"Things will be quiet for a while, then something else will happen to one or more of you in Karistos and it will be bad. And then you'll get the offer for bigger and better. Next thing you know, we're an arsenal." She felt the rage build, heard the shudder in her voice, and bulled ahead anyway. "And things here will never be the same."

She sensed Lucien's approach, heard his muttered multilingual pleas to *steady on*. Looked to the warehouse crew, who stepped back as one when she met their eyes. "I grew up in a place like that. I watched it happen in real time. My father beaten for not going along. My mother's business destroyed just for the hell of it. They're only nice to start. But their protection has a price, and it's everything." Her eyes stung. Her fists clenched. *"Is that what you want?"*

Breathe. She drew up tall. Remained silent until the slow pound of her heart lessened. "I know how much you hate to tell me things, but I would greatly appreciate if from now on you follow procedures and let me know who in hell you want to buy from and what they're selling, because odds are that I know them and how far they can be trusted. *Kalá?*" The switch from Commonwealth English to the Elyan Greek *okay* made a few of the natives jump. A beat later, a few replies reached her, barest whispers of acquiescence. She nodded in acknowledgment, then headed for the exit. Her legs felt weightless, her step too rapid, as though she had just stepped off a moving walkway. *Adrenaline.* Damn. She had been angrier than she realized.

The Elyan sun hit her full-face as soon as she stepped outside, the warmth of a calming hand. She walked to the skimmer, then waited for Lucien to catch up. Some time passed before she realized he had yet to join her. She looked back, and found him standing halfway between her and the warehouse, well beyond her reach.

"Back in Chicago, right before I came here, I attended a challenge as an honored witness. Two of the embassy Haárin, friends of Dathim. I think it was over Tsecha. One of his writings." Lucien looked not at her, but at the ground at his feet. He toed a rock, then bent and picked it up. "One of the challengers was female. Dark, like you. And so angry. Her shoulders—" He hunched for a moment, then straightened. "The judges, referees, whatever the hell you call them, had to stop the bout several times and warn her. I knew they'd have to end it before declaration was made because otherwise she would kill her opponent, and they did. I could tell from the look on her face. She wasn't going to stop." He tossed the rock into nearby scrub. "You reminded me of her, in there."

"You don't think I can control myself?"

"Maybe you can, now." Lucien brushed sandy grit from his hands. "But I'm not looking forward to the day when I need to drag you off some poor bastard."

Jani did a quick self-assessment. She could feel the ground on which she stood. Her heart had quieted. "If the situation arises, I'll try to refrain." She inserted herself into the skimmer cabin.

"I'm just saying." Lucien waited for Dathim and his cohort to board, then lowered the gullwings and activated the vehicle.

Jani watched the rocky scenery slip past. "Why didn't you tell me about the security scans?"

"Because, micromanager of the year, we're still trying to figure out what happened and why. When I had answers, I would've told you." Lucien quieted as he steered around a pile of fallen rocks and maneuvered uphill, then relaxed as the road leveled off and the Main House came into view. "Right now, it looks like simple failure. Sand got in through a crack in the primary relay housing because it's the bloody flat and the sand gets into everything."

"Or someone sabotaged it."

Lucien drummed his fingers on the steering wheel. "You sure it's Morwenna the warehouse bought from? You always said that most of the smugglers you dealt with are dead."

"There's a lot of churn at the scrub level, which was where I worked. The idiots and careless get weeded out. The survivors rise up the ranks and tend to hang around. She was one of them."

"You survived. Why didn't you move up?"

"My physical changes had become harder to hide. I had to move around a lot." Jani rubbed her eye, thought back to the time when such a simple act would've led to a split film and the risk of discovery. "By the time the Service pulled me in, my time was running out." She buried her face in her hands. "Almost three years here, no problems. But these last few months..." She slumped back. "Get Roland out of there. He's going to get us into an absolute mess."

"He spends a lot of time at the clinic. There's something screwy about his hybridization. I overheard a couple of the techs talking about it." Lucien rolled his eyes in reply to Jani's unspoken comment. "We've talked about this. If either the Service or one of the ministries had developed a hybrid spy program, I'd have heard about it."

Jani shrugged. "Seems obvious to me."

"It certainly adds new meaning to the term 'deep cover.'" After a beat, Lucien shook his head. "They'd have a helluva time recruiting. It's not like you can become human again after you get pulled back in. The process isn't reversible."

"Did the Service explain everything to you about your augmentation? No, they just did it and you had no choice because you'd passed the screening and it was an order." Jani focused on the Main House as it loomed into view, like a massive vessel easing into its dock. "Reassign Roland. Stick him somewhere he can't order anything. Cancel his access codes and accounts." She watched a pair of hybrids females pick flowers from roadside planters and load them into baskets. *Lunchtime.* Each table would have a centerpiece, and the scents would fill the air. "I tell them we're part of the Elyan Haárin enclave and they will take us in if anything happens. But I'm not sure it's true. Maybe if I left—"

Lucien looked up from his examination of dashboard scans. "What?"

"Maybe if I left, Feyó would be satisfied. John might come back, bring his people. Dieter's a born administrator, he could—"

"If you left, this place would fall apart." Lucien steered up the last incline. "You were the first. From all I overhear, it means a lot."

Does it? Jani fought back a sense she hadn't experienced in years. That something brewed. That soon, she'd need to run.

Chapter Six

Discussion faded as they pulled into the tiled parking circle outside the Main House. The visible portion of the four-story building, which housed meeting areas and living quarters, had been walled with reflective glass that currently flashed back scenes of the bay and seemingly endless sky. The business half, which contained laboratories, medical facilities, basements and subbasements housing siloed data and communications hubs, lay hidden within the cliff, built from materials designed to withstand quakes.

Couldn't survive a shatterbox hit, though. Jani gave herself a mental kick. *Lighten up, dammit.* She squelched thoughts of bombs by concentrating on the images that Dathim and his crew of tilemasters had set into the updated parking circle. Flocks of sandies with their rainbow feathers. Desert flowers bright against rock and scrub. She avoided stepping on the mosaic flora and fauna, her occasional sideways hop eliciting an arched brow from Lucien, who preceded her to the double-wide entry and held it open for her.

"After you, Skippy." He followed her inside, then left her to talk to two of his staff stationed nearby.

Jani leaned against the wall, inhaled warm air scented by the flowering plants and trees that encircled the central courtyard, and felt the disquiet ease just a little. In one corner, a trio of Haárin youngish played some complicated game that looked like a cross between checkers and jacks. At scattered tables and couches, Haárin and hybrids sat working or taking meal breaks. Above, they gathered in the open stairwells and landings that coiled upwards to the glass ceiling, calling out greetings from one side of the cavernous space to the other, laughing, chatting.

So normal. Jani wandered deeper into the courtyard and spotted a table of new arrivals, four human hybrids and one Haárin, receiving their orientation instruction. When Lucien joined her, she pointed to the gathering. "So, who don't I know?"

Lucien pointed to a dark-haired, twentyish pair. "Mark and Belinda, brother and sister from Guernsey. The older woman is Marta, from Felix. The man is Lucas, another virus survivor from Amsun. Roland sponsored him."

"Keep an eye on him. No warehouse."

"Done." Lucien nodded toward the Haárin, a male with the blackened bronze skin of Pathenrau, the current ruling idomeni sect. "Ní Lano Qes. He said Wuntoi is cracking down on his Haárin. More combat training. Behavior restrictions. The Oà threat has grown more serious and talk of war is common."

"That explains Shèrá shutting down supply lines to Samvasta. They're conserving resources." Jani watched the male look around the courtyard, head high and back rigid, right hand cupped in question bordering on confusion. *Don't worry, ní Lano. You'll be all right.*

"Their background checks are completed. I will send them along forthwith." Lucien tossed an 'in a minute' nod to one of staffers, then drew close to Jani and lowered his voice. "How much of this edge is due to your worry about Pierce?"

"He's not my worry, remember?"

"Uh-huh." Lucien turned to leave, then paused. "I'm sorry."

Jani watched him pull something from his pocket, a vend token or old coin, and work it between his fingers. She had known him for over four years, interacted with him in most every way possible. He'd thrown her a fair number of emotional curveballs in that time, but sympathy had never been one of them. "Are you feeling all right?"

Lucien exhaled in a rush. "I know he's your friend and you care about your friends." He stuffed the coin back in his pocket. "Forget it."

"Lucien." Jani waited until he looked at her. "Thank you." She struggled to find the right words, knew that the flippancy they usually tossed at one another wouldn't do at a time like this. "I'm not used to commiseration from you is all."

"I'll try to keep it under control." Lucien made as if to say more, then hurried out without another word.

Jani stared at the spot where he'd stood. *He can't really feel sorry about anything—they engineered that out of him.* How many times had he told her that he couldn't love, that emotional give and take was a language he could imitate to a point but never truly comprehend? *Don't do this to me, not now.* When her handheld dinged, she gave silent thanks for the interruption until she saw the face form and sharpen in the display. "Theo, I could really use some good news right now."

"Sorry, boss." Theo Simonides, who headed one of the research teams that operated outside Feyó's detection limit, started to say more, then stopped and covered his mouth to stifle a yawn. His narrow face proved a study in exhaustion. Hazel eyes dulled by fatigue and undercut by dark circles. Pale gold skin dull and slack. "Sixty-two percent of the organoids failed within twenty-four Common hours."

Jani rocked her head back and forth. "That means thirty-eight percent are continuing to develop, right?"

"For the moment." Theo scrubbed a hand through his black hair. "Thousands of samples, all dross for the incinerator." He slumped back in his chair. "I didn't think growing a hybrid brain would be this difficult."

Jani probed under her sleeve and fingered one of the tiny scabs that dotted her arms and torso, the sites where Theo had extracted adipose stem cells. Then she reached behind her neck and felt along her hairline until she found a much older scar. A tiny bump at the base of her skull, courtesy of a Service Medical cannula. "Maybe you need to start with brain cells instead of stem cells."

"We don't have the proper equipment to sample you in that way." Theo took a deep breath. "We're also running low on growth media and analytical supplies. They're specialized. We won't be able to hide them from Feyó's watchdogs for much longer. They'll figure out what we're doing."

"We can continue to bury it all under agricultural and clinical if we code it properly. Let me do some digging." Jani was just about to sign off when she glanced at Theo's face and saw the set mouth and narrowed eyes that had become all too familiar of late. "How many?"

"Three more. Two were general tech staff—rough losses, but not irreplaceable. But Li Song was our top therapeutician. She treated the problem cases."

"John Shroud is still headhunting?" Jani tried to analyze Theo's slow, careful nod. "Have you been approached?"

Theo looked down at his hands. "Yes."

Jani took a deep breath of her own. "You know, if you feel that moving on is in the best interest of your career—"

Theo's head shot up. "I had to flee my home in the night. You took me in when no one else would. When I opted to hybridize, my own family tried to—" He quieted, looked away, blinked rapidly for a few moments, then settled back into his usual businesslike mien. "I'm not going anywhere."

Jani said nothing, only nodded. She would never forget Theo's case. He had arranged for hybridization after contracting a particularly deadly virus. But his parents filed suit to countermand his decision. At first, they claimed the effects of his illness had rendered him unable to act in his own best interest. But as the case wended its way through the courts, the truth emerged from the depths.

We would rather see our son dead...

Jani forced a smile. "Keep me posted. Let me know if you need any more bits and pieces of me." As soon as Theo's face faded, she found a quiet corner and an empty lounge chair in which to sit.

Dammit, John. Couldn't you take it out on me and leave everyone else out of it? She spent a few minutes gathering her thoughts, then took up her handheld and made ready to activate another contact code when she heard footsteps. She looked up from the screen, and shook her head. "Rudo. Telepathic as always. I was just about to call you."

"I am on my way to a meeting at Government Hall. I am hopeful that by the time it ends, we will no longer have to pay Commonwealth surcharges on our Elyas Station dock leases." Rudo Sikara, the head of Thalassa's legal department, set down his brief bag and sat across from her, back straight, hands resting lightly on his knees. Slim and slight of build, dark of skin and eye, he wore his usual black daysuit and white shirt, the only shot of color his neckpiece. Today's choice was paisley in purple and green, bright yet soothing, like a spray of flowers. "I heard about Niall. I wanted to see how you were doing."

And to make sure I hadn't gone off after him. Jani adjusted a control in the chair arm, activating a privacy shield that enveloped them both. "Feyó's already laid down the law. He's not my problem."

"But he is your friend and I am aware of your compulsions. You are the body in motion that tends to remain in motion." As always, Rudo spoke softly but firmly, legal advice presented in a fatherly wrapping. "But now is the time for you to remain still. You would do him more harm than good if you went after him."

"Lucien said pretty much the same thing."

"In matters of Service and Family machinations, Lucien is wise beyond his years. You could worse than listen to him. Much worse." Rudo sat back, elbows set on the arms of his chair, hands folded in his lap. "What else is bothering you?"

"What makes you think there's something else?"

"You have that look on your face." Rudo sighed. "What has John done now?"

Jani started to protest, then realized it was pointless. Rudo, unfortunately, knew the situation all too well. "He's still poaching our medical staff."

"Not a surprise. He feels you stole his company."

"I stole nothing. I kept Chicago from taking it over. It gave you room to negotiate a better deal. A more equitable split. It was still his to run."

"But it became a Thalassan holding. His control is no longer absolute. You know that would matter to him." Rudo brushed a nonexistent blemish from his trouser leg. "You're each of you expert at injuring the other, even when the pain isn't the point. You knew John's weakness was his company. He knows yours is this place." His gaze drifted around the sitting area, then overhead to the upper floors, the glass roof that allowed a view of the sky, blue tinged with the barest hint of purple. "We are still in the process of sorting out what we are and what we can and cannot do. That portion of Neoclona that is now under Thalassan control is no longer subject to Commonwealth law regarding noncompete agreements and industrial espionage."

"So we have no recourse?"

"Given that, as you just stated, the company is his to run, one could argue that he is simply shifting personnel as he sees fit. You may feel that he is attempting to cripple your medical research capabilities, but intent in these matters is very difficult to prove." Rudo shrugged. "Also, there is the minor detail that no court exists that could hear the case."

"We're making all this up as we go."

"Yes, we are. And of late, much of my focus has been on advising those who are defending Commonwealth citizens who are being impeded in their wish to hybridize."

"Yes. And that is most appreciated."

"I wish it wasn't necessary." Rudo held up one hand, the first hints of gold shading the near blue-black. "I too have felt the sting of rejection." His own decision to hybridize rather than live with a progressive neurodegenerative disease had cost him his marriage, his Commonwealth law license, and a career built over half a century. "You and John are capable of working this out between you. The fact that neither of you is willing to make the first move is a comparatively minor consideration given all the other issues we currently face."

Jani hugged herself. "In other words, grow up and figure something out."

Rudo smiled. "I would never be that blunt. That's your style." He stood, hefted his brief bag, turned to leave, then paused. "Given Niall's past, is what happened really a surprise?"

"You are the third person in the last two hours to say that."

"Perhaps you should call that a sign."

"I would call it damned convenient."

"Your mind is churning." Rudo's brow furrowed. "We are in a delicate place here. You know this even more so than I. Holding back is not your way—I understand this. But you're now in a position where hard choices are the norm. Trust me when I tell you that it will never get easier."

"Is this your idea of a pep talk?"

"You always asked for the facts. That's one of the reasons I appreciate working with you." Rudo rested his hand on Jani's shoulder. "What is it that all those tiresome football announcers always say? Eye on the ball?" A quick pat and a nod and he departed, a dark-clad knife amid the colors and the brilliance of the day.

Jani watched him go, deactivated the privacy shield, debated lunch as her stomach gurgled. Eating had become a chore more than a pleasure of late. Being almost twenty years farther down the path than every other hybrid in existence meant she stood alone, a race of one, unable to fit in comfortably with any of the other Thalassan cohorts. Even their spiciest foods tasted like nothing, while most Haárin offerings still proved too strongly flavored.

Maybe that fusion restaurant in Karistos delivers. But that would remind her of Niall, the look on his face and the fear in his eyes. She had resigned herself to a trip to the kitchens to see what she could scrape together when her handheld dinged. She glanced at the caller code and immediately reset the privacy shield, her heart thudding. "Dieter."

Dieter Brondt's round face filled the small screen like a worried moon. He paused to rub his eyes, their startling yellow-green muted by the harsh station lighting. "How are you holding up?"

"Trying to stay busy, keep from jumping out of my skin." Jani sat back and let her suborn's concern wrap her like a warm blanket. Sympathy from him, she understood. "So?"

Dieter's hands flicked across his touchboard. "At least a hundred long-range ships have arrived and departed over the last eight hours."

"What about the scavengers?" The docks that took any business, usually paid for in untraceable credit chits or stolen goods.

"Unusually quiet, which may mean nothing or something, depending." Dieter slumped back in his chair, the ergoworks buzzing like a swarm of bees to compensate. "I've tapped all my usual sources, up here at the station and on the ground. They're all...let's say they're taken aback. Kidnapping a Service officer, especially Pierce, the Admiral-General's right hand? It's just not—" He glanced off to the side, then leaned closer and lowered his voice. "The Service is setting up monitoring loci and throttling unnecessary communications. This channel is secure, but it may not be for long. They're looking for him, Jan."

"Or they're making sure he's well away."

"You have your reasons to think that, I suppose." Dieter again glanced to one side, and frowned. "I'm detecting interference. I need to sign off." He had undone his tunic collar, and his usually neat hair looked as though he had combed it with his fingers. "I'll keep a weather eye out. But Service is on it, and their reach is a hella farther than ours. They're already way ahead of us. If they can't find him..." He made as if to say more, then signed off with a silent shrug.

Jani watched his face fade. Whether the Service had in fact

launched a search, covered their tracks, or simply went through the motions, their infiltration of Elyas Station would staunch all information flow in and out. *I'll be cut off from everything.* Whatever diplomatic pull Thalassa possessed rested in Feyó's hands. Only she could request a progress report on the search. *Which she would never do.* And even if she did, the Service's first question would be why the Elyan Haárin wanted to know.

Jani drummed her fingers on the arm of her chair. Another time, another place, she'd be out the door, sending out feelers and pulling in markers until she wrangled transport to Elyas Station. Once there, she'd suss out the situation, play it by ear. *Just like the good old days.* One leap into the unknown at a time.

The flash of her handheld display shook her aware, the steady red beat of the incoming message illumin. Dieter, with one last update before the door slammed shut? Or one of her key informants?

She activated the display. The messaging account, carefully anonymized and stripped of all formatting, should have shown plain text only. But each letter of this three-word message showed as a different font and color, some throbbing while others whirled like wheels against a background of sparkling stars.

A scavenger hunt!

"Dammit." Just a junk message that had somehow managed to evade Lucien's filters. Jani reached for the purge key, then stopped as the pulsating banner vanished.

For a moment, a blank, black display. Then came a grouping of six numbers and letters. A space. Four symbols. Another space. Another alphanumeric grouping, this one with ten characters. A pause.

A second line, different numbers, letters, symbols, but the same pattern.

A third.

A fourth.

Jani squinted, blinked. Then her gut clenched. Encodes. Old ones, that only a few documents examiners would know. She and

Hansen and Dolly and the others. The first dexxies, who had learned all about paper from the idomeni, then developed the systems used by the Commonwealth to this day.

Again, the display blanked. Then came words, in plain text this time, the requisite, Lucien-approved green-on-black that one only saw on the oldest, most stripped-down systems.

> *If you want to see him again alive, Two of Six.*
> *Find the paper. Better be quick.*
> *Tell no one—abide by that vow.*
> *You have three days Common starting now.*

The screen blanked a third time. Jani stared, heart pounding, waited for...what? More encodes? Another taunt? When minutes passed with no further message, she dug out a stylus and a scrap of parchment from the recesses of her overrobe and scribbled the strings, hand shaking so from nerves that she had to more than once cross out characters so illegible that not even she could read them.

When she finished, she slumped back. Every instinct honed over her years in hiding screamed for her to run even as she realized that would be the worst thing she could do. She had three days to find old paper. Old *Commonwealth* paper. The logical place to start would be the nearest Registry archive. *But I don't have clearance anymore.*

Once again, Niall's words drifted through her head, spoken in a Victorian twang rendered dull and uncertain by fear.

Do you ever think, with all the shit you've done in your life, that something might come back to bite you?

"Yeah." Jani pushed a hand through her hair, dug fingertips into a scalp gone tight. "But not this."

Chapter Seven

Niall Pierce opened eyes hot and grainy as the Karistos sands. Blackness greeted him—he felt the soft pressure of blindspecs pressing against his temples, the bridge of his nose. Nasty things. Zapped your eyes if you tried to take them off, turned the innards into scrambled eggs.

Well, we've gone and fucked ourselves good and proper, haven't we, boyo? He peeled his tongue from the roof of his mouth, took a deep, steadying breath, then pulled out the mental checklist and started ticking off.

Cot. I'm lying on a cot. He ran his hands up and down the rough polycloth, felt seams and edging, and knew the thing had been cobbled together from old framing and a piece of tarpaulin, hand-stretched and hand-sealed. He inhaled, and caught the faint tang of sweat mixed with stale damp and hints of metal and plastic. *Not a ship.* He detected the slightest difference in the taste of the air. *Orbiting station.* And a poor one at that. If a secessionist group held him, that was to be expected. If this were one of the former smuggler buddies he feared most, the equipment would've been top-notch.

Only the best for the gangs. To prove they could afford it, that they were successful.

Memories of a hardscrabble youth flooded back, all thanks to the touch of scavenged cloth. *Not a Service brig, then.* Which meant Roshi hadn't been arrested and imprisoned, or worse. Not the likeliest possibility of all the ones he and his A-G had discussed over the last months, but one that needed to be considered.

Something's going on, Roshi. I'm digging, putting out feelers, but I keep hitting walls.

I'm not getting anything here, Niall.

It feels like the old days.

Then Roshi had followed up with the usual questions. How had he been feeling? Had he been dreaming again? *At least he didn't ask about my drinking.* That would've hurt.

Niall shifted, wincing as various damaged parts of him cramped and complained.

Then his stomach flipped and saliva flooded and he barely got his head over the side in time.

"Yes, the sedative you were given does have that effect, I'm afraid." A voice, rendered anonymous and tinny by tonal filtering, oily with fake sympathy. "Perhaps you'd like a shot or two of Scotland's finest to wash out the taste?"

Niall flopped back on the cot, wiped his mouth with his sleeve, choked down the acid that seared the back of his throat. The very thought of liquor—it sickened him. *Not so far gone, then.* He worried sometimes. That he'd wind up a captive of the bottle like so many others he had known. Fuck up beyond Roshi's ability to shield him and drink his pension until his demons came to claim him. *Jani'd get the call.* He had named her next of kin months before. *Did I tell her?* He couldn't remember. *Least of your concerns now, boyo.*

He worked his jaw, stiff and achy from that last punch that had put him down. Tried to raise his head, but his gorge rose with it and he slumped back. "Water." His voice rasped. "Just. Water."

As the sounds of clinking vessels and the slosh of liquid reached him, Niall tried to gauge direction and distance. They'd failed to shackle him to the cot. Big mistake. His captor would likely blind him for his trouble, but there was always the chance they wouldn't react in time. Besides, darkness meant nothing. He could do what needed doing by feel.

Footsteps. Approaching from his right. Slow. Heavy. *One...two...three.* Then they stopped.

"Place your hands on the metal part of the frame, if you please, Colonel." The oil congealed into something harder. Crueler. "I won't ask again."

Niall rested his hands on the cold tubing, then stiffened as sick sensation pulsed through him. Like worms, crawling under his skin, burrowing into his muscles, snaking up his spine. His back arched and his teeth chattered and no matter how he tried to straighten his fingers, they remained locked in spasm around the cot frame. He dug deep, forced words as his jaw clenched and worked as though he gnawed leather. "What—the hell—do you want—from me?"

"All in good time, Colonel. All in good time." The voice held a smile. "Do you like our immobilization field? If you're a good boy, we'll only use it as needed. If you're not, we'll leave it on all the time. It does do some damage after a while, I'm told. Motor control suffers. Leave it on long enough, we'd be able to turn it off for good." Then came the clatter of metal on the floor near the cot, followed by more footsteps, this time walking away. "There's a sink in the corner. Soap and a towel and such. Time for a wash-up before supper. And do clean up your mess, Colonel, before the stink gets in the venting. Unfortunately the filtering around here leaves something to be desired." Soft hisses sounded as the door opened and closed, followed by the buzz of locks locking and bolts sliding. Then, finally, silence.

A heartbeat later, the field cut out, and Niall slumped back down on the cot. The worms stilled almost immediately, but minutes passed before he could control his shaking hands, ease his trembling legs over the side, steady himself so he could lean down and pick up the cup without toppling forward onto the floor. He knew the owner of the voice wouldn't take kindly to that, would think it was some kind of ploy to draw them back inside. They would reactivate the field and leave it on for hours, just to show they could. Pretend to leave, but instead watch their prisoner convulse again and again.

It's the voice. Almost stilted in its formality, it held a touch of the sadist. But whether they were a true hard-ass or a coward in wolf's clothing, Niall lacked the data to conclude. Best to assume the former, at least for the time being.

He held the cup with both hands as he drank, small sips only to keep from choking. Fixed on his checklist to settle his nerves. *Cobbled together.* Shoddy cot, but advanced immobilization field. *Stale air.* But the water tasted good, not like the flat, over-filtered stuff one usually found in stations.

Not a pro. The conclusion dropped into Niall's head and lodged itself, based on nothing but feeling, that career criminal's sixth sense that had never left him. *Damn.* Professionals followed certain patterns. They were consistent. Once you figured them out, knew where you stood, you could determine next steps. *This is different.* Jailer duties fell to underlings in his experience, but this time he felt sure that his visitor was the one in charge. *Just as I thought. Sadist.*

Or, possibly just short-handed.

Still need to figure things out, Roshi. When he had first broached the proposal that he would try to infiltrate, by any means possible, one of the criminal groups that he suspected had snaked its way into Outer Circle bases, his supreme commander and good friend's commentary had been short and to the point. *Don't be a bloody idiot.*

Fast-forward two months later. *One bloody idiot reporting for duty, sir.*

Maneuvering as best he could in the blindspec dark, Niall found the sink and washed his face. Tottered back to the cot, lowered to his hands and knees, crawled around until he found the puddle of vomit, and cleaned that up. As he moved, he counted steps from the cot to the sink, then from the sink to the far side of the cell, where he found a pull-down sheet metal table attached to the wall and a metal stool bolted to the floor. *Just getting a feel for the place.* Building a map of the room in his head. His captors would expect some exploration. He would be fine as long as he didn't wander too close to the door. Not that he needed to, given that he had sensed its location when his visitor departed.

He returned to the cot and lay back down, folding his hands across his stomach. He felt better for having moved around, which he hoped meant no debilitating injuries. *Christ, I'm too old for this shit.* Sure, he'd sensed something rotten in Denmark over the past few months, but part of him had hoped it would prove nothing more than a periodic uptick in his usual baseline paranoia.

He listened to the air whisper through the venting, and wondered if his absence had been discovered. If the "here's what I've done if you don't hear from me in a while" message he had sent to Roshi had made it through. If Jani knew. He had left a message that she would understand. Now he wondered why he had bothered.

You're not her problem anymore. She was a Thalassan official now, concerned only with the health and wellbeing of a growing band of hybrids and a few Haárin hard cases. Feyó had clipped her wings and political tensions had done the rest. *Fucking mess.*

He pushed thoughts of blown friendships from his mind. Eventually, the first seeds of an escape plan formed, but he pushed them aside. He needed to stay put for as long as possible. There were risks, of course, but to be honest, given how he had been digging he wondered why they hadn't yet killed him. *They need something from me.* That gave him somewhat the upper hand, no matter how the oily voice threatened.

I still need to step lightly. Until the time was right, he would do as he had in the past when he had been captured or arrested. He would follow orders without question and monitor the gaps and the lapses. Once he had learned as much as possible, he would make his move. His best chance, most likely his only chance, would be the first one.

Exhaustion settled. Sedative hangover. As Niall hovered on the edge of troubled sleep, he thought back to his visitor's voice. For all the engineered tinniness, there was something familiar about it. *They called me Colonel.* Not *Niall,* or *Pierce,* or *you sonofabitch.* A more recent acquaintance? Well, that opened up an altogether different can of worms, didn't it?

Chapter Eight

Jani decamped to her office, a subbasement cell the location of which Lucien had insisted upon in the interest of safety. Like Niall, who had managed her security until politics made it impossible, he had an aversion to windows.

She paced from one end to the other and back again, over and over. She normally hated the lack of natural light, the sensation of being imprisoned. But at that moment, it was the privacy she valued more. No distractions. She needed to think.

Notify Dolly. As Head of the Documents Registry, Dorothea Aryton would have access to any paper created by the Commonwealth, whether government, military, or commercial. *She'd give it to me.* They had never gotten on particularly well, but their old Rauta Shèràa Academy tie still had to count for something. Besides, the paper in question wasn't confidential—the encodes were for commercial dock slip applications for Station Louis-Phillipe, which orbited Phillipa. *Jewelers Loop world. The colony nearest Shèrá.* All personnel and supplies had passed through there on the way to Rauta Shèràa Station, one last check to make sure no foodstuffs or other contraband that might offend the idomeni made it through during those tense prewar days.

An ultra-high security Misty would reach her in time. Maybe. Except that most Message Central Transmit relay stations were controlled by NUVA-SCAN or the Service, neither of which would be inclined to give a Thalassan missive top priority. *Assuming they let it through at all.*

Jani rounded her desk, fell into her chair. Sat forward, elbows on knees, and buried her face in her hands. The last time she had seen Dolly in person had been during her Chicago days, over two years before. She had browbeaten her former schoolmate into agreeing to some highly suspect activities, and while the outcome had been successful, a young dexxie had been seriously injured and the fallout hadn't done much for Dolly's Familial relations. So, while that bridge may not have been burned, it had sustained significant structural damage. *Besides, Dolly's human and I'm not. I'm also no longer Registry.* Reasons for not helping had now gone from intense dislike to matters of Commonwealth security.

Jani took her scanpack from its holster, pressed her hand to the underside to activate it. The unit remained dark for a time, a balky wodge of cloned brain tissue encased in an oval of worn black poly, of more use as a doorstop than a documents device. Then the surface illumins stuttered to life, flashes of yellow indicating an incomplete initiation sequence. A few moments of twinkling followed. Then, darkness.

Device in hand, Jani adjourned to her bathroom. She washed her hands, then tried once more. The reduction in hybrid skin oils did the trick—the scanpack activated fully, one green illumination after another indicating active quadrants, relays, sensors. She returned to her desk and scrabbled through stacks of files until she found a receipt from a Karistos spice vendor. *Cumin. Cardamom. Speciality Blends. Amounts. Delivery time and date. Payment verifications codes.* As she passed the scanpack over the document, all the appropriate alphanumeric strings and symbols scrolled across the display, followed by the steady green light indicating clean paper. Save for the odd stutter, her brain-in-a-box had performed perfectly.

This time. On one of the simplest documents imaginable. Jani lowered to the floor behind her desk, drew her knees up to her chin. *Most invoices and manifests aren't that much more complicated.* Then there were docking logs like those Niall's apparent captor demanded she retrieve, documents so simple they made invoices look like Family contracts.

But the encodes she'd been sent were for some of the first documents the fledgling Commonwealth Registry had developed. Designed on the fly. Error-prone. *Messy.*

Her auditor alarms pinged one by one as she considered why someone would want her to dig up that particular paper.

Proof of arrival of a ship at a registered dock. The first in a stack of commercial paper that would confirm ownership of a shipment.

She recalled the scrum that Station Louis-Philippe had been in those days. Supply ships from all over the Commonwealth. Every dock slip filled. Protocols written in days and sent out to the colonial stations for immediate implementation. No training. No guidance. She had written more that a few of them herself, had tried to keep them simple, straightforward, fool-proof. But even so, so much confusion. So many mistakes.

Or, depending on your point of view, so many opportunities.

And then there was Niall. A twenty-two year old corporal stationed at Fort du Lac on Phillipa. Up to his eyeballs in the rackets and one baby step away from a life sentence to a Service stockade. *Oh, Niall—what the hell did you get yourself up to?* And why was she getting dragged into it? Anyone who knew enough to send her those encodes would have to know that she no longer had access to that paper.

Of course they know. It was all part of the fun, this yank of her chain. *Find what we want in three days.* So what if it's out of reach. Figure it out.

Or Niall Pierce dies.

Jani eyed the wall clock. *One hour gone.* Seventy-one to go.

She boosted to her feet, tucked her scanpack into its holster, walked out into the corridor and exchanged greetings and smiles with the laboratory techs and clerks she encountered as though it were any other day. Rode the lift to the fourth floor and wended along the maze of hallways to the cavelike depths within the cliff, where her and Lucien's quarters were located. Another windowless space, cell-like for all its capaciousness and the sterling quality of its furnishings, the holograph nature scenes on the walls a poor substitute for the real thing.

Jani entered a closet larger than most of the apartments in which she'd lived and grabbed one of the few items resting on the overhead shelf. A small Service duffel, battered, the dark blue surface worn to gray in spots. *Jani's Noah bag,* Lucien had dubbed it. *Two of everything in case of disaster.* She adjourned to the bathroom, locked the door, then dumped the contents of the bag onto the mosaic-tiled floor and hunted through the coveralls, underwear, socks, and assorted necessities until she found a small silver metal box. The bottle it contained hadn't been opened in years—Jani had to hold it under the hot water faucet until the cap loosened enough that she could open it. She drew up some of the contents into the attached dropper, a thick, dark green substance that had the unfortunate appearance of pond scum.

Yes, you are a little old. Jani recapped the bottle and gave it a good shake, then tipped back her head and went though the motions that had once been habit but now seemed so strange. One drop. Two. First the left eye, then the right. *Hold the lids open for ten seconds, fifteen to make sure. Blink.*

She looked in the mirror, studied the eyes that stared back. A dark green-brown, more moss than honey, surrounded by bright white sclera. Human eyes. *Like Val's.* Her friend, Val Parini, who she hadn't seen in so long. *A year.* Twelve months of the Common calendar, give or take a few weeks, during which she had driven off one lover and found another and struggled to build a future for herself and an ever-growing band of others who had through no fault of their own been rendered as rootless as she had once been.

Do you ever think, with all the shit you've done in your life...

As for her past, she had made a peace of sorts with parts of it. The rest, however, she had simply buried, only to have it bubble to the surface at moments like this. How many times had she locked herself in a bathroom and filmed her eyes or examined the membranes for fissures. Coaxed the last few drops out of a bottle of film former, then scrabbled for enough untraceable credit chits to buy more. Her time on the run had consisted of stretches of continuous fear interspersed with bursts of panic and the rare sweet or tender interlude. She could never look past the next hour. The next day seemed eons away. The possibility of payback years down the road had never entered her mind.

I killed people too, Niall. How many times had she told him that during one of their dark discussions, their remembrances of crimes past.

Yes, he would answer, *but you killed to protect others. To save them.*

But there were times when she sat in a cell much like the office she had just left, furnished with a chair and a desk stacked with binders and folders and piles of paper. A cell in which she had done her job even as she knew in the back of her mind that if she was successful, people might die, and that some of them were innocent. Wrong place at the wrong time. Unfortunate in their choice of friends.

But she kept her head down and did whatever the job entailed because she needed to stay close to paper and all that supported the process, because a palm-sized unit that contained a cloned mass of her brain tissue needed to be fed, cleansed, updated, overhauled. Because without her scanpack, without that quest for knowledge that had driven her to leave her home and consign herself to a culture that despised her, she didn't know who or what she was. Her time at the Rauta Shèràa Academy, in the Commonwealth Service, in the wilderness, even in Thalassa, had all been means to an end. She was a documents examiner, a dexxie, a puzzle solver and investigator, a turner-over of rocks of all shapes and sizes, all ranks and classes. And all during that time, she had learned so much.

And all during that time, she had made enemies.

She had also, along the way, stopped believing in coincidence. Niall's unrest? The threats to Thalassa? *Related.* Had to be. She didn't know how, but she would find out.

Jani pressed a hand to her scanpack. "You need to get me through this. You need to work. After all I went through for you, you owe me." Then she stuffed the clothing and other items back into the bag, checked the sheathed secret compartment for her old Service shooter. Doffed her overrobe and hid it in a stack of towels, then shouldered her bag, unlocked the door, walked out—

—and collided with Lucien.

"Going somewhere?" He stepped back and surveyed her from head to toe and back again, finally settling on her eyes.

Jani looked away even though she knew it didn't matter. "You were out here waiting for me?"

"I came by to change my shirt. Saw the door closed, and waited. You only spend that much time in the bathroom when we're in the shower." Lucien sighed. "And here I thought that this one time, you might listen to reason." He pointed toward the sitting room, then gestured for Jani to get in front of him. "So. What the hell are you doing?"

Jani hesitated, then resigned herself to the inevitability that was Lucien Pascal and took out her handheld. "Better to show you."

"I want to know how the hell they broke into a siloed system." Lucien flipped the handheld across the coffee table into Jani's lap, then grabbed it back and glared at it. "Even Service-grade scans can't detect it. It officially does not exist."

Jani shrugged, then paused to take a swallow of some badly-needed coffee. It tasted like water, but luckily the caffeine still had the same effect on her hybrid system. "Local assistance. Someone on your team. Someone sleeping with someone on your team. Someone here who didn't bother to tell anyone how good they are with systems. With the right tech, it could even have been a long-distance break-in. Someone worlds away. Take your bloody pick." She glanced at her timepiece. Another half-hour gone.

"I vetted everyone."

"We're a work in progress here, Lucien. You're building a security system on the fly while trying to run checks on refugees from all over the Commonwealth who we can't turn away because they have nowhere else to go. You're trying to hit an ever-changing target."

Lucien's eyes narrowed. "You're so understanding."

"I've had time to think." Jani hugged her coffee mug close, drew what comfort she could from its warmth. "Whoever took Niall did it to get to me. It has something to do with a shipment that arrived at Station Louis-Philippe just before the War of Vynshàrau Ascension. They want me to excavate the documents, only I can't do that legally anymore because I've been struck from the Registry. That means I need to do it illegally."

Lucien sagged back in his seat. "And how can you do that?"

"Whoever has Niall knows where I am, and they gave me three days to find the paper. That means there's an archive within that window of travel time." Jani took back her handheld and tabbed through screens until she found a listing of Registry outposts. "The closest one is located in Padishah Station, and as I recall, we have an agent embedded there."

"Teddy Honore. He's in dock scheduling."

"The perfect location." Jani shouldered her bag and started to rise, but the expression on Lucien's face caused her to sit back down.

"You're kidding, right?" Lucien's provincial French accent thickened, a telltale indication of mounting agitation. "Forget all the delicate diplomatic bullshit—you'd be disobeying a direct order from Feyó."

"What else can she do to me? Take my scanpack? It has weeks left, maybe. Lock me up in here? That's been pretty much my life these past few months anyway. Order everyone to shun me? Some will. Some won't." Jani slumped back. "Kill me? I know she'd like to. The only thing that stops her is the knowledge that Tsecha would object and maybe she'll get past that." Her gaze moved to one of the floor murals, a touch of beauty among so many. "This is the only place I can live. The only place I can call home. And someone, some group of someones, wants to destroy it or corrupt it. Wreck the lives of a collection of medical outcasts who came here because they had nowhere else to go." She pointed to her handheld. "This is the start of it. I'm going to find out who's behind it, and I will stop them."

Silence settled. Then Lucien drummed his fingers on his thighs. "It's going to take a hell of a lot more than filmed eyes to get you to Padishah undetected."

"I can change clothes on the way. Straighten my hair. Color it. Stick to the areas of the station without monitoring—"

"There are no areas without monitoring."

"Every station has open places and you know it." Jani tried to avoid looking at her timepiece, the wall clock. Felt her heartbeat tick away the seconds. "I avoided an active manhunt for eighteen years, and the only reason they found me was because Evan put an entire ministry to work tracking me down." Evan van Reuter. Former Interior Minister. The "V" in the NUVA-SCAN conglomerate, and the love of her much younger life. *My idiot days.* She was so much wiser now, wasn't she? *Don't answer that.*

"You've been all over the newssheets for the last two years. You'd be spotted within the day." Lucien pinched the bridge of his nose, the sign a headache had come to call.

Jani sat back and pondered. One thing she had learned over the years was that human powers of observation could prove surprisingly weak. She always took care to wear a very specific wardrobe when in public, tailored shirts and trousers in shades of brown topped by the off-white overrobe of an idomeni secular dominant. Lose the overrobe, add different clothes and a wash of make-up, and most humans wouldn't recognize her at first glance, which was usually all the time she needed. Yes, there were other stumbling blocks, but she had learned her way around those as well. *I can do this...I have to do this....*

Then she studied Lucien the way she used to, when words unspoken mattered more than anything they said aloud to one another. Saw him as he had been, such a short time ago. Captain Lucien Pascal, officially assigned to Service Intelligence. *But unofficially....* She waited until his hand fell to his lap and he stared back. "You used to kill people for a living."

"Uh-huh." Lucien's voice emerged flat.

"You can't tell me that you did those jobs looking like you."

"Perhaps I did."

"What, uniform and all?"

"Are you telling me I'm memorable?"

"That's one way of putting it." Jani paused. Considered the odds, and decided they couldn't be worse than they were already. "I know there were materials that some people used to alter their facial appearance." She poked her cheek with her forefinger. "Injectables that melded with bone and soft tissue. Undetectable. As I recall, they didn't work very well. They didn't last long. They moved around. The really bad ones contained materials that damaged bone and nerves and wound up making a real mess. I am guessing that whatever you used during all those times you disappeared for weeks on end worked much better, but that given how well it worked, it was quite closely controlled."

"Nothing works that well. It wouldn't have been approved if it wasn't detectable."

"Hence the close control. But it would have to be undetectable or you'd have been vulnerable. What if your target suspected you? Tested you in some way?"

"It wouldn't have mattered—" Lucien clamped his mouth shut.

Jani feigned surprise. "So it is undetectable? Really?"

"In case you've forgotten, we became rather close during that time." Lucien looked at the floor, the ceiling, everywhere but at her. "If I'd been injecting things into my face, you would've been able to tell."

"I never saw the difference. I never felt the difference. So you either need some compound to reverse the process or it wears off on its own." Jani sat forward, elbow on knee and chin propped on fist, and took what pleasure she could in the fact that she had once again made the unshakeable Lucien Pascal squirm. "Must've been really good stuff." More minutes she didn't have to spare ticked by, but she told herself it would be worth it. *Stay frosty.* Panicking wouldn't do anyone any good. Least of all, Niall. "Think you could get hold of some?"

"Assuming what you're asking for is even available at a pit like Fort Karistos, what makes you think I could lay my hands on any? I'm to the Service what you are to Registry, a non-entity."

"Within the next hour would be great. Unless, you being you, you held onto some of it. Tucked away for a rainy day."

"Why the hell would I do that?"

"Like I said." Jani smiled. "Because you're you."

Lucien's gaze shifted, fixing on a point on the wall opposite. Eventually, he sighed. "A few days before they kicked me out, I don't know, I just had a feeling. Your warnings, mad mutters in the back of my mind. I went to my quarters, my locker, cleaned out the stuff I wanted to keep and left the rest for them to do with what they would."

"Sounds familiar." Jani nodded. "Give them something to find because after that, they stop looking."

"Something like that." Lucien stood and walked across the room to his armoire. No rummaging for him—he found what he needed in the first drawer he opened. A Service issue toiletry case, this one a crisp silver-grey. "I don't know why I bothered. Perhaps I thought that someday, I would just, how would you say it, play a game." A corner of his mouth turned up, the barest of smiles. "Or perhaps I always knew deep down that eventually they'd give it to me in the neck, and that I would get back at them for pushing me out. Some swindle or other."

"And all during that time, nobody followed up to make sure you turned everything in?"

"Being under Anais Ulanova's umbrella had its benefits." Lucien shrugged. "Paperwork fell by the wayside. Follow-up didn't happen. And believe it or not, I wasn't greedy. I built up my supply over time —a little here, a little there." He returned to his seat, unzipped the case, and removed a bulky cloth roll. "Plus I did everything they asked of me, and I did it well. What Ani's influence didn't cover, that did. Until it didn't." He cleared the top of the coffee table, then set down the roll and unfurled it, revealing two rows of small pockets stuffed with smaller metal vials and an assortment of instruments.

Jani spotted the injectors, long metal tubes enclosing the metering mechanisms. "A stash of this could've saved me so much trouble over the years."

"Perhaps. You have to know what you're doing." Lucien took out one of the injectors and held it up between thumbs and forefingers. "It requires patience, and a steady hand. You want a natural-looking face, not a lumpen mask."

Jani picked up one of the injectors and read the label. "This says 'Jawline.' It comes with instructions. The device controls the metering."

"Those only go so far." Lucien plucked the device from her grip and returned it to its slot. "My appearance was designed by an identity team. Sculptors. Bioaestheticians. They would administer the injections on base. I would lie low for the few days, then depart with the rest of the evening rush hour crowd, like any anonymous contractor."

Jani forced herself to not look at her timepiece. "We don't have an identity team, or a few days. We have a couple of hours at most."

"So we need to inject now, then get to Elyas Station as quickly as possible. The next problem is, we need IDs. Just the basics. Standard personal ID. Station general staff."

"You didn't hold on to any of those?"

"Those, they made sure I turned in." Lucien muttered foul French. "The Intelligence dexxies were a fucking pain in the ass." He rolled up his face-altering kit, then unrolled it again. "Unfortunately, everyone I know in Karistos who makes good fakes is a Service or Government Hall informant." His shoulders sagged.

Eventually, he looked across the table at Jani. "You're awfully quiet for someone whose rescue mission has just gone off the track."

Jani pulled her bag onto to lap and dug into one of the harder-to-find pockets. "I have some basics. Station staff. Simple ID cards."

"Where did you get—?" Lucien's mouth worked soundlessly for a moment. "You have clean fake IDs?"

"My 'pack's been acting up."

"I know."

"So every so often I tested it—"

"—by making up fake documents."

"I wasn't intending to use them. I just wanted to see if I still had the touch."

"The touch."

"I mean, I wanted to see if my 'pack—"

"I think you said it right the first time." Lucien's expression lightened. "And do you?"

"I think so. They come up green." Jani dug into her duffel's secret compartment, pulled out a small stack of cards, and spread them across the table. "The problem will be insetting the right images. We'll have to leave before our faces are through...developing. So we'll need multiple sets—one for the Elyas Station stopover, one for Padishah, and one for where we wind up going next."

"Can't you edit the same cards?"

Jani shook her head. "The insets degrade if you try to alter them once they've been closed out. After that, they don't work."

"I thought you couldn't update your scanpack anymore. That means it's probably a few versions behind on everything. Doesn't that matter?"

"Elyas Station hasn't updated their read system in a while. I am guessing that the more out of the way areas of Padishah haven't, either. Plus, the chips I used were one version ahead of Elyas. I always tried to stay one version ahead of wherever I was. Breathing room." Jani looked up from her ID stash to find Lucien regarding her with his hand over his mouth. "What?"

"How long have you been planning to bug out?" He spoke through his fingers, but the grin in his voice came through. "Were you going to tell me, or was I just supposed to wake up one morning to find you'd gone?"

"I wasn't—" Jani struggled for the words. "I wanted to make sure I could still make them. With all that's going on, I can't help thinking that someday we're all going to need them." She gathered up the cards. "We should get started." She paused in mid-shuffle. "But we can't—"

"—prepare here. Everyone knows everyone here. There's no way we wouldn't be spotted trying to leave." Lucien swore some more.

"You have a flat in Karistos."

"I used to have a flat in Karistos. I gave it up when I took over from Niall."

"I thought you'd keep it."

"Why?"

"Days off. Place to, I don't know—?" Jani shrugged. When they lived in Chicago, Lucien had occasionally gone off on his own for the evening. *Sometimes longer.* She hadn't cared—they didn't have that sort of relationship, and there were times when she savored being alone.

But since settling in Thalassa, Lucien had become, well, sticky. She couldn't recall the last day off he'd taken, the last time he'd told her he was headed to Karistos and she shouldn't wait up.

Lucien shook his head. "We wouldn't be able to go into Karistos even if I had a place. One of Feyó's informers would spot you and you'd be rounded up—"

"Because I'm not supposed to be there." Jani ran through the short catalog of places where they could prepare. "The smuggler shacks on the flat are out—they're all booby-trapped. The nearest mountain settlement is three hours away and they know me there, too."

Lucien drummed his fingers on his thighs. "I can think of one place." He eyed her from beneath his lashes. "You aren't going to like it."

Chapter Nine

They left the Main House separately, and went in opposite directions. Lucien carried their bags and headed for the vehicle depot to sign out a skimmer—if anyone asked, he was going into Karistos to meet with a security systems vendor. Meanwhile, Jani walked out into the wilderness area that bordered the flat, something she had done often enough that no one would think it unusual. House monitoring would pick her up on the scans, then set her trace on automatic and ignore her for the hour or so that she commonly spent strolling through the scrub. As for Feyó's spybots, experience indicated that they were concentrated on the routes between Karistos and Thalassa, with little if any flyover of Thalassa itself.

That will change. Jani kicked at stones, forced herself to not look back at the House to see if anyone followed or watched her. She and Lucien were exploiting every weakness they could find in House security protocols. This was their shot. If they got caught, all the holes would be plugged. Feyó would seal her in and probably expel Lucien—she wouldn't give a damn about the reasons why whoever had kidnapped Niall wanted old war-era paper, or that Jani's failure to follow through would likely condemn him to death. *Humanish problems,* she would tell Jani. *Commonwealth problems. Neither are your concern.*

Breathe. Jani had to keep reminding herself as old memories flooded back. That sense that it was time to run, which direction to head, where to go next. She shivered despite the heat, the press of the sun on her back. The distant air shimmered and the only sounds were the crunch of her boots on the rocky ground, the occasional wail of a sandie. She half-walked half-slid down an incline that was just steep enough to block her view of the House. Sat on a rock, and waited. Checked her timepiece. Another hour had passed since her receipt of the message from Niall's captors. *Seventy to go.*

Minutes later, the soft hum of a skimmer reached her. Soon, a nondescript brown four-door glided into view. It stopped a little distance away, the front gullwings slowly opening like a bird stretching its wings. Lucien emerged and tossed something into a nearby rocky niche.

Jani stood, then paused to brush sand from her clothes. "Is that the tracer?"

Lucien nodded. "When they ID the signal, they'll see it's from the skimmer I checked out. It should serve to keep them away from this area for the next hour or two, at least."

"Because they'll think—" Jani whacked him in the arm as she passed him on the way to the vehicle. "You would set it up that way."

"Can you think of any better reason for them to stay away from here?" Lucien didn't bother to hide a rakish grin.

Jani opened her mouth to argue, then admitted to herself that he was right. The hybrids on Security might crack raw jokes, and the Haárin would wonder once again at humanish ways of mating. The one thing they wouldn't do was interrupt an assignation between their dominant and her lover.

She flopped into the passenger seat and strapped herself in. "Even without the tracer, we're still going to show up on the roadway monitors."

"Just as an anonymous vehicle." Lucien got in behind the steering mech and lowered the gullwings. "And the faces they see won't be ours." He steered out of the depression and drove deeper into the rock-strewn wilderness. They flitted over ravines, dodged clumps of dull green vegetation, the odd weathered tree.

"So where are we going that I won't like?" Jani turned her timepiece so she couldn't see it, and debated covering the dashboard clock.

"You'll find out soon enough." Lucien eventually turned toward the bay. The skimmer, a standard design more suited to city streets equipped with guidance systems, shuddered and wobbled as it struggled to maintain an even keel without the steadying signal of a skimtrack to guide it.

"Are you sure this thing can run over water?" Jani gripped both sides of her seat as the vehicle shot over the edge of the cliff and down to the bay below. Swallowed hard as her stomach went floaty and what little she'd had to eat and drink that day bubbled up to the back of her throat.

"We won't be doing that for long."

Jani felt a nervy shudder as the Karistos skyline came into view. Then her heart thumped as Lucien steered the skimmer off the water and onto a stretch of beach. "Oh, damn."

"I knew you wouldn't like it." Lucien soon maneuvered up a steep incline, then skirted a cliff edge before turning onto a stretch of rocky land sliced with ravines. "But everyone avoids it. Even the poachers don't go there. They claim the whole area is haunted."

"We're getting a little close to Karistos. We should be inside Feyó's surveillance range."

"Do you really think she would monitor this place?" Lucien slowed as they approached a ruined house, a tiny white box partially collapsed by fallen rocks.

Jani rubbed hands gone to ice, then tucked them between her knees. A little over a year before Lucien had brought her here in the night and her world, already shaken to its core, had suffered that final shattering blow. Tsecha, her dominant, her friend of so many years, killed, felled by a Vynshàrau assassin who had used this house as her base of operations.

Lucien maneuvered the skimmer into a gap between the house's rear wall and the fallen rocks, shut it down, then waited. "Are you all right?"

"Fine." Jani rubbed her hands together once again, then tucked them under her arms.

"Having second thoughts?"

"Bad memories."

"Understandable." Lucien made a move to disembark, then hesitated. "If you'd rather go somewhere else? Someplace near the shuttleport?"

"Too risky." Jani got out, then rounded the vehicle and waited for Lucien to open the boot. She hefted her duffel along with another bag containing an assortment of documents gear, and headed for the entry. Wished that one of the area's occasional quakes had finished the job that a long ago rockfall had started. "Who do they think haunts this place? Not Tsecha?"

"Who else?" Lucien followed close behind. Along with his gear bags, he also lugged a small folding table and a rolled blanket, which he motioned for Jani to take.

Jani shook out the blanket and spread it carefully to avoid raising the fine stone dust that coated every surface. "Ghosts are human inventions. Once Tsecha's soul departed for the First Star, that was it. He was at peace. No reason for him to return."

"So what are their demons?"

"Idomeni demons aren't fallen souls. They're something else."

"What?"

"Embodiments of chaos, mostly. Inflictors of disorder." Jani paused in the middle of setting out her paper gear. "Since when did you become interested in idomeni theology?"

"Just trying to ease the tension."

"I'm not tense."

"If you say so."

Jani walked to the room's single window and looked out toward the bay. *She stood here.* Her name was Rilas. After she released the device that killed Tsecha, she fled back to the idomeni homeward of Shèrá. *But I tracked her down.* And so another name was added to the list of Jani Kilian's dead. "There was talk of turning this place into some kind of memorial, but it fizzled. Hard to escape the sense that we would be honoring the assassin and not the victim." She returned to the blanket and continued to prepare the ID blanks for imprinting. "I hope I can keep these clean with all this dust around."

"First things first." Lucien beckoned her to the table on which he'd set out the injectors. "Sit or stand—whatever you do, you have to remain still."

"I'll stand." Jani rested one hand on the table to steady herself and stared straight ahead as Lucien traced one injector along her jaw, a second around her eyes, and a third across the bridge of her nose with unsettling speed. First came tingling on the surface of her skin, followed by warmth beneath. Then came pressure, as the biomaterial expanded, bonded to bone, and infiltrated soft tissue.

Jani looked at herself in the small mirror that Lucien handed her, saw only the faintest line of purplish speckling where the needles had pierced. "You've done this before." She tried to rub a place on her cheek that had started to itch, but Lucien pulled her hand away.

"Possibly." Any hint of lightness or flirtation had given way to somber focus. "It takes surprisingly little change to give someone a face that's just different enough."

"After you described an entire team—"

"They built me a life, a past. Assembled the right clothing. Gave me instruction in language. Customs. We just need a few days of confusion. I hope." He took another, larger, bottle from his array, started to hand it to her, then paused. "Speaking of confusion, how are we planning to finance this excursion of ours? Feyó needs to approve all transactions, so we can't borrow from any accounts."

Jani pointed to her bag. "I have unused chits."

"How much? Those Chicago reserves must be getting pretty low."

"Enough for a couple of weeks' worth of third class berths and vend alcove meals."

Lucien grew thoughtful. "I have some." He shrugged off Jani's questioning look. "I have a locker at Elyas Station. Leftovers from an old job."

"I didn't know you'd worked out here." Jani tried to sneak a scratch of one of the injection sites, but Lucien's grumble cut that short. "This is the most you've revealed about your old job since I've known you."

"You know the most important part." Lucien finally handed her the bottle. "I don't do it anymore."

"Well, I just never knew it was this involved." Jani read the bottle's label. "Skin dye?"

"It's as close to your shade as I can make it. It will cover the gold undertone." He looked around at the stark white of the stone walls, the sunlight streaming in through the window, the cracks in the walls and ceiling. "It's really obvious in this lighting." He picked up an injector and turned toward the mirror. "You could work on that and on your hair. Then we can get started on the IDs."

Jani gave the dye bottle a good shake, then undid her shirt cuffs and rolled up her sleeves. *Oh, shit.* "Do you have anything to cover these?"

Lucien stared at her scarred forearms, then pushed up one of his sleeves to reveal his own à lérine mementoes. "I have something to cover scars, but these may be too deep. We'll just have to stick with long sleeves." He worked with speed born of practice. Within minutes, he had darkened his white-blond hair and eyebrows to nondescript light brown. Meanwhile, his sharp jawline had already altered, become more rounded, looser.

Jani massaged dye into her arms and straightener through her hair, then followed with hair color that dulled blue-black to dark brown. "What about pubic hair?" She waved off Lucien's glare. "I'm completely serious."

"If we're strip-searched, we're done. That dye only goes so far." On that uncomfortable note, they continued their preparations.

As soon as her skin dried sufficiently, Jani dragged on a gray jumpsuit she had salvaged years before from a station's lost lambs bin. She had never worn it before—it would have been too dressy for her past situations, too casual for the life she lived now. She checked herself as best she could in the small mirror, then tugged at the thighs and waist. But the jumpsuit stubbornly refused to bag in a manner she considered suitable, rendering her a trim column instead of her usual draping sag. The straightener and hair color had converted her short black waves into a skull-fitting coffee-colored cap, while the skin dye had squelched the idomeni gold.

And then there's my new face. She'd had her doubts about the usefulness of Lucien's ministrations, but she had to admit that they'd had the desired result. A slight squaring of the jaw and widening of the bridge of her nose had replaced fineness of bone with stolidness, while the injections around her eyes had filled out her upper lids, causing them to droop. Aging her.

"I may have overdone it with your eyes." Lucien stood behind her and studied her reflection. "I don't usually see swelling."

Jani fingered the puffy mound beneath one eyebrow. "It occurs to me that this stuff is made for humans. I just have to hope it's compatible."

"I guess we'll find out."

"How long does this last?"

"Ideally, one to two weeks." Lucien gathered the injectors and returned them to his bag. "The problem is, some of this is expired, and I don't know how much it's degraded." His voice came halting, as though second thoughts had come to call. "Thing is, that's not the hard part."

Jani nodded. "Characteristics. Voice. Walk. Behavior. Anything that makes us easy to spot." She took in the changes that had already overtaken her partner in deceit. His face had lost that distinctive carved aspect—it now looked softened, puffy. His nose had widened and taken on a crooked bumpiness that hinted at multiple breaks left to heal without benefit of medical intervention. He had switched out his usual fitted apparel for baggy black trousers and a stretched-out dark blue pullover. *Enter Lucien's less fit, desk-bound cousin.*

"This is an awful lot to pull together in a very short amount of time." Despite his expressed concern, Lucien's voice had already changed, pitch slightly lowered and provincial French accent grown thicker.

"But you're not trying to talk me out of it."

"What good would it do?"

Jani didn't answer right away. Instead, she leaned against the wall and assessed Lucien's transformation. *He's just sliding into different skin—is he even aware he's doing it?* He had of course told her many times of his past exploits, but she had never been this close to the actual working killer. *Well, except for the two times he was supposed to kill me.* But both those times, he'd worn his real face. "No," she said finally. "That's not it."

"No, you're right." Lucien folded his arms and adopted a wide-legged stance that accentuated the poor fit of his clothes. "I think it's because when they capture us and shove us in an airlock, I want to be able to look you in the eye and say 'I told you so' before they release us into the void."

Jani managed a laugh. "That's not it, either."

Lucien opened his mouth to speak, then shut it. Tried again, and failed. Looked down at his hands. "Insanity," he said finally. "Living with you. It was bound to happen."

"Your job is to keep me from getting killed. My job is to work in spite of that never-ending threat. Will this really be so different?"

It was Lucien's turn to laugh. Then he wiped his hand over his face. "Tell me the truth. Are you really as confident as you appear to be?"

Jani pondered, shrugged. "My scanpack is dodgy—every time I

fire it up, I wonder if it will be the last. I have to either talk documents staffers into risking their Registry rating to give me paper I no longer have a right to see or figure out a way to steal it. We may get lucky at Padishah Station, but what comes after? I assume it will be more difficult." She checked her timepiece. *Sixty-nine hours to go.* "Niall's in trouble because someone is using him to get to me. What choice do I have?"

"But you're looking forward to it. It's like old times for you. Wading into the shit with your little brain-in-a-box." Lucien kicked a small pile of stones, scattering them. Then he stilled."With me, it's self-preservation. I have to come with you. As soon as they figured out you'd bolted, they'd roll me up and stick me in a cell."

"They wouldn't do that."

"I'm the only human in Thalassa, Jani. Feyó doesn't trust me and all the hybrids keep asking when I'm going to make the switch." Lucien knelt on the blanket and gathered the injectors and other gear. "IDs."

Jani watched him work, head down, expression grim. Then she lowered to the blanket and unpacked her documents bag, spread out the ID blanks, inset chips, and other markers. She wiped her hands with an oil-stripping cloth, then activated her scanpack. *Please behave.* It balked at first, then steadied. She paused, listened to the silence, and looked up to find Lucien pointing at the ID blanks.

"Those are genuine Commonwealth-issue."

"Yeah. I said that before, didn't I?"

"No, you didn't. Where the hell did you get them?"

"I...acquired them over the years. The versions don't go out of date very often, and even the old ones usually work." Jani picked up one of the blanks by the edges, and held it to the underside of her 'pack. "Do you have a preferred name?"

Lucien sat back on his heels, arms folded. "Surprise me."

Jani tapped in a code string. "Justine Valery. Lop off the 'e.'"

"You have a name randomizer installed in your 'pack?"

"I went through a lot of them over the years. It was hard to keep track. Couldn't risk repeats." Jani met Lucien's questioning look, as though he had never seen her before. "Lucien, how do you think I managed to survive for eighteen years?" She gestured toward her face, then his. "Is this done cooking—can I image you now?" She held up her 'pack and edged it back and forth until the visual and focus indicators blinked green. "Don't smile." She transferred the image to the ID card, then handed the card to Lucien. "Check everything. Then I can close it out."

"Well, that took you all of two minutes." Lucien held the ID by the edges, as though afraid it might crumble. Examined both sides, then gave it back to Jani. "I confess amazement."

"Yeah, it's been an educational time all around." Jani closed out all the entries, locking them in place. Then she imaged her face, added it to her own ID. *And my new name is...Lita Mansour. A Padishah name. Three main languages, colonial dialects of Arabic, Hebrew, Farsi. And I can't speak any of them.* She closed out the entries, then collected her gear. Hesitated, then stuffed a few of the blanks into the scan-proof compartment of her duffel. *Five years in the Lunar shipyards for possessing these.* Except she wasn't human anymore, so she would likely be turned over to Thalassa, and any punishment would be Feyó's to mete out. *I'll take the shipyards.* "I should drive."

Lucien paused in the middle of his own packing. "God help us."

"You always drive. If I drive, it's one less reason for them to think it's us."

"I want to get to the station in one piece, okay? You drive like the hounds of Hell are on your tail."

"That's because they usually are." Jani cut short further argument by handing her documents bag to Lucien—as he bundled it with his own gear into a larger, weighted bag, she stepped around him, headed out to the skimmer, and slipped into the driver's side.

There were a few moments when Jani wondered if she should turn the controls over to Lucien. Months had passed since she driven anything more complicated than a scoot, and the rough, trackless terrain challenged her rusty skills. First she swept down the slope and out over water so Lucien could toss out the weighted bag. Then she had to maneuver back up the slope and onto the road that led to the shuttle port. "You didn't tell me you were going to dump all that valuable equipment in the bay."

"It's tagged. I'll retrieve it when we get back. If we get back." Lucien leaned into every turn, sitting up straight or slumping as their close brushes with other vehicles demanded. "Assuming we make it to the shuttleport alive."

"Fine." Jani turned onto an access road that led to a cluster of vacant storage sheds. "I can walk the rest of the way. We need to leave separately anyway, then hook up at Padishah. They'll be looking for us within the hour, assuming they haven't already figured out we're missing. They will contact Dieter and ask for all passenger lists for incoming shuttles from Elyas, and they will be looking for couples." She squeezed the steering wheel, then loosened her grip, over and over. *Bolt nerves*, she had once called them. The overwhelming urge to *get out now*. "Check your ID again. If anything's off, I have time you a new one."

"It's good." Lucien looked at the card, then at her. Shaking his head, he tucked the ID in his pocket.

"The safest area is F Concourse." Jani closed her eyes, saw the layout of the station in her mind, the Main Concourse, the secondaries and the docks, the twists and turns. "The planet side, near the general service docks. Hang around there. That's where day jobbers gather. They're usually looking for loaders and doc techs. You may stand out—I don't know. Sometimes they look for regular office staff, too. There's also an unlicensed casino behind one of the bars. It's Stash Markos's favorite evening hangout."

Lucien nodded. "So, no cams."

"No cams. There may be physical security, because Stash isn't an idiot. They're easy to spot. Just stay out of their way." Jani glanced at Lucien to find him regarding her with the steady stare she had long ago labeled his *knock it off* look.

"You know, I do know all this." His changed face, narrow-eyed and fleshy, gave his quiet reproof an edge of annoyed boredom.

"Sorry." Jani sat back, folded her arms and tucked her hands underneath, hugged herself. "It's just that it's been a while. I keep thinking I'm forgetting things. I thought my bug-out days were over." She checked the dashboard clock. An hour's wait until the next shuttle to Elyas Station. A ninety-minute trip, give or take, depending on how long they needed to wait for a dock. *Sixty-five hours.* "I should get going." She reached down to gather her duffel, but stopped when Lucien took hold of her hand.

"You know, if things go badly, we may never see each other again." He leaned close, bringing with him the faint hints of his favorite musky soap and his own indefinable scent.

"Ever the optimist." Jani's heart stuttered despite the growing tension, fear, worry. Lucien spoke with his real voice, a disquieting contrast with his retooled self. *Except for the eyes.* Deep brown, as ever unsettling, a veneer of warmth that failed to hide the icy intelligence of a predator. "We really don't have time." She tried to free her wrist, and would've had more luck shaking off an iron band.

"The next shuttle doesn't leave for an hour. It's a fifteen minute walk." Lucien had already tweaked the controls so that the windows darkened. "You're on edge. I'm amazed we survived the drive here. We're headed out into the unknown. We both need a break."

"Break from what?" Jani sagged into her seat. "We haven't even gotten started."

Lucien shifted so he faced her, rested his head on the seat back, studied her for a long moment. "First time we met, on van Reuter's ship." He shrugged. "I'd read the info about you that Ani had given me, and I thought, okay, this is different, but nothing I can't handle." A light laugh, touched with wonder. "But I could not get through to you, no matter what I did. Every time I felt I was getting close, you'd just—" He mimed brushing something off his shoulder. "—as if to say, *piss off, petit.*"

"You had been sent to spy on me."

"Details. I don't believe my pride has ever recovered."

Jani had to smile. "If it's any consolation, there were a few times when if you'd applied yourself just a little more..." She held up one hand, forefinger and thumb a hair's breadth apart.

"Now you tell me." Lucien released her wrist, and took hold of her hand instead. "The way you were then, and when we were in Chicago. And here, too. Working within the rules. Trying to, at least. That's the you I was used to. The Jani I thought I had finally gotten through to." His eyes brightened, as if he'd just received a long-desired gift. "This is new. I've never seen the outlaw before."

"Maybe you're enjoying it." Jani tried to pull away at first, then stopped. As always, despite all she knew about him, the engineered creature that he was, she found his touch comforting. "I'm not."

"Really? Not even a little?" He leaned closer, then closer still, a little bit at a time. As always, never assuming. Always making sure. Then, when she made no move to stop him, he gathered her in his arms and kissed her hard while his hands moved everywhere at once—undoing the front of her jumpsuit, pushing down her top, pulling her onto his lap.

Jani struggled to untwist a leg of her jumpsuit. "This isn't going to work."

"I think we can manage." Lucien undid his trousers with one hand and pulled her closer with the other. "It's not like we haven't done it before."

Jani fixed on his voice, his eyes, the touch and feel of him and the smell of him. Not his face, that temporary thing that would fade away in days, like other faces from her past that had faded away in less time than that. She let him guide her and pushed thoughts of the next hours, the next days, from her mind for just a little while because yes, he was right. They needed a break.

And yes, he was right. They managed.

Chapter Ten

Elyas Station had a well-deserved reputation as the strangest in the Commonwealth. A bizarre combination of sacred and profane, a spaceship cathedral complete with gargoyles, fake stained glass, and statuary scattered about like a throw of odd-shaped game pieces, it needed only incense and the distant crash of organ music to complete the picture.

And maybe a prayer or two. Jani held her breath as she scanned her Lita Mansour ID at the check-in kiosk. Never before had one of her creations betrayed her, but there was a first time for everything, wasn't there? When the scanner illumin flashed green and the entry gate swept aside, she hesitated until the mutters of the passenger behind her spurred her to move.

Wake up. She hitched her duffel higher on her shoulder and hurried into the Main Concourse, where passengers, station staff, and ships' crew members pressed in from all sides. *Nice and crowded—crowded is good.* Easier to push the limits of the station's recognition systems, which, like those of most Outer Circle stations, was out of date bordering on obsolete. No doubt that it would still function well enough to highlight tallish human females who bore a resemblance to

Jani Moragh Kilian, but Feyó's team wouldn't yet know that she had altered her features. By the time they figured it out, she hoped to be well on her way to Padishah.

Assuming they can even request a search. Feyó only had authority over the Elyan Haárin section of the station. Only ComPol, various Cabinet offices, and Service Investigative could initiate searches in the human section, and their primary interests would be persons wanted by Chicago, NUVA-SCAN, or the Service. A request from the dominant of the Elyan Haárin to hunt for a wayward hybrid likely wouldn't receive top priority.

Although, given that she was the hybrid in question....

Better keep moving. Jani would be able to relax a little once she reached Concourse F. But until then, best not to gamble on how much influence ná Feyó Tal could bring to bear if circumstances demanded.

As she turned off the Main Concourse onto the walkway that led to the secondary concourses and general service docks, she spotted a trio of Haárin docks staffers headed in her direction. Her step faltered. Sweat bloomed and trickled despite the station chill. She snatched glimpses of their sand-colored overrobes, their breeders fringes. *They're conservative.* So they wouldn't look at her face. *But they might know Jani Kilian's walk, her bearing.* She slowed her pace, adopted the aimless saunter of a human female with no particular place to be or time by which to be there. She paused in front of a shop display as they approached, held her breath as they passed within an arm's length, and didn't release it until they had disappeared around the corner.

No reason to assume they were looking for me. After all, they were headed toward the Haárin end of the station. *They're off to meet someone.* Possibly a delegation from Shèrá, or one of Feyó's many traveling trade representatives.

Or maybe I just dodged a shooter blast. Jani checked her reflection in the shop window, took some comfort in the strange face that looked back, and continued on her way.

As she approached Concourse F, she kept an eye out for Lucien, hoped like hell that he had done as she asked and delayed his departure. She shivered again, dug a light jacket out of her duffel, and dragged it on. *Freezing.* She shoved her hands in her pockets to keep from rubbing them together—she knew she needed to take care. The humans around her all wore light clothing, short wraps, desertweight uniforms. Someone who appeared cold would stand out. Any human familiar with the Haárin would tuck that detail away, then disgorge it later in answer to the usual questions. *Did you see anything unusual? Anyone behaving oddly?*

Jani stood against a wall, pretended to search through her duffel, and drew a long, steadying breath, then another, as the scores of questions, self-assessments, and observations that had once informed every waking moment scrolled through her mind in a continuous loop. *How soon we forget.* What had once been second nature now required conscious thought. *Settle down, Kilian.* Instead, she forced herself to think of Niall, which led to a different flavor of fear. Was he aware of what had happened, or had they sedated him? Did he know where he was? There had been blood on the walls of his office—was it his? Was he hurt, injured, in pain?

Or had he been the cause of same? The thought brought a smile. *Hang on, old friend.* She checked her timepiece. There had been a delay in departure thanks to an accident at one of the docks. *Sixty-four hours.* She looked toward the ticketing kiosks, where the lines already stretched out into the corridor. A mix of singles and couples. Families with small children. The odd low-level official, uniform tunic and trousers in severe contrast with all the casual wear, shaking their head at the wait.

Jani adjourned to a restroom. Checked her eyefilms as she washed her hands, then examined her neck for any telltale signs of Lucien's recent attentions. Fixed a jumpsuit clasp that she hadn't refastened properly, and allowed herself a quieter smile at the memory of their hurried interlude. They had held onto one another afterwards, that human desire for connection in which neither of them often indulged. *Simple nerves—we're both out of practice.* She finger-combed her hair, gave herself a final once-over, and headed out.

She passed the lines, which had grown even longer during her brief absence, and instead made her way to the general service docks. The companies with slips there were usually the poor relations, unaffiliated with NUVA-SCAN, that couldn't afford to maintain their own facilities. So they shared docks, or rented as needed.

But sometimes they weren't so poor. They simply didn't want the attention.

Jani wandered up and down the rows until she found a smallish Corsair class ship with an indy designation and a posted manifest showing "general agricultural cargo." It straddled the dull center in every category—crew size, cargo capacity, GateWay rating. The *Agneta*, registered on Whalen's Planet.

For this run, anyway. She stood in the display port and watched the loaders move unmarked crates in and out of the hold.

"Can I help you?"

Jani turned and found herself face to face with a wary-looking older man in a dark blue coverall, *Billy* in faded letters hand-etched over one shirt pocket. "Stopping at Padi?"

"Not really a stopover—just in and out."

"Taking anyone on?" Jani forced a smile. Just another Outer Circle scrub looking for work.

"What's your spec?"

"I have some doc tech experience."

"Any doc work would have to be off-log."

Jani kept the smile fixed. The ship was rated for one documents technician. If they took on another, that rating would be upgraded, which meant higher docking fees. If she had needed to track hours to keep her professional rating, well, she wouldn't have earned them on this flight. She pretended to hesitate, then shrugged. "General crew's fine."

Billy's eyes widened, that *think I got a live one* goggle. "We're topped out for crew, too, to be honest. Better if I keep you off-log period."

Which means there will be no record of my arrival on Padishah. That was the good news. It also meant that she probably wouldn't get paid, which would stink if she actually cared. Meanwhile, Billy would tell the poor official doc tech that he would have to chop their pay in order to cover hers. *Then he'll pocket the difference.* She reached into her jacket for her ID, and was about to hand it to the man when he waved it away.

"We head out in fifteen minutes." He pointed out the door that led to the crew entrance.

And thus does Lita Mansour disappear. Jani boarded, took care to choose the smallest cabin, and waited for the *Agneta* to get underway. Then she maneuvered the warren of short corridors until she found the office of the official doc tech, a young man named Sadi who wore the hangdog expression of one who knew his pay had just been sliced *again.* A few minutes later, she sat nestled in a cubicle with barely enough room for a half-desk and chair, and began working through a stack of invoices. Later, she would destroy the Mansour ID and make up a new one, and she'd be one step farther along a path she had negotiated so many times before.

Some moments later, she realized she was humming. A song from her childhood, about returning home after a long journey.

———

Arrival at Padishah Station was announced by the squeals of docking alarms and the soft clicks of airlocks. Jani tumbled out of her cabin berth, scrabbled for her duffel, and was halfway out the door before memory caught up with motion. She lowered to the edge of the thin mattress, and breathed slowly and deeply until her heart stopped pounding.

She dug through the cabin's supply drawer until she found a self-heating mug and a packet of instant coffee. *John Shroud would be horrified.* She drew water from the cup-sized sink, stirred in the coffee powder, and pulled herself together while she waited for the mug to heat.

She examined her face in the mirror, crossing her fingers that nothing had grown, shrunk, or shifted overnight. She thought her jaw had gotten a bit heavier on one side, but decided that if anyone said anything, she'd blame a toothache. Her eyefilms had withstood the stress of her nap, but she played it safe and applied fresh, then drank her coffee and ran up a new ID while she waited for them to set.

She skipped out while Billy and his crew argued with dock personnel, and vanished into the innards of Padishah Station. The place had upgraded since her last pass-through. What had been an average-looking warren of concourses and corridors was now a pleasant, airy facility replete with tree-lined walkways and tiny hidden gardens. She cobbled together breakfast from a row of vending machines—a cup of foamy espresso, spicy soup, a sugary bun—then parked on a bench to eat and people-watch and wait for the first-shift bell to chime. Then she followed the signs until she found the corridor leading to the dock management offices.

She found Scheduling at the end of a short hallway, a glass-walled office furnished with a circular bank of workstations at its center and systems hubs at the four corners. In the middle of it all stood Teddy Honore, a short, dark man in sand-colored shirt and trousers, black curls twisted into a topknot, earpieces in both ears. He had been born on Padishah, spoke the colonial and Earth provincial dialects of all three languages plus standard English and Hortensian German, and felt the same passion for the intricacies of scheduling as Jani did for paper. His official title was First Shift Dock Scheduler, Padishah Station. He'd applied for the position as fully human, and was hired because Padishah had yet to require gene scans for job applicants.

That will change. Someday soon. Until it did, his unofficial duties involved protecting Thalassan interests, guarding against adulterated shipments and fake licenses, and general intel gathering. Jani liked him. He reminded her of Dieter. Steady. Persistent. Hard to ruffle.

Here's hoping he remains that way. Jani rapped on the glass panel door. Teddy ignored her for a time, concentrating on the numerous screens and the columns of numbers and letters that ribboned through the air in front of him. She rapped again. That earned her an annoyed glance. When she raised her fist to knock a third time, Teddy waved the columns away and barreled to the door. *"What the hell do you want?"* Or words to that effect, Padi Farsi muffled by the thick glass.

Jani answered in Elyan Greek. "Is this where I'd come to track down a friend?"

Teddy hesitated. Just a single hitch in the beat, but enough to indicate that he understood the question for what it was, a request for help from another Thalassan agent. His hybrid eyes, filmed brown rendered black by the harsh interior lighting, widened for an instant before narrowing in feigned anger. "This isn't a matching service." He turned on his heel and returned to the workstations, bringing back the ribboning figures with a magician's wave of his fingers.

Jani left the way she'd come in. She wandered for a little while, alternating between checking her timepiece and watching the corridor. But there were too many station security and ComPol about for comfort, so she hunted for a more suitable meeting place.

She found it on the floor below, near the entry to a secondary corridor, well away from the crowds. A pocket garden consisting of a few shrubby fruit trees and a two-tier fountain arranged in a circle around a stone bench, illuminated by a beam of fake sunshine. She collected a second cup of vending machine espresso, sat on the bench, and watched who passed by on their way down the corridor. One couple. A few minutes later, another. A few minutes after that, the first couple exited, parting ways before reaching the heavier foot traffic of the main corridor. Nothing handed off. No backward glances. Whatever the transaction involved, it had been completed out of sight.

The cycle repeated a few more times with the same two principals, a young man and a young woman. Add to that a distinct lack of the ComPol presence that existed most everywhere else, and Jani knew that whatever all-seeing eyes the station had installed, they didn't reach this particular spot. She relaxed a little. She wouldn't be able to remain there long. Whatever went on in those out of sight rooms was not for public viewing—someone would be bound to notice her and take exception. She would wait as long as it took to finish her coffee, then figure out a new way to draw Teddy's attention.

I can't just order him to help me—he's not my agent. He reported to Feyó's security dominant, he had a very specific job to do, and he needed to do it with care. Tracking licenses meant dealing with the sort of people who controlled out of the way places like the one she sat in now. It would be safe to say that he sometimes had cause to watch his back, even fear for his life. For all she wanted to scream as the minutes ticked away, this would need to be played at his pace. Assuming he wanted to play at all.

At least she didn't have to wait long. Teddy soon strolled into view, earpieces dangling around his neck on a thin cord. He went directly to the vend alcove, made his purchases, then ambled over to the bench. He paused, waited for her to nod, then sat so that he faced the corridor as well.

"I admit to feeling a little at sea." He uncapped a dispo of a beverage so green it seemed to glow, and took a swig. "I don't believe we've ever met, but you do seem vaguely—" He leaned closer and stared into her eyes, then jerked bolt upright. "Oh, holy shit."

Jani felt a jolt, the icy finger that had touched her heart in years gone by every time someone stared too long. Every time she feared she'd been recognized. *This is Teddy, dammit. You want him to know it's you, remember?* "I thought they looked pretty good."

"We hybrids can usually spot one another." Teddy tapped the corner of one eye. "Sometimes there's something about the sclera coloration that's just a little off. Other times, the irises are too, I don't know, not enough detail, maybe." He looked around, a faint smile forming as he watched the slow, steady parade up and down. "But then, you know, sometimes it's a voice you remember from a training class about how to spot jazzed documents without a scanpack. I will add that if you can spare some of that—" He scratched his nose, rubbed along his jaw. "—I'd love to take it off your hands." Another green swig. "So, ná Kièrshia, why are you wandering Padishah Station wearing a face not your own?"

"What have you heard?" Jani sat back, fingers laced around one knee, and tried to convince herself to relax.

"I may have received a ping from Thalassa to keep an eye out." Teddy opened a bag of coated nuts, the foil crackling like a small flame. "It was sent to all agents in the Outer Circle and Pearl Way. General howl of dismay sort of thing. They don't know where you are." He held out the bag to her. "A warning about the food here. These are called 'crunch nuts.' Macadamias with a laser pepper coating. Most humans can only eat a couple before the pain starts, so don't go popping them in your mouth like, you know, candy. At least not where anyone can see you." He made a show of biting one with care, chewed slowly, pretended to cough. "Company called 'Jaki Pax.' First vend stuff I've ever seen made for Haárin tastes and tolerances."

"Is there contact info on the package?" Jani took one of the bright yellow confections, bit it, felt the wash of heat fill her mouth. "They'd love this back home."

"A general mailbox. Just the name. That'll change. It's a big hit. The Haárin usually clean out the alcoves when they pass through." Teddy studied her face, then shook his head. "I can guess why you're here." Another nut crunched. "Pierce missing."

Jani checked the wall chrono. *Fifteen hours since I left Thalassa. Fifty hours remaining.* "Any rumors as to who?"

"No names. Just the usual judgement calls. Chickens come home to roost. I mean, I like the guy but you have to admit he must've made some hard friends along the way." Teddy's eyes narrowed. "And I could've answered any questions you have via Misty, so?"

Jani hung her head. *And so it begins.* "I need a document."

"And what does it have to do with Pierce?"

"It may be related." Silence stretched, and Jani knew Teddy was perfectly willing to wait and let her fill it. "An old docking slip."

"How old?"

"Prewar."

"By that you mean the last idomeni war? And you need me to pull it why?"

"You have access because it's your department. I don't have general access to archives anymore. I was booted out of Registry seeing as I'm no longer human."

"Human's overrated." Teddy took another nut, but instead if eating it, he rolled it between his fingers. The shiny coating flashed light like a jewel. "Timing is everything, you know?" He shook his head. "I may not have it anymore. Registry's been rounding up old paper. The dock archive got the message yesterday morning. Priority the first. We crated up the stuff *tout de suite* and sent it to Staging."

Jani's heart skipped a beat. If she were still Registry, she would've heard of those plans during the initial stages. She would've known to hurry. "Docking slips. Anything that shows provenance. Chain of possession."

"You have any ideas as to what the hell Registry's thinking?"

"Maybe pending lawsuits. Some Family inheritance squabble." Jani struggled to focus as her mind raced. Could she talk her way aboard the ship that carried the documents? Could she break into a secure hold without triggering alarms? *And you thought this would be simple.* Her chest ached. *When was it ever?* "I know you don't have to help me. I know it's better for you if you don't. It doesn't concern you. It's not supposed to concern me."

Teddy rocked his head back and forth. "Yeah, I should just go back to the office. Forget I ever saw you. Or maybe even earn a few gold stars and rat you out."

Jani started to offer a Vynshà Haárin gesture of acquiescence, but stopped herself in time. "If you could give me a couple hours head start, I'd appreciate it."

Teddy slumped. "You really think I'd do that to you?" He leaned close, lowered his voice to a whisper. "Thalassa would still be a hundred hybrids living in the Main House if not for you. I mean, I know Shroud and his crew make us what we are, but—but I know that you're the one who talked Feyó's security into convincing her to send us out here to watch and—and learn shit and cover our asses. Build a world." His voice grew rough. "You give us something to aspire to. You're trying to make us a people." He looked away for a moment; when he turned back, he blinked, dabbed the corners of his eyes. "Besides all that. You get the feeling, you know, that something's going on. It's in the air, like a faint stink. You can't place it, but dammit you know it's there."

Jani nodded. "I know that feeling."

"Everything's Family lately." Teddy finished his drink, crumpled the dispo, and flicked it into a nearby recycler. "Shipments getting leap-frogged to the front of the line. Dock reservations getting bumped. Crews being bribed to jump ship. The kickbacks must be flowing like wine into the main station coffers. I'm tearing my hair out trying to keep it all straight because half my staff quit yesterday to work for Family companies. It's like they're getting ready for something, you know? Gearing up." He quieted for a time, head down, hands hanging between his knees. "Maybe transfer hasn't been closed out yet. I can go down there, give them some damned excuse. A screw-up. Wrong paper in the mix. But I can't promise anything."

"I appreciate it. More than I can say." Jani dug a stylus and a scrap of paper out of her duffel, wrote out the code strings, and pushed the note along the bench to Teddy, who set his bag of nuts on top of it.

"What the hell, you know?" After a beat, he picked up the bag with the note and stuffed both in his pocket. "I'm already on Feyó's shit list. Always getting questions about my expenses. Like they think I'm getting rich on this job. It's insulting."

"I don't think she believes in agents. Spies. Tsecha's assassination caused her to turn against those sorts of activities."

"Well, she better wake up, because if she wants to deal with humans, those sorts of activities have to be on the top of her to-do list." Teddy seemed to sense Jani's nerves. He gave her hand a tentative pat, then pulled away as though he feared crossing some line. "I'll do what I can."

Jani's tension ebbed. A little. "I appreciate it." Nothing to do now but wait. *Sit on my hands.* Keep from going mad. "Any way I can come along?"

Teddy shook his head. "Sorry. Access is limited. High-level clearances only." He stood, started to leave, then stopped. "I'd really love to know what the hell is going on."

"I'm not sure myself. When I learn anything, I'll get word to you." Jani stood, and found herself the focus of an irritated look from the young woman, who currently escorted her fifth new partner down the corridor. "I think I had better find another place to land. I've worn out my welcome here."

Teddy turned to watch the pair pass, and grinned. "A fencing operation. Brother and sister. Vending licenses, I think." He waited for Jani, and they left the garden together. "Hate to say it, ná Kièrshia, but I think I know why Feyó keeps you on a short leash." He laughed silently. "Tries to, anyway."

"If they corner you, give me up. I should be out of here by then." Jani smiled.

"For she is like the wind." Teddy shook his head, then pointed towards the ceiling. "Give me two hours. Fifth level, above the garden we just left. High end station offices, so no monitoring. There's a planter wall with decorative niches. Around the back, left side, six up, five over." He plugged his ear pieces back in and veered off in the direction of the dock offices.

Chapter Eleven

Five minutes after the effects of the tranq wore off, Niall would've happily done murder for a nicstick.

They left him alone for the better part of the...well, he assumed it was the day. He wished he knew whether it was station day or night, just so he could have some solid fact to hitch his thoughts to.

He heard footsteps in the corridor, assumed a shift changing of the guard. He stepped as close to the door as he could without setting off the proximity alarm. "Hey? What time is it?"

No answer. Just the sound of those footsteps, receding.

He wished to hell he could see. He touched the blind spec earpiece, then jerked his hand away as the device emitted a warning *beep*. Paced from one end of the cell to the other, thought back over the last weeks, every new face and odd occurrence, and tried to figure out who the hell had taken him and what that meant.

Smuggling. Yeah, no stretch there. That had always gone on to some extent at colonial bases. But other alarms had ramped up over the last few months. Shifting personnel, names he recognized replaced by names he didn't. Changes in who signed off what.

Switching out colonial Spacers for Earthborn—he didn't agree with that, but Regionals got whatever they wanted as long as they could justify it to Supreme. Which meant Roshi. Who was Earthborn.

If I survive this exercise in overreach, Roshi, we really need to talk about your Earth bias. Niall dropped to the floor, managed thirty push-ups before his arms gave out, then rested his chin on the cold lyno to support his head the best he could. *You're being played.* They all were. *Earthborn Spacers.* Fresh out of Boot, most of them. The sweet little pumpkins couldn't recognize what was happening right in front of their eyes, signs any colony kid could spot a light-year away. *They can't deal with Haárin, either.* Even the damned hybrids scared the pants off them.

He stood, then resumed pacing, swinging his arms and working his shoulders for good measure. Whoever they were, they didn't seem to be in a hurry to grill him. *They're giving me a chance to stew. Get nervous.* In years past, he'd have psyched them back. He'd have pretended to sleep, and snored loud enough to rattle rafters. Shouted obscenities at irregular intervals. Sung the same song over and over, an irritating bit of sap like "Oh, Carry Me" or "Your Shining Eyes." Back then, he'd often earned a beating for his trouble, but there had been a few times where he made an impression and was hired to join the scrum. He got some of his best jobs by being an asshole.

And then there were other times where, if you pushed them hard enough to come after you, it was like that first fault in an ice sheet. That first hint of weakness. And like that physical crack, the psychological one always radiated. Then you knew you could use it like the weapon it was. To wedge, play one against the other, divide. Learn things. Information could prove as valuable as merchandise sometimes.

Niall stilled, hung his head. *That said, I really am too old for this shit.* Maybe you did reach the point where you lost your nerve, your patience. Maybe—

The whispering slide of the cell door lock mech cut off his inner ramble. He reached for his belt, the shooter that wasn't there.

"Back on the cot." A rough voice. Male. Manxman, from the sound of him, all the words running together in one long garble.

Niall shifted so he faced the direction of the voice. "Why?"

"Because I said so." A ringing clatter, like shaking chains. "Need to dress you up. Time to go visiting."

Niall sidestepped to his cot and lay down. This time, he rested his hands loosely on the bed frame, fought the urge to tense up as he braced for the sick shudder of the immobilization field. It helped, a little. Instead of worms under his skin, he felt a weird pulsation, as though his whole body rippled in a breeze.

"Put your hands together. I'm going to cuff you. If you try anything, Bennu here will smash your kneecap."

Niall did as he was told—it would be suicide to try something now. He winced as the cuffs dug into his skin. After they shut off the field, they needed to pull him to his feet, then drag him until he regained control of his legs. He counted steps, gauged direction. Listened. Smelled the air, caught hints of cooking odors and the sweat stink of his escort.

And then, something else. Faint, and gone so quickly he wondered if he'd really smelled it at all. Jarring, because it didn't belong amid the stale and the rank. A light scent. Floral.

Like perfume.

———

The room they dragged him into felt cooler and smelled better. They pushed him into a stiff frame chair, then stood on either side and took hold of his arms, cracked his cuffs' magnetic locks, then pulled his arms behind the chair back and refastened the cuffs. The chair back was too wide, the side edges sharp plastic that dug into the undersides of his arms. He pressed against the chair back and rolled back his shoulders in an effort to ease the pressure, which forced him to pull his hands apart and caused the cuffs to dig into his wrists even more. For the next few minutes, he alternated between easing the pain in his arms and his wrists, and wondered if his guards had done this on purpose or if it was just a combination of rotten luck and a crap chair.

He waited, and wondered what would happen next. *It's the waiting that gets you, and don't think for a second that they don't know that.* Problem was, years had passed since his last bout of survival training and he wasn't sure how he would respond. Physical pain, he could handle, probably—his augmentation would see to that. Drugs, though. Drugs worried him. The old ones—Sera, Ascertane— could be countered if one's augie functioned as it was supposed to. But now the medicos were finding that augmentations could deteriorate over time in some individuals. *And there are always new drugs.* Always new ways to break you.

He almost groaned in relief when he heard the door open, but swallowed the sound in time.

"Good afternoon, Colonel." The first voice he had heard, the filtered, indeterminate one, sounding too cheerful by half. "I trust you're feeling better, more settled."

I'm wonderful—thank you for asking. Niall swallowed that back just in time, too. Debated not answering at all, even though he knew he had to give them something. *Stick to simple answers for the time being.* Let them think him cowed, rattled, off his game, for now. "Yes."

"I can't hear you, Colonel."

"Yes." Niall relaxed his shoulders—once more, the strain on his wrists eased as the sides the chair back dug into his arms. *C'mon, augie, dammit.* It wouldn't prevent the physical damage, but it would deaden the pain, allow him to concentrate on his answers instead of trying to figure out how to sit.

The clatter of ice tumbling into a glass broke through his thoughts, followed by the sound of pouring. *A drinker.* A fact to file away. *Damn.* Drinkers could be hard to manage. Depending how bad they were, the littlest thing could set them off and next thing you knew, your face was getting splattered across the walls.

"Hard to sleep on stations. Too quiet. You never realize how much noise there is in a planetside building, in a supposedly quiet room, until you're out here." A sigh. "I never liked silence. Nothing to focus on to lull you. Too many opportunities to think." Footsteps, back and forth. Pacing. "How is ol' Roshi these days?"

What? Niall shrugged, and earned raking pain in both arms for his trouble. "I trust he's well."

"You *trust* he's well?"

"We haven't spoken in some time." Better to claim ignorance of anything going on at Supreme Command.

"Is that why you went to Karistos, to get away from him?"

"I go where I'm sent."

"Sending back updates about all those Thalassan mongrels? Whatever science experiment John Shroud is cooking up this week?" The screech of a chair being pulled across the polycoated floor, followed by the hum of ergoworks. "Tell me about Jani Kilian."

What—? Scattershot questions—was this the plan? Well, that made Niall's attempts to determine what in hell they wanted from him more difficult. Without a discernible pattern, he'd have a harder time figuring out where they were headed, what information they were really interested in, what he could learn. "What do you want to know?"

"What's she been up to?" Words steeped in annoyance, their flow broken by intermittent gulps. "For a while, she was everywhere. Every time I turned on the bloody—" A hitch. A grumble. "Every-where. Then she fell off the edge. Almost a year gone, it's like she no longer exists." A pause. "She's not dead, is she? That would be too much to hope for."

Niall sat silent, head down, as multiple scenarios whipped through his head.

Loyalty test. The Service had kidnapped him to find out whether his and Jani's friendship had crossed security lines.

Service factions. One of the anti-idomeni cells, wanting to learn more about Thalassa, the Elyan Haárin. Armaments. Supply lines. Capability.

Secessionists. They hated the idomeni as much, if not more, than they hated Chicago. They wanted their worlds free of interference from both sides, which meant no hybrid contamination. They would want to know Feyó's plans for Thalassa, whether more hybrids were being made. What role Jani Kilian, the first hybrid, would play.

Or maybe it's my old friends. He suspected that some Thalassans had dipped way more than a toe in the smuggling pool. Had a deal gone awry? *So why drag me into it?* What could he—

He fought for balance as a hard punch to his chin knocked him half out of his chair.

"Colonel?" The voice shook a little. "Please pay attention when I'm talking to you."

Man's hand. Niall filed away that bit of information as he worked his jaw back and forth, then probed with his tongue to see if any teeth had loosened. Tasted blood. "Just wondering why you're asking me about her." His voice came thick as that all too familiar coppery taste filled his mouth.

"Yours not to reason why. Yours but to do and, well, not die, we hope. At least not right away." A wet chuckle, followed by more clinking ice, more pouring. "So, answer my question. She didn't die, did she? You'd think word would've gotten out if she had. Bloody Commonwealth holiday."

Niall detected the barest sweet scent of whiskey in the air. "Little early in the day, isn't it?" He swore at himself before he finished speaking, but bulled through regardless because he needed a fucking 'stick and he was sick of the blindspecs and his wrists ached and his arms felt sliced and his shoulders burned and where the hell was that fucking augmentation when you needed it?

The second blow had more behind it than the first. He spit blood this time, along with at least one tooth, and felt his lip grow hot and swell.

"Well, now you'll have matching facial ruts. You'll look quite snarly, I'm sure."

Niall swallowed, tried not to cough, and failed. He craved water. Even an ice chip would do, something clean and tasteless. *If I ask, he'll give me whiskey.* He winced at the thought of alcohol washing over open wounds. Cleaned the inside of his mouth with his tongue, swallowed once, then again. "Jani's fine."

"She's *fine?* I thought she was your great and good friend." A snort of disgust. "Still banging Shroud?"

What the fuck? "We don't discuss our social lives."

"It's not her social life I'm asking about, though, is it?" A bark of a laugh. "Not that blond? Anais' old piece?" Another chuckle, this time with added wheeze. "They deserve one another."

Niall closed his eyes. Wondered if he were in fact unconscious, and this was a nightmare.

Or dead, and this was hell.

———

The discussion continued for too long, questions about Jani interspersed with raw comments that under different circumstances would have earned the speaker his very own punch in the mouth. Niall tried to keep his answers vague. Unfortunately, that only served to irritate his interrogator, whom he'd dubbed "Whiskey." He struck Niall one more time, hard enough to loosen another tooth.

Soon after, Niall's guard arrived to collect him. He walked elbows-out, felt the cool air sting and dry whatever damage the chair edges had inflicted as every step sent vibrations up his spine and neck to his aching jaw. *You pathetic old man,* his younger self mocked him. *Crying over paper cuts.*

Once he reached his cell, he stood with his back to the door until it shut. Then he turned and thrust his hands through the meal tray slot. Sagged with relief as his guard unlocked the cuffs—he worked his fingers as he paced, as the numbness gave way to pins-and-needles that aggravated the pain in his wrists and arms. Eventually, fatigue and sedative hangover ganged up on him, and he lay down on the cot and tried to figure out what the hell had just happened.

Yours not to reason why. Fucking Tennyson. Never a favorite, that poem. Too damned kludgey. He replayed every word spoken, every question and response, every sound. *I know you, you bastard.* But how?

Eventually, pain dulled and bleeding stopped on its own since augie, that pissant wanker, had let him down. He'd have to see the medicos if he got out of this mess, find out what was going on. *You picked a hell of a time to abandon me, little friend.* He had a nasty feeling that sooner rather than later he was going to need all the pain-deadening help he could get.

As he pondered, sounds drifted in from the corridor. Cheers and whistles. A rabid announcer. *Football?* Then it hit him. *Oh hell—the Commonwealth Cup.* The elimination rounds had started the previous week. Acadia Central United and Victoria had drawn the same flight, and he'd been looking forward to talking Jani into wagering. *She hates her singing voice.* So, he had planned to make her learn the Victorian team song if his Auld Vics carried the day. "Who's playing?" His voice emerged a rasp barely above a whisper. He doubted anyone heard.

But then he heard the scrape of footsteps. "Guernsey Freehold. Whalen." A mutter of disgust in thick Manx English. "Fuckin' Whalen. Fuckin' joke."

"Llongo still out with his leg?"

"Aye, the bastard." Silence for a time. Then the sound of more shuffling footsteps. "You're fer Auld Vic, then?"

Niall worked to his feet and edged closer to the door, one hand in front so he could feel for the wall. "That I am." He winced. His jaw had already stiffened and his wounded lip pulled even though he tried to move it as little as possible.

A snort. "Albritton's overrated. Lowery's good, though." A pause. "Face hurt?"

Niall debated how best to play it, decided *tough old bird* the better path. "I've had worse." At least that had the benefit of being true.

Quiet on the other side of the door, followed by muffled conversation. "Supper's coming up soon. Told Bowa to slip something cold on your tray."

"Thanks." Niall felt that mental knock back on the heels that came from receiving a kindness from an unexpected source. He'd known plenty who thought nothing of their charge's suffering. He'd never been a particularly sympathetic soul himself, especially in his youth. *'Course, it could just be an act.* Yet one more way to glean information. *Good cop, bad cop.* Anyone would seem kind compared to his punch-loving drunk.

He leaned against the wall and listened to the game. *Is it a local transmission?* If so, that meant the station hosted a relay. *Announcer's speaking what?* Sounded like either Hortensian German or Josephani Dutch—he couldn't hear enough to tell which. That meant they could still be in the Outer Circle, where most every world hosted its own Service base. Depending on the size of the station, there could be Service presence here, as well. If he could just figure out a way to attract attention, cause some damage that would signal an emergency team. *And manage not to kill myself in the process—*

Chapter Twelve

Commotion in the corridor derailed Niall's escape planning. Voices he hadn't heard before, multiple sets of footsteps.

"Lay down, now," his guard rapped the door for emphasis.

Niall stumbled back to the cot and stretched out just as the lock mechs hissed and the door opened.

"Hello, Niall."

Niall's ears perked. A woman's voice. *Definitely a woman.* No filtering or other attempt to disguise. Hint of an accent he couldn't place, except that it was colonial.

Then he sniffed, and caught a whiff of the same perfume he had smelled earlier. "Have we met?"

"I don't think so. I believe I'd have remembered." A sigh. "Artur, take off those 'specs. They're inhuman."

"But he said—"

"I said, take them off." Still the same vocal silk, except this time coated with frost.

"Ma'am." The click and hum of a device being activated. "Assume the position."

Shit. But just as Niall braced for the sick shudder of the immobilization field, he heard the woman sigh once more.

"I don't believe that's necessary, Artur. I'm sure the colonel can be trusted to behave himself." The frost had melted, mostly, but the barest hint of warning chill remained.

"Ma'am." If Artur had any objections, this time he kept them to himself.

Niall sat up, stuffing his hands beneath his thighs to show that he intended to be a good boy. Heard a soft buzz as Artur inactivated the blindspecs' locking mechanism and slipped the damned thing off. He worked his neck, rocked his head from side to side, heard his cervical spine crackle like old paper.

He tried to open his eyes, then squinched them shut as the brightness stabbed, triggering a round of sneezing that reopened every wound and reactivated every ache and pain. He covered his face with his hands and pressed the spot beneath his nose, breathed in slowly, felt the heat rise and flood his cheeks. *A sneezing jag? Really, Pierce, you dumb—*

He flinched as fingers encircled his wrists, eased his hands down. He forced his eyes open, blinked like mad as the tears fell, smearing a face only inches from his own.

Slowly, his vision cleared and details sharpened. Rose-tinged skin. Freckles splashed across a high-bridged nose. Russet, shoulder-length hair. Full mouth.

"You poor man." She turned to the guard standing beside her, Artur the football fan, who proved to be a lantern-jawed hulk with a fully-loaded belt that held cuffs, a pulse-charged truncheon, and a shooter. "Bring me a med kit." She wore the sort of long-sleeved utility coverall that Jani used to live in, but while Jani wore hers so loose you could fit another person in there with her, this woman's was definitely...fitted.

That body. Niall tried to speak, but his mind had blanked. *Those eyes.* If filmed, they were a color he had never seen before. If real... *damn.* Clear, brilliant turquoise, like the waters of the Caribbean.

Dammit. He shifted in his seat, wondered if crossing his legs would be too obvious, settled for dropping one hand over his dick as unobtrusively as he could. *Steady on.* He fixed on a point on the wall opposite, tried to think about the report he'd have to write once he got back to Fort Karistos. The hours of debriefing.

"Oh my, Colonel, what did he do to you?" She stroked along his aching jaw, then unbuttoned his shirt and checked the undersides of his arms, fingers lingering just a moment too long, her soft scent sweet as life.

Wake up, you fuckin' idiot. She and Artur had slipped. *They both said "he."* Niall had felt sure Whiskey was a man, but it was nice to have confirmation. That little triumph helped him focus, calmed his sexual shakes. *Grow up, old man. It's the oldest trick in every book ever written.* But still, he couldn't stave off that oldest of unsettling feelings when he looked into those eyes.

Artur returned too soon. He handed off the med kit, then tossed a knowing look at Niall before leaving to stand out in the corridor.

As his sea-eyed nurse rummaged through the packets of meds and bandages, Niall worked his jaw, concentrated on calm. He scanned the cell, compared the map he'd formed in his head with the reality. *There's a mirror over the sink.* Unfortunately, it would be fashioned from polished metal or coated poly. No way in hell they'd be stupid enough to allow him a sheet of glass. *The lip of that table looks interesting.* He wondered if it was all one piece, or could be removed. "Thanks for getting him to remove the 'specs.'"

"There's no reason for them. My partner tends to be overly cautious." Sea-Eyes soaked a pad with antiseptic and leaned close to wipe Niall's jaw. The top of her coverall gapped open, then closed, with every move.

Niall forced himself to stare over her shoulder. "Does your partner have a name?"

"He does. He wants it to be a surprise."

"Do you want yours to be a surprise, too?"

Sea-Eyes smiled, but kept her attention focused on her task. She worked silently, dabbing, cleaning, applying skin adhesive and anesthetic cream. "That's better." She tucked everything back in the medkit, then cleaned her hands with an antiseptic wipe. "You look raffish rather than dragged through a gantlet." She had been kneeling at his feet. Now she sat back on her heels and gazed up at him, head tilted to one side. "Niall Pierce. The Admiral-General's Colonel. I've heard so much about you over the years." She leaned forward and pressed her arms to her sides—the move pushed her breasts together and allowed a glimpse of lovely cleavage. "Can all of it possibly be true?"

Oh fuck—she's good. Niall bit back the urge to brag, to make those eyes shine brighter and that mouth smile. Forced images from his mind of all the things they could get themselves up to, even with the cell door open and Artur of the Knowing Look standing just outside. "The story about the llamas may have become embellished over the years."

"Oh, that's the one I wanted so much to be true." She laughed. Then she held out her hand. "I'm Morwenna MacCallan. You may have heard of me."

"You're—" Niall stared, as that enlivening flame of lust flickered, then died a smoky death. "Yes, I believe I may have heard your name mentioned once or twice." He gripped her fingers lightly, then released her as though she burned.

"During those misspent days of your youth?" Morwenna boosted up on her knees and leaned forward, resting her elbows on the edge of the cot. "What about more recently?"

"More recently?"

"You've been on Karistos for how long now? Two years?"

Niall started to smile, but the stiffness of his jaw stopped him. *This is where it really starts.* Whoever Whiskey was, he was an amateur. A sideshow. Morwenna had been a player in the game for over twenty years, since the first glimmers of the War of Vynshàrau Ascension. *What does she want from me?* He struggled to fight down that part of him that wanted to savor that smile, and concentrated on the danger that he now found himself in.

He focused on taking in as much as he could of his surroundings. The construction and lock style of the door. The lack of any interior controls, which meant his room had always been a cell. Filed it all away because he knew the blind specs would soon be snapped back on and who knows when they'd be removed again? "Two years. More or less."

"How can Mako go without his colonel for so long?" Morwenna's voice was pleasantly throaty, an alto with a touch of a morning growl. "Has he replaced you? Found a new Niall? Sent you away for good?"

"Are you asking if I'm on his shit list?"

The sea light flared, but softened almost instantly. "I'm just curious."

Careful, jackass. Niall had heard stories during his wilder years. Anyone who pissed off Morwenna tended to pay for their sins. "We communicate on a regular basis." Better to feed her enough information to keep her interested, and hint that any mistreatment of him could have consequences. "Why do you ask?"

Morwenna shrugged. "I can always use a friend in the Service. Especially a highly-placed one like you."

"I see. You just want me for my mind."

"Well, Colonel. We have to start somewhere." Morwenna buttoned his shirt. Then she took hold of his chin, turned his head one way, then the other. "I'll make sure you're seen to by more professional hands than mine." She clucked her tongue. "There was no reason for this. I will have to have a little discussion with my associate." She stood, managing to brush his arm in the process. "You and I will talk again soon."

"I look forward to it." Niall touched his injured cheek. Already, it felt cooler, less puffy. "Think you could leave those 'specs off for a little while longer?"

"Of course." Morwenna's smile held warmth now, along with a touch of kindness. "As long as you don't try anything foolish, I think you'll find that your time here could be quite comfortable." She collected the medkit and left the cell, leaving behind her scent and a last view of her lovely figure.

Definitely the good cop. For now, at least. Niall stood and walked to the sink, washed his hands, checked his face. *Jesus.* Morwenna had been kind—he looked like he'd been rolled in an alley. His puffy cheek and lip made his face look lopsided, the split had bloomed into an angry red gash spotted with scabs. Some swelling and bruising around one eye. He opened his mouth, checked the gap where his tooth had been.

A highly-placed friend in the Service. Was that all she wanted? *Like hell.* Shipment information seemed more likely—stations, dates, number of Spacers in the escort. Everything she would need to arrange for the hijacking of armaments. Special systems components. Official parchments and other documents supplies. *Yes, she'd love to have an old fool like me in her pocket.* She'd grant him a cut of the proceeds, of course. She might even grant him more personal favors. *For a while.* Once she had him good and compromised, she'd work her fingers through his short hairs and twist.

That said, if the situation presented itself, he would willingly sacrifice his body for the good of the Service.

The things I do for my Commonwealth. He bent over the sink and laughed silently until the gash in his lip reopened and the blood dripped.

———

As Morwenna had promised, more practiced medical care arrived. Someone retrieved his tooth from the interrogation room, and a brusque older woman with gray hair like sprung wire reinserted it into the socket. Niall's augmentation had finally kicked in by that point—all he felt was the pressure, the odd twinge. Then came an injection into his gum, followed by advice to chew on the other side of his mouth for a few days.

Guess that means they don't plan to kill me right away. He nursed a hope that Morwenna would stop by to check up on him, but was doomed to disappointment. Instead, supper arrived courtesy of Artur, who cracked wise about Victoria's chances in their draw and hinted at the possibility of a wager.

The contents of the tray proved the usual. Vat-born chicken and reconstituted carrots—damn, but he already missed the fresh produce from the Thalassan hydroponics sheds. Coffee that stank like it had sat on the heat for days. The promised cold treat proved to be ice cream, but he knew from its candy-pink color that it was the vat-made stuff, so stuffed with stabilizers that it wouldn't melt even when placed over an open flame.

But, surprise of surprises, nestled beneath a dispo napkin, three beautiful, wonderful nicsticks. Without thinking, Niall grabbed one, bit the tip, and took the deepest drag a human being had ever taken in their entire sorry life. *Shit. Menthol.* An abomination under normal circumstances, but for now he didn't care. He shivered as the nicotine hit his system and his mood lightened and the thought occurred that he might be able to talk his way out of this whatever the fuck mess he had gotten himself into after all.

Then he looked down at the half-spent 'stick, at the two remaining on his tray. He wanted to think that someone—Artur, maybe, or one of his cohorts—had pulled them from their own stash and tossed them his way out of pity. But he had spent too much time on both sides of the bars not to realize that it was a statement. *Three 'sticks.* Enough for a couple of hours' enjoyment, but not enough to allow him to assume that more would be forthcoming unless...*unless I give them something they want.* Only exactly what that something was seemed rather vague at the moment.

So, he snuffed out the 'stick, rolled it up in the napkin with the others, and stashed them in his shirt pocket. In his younger days, he might have felt nervy enough to shove them up his ass for safekeeping, except that he had been on both ends of that search both literally and figuratively and it never worked out well for anyone.

Then he laughed, silently, bitterly. *You've fallen right back into the muck, haven't you, boyo.* A far cry from a master's thesis on the finer points of Adama's many interpretations of *King Lear. It's like you never left.* The hardscrabble colony orphan, again and always.

Niall sat quietly for a time, then started picking at his meal. Despite the lack of pain, he found he couldn't open his mouth very wide. He managed to eat by cutting everything into small pieces and inserting them between his teeth. As he chewed, he pondered the odd interview with Whiskey, the questions that made no sense. *All about Jani.* It meshed with his surmise that his captor was a more recent vintage, since he knew of their friendship and a little about Thalassa.

Someone who knew us both. And had reason to dislike him and Jani heartily. That list was, unfortunately, rather long. The last few years had been a little too eventful. There had been a number of thwarted incidents he'd never told Jani about, both during his time as her security chief and afterwards. He'd informed Pascal, of course, and over time had come to acknowledge the younger man's competence. *Those two.* If he lived to be a hundred—a prospect that was by no means a sure thing given his present predicament—he'd never understand that relationship.

His pondering were interrupted by Artur, who entered bearing the hated blindspecs.

"Lights out time, Victoria." The man gestured for Niall to lie down.

"Couldn't you leave them off for the night?" Niall made a show of massaging his neck. "They make it hard to sleep."

"Sorry, Vic. Lady's orders."

"Morwenna?" Niall felt a stab of disappointment. "I thought she told you to leave them off. Give me a break."

Artur laughed, a hacking sound like he cleared his throat. "She had a little back and forth with her partner. Break time's over, man. You had your treat for the evening." He held up the blindspecs. "Sleepy time for you."

Niall pushed away his half-eaten meal. Took one last look at the ceiling, and noted the location of air vent. *Probably too small for me to crawl through.* Before he could gauge for sure, Artur set the blindspecs in place and activated the lock. The world went dark.

"'Nighty-night, Victoria. Sweet dreams." Another damp chuckle. The slam of the cell door. Silence.

Niall rolled his pillow and tucked it under his neck, then his head, in fruitless struggle to balance the weight of the 'specs. Listened for any noise out in the corridor, footsteps or voices or sounds of a football match. *Station night.* Instead of a guard outside his cell door, he wondered if Morwenna's security monitored him from a central console? *Could they be shorthanded?* Somehow, after meeting his hostess, he doubted that would prove the case. Smugglers at her level didn't make mistakes. Too many competitors eager to fall on them when they did.

He yawned, jaw cracking as he fought against opening his mouth too wide. Wondered if they'd drugged his food. Nothing serious, just a mild tranquilizer. Enough to keep him quiet for a few hours.

His thoughts drifted back to Chicago days. *Jani and Pascal.* They had met just before Jani arrived on Earth for the first time. Anais Ulanova, Exterior Minister and Pascal's...sponsor, had dispatched him to learn more about the woman Interior Minister Evan van Reuter was transporting to Chicago to investigate his wife's death. *How did that work out, Evan?* Not so well, unfortunately for the last van Reuter. Crimes came to light thanks to Jani's investigation, the wartime murders of Service personnel. Not only was he removed from office, but the other NUVA-SCAN Families stripped him of his fortune, his properties and licenses, on Earth and in the colonies.

Not a damned thing left to his name. Niall had met him briefly during the discussions as to his fate. There would be no public trial for the V in NUVA-SCAN, no matter how heinous his crimes. Just quiet negotiations between various lawyers, and relocation to a secured residence-slash-prison outside Chicago.

He should've been executed. Whiny bastard. Niall could still see him, a tall, dark-haired drink of water, surrounded by the faint aroma of liquor and bitching about how Jani—

Niall's eyes snapped open, the tranquilizer haze shredded and gone. *Evan van Reuter is under house arrest.* How the hell could he turn up on a station at the ass-end of the Commonwealth?

It couldn't be, could it? How in the hell—

No. No. Van Reuter was like most Family, helpless without staff. Lots of staff. Hell, he probably couldn't even dress himself, especially now that he—

"Now that he's half-toasted all the time." Niall wiped a hand over a mouth suddenly gone dry. "Oh shit." That would mean what? That wasn't about him at all, was it? That he was just the bait, someone for Morwenna to toy with.

He would want Jani.

Chapter Thirteen

After Teddy left, Jani found a restroom, tucked into a stall, and ran up a new ID. *Zara Marté*. A good Pearl Way name.

After that, she wandered. She checked out several vend alcoves and bought an assortment of Jaki Pax, which she stuffed in her duffel for later evaluation. Counted the passing minutes. Monitored display boards for incoming flights from Elyas, and tried to push the thought from her mind that Lucien had been waylaid and even now underwent questioning by Feyó's security. *They'd have to drug him to get him to talk.* And it would have to be the right drugs, not the ones that his augmentation blocked. But given that Feyó didn't like Lucien anyway, the attempt would pretty much be guaranteed.

She stood before a shop window and pondered whether she could continue without Lucien. One of the shop's ChanNet screens shimmered to life when it sensed her presence and before she could wave it blank, an all-too-familiar figure filled the display. Her jaw clenched as she watched newly-appointed Deputy Exterior Minister Anais Ulanova sweep across a stage to loud applause. The woman wore a tunic and trousers in darkest blue, black hair combed back and bound in a tight chignon that accentuated her narrow face and high-bridged nose. The severe styling harkened back to her earlier political career, which had crashed thanks to Jani.

Well, she did try to kill me first. Or rather, she had sent Lucien to do the deed, a move which most definitely had not worked out as planned.

Jani caught a flicker out of the corner of her eye, a reflection in the glass. A man standing off to the side, watching her. She started to edge in the opposite direction, then stopped and turned. "Never come up behind me like that again."

"I wanted to surprise you." The station's fake sunlight caused Lucien's altered eyes to appear more hooded. "Perhaps that wasn't the best idea."

"I'll be glad when we have our own faces back. I catch sight of my reflection and it's like I'm not really here." Jani turned back to the display. "That's the third time I've seen her on ChanNet this week."

"She's navigating her comeback." Lucien gave his former patroness a bored once-over. "She allowed a reasonable amount of time after Scriabin's death."

"Four months?"

"He was only a nephew, not a child or a spouse." Lucien did a quick count on his fingers. "Six months would've been more seemly given he was prime minister, but I'm guessing she's grown impatient. She's been out of the spotlight for over a year."

Jani watched a second clip play. Anais wielding a shovel at a groundbreaking on Amsun, which had been the headquarters of her Exterior Ministry offices as well as the traditional base of operations for her Family. "You think she arranged it?"

"Death of a close relation?" Lucien folded his arms and stroked his chin, a pose that made him look stodgy. "It's happened in the past. The Families tend to prefer other forms of destruction. Financial. Reputational."

"I'm not looking forward to her sticking her nose back in Outer Circle business."

"She can't touch you."

"You really think she won't try?" Jani motioned for him to follow. "I've talked to Teddy. Assuming he can find the document, I pick it up—" She glanced at her timepiece. "—in about an hour." She flinched as Lucien pressed close. He moved his sling bag to his other shoulder, took her waist and pulled her closer. "What are you doing?"

"We never touch in public." He draped his arm over her shoulders and steered her along the line of display windows, the side of his hip brushing hers with every step. "One less reason for any scanner to think it's us."

"I'd say 'good thinking' if I didn't also know it was just an excuse to feel me up."

"There's that, too." A hint of familiar grin, turned smirk by fleshier features. "What do you mean, if he can find it?"

Jani explained about the paper activity and the worry that the document she needed may have been shipped out. "Teddy can tell me where it's going. I can try to get on the ship and—"

"And what, steal it? Break into a Registry ship documents hold?"

"I've done it before."

"When?"

Jani started to reply, then hesitated. "It's—it's been a while. I'll get to the ship, and go from there."

"No. If Teddy doesn't get it, we're done." Lucien pulled her closer, whispered in her ear. "Whoever contacted you. Perhaps they knew the paper was getting moved and thought you could get hold of it before it was. Or they sent you on a mad chase on purpose, knowing you wouldn't be able to get it. Jerking your chain for the fun of it."

"That doesn't make sense."

"None of this makes sense. Who did you know who'd want to taunt you like this?"

Jani's step slowed. "I've been thinking about that." She stopped in front of a toy store—one of the displays showed a child darting back and forth as she tried to grab a bird-shaped drone out of the air, crying out in frustration as it swooped and glided just out of reach. "Unfortunately, the list isn't short." Faces flickered in her memory, some dredged up from the depths, others, never more than an absent thought away. "Someone I thwarted when I was auditing Service supply streams. An old acquaintance from my less lawful days. They wouldn't have any trouble finding me. I'm in the newssheets. On ChanNet."

"That's not helpful."

"I won't be able to narrow it down until I see the manifest that goes with the docking slip. Odds are that it will be the next thing they send me to find." Jani tried to work out from under Lucien's arm, but he tightened his grip and held her fast. "Once I know what they're looking for, I'll have a better idea of who they might be."

"You think we're going to get dragged someplace after this?"

"It is a scavenger hunt. That's how they work." Jani counted out on her fingers. "There are three archives within easy reach of this station. New Indies, Tsing Tao, and Abercrombie. I am pretty certain that whatever they're looking for, it will be in one of them."

"So we're leaving after you pick up the document?"

"There are flights to all three stations leaving within the next few hours. I know they will set another time limit, and I want to add in as much buffer as possible."

"Why the rush, I wonder?"

"Teddy said Registry was calling in all old paper. I am guessing whoever has Niall knows this, but for whatever reason can't get what they need."

"So you're their cat's paw?"

"I guess."

They continued to wander the concourse, sticking to the crowded areas, examining shop displays. Jani checked time's passage on various clocks, listened to Lucien's critiques of the merchandise, and realized after a while that she no longer minded his arm around her. It felt comfortable, even a little comforting. Like a favorite jacket, or the Thalassan sun on her face.

———

"He said fifth level, above that little garden." Jani stepped off the lift and scanned the area, a carpeted mezzanine that overlooked the main concourse. Here and there were benches and tables that at any other time might have been filled with office workers on break but that now, thankfully, stood empty.

She spotted the planter wall, a freestanding divider at the far corner of the space, alternating rows of stone and brick dotted with inset niches and pots of flowering plants. She hurried toward it, Lucien at her heels.

"Slow down." He gripped her elbow and tugged.

"I know." Jani inhaled deeply then exhaled once, then again. "Should be around the back."

Once they reached the wall, Lucien stepped ahead of Jani and made sure all was clear. She then followed him and headed for the left side. *Six up.* She counted the rows of stone and masonry from the floor up. *Five over.* She tapped each brick in turn, came to the one occupying the fifth space, gripped the rough jutting edges, and eased it out. Reached inside the gap, gasped as her fingers brushed plastic, and realized she had been holding her breath. Pulled out a long, thin document tube.

"I haven't used a dead drop since primary school." Lucien leaned against the wall, hands stuffed in pockets.

"Then this was a nice refresher for you." Jani shoved the brick back into place. Then she pulled up a leg of her jumpsuit and tucked the tube down the shaft of her boot. "We need to find a quiet spot so I can examine this, then notify who the hell ever that I have it." She heard voices and pressed against the wall. Looked around the end and saw a trio of young women in daysuits standing at the railing at the front of the mezzanine. They waved to someone in the concourse below, then hurried to the lift bank.

Jani pressed her face to cool stone, waited for the *ping* that announced the arrival of the lift car, the sound of closing doors. Sensed Lucien's approach, felt him press against her.

"Anyone finds us here, they're just going to think we're making out."

"Dammit, sometimes you say the wrong thing at the wrong—" Jani knocked her head against the wall once, then again. Stopped when Lucien pressed his hand to her forehead, like a cushion.

"Jani?" His voice was even, steady. "We'll find him." He wrapped his arms around her and rested his chin on her shoulder.

Jani felt the tension ease, her heart slow. She grew conscious of Lucien's breathing, how it kept time with her own.

After a few minutes, he released her. "We should go." He checked the mezzanine, then beckoned for her to follow. "Find a place where you can work."

They boarded the lift, and Jani hit the pad for the main concourse. "There's usually office space you can rent by the hour. After I figure out where we're going next, I'll reply to the account that sent the original message—" She watched as the indicator for the Main Concourse flashed, then blinked out.

Problem was, the car didn't stop.

"What the hell?" Lucien extracted his shooter from his slingbag and tucked it into his waistband, then let the bag slide to the floor. "Stand in the back corner."

"I know where to stand."

The car continued its glide down, past the commercial dock floors, the facilities offices, maintenance and storage.

Jani hit the STOP pad, the alarm, the pads for the upper floors, but none responded. She excavated her shooter from the depths of her duffel and smashed the ceiling illumination case with the butt end, plunging the interior into darkness. Then she took her position on the opposite side of the car. "You ready?"

"Never a dull moment with you, is there?"

"Could be a VIP override."

"Uh-huh. Sure." Lucien activated his weapon—the soft hum seemed loud as a shout. "Stay in here. Let me handle it."

Jani fired up her own shooter. It vibrated ever so slightly, as though coming alive. "You know there'll be more than one."

"This isn't what you do." Lucien pulled more weapons from his bag—a knife, another shooter—and stashed them about his person. "Stay. Put." He snapped a band around his wrist, a device that would block any equipment monitoring his approach. "If anyone comes in here, take care of it. You've done that before. Otherwise, I want you to be here when I get back because we're going to have to move."

"You don't even know what's out there."

"While you were wandering around waiting for Teddy to stick your document in a hole in a wall, I was studying the layout of this station." Lucien's voice came harsh and low. "That's what I do." He handed her an earbud, then inserted its twin in his ear. "Let's keep the chatter to a minimum."

Jani shoved the bud in her ear as she watched the floor indicator flash. They had reached the subbasements, the very depths of the station. One blink. Another. Then, finally, they stopped.

"Sixth level down. The car opens onto a landing area with two ways in and out." Lucien raised his weapon in a two-handed grip. "You can see the one on the left from where you are. I will go to the right—that feeds into a maintenance chase and from there to the emergency exits to the docks. That's where they would've gotten in."

"And if they're waiting for us when the door opens?" Jani brought up her weapon.

Lucien said nothing. He kicked his bag toward her, then braced against the wall of the car.

The door slid aside to reveal darkness tempered by a string of emergency illumins dotting the ceiling, their thin, green light like a view underwater. Lucien slipped out, the soft padding of his shoes on the bare composite floor the only sound.

Jani stepped to the front of the car to check the left hand corridor and cover Lucien's back. Watched him fade into the dark. After a few moments, she retrieved his bag and slung it over her shoulder so it covered her front as her own duffel protected her back. Not the best shielding in the world, but at least it was something. Then she set out after him.

Because not listening is what I do. She hugged the wall, one eye on the left side exit. Did it wrap around to the chase, or was it a dead end? *Would've been nice to know, Mister I-studied-the-layout.* Despite the uncertainty of what lay around every corner, of what the hell was happening, she felt oddly...focused. *Augie's dead.* Her Service-implanted chill was no more. All she had now was adrenaline and experience—

—and anger. Cold anger. At this attack from persons unknown. At being jerked around like a puppet and threatened with the loss of a friend if she failed to comply. At her deteriorating scanpack and having her profession yanked out from under her and the entire fucking mess of it all.

Focus goddammit. She edged forward in the green-tinged dark, saw a crumpled heap in the opposite corner, a spreading pool of dark beneath. *Light-colored clothing. Not Lucien.* She hadn't heard a shooter blast, which meant he'd used his knife. Between that and the block, whoever awaited them up ahead wouldn't know he was coming.

She edged forward, stopping when her foot brushed another body. She stepped around the blood and entered a narrow corridor lined with access doors and instrument panels. She slipped inside just as Lucien knifed a third assailant, a man who managed to fire off one errant blast before collapsing—it ricocheted off bare metal fittings and pipes before dissipating along the coated ceiling. The crack shattered the very air within the narrow space.

Jani's ears popped. She smelled ozone. The odor triggered memory. Memory triggered reaction. She let the bags slip to the floor when she heard the pound of boots on the other side of the instrument wall. Saw the hatch nearest Lucien open, a man scramble through.

Lucien, still hunched over his kill, turned toward the opening door. He pulled his blade out of the body, reached for his shooter with his free hand.

The man had already sighted down. Point blank range.

Jani raised her shooter.

Fired.

The pulse packet glanced off the man's chest, struck the bare metal hatchway and rebounded, hitting him in the neck. He yelled and collapsed against the wall, limbs shuddering, smoke rising from his blistering skin, boots sliding on the smooth floor as he struggled to get his feet under him.

Lucien raised his weapon to finish the man off, but Jani got to him first. He still held his shooter, but his hand, spasmed from the pulse, couldn't close around it. He looked up at her, eyes narrowed and lips curled, and swore at her in Phillipan French, words ragged from his damaged throat. She shoved her shooter in her belt, took his head in her hands, and twisted. Heard the muffled crack of his neck, and staggered back as his body slumped against her, then slid down to the floor. She watched it twitch, then sag. Smelled the tangy stink of urine as it flowed from the body.

She bent low and looked out through the hatch. Saw only an empty corridor, the same sickly green lighting. "I don't see anyone else." After a moment, she felt jostling, a hand gripping her arm.

"Jani? We need to move."

She pulled the hatch closed, then turned and followed Lucien. She helped him pry open the cover of a vent access port. Then, one by one, they wedged the bodies into it, cleaned up the mess as best they could, and headed for the lift. This time, the floor pad worked.

Jani checked her clothes for blood. Sensed Lucien's stare, and found him looking at her as though she were a stranger.

"Are you all right?"

"I am." Jani looked down at her hands, her cool, steady hands. "I am."

"Okay." Lucien spoke slowly. "We need to find Teddy. I would like to talk to him."

Jani thought for a moment, then nodded. "Yes, I would, too."

———

Teddy's work name at Padishah Station was Raoul Sebastien and it was under that name that Jani and Lucien found his flat on the tenth floor of the station's residential sector. The flat blocks were densely-packed, utilitarian, the corridors blank beige poly broken at regular intervals by darker beige panel doors bearing clear placards displaying address codes. Lucien touched the door chime, then stood, hands at his sides. Waited, then hit the chime again.

Teddy finally opened the door on the third ring. He didn't look happy to see them. He stood in the entry, shirt collar undone, shoes in hand. "Executive asked for the quarterly report a week early. I just got in." He stuck his head out and looked up and down the corridor, then stood aside with a weighty sigh. "You had better come in." He checked again after they entered, then locked the door. "Why have you—" Speech gave way to grunts of protest as Lucien grabbed him by the shirtfront and rammed him against the wall.

"What the—fuck—" Teddy struggled to breathe as Lucien took hold of his throat and squeezed.

"Lucien." Jani tried to loosen his grip, but he elbowed her out of the way. "I don't think he knows."

"Oh, I think he does." Lucien's voice emerged too calm. "They overrode the lift system. That means an inside job." He shook Teddy so hard the male's teeth rattled. "And who's the only one who knew we were here?"

"What the fuck happened? Just tell me what happened I don't know what just tell me please." Teddy stared, wide-eyed and gasping for breath.

"Dammit, let him talk." Jani took hold of Lucien's thumb and pulled it back until he released Teddy's throat.

"Why should I?"

"Because Dieter trusts him and if he trusts him, then so do I." Jani wedged between the pair, pushing against Lucien until he backed off.

Teddy sagged against the wall and slumped forward, hands on knees, head down, until his breathing slowed and steadied. When he finally looked up, he fixed on Jani. "What the fuck happened?"

Jani tried to act as a barrier between him and Lucien, who attempted to step around her every time she moved to block him. "I had just picked up the doc. We were on the lift headed down to the Main Concourse. They overrode the lift mech. There were four of them."

"So then what—?" Teddy glanced at Lucien. "Oh, shit." He walked to a chair and lowered into it. "Where are they?"

"A secondary vent shaft next to the section cut-off. Didn't look like anyone had opened it in years. They'll keep." Lucien pulled over a chair, set it directly in front of Teddy, and sat, leaning forward, elbows on knees. "So?"

Teddy's skin greyed. His eyes glittered. "I didn't say anything to anyone about you." He shook his head so hard his neck crackled. "Do you know how many gangs have bases here?"

Jani shrugged. "That doesn't explain why one of them would've come after us. We just arrived a few hours ago."

Teddy's gaze flicked over the room, as though the answer lay hidden amidst the furniture. "Maybe someone from the fencing operation took exception to you."

"What fencing operation?" Lucien turned to Jani, his expression shading from murderous to merely irritated.

"Four armed men seems like overkill for a couple of license boosters, don't you think?" Jani stifled a yawn. She felt as though she viewed the proceedings through a curtain, that post-augie haze that she wasn't supposed to experience anymore. Then her stomach rumbled—she lowered to the floor and dug one of the snack containers out of her duffel. *Purple Passions.* She shook out a piece of candy and bit into it—the combination of sweet, spicy, and hot shook her out of her daze.

Lucien stared at her as through she'd erupted into song. "You're eating?"

"I'm hungry." Jani held out the container to Teddy, who shook his head and regarded her much as Lucien had. "What about the doc request? Could that have triggered someone?"

"I didn't formally sign it out. I did what everyone else does around here—I just went in and took it." Teddy looked away. "Sorry. I know you don't approve of that sort of thing."

"I'll overlook it this one time." Jani shifted her foot, felt something rub against her ankle. *The document.* She needed to let her puppet master know she had it, then figure out where she and Lucien needed to go next. She checked the clock on Teddy's wall, counted the hours until her deadline. *Thirty-one.* She shoved another candy into her mouth, chewed fast, and swallowed. *Maybe it's just low blood sugar.* The first thing John used to ask her when she complained of feeling wobbly was when she last ate. "We should get going."

Teddy boosted to his feet and headed for the door, his relief palpable. "Don't worry about the bodies. You would be surprised how often they turn up in the lower levels." His smile was tight and vanished as quickly as it appeared. "And you'll be long gone before they're found anyway." He flinched as Lucien brushed past him on his way out.

Jani squeezed his shoulder. "Thanks for your help." She headed for the door.

"Ná Kièrshia."

She turned.

"I swear I didn't say anything to anyone." Teddy's eyes welled. "I swear."

Jani nodded, then left him standing shoeless in the middle of his living room. Walked out to find Lucien leaning against the wall opposite, arms folded, head down.

"You're the only reason he's still alive." He set off toward the stairwell at the end of the hallway, then stopped and waited for Jani to catch up.

Chapter Fourteen

The office kiosks were located on the Main Concourse level, along a quiet, carpeted corridor well away from the shops and restaurants. Jani knew she and Lucien, rumpled as they were, looked out of place, and hoped the daysuited patrons who bustled in and out were too preoccupied to notice.

She inserted untraceable chits into the kiosk payment slot, keyed into the office, activated the privacy barrier, then dug out her scan-pack and handheld. "What if Niall's captors arranged the attack?"

Lucien wedged into the tight space, glanced around for the nonexistent second chair, and made do with perching on the edge of the desk. "That makes no sense."

"It does if Niall's dead and they want to shove it all under the rug. The only connection we have to them is their message on my handheld." Jani shook the dock slip out of the tube and laid it atop the desk—the government-grade parchment flattened with nary a crease. She took out her handheld, imaged it, then saved the fiche.

Lucien dug a hastily-bought meal out of his bag. A sandwich. A dispo of soda. "You're really going to wait until the last minute to send it?"

"I've given it some thought. I want as much time as possible to find the next one. I doubt it will be as simple to obtain as this one was."

"You call what we just went through 'simple?'"

"But for the attack, it would've been." Jani paused in mid-examination. "I know how that sounds."

"No, I don't think you do." Lucien wrestled with the dispo closure. "What if that's not the doc they're looking for? What if Teddy screwed up? What if you're wrong?"

"Teddy didn't screw up and I'm not wrong." Jani checked her timepiece. "Thirty hours to spare and counting." She sat back and stared at the slip of pale blue parchment. Then she uncased her 'pack. It took three tries to activate. Then it stuttered through the scan, the indicators flickering between yellow and green with the occasional concerning flash of red. But despite all that, she could still read the information in the encoded inlays and chips. It wasn't much, but it was enough. "I knew it."

"What?" Lucien alternated between taking bites of his sandwich and picking out bits that he flicked into the trashcan.

"A Family document. A Family dock." Jani nodded. "Not surprised. This request is for a Family dock."

"Which Family?"

"Scriabin." Memories tumbled like the pieces in a child's game— she could almost hear them click into place. "At the smaller stations, Families shared docks. During the war, we had to revise the docking requests because they would play games, name primary and secondary owners and switch designations back and forth so quickly that we'd lose track of who owned what, who owed the docking fees." She massaged her temples. "I get a headache just thinking about it."

"You sure it isn't these things?" Lucien picked up the Purple Passions container and shook one of the candies onto his hand, rolled it between his fingers, then touched it to the tip of his tongue. "Damn." He winced, then rinsed his mouth with soda and spit into the trashcan, the liquid sizzling as it hit the inset incinerator.

"Don't waste them." Jani snatched the container away. "It's nice to be able to taste something for a change." She popped three of the candies into her mouth for emphasis. "It was always about taxes. No, I take that back. Sometimes, it was about transferring ownership to another Family for a nominal price, so the shipment would be downgraded. Then they'd take that same shipment and slip it into the the black market sales channel, raise the prices back up, but only pay tax on the lower value."

"Why bother with the transfer at all?"

"Close out the paper trail. As far as we would ever know, the shipment stayed within the Families. It wasn't my job to follow up and make sure that the new owners actually had the goods. That was External Revenue's job." Jani nodded to herself. "Like I thought, this does involve ownership of a shipment. A small commercial vessel carrying who knows what docked at a Family dock. And now, years later, someone wants to get their hands on whatever that shipment was."

"I don't know how you did that all without screaming."

"I spent more hours in tiny offices stuffed to the ceiling with tax attorneys and accountants arguing depreciation minutia than I care to remember." Jani chased down the memories with more candy. "It could get pretty scream-worthy." She poked at the dock slip with her finger. "I just didn't think it would be this easy. Should it have been this easy?"

"You don't know what else they have planned. Perhaps you better take your definition of easy where you can find it." Lucien downed the last of his soda and dumped the containers in the trash. "So now what?"

"I tell my cage-rattler I have the doc and wait to hear. I'll be surprised if they reply right away. They'll draw it out, so I'll worry if they received it. They want me to panic, send follow ups."

"You've been through this before?"

"I've been on the sidelines for a few kidnappings. Smugglers invade one another's turf, so someone will get grabbed and held until a deed or title is officially transferred." More long-forgotten faces appeared before her mind's eye. "I met more than one deregistered dexxie who was happy to take that job."

"You were never tempted?"

"Dexxies who crossed that line didn't have very long life expectancies. Like the accountants, they knew too much. I always stayed low-level. Tried not to attract attention." Jani glanced up at Lucien to find herself the focus of his *concerned* stare. Always an odd sensation, like being worried over by a shark. "If you have something to say, say it. Since we left the basement, you've been looking at me like you're afraid I might explode."

"Since we left the basement." Lucien's brow arched. "What happened down there?"

"I know I should've stayed in the elevator."

"That's not what I meant." Lucien slid off the desk and lowered to the floor at Jani's feet. "If you think I'm upset that you possibly saved my life, perish the thought."

"You'd have been fine." Jani leaned forward, and brushed a lock of hair off his forehead. "You saw him coming. I could tell."

"Okay, but I likely would've been shot or otherwise injured, and then we would've had to deal with finding medical help along with everything else." Lucien's brow furrowed, but given the changes to his features, it made him look more angry than puzzled. "I know your history. I read the background reports. It's just the first time I've worked with you in the field." He hesitated, his jaw working. "It was educational."

Jani held up her hands, palms facing each other. Saw the man's head clasped between them, and pushed the image from her mind. "I killed Durian Ridgeway with my bare hands."

"That was your augmentation. That's supposedly not functioning anymore." Lucien paused. Another frown. "Are they sure about that? It would explain it."

"They tested it. It no longer activates."

"By 'they,' you mean John Shroud." Lucien spoke the name as he always did, like he'd just tasted something sour. "He's lied to you before."

"He wouldn't lie about this."

"And you know that how?"

Jani started to reply, then stopped. *I'm pretty sure he wouldn't lie about this.* She would have to discuss the matter with him. *Assuming he ever wants to talk to me again.* "Of the three closest documents facilities that house archives, only the one at New Indies is equipped to handle Family documents. That's where we need to head next."

Lucien's head dropped. His laugh held no humor whatsoever. "I shouldn't even bother to argue, should I? Tell you that you should send that thing out and let them tell you where to go next instead of guessing?"

"New Indies is a major archive, unlike Padi. Better security. It would be further down the recall list because it's more trustworthy." As Jani worked through the likely location of the next step in her paper chain, she felt herself calm, settle. Up to that point, she hadn't realized how tense she'd been. "If their stuff's already been recalled, that means a trip to Chicago, and I don't believe that would serve the purposes of whoever is directing this production. They need to stay one step ahead of Registry so they can claim an old shipment. Whatever it is must be worth a lot of money, even after twenty years."

Lucien yawned. Started to rub his eyes, but stopped before he damaged any injection sites and pressed the heels of his hands to them instead. "Families employ their own dexxies. I'm sure the larger smuggling operations do as well. Why get you involved?"

Jani shut down her scanpack, packed up her gear, rolled up the dock slip and returned it to its case. *Did you ever think, with all the shit you've done in your life....* "We should get going."

———

Lucien handled their boarding. He bought the billets, carried his and Jani's bags, and herded Jani ahead of him to their cabin. It wasn't big enough for both of them to stand at the same time once he pulled down the bed, so Jani sat cross-legged on the narrow platform while he set out one of the oversize T-shirts she wore as a nightgown, then pulled out his own sleepwear and undressed.

Jani watched as he stripped down to his underwear. Admiring his body had always been one of her simple pleasures, but this time all she could see were the bruises that had bloomed on his thighs, ribcage and back, the scarlet shooter burn on the side of his arm. "Hold on." She pulled a first aid kit from her bag, ignored his protests as she cleaned his wound, then dabbed anesthetic cream and repair boosters. Under normal circumstances, the intimate nature of her activity and the close quarters would have led to the usual outcome.

But these circumstances were far from normal. She sensed it in the air, in the way that Lucien would meet her eye in the sink mirror, then look away.

After she finished, he started to wash his face, then paused halfway through and stood still, hands gripping the sides of the sink bowl as through he might vomit. Not an unexpected reaction from the average person, but post-killing backlash wasn't part of his programming. "Looking after you is turning out to be a much bigger job than I imagined." He straightened and flexed his injured arm, wincing with every movement. "Niall warned me when he handed off. Feyó's lack of support. Rising tension between Chicago and the outer colonies. His concerns about you." He resumed cleaning up, then pulled on a T-shirt and shorts.

Jani changed into her own sleepwear, then maneuvered to the sink as Lucien took her place on the bed. "I don't mean to cause trouble."

"No, you just can't help yourself." He lay back, his good arm bent beneath his head, gaze fixed on the ceiling. "So?"

Jani studied her face for a few moments, ran a finger along the injection sites, then continued washing up. "How do you feel right now?"

Lucien shrugged. "I never feel much of anything. We needed to get from one place to another and they were in our way, not to mention they were trying to kill us."

"You kept souvenirs in Chicago. I saw them."

"Old time pilots used to paint symbols representing their kills on the sides of their aircraft." Lucien raised a hand, let it fall. "I left those behind when I left Chicago. I didn't see the point anymore."

Jani folded the disposable towel, shook it out, then folded it again. "I lit a candle for every being I ever killed. Maybe not right after, but eventually."

Lucien raised his head, and met her gaze in the mirror. "Even Ridgeway?"

Jani nodded. "It didn't matter how I felt about them, or even if they would've killed me first. It was just...acknowledgment." She looked again at her face in the mirror. She had examined her filmed eyes so many times over the years, but now even they seemed like they belonged to someone else. "This was different. I'm not sure how to describe it, except that it didn't feel like augie. Augie used to talk to me, encourage me."

At that, Lucien boosted up on his elbows. "You're kidding."

"No. There were times when, if it had been human, I'd have shot it just to shut it up. This time, it was all me, and I didn't think twice.

"So you're like me now?" Lucien frowned. "I don't know how I feel about that." He scooted to the edge of the bed as Jani clambered over him and stretched out, her back pressed to the wall.

After a few minutes, the cabin illumins dimmed. Jani waited for the sounds of soft snoring or some other indication that Lucien had fallen asleep. But he continued to lie with his eyes open, staring at the ceiling, as aware of her as she was of him.

"I know I'm not the woman you met on the *Arapaho*. I'm not who I was when we lived in Chicago, or when you first came to Thalassa." Jani held her hand above his body, felt his warmth radiate, but didn't touch him. "I'm the frog in the pot, and the water is heating. I don't see it myself, what I'm becoming. I see it in the faces of those around me. When I blurt out something inappropriate, or laugh at the wrong time. When I get angry." She formed a fist, shoved it under the too-small pillow. "Except, every so often, like in the basement, I sense the temperature change. Then, I see what you see. The difference."

Lucien exhaled shakily. Discussing feelings made him uncomfortable. It made him feel lost, and it showed. "We dock in seven hours. You'll feel more like yourself after you get some sleep." He closed his eyes, turned his face away. Soon, his breathing slowed, deepened.

Jani listened to the rise and fall, which combined with the distant rumbles of the ship and the occasional ping of a cabin door to signal the start of a quiet, routine trip. *Except nothing about this is routine.* She prayed for the first time in months, asked her Lord Ganesh for wisdom, and that he remove all obstacles that would prevent her from rescuing Niall. Wondered where the next document would lead them, and what she would do when she got there.

Chapter Fifteen

Jani awoke an hour or so before the scheduled docking at New Indies Station. She crawled with care over Lucien to keep from waking him, dressed in the dark, and crossed her fingers that her facial alterations hadn't taken any interesting turns during the ship-night as she slipped out into the corridor and made her way to the observation deck.

The ship had already passed through the New Indies GateWay and now readied to make its final approach to its assigned slip. As it circled the station, Jani saw the first in what turned out to be an array of warning buoys set out some distance from the commercial docking section. A few moments later, the reason for the warning became apparent, a stretch of open grillwork around which buzzed construction 'bots and the odd human worker. Through the lacy polymetal frame, she caught glimpses of the crosshatched red and white of the temporary barrier that walled off the repair site and served as an additional warning to other craft to stay clear.

"Helluva collision." Lucien moved in beside her. "Somebody got sent back to pilot school." He handed her a dispo of coffee, then took a sip from his own. "So what's the plan?"

"Once I get the information about the next document, find the archive. It's possible they may not have received the notice about my delisting, but if they have, I'll see if I can talk someone into pulling it for me." She met Lucien's questioning look. "What?"

"How will you explain your face?"

Damn. One of the problems with disguising a famous face was that sometimes that fame came in handy. "Undercover mission." Jani walked to a seat as the first of the approach alarms blared and buckled herself in. "We don't have any agents here, do we?"

Lucien settled into the seat next to hers. "We don't do any business with New Indies—you know that. Most of the vendors who trade with Elyas come from the Channel Worlds via Amsun."

"I know." Jani tried the coffee, which like most human-made brew tasted like hot water with added hot water for flavor. "Just thought we might get lucky."

"Another Teddy? That's all we need." Lucien jerked his chin towards Jani's bag. "Are you going to report in?"

"We still have twenty-two hours."

"What if we have to get to a different station?"

"We're right where we need to be, oh ye of little faith." Jani looked out at the bulk of the approaching station and tried to ignore the pressure of Lucien's stare until, with an array of Acadian French curses, she buckled. Dug out her handheld, activated it, sent the fiche.

"Thank you." Lucien settled back. "Forward me the reply when you get it—I want to see if I can trace it."

"You tried tracing the first one—you didn't get anywhere."

"But now I'll have two messages. If they originate from the same place, there will be some common code in there that I can dig out." The subdued lighting cast odd shadows across his altered face, rendered his eyes to slits. "How are you feeling?"

Jani fixed her attention on her handheld. "Clean and green." If the dexxie slang for a good document reassured her companion at all, he kept it to himself.

Minutes passed. Just as the ship entered the dock breezeway and the communications dead zone that would persist until they disembarked, Jani's handheld pinged.

"That was fast." Lucien leaned over so he could read the screen. "That means they're nearby."

"Or they have top tier access. Which means money, influence, or both. Which means Family."

"You have Family on the brain."

"With good reason." Jani's heart stuttered as she opened the message and fear touched her. Had she chosen the wrong archive after all? Would they have to rush to another station, lose time, and put Niall's life at risk? Had she messed up, lost her touch?

The text scrolled down the screen. She read it once, then again. "Well."

"Are we in the right place?" Lucien leaned close and tilted the display so he could read it.

"Yeah." Jani brushed his hand away, and read the message once more.

Two of Six, congratulations!
Such a clever gel
Find what's next in four days' time
Or you'll send your friend to Hell

"That's it?" Lucien slumped back. "What does it mean?"

"It means I have no code strings or any other info to identify the next document so someone can pull it for me." Jani powered down the device and tucked it back in her bag. "It means I have to get into the archive and dig it out myself."

———

"If you can't get into the archive, how are you going to get your hands on the document?"

"I don't know."

They had disembarked as soon as the ship's doors opened, and now hurried through the arrivals concourse as though Feyó herself was on their heels.

"So we're rushing like hell to get where, exactly?" Lucien took hold of Jani's elbow and pulled her to a stop.

"To find the facility. See how well it's guarded." Jani tried to shake off Lucien's grip, but every time she managed, he grabbed her again.

"You think you're just going to waltz in?" He steered her into a sitting area and pulled her down next to him on a bench located on the edge of the crowds.

"Of course not." Jani sat back. Breathed. Scanned the passengers moving through the airy glass tunnel, dressed mostly in casual clothing rather than daysuits given New Indies' status as a prime vacation destination. "But it's a room full of old paper. Maybe they don't guard it well. Or, like I said, maybe they haven't changed my status in their system yet, so I can still get in. Whichever it is, I'd rather know sooner rather than later so I can figure out what to do next." She took out her handheld. "I'm forwarding you the second message."

"Thank you." Lucien pulled out his own device, opened the file, and got to work. "The message bounced all over the place. Multiple relay points."

Jani watched his fingers flick across the input pads. "No point of origin?"

"It's masked. No surprise there, given they don't want you to know where they are until you have what they want." He sat back, rubbed his chin, interest piqued despite his irritation. "I think this may take a while."

"There's something else."

"It's so expensive to route this way." Lucien eyed her sidelong. "What you said about resources and access."

"So Family."

"Or Service. Or a high-end smuggling operation." Lucien set down the device and looked out at the passing throng. "I'll ask again. Any idea who it might be?"

A distinctly unwelcome face formed in Jani's mind's eye. "Anais Ulanova? She lost her ministry because of me." She glanced at Lucien. "And then there's the little matter of you."

Lucien held out a hand, rocked it back and forth in a so-so gesture. "The thought crossed my mind. But I think I would need to be involved to a greater degree if it were she. I think she'd want to injure us both. Perhaps even hurt me more than you."

After a time, Jani nodded. "You know her better than I do." She dug out some credit chits, headed to a nearby vend alcove, brought back a second round of coffee for them both. "Do you think any born-sect idomeni could be involved?"

"Only if they've figured out how to infiltrate our Misty network with perfectly duped coding, which would be really, really bad." Lucien stared into the distance, then shook his head. "I still run into some of the Fort Karistos com folks. If they were seeing that, I would've heard something."

Jani forced down the coffee, supplementing it with another Jaki Pax offering, crunchy cookies with a spicy sweet filling hot enough to make her cough. "How are your Chicago connections?"

"I still have a few. Any message there is going to take a while to run the circuit."

"I know." Jani debated letting the matter drop. Told herself it was an utter waste of time and funds. "Ask them about Evan."

"Van Reuter? He's under house arrest in the Bluffs."

"I know that."

"He's never getting out."

"I thought they worked out a deal. Five years' house arrest, then things loosen up. He gets some assets back."

"That won't happen. Anais will see to that. I think she may hate him even more than she does you."

"Thanks." Jani thought back to the last time she had seen Evan

van Reuter. He had brought her to Chicago under false pretenses, and from there the situation had gone pear-shaped in every way possible. "Maybe he managed to hire someone. Maybe he has friends out for revenge on his behalf. Just ask."

"Fine." Lucien drummed his fingers on the arm of the bench, then made entries into his handheld, dug out credit chits so he could scan the codes and pay the undoubtedly expensive fees. "He was stripped of everything, you know. Family assets were all divested but for funds to cover his maintenance. He sure as hell has no access to any unmonitored communications."

"I know. And I'm the one who set that all in motion." Jani mined her memory for some reassurance, some reason to remove Evan van Reuter from the list of people who hated her enough to kidnap her good friend and send her on a paper chase to save his life. "He was the 'V' in NUVA-SCAN. There has to be someone willing to put themselves on the line for him."

"I still think it's a stretch."

"Just covering bases." Jani felt numbness, that deadening sense that settled when an unpleasant memory revisited. "I heard things when I was still in Chicago. Let's just say that no tender feeling remains."

"No surprise there. You blew up his life."

"He blew up mine first." Jani disposed of her trash, shouldered her bag, and headed down the concourse, ignoring Lucien's grousings as he hurried to catch up.

———

Since it contained a major archive, the New Indies documents facility took up an entire wing of the station. That meant significant staff, a training center, and, unfortunately for Jani, up-to-date systems.

She placed her hand on the first level entry pad, watched the red access illumin remain red and the door to the reception area remain closed. Unlike with her scanpack, washing her hands didn't help. She tried once more, then again. On her fourth failed attempt, the pad sounded a warning beep.

"May I help you?"

Jani's heart thudded. She turned, forced a smile. "I wondered if you were hiring."

The young woman looked her up and down. All business, judging from her crisp black daysuit and tight expression. No interest in or time for nonessential conversation, much less allowing a potential job applicant inside the archive for a tour. "Non-registry jobs are listed on the station's employment board, documents section." She brushed past Jani, passed the ID scan with the proverbial clean-and-green, and disappeared into the sanctum.

Jani wandered the area for a few minutes, pretending interest in the news feed that ran along one wall before adjourning to the outer lobby to figure out next steps. Lucien had left her in order to track down gray market systems brokers, who usually lurked in the less-traveled corners of stations; this allowed her time to sit and observe the parade that passed in and out of the doc center. Documents examiners, holstered scanpacks bumping their hips in time to their strides. File-laden technicians. Vendors, identifiable by their sample cases and harried airs, hustling past her at irregular intervals. One, a departing woman juggling a sample case, a parchment portfolio, and a briefbag, stumbled as her burden shifted, spilling the contents of her briefbag across the carpet.

"Let me help." Jani hurried to assist her, kneeling on the carpet to gather the scattered business cards, handheld, and personal items. The woman's vendor ID, she blocked with her knee, tucking it in her pocket when the woman turned her back.

"I'm so late." The woman collected her gear and hurried away. "Thanks."

"You're welcome." Jani waited for a few minutes in case the woman realized her loss and returned. Then she pulled out the ID and examined it. *Ilsa Meck. Sales. Birdwell Systems.* One of the many commercial chip manufacturers. Fine. She could manage intelligent chip talk in her sleep. Problem was, she knew nothing about Birdwell products specifically. *Don't give anyone the chance to ask.* All she needed to do was get inside.

Just then, a pack of assorted staffers bustled in, bags and trays of food in hand. Jani followed them, took hold of the door from the older man who opened it, and held it as everyone filed inside. She then entered after them, holding up the ID when one of them glanced at her. Waited for the staffer at the front desk to stop her, but he didn't even look up as she passed.

I'm in. Jani followed the snack crew along a series of corridors, then ducked into an empty conference room and hunted for a hard-copy of a site map, which she found hanging on the wall next to the images of the prime minister and Dorothea Aryton, the head of Registry.

Hey, Dolly. Jani studied the severe face. *You've gotten a little grayer since last we spoke.* She took out her handheld, imaged the site map, then scooted across the corridor and into the restroom. Locked herself in a stall, and worked out where to go next.

Oldest paper. The historical documents that no one ever touched, that sat and moldered in boxes and folders until their destruction ticket got punched. *Except now Dolly has called them in.* She lifted her feet when she heard the restroom door open, and listened to a pair of techs bitch about their dexxie and share a flask of, if her New Indies French could be trusted, tequila. After a few minutes, she worried that her thighs would cramp before the two finished drinking. When they finally did, she dropped her feet to the floor with a groan, and resumed her study of the map.

Section H-4B. A twisty journey from her current location. Probably additional security. More doors requiring properly registered hand prints, possibly with added retinal scans. *A few weeks ago, I could've just walked in.* Jani swallowed the anger that insisted on bubbling up whenever she considered her deregistering. *I was struck from the list.* And indeed, it felt like a physical blow, as if they deleted over two decades of knowledge and experience along with her name. *Concentrate.* That didn't matter. She knew what she was. She knew what she knew.

She ran a quick search of Birdwell Systems. They specialized in chips for agriculture-related documentation. *Hydroponics?* She could invent a meeting, invent names—she knew enough about the paperwork and regulations related to the Thalassan sheds to bullshit her way past simple questions. With luck, no one would try to confirm what she said. The facility was large. Odds were that entire departments were unaware of one another's existence.

I can do this. Jani looked down at her jumpsuit, which was starting to look distinctly travel-rumpled. She rubbed away a coffee splatter, dug a make-up kit out of her duffel and applied some color to her lips and cheeks and finger-combed her hair. Set her professional face. Serious. Focused. Shouldered her bag and stepped out of the stall, washed her hands, gave her eyefilms one last check in the mirror, and left.

Years had passed since Jani had last walked through a major documents center, and sense memories returned en force. Fresh parchment had its own distinctive odor, like sun-warmed cloth. Inset chips and inks smelled sharp, chemical, like a skimmer battery after a long drive. Old paper reminded her of Niall's books, vaguely dusty with a hint of vanilla. Add in the whiff and tang of scanpack innards, which always seeped out of the maintenance labs no matter the quality of filtration. Then add in the people, their perfumes and native smells, that vaguely meaty scent specific to pure human. And finally, station air, that always smelled like it had been run through a used sock no matter the location or stature of the station in question.

Jani stopped in mid-stride, stepped off to one side. Leaned against the wall for a moment, then crouched, and pretended to hunt through her duffel. She had expected to be on edge, mindful of being exposed. But overwhelmed by simply being in a place—that shook her. She had always moved quickly, without looking back. She had never had time for the luxury of regret. But now, at that moment, she wondered where she would be if the war had never happened, if she had simply served her time at the Rauta Shèràa consulate and moved on. Would she have remained in the Service, or would she have left and joined Registry? Or would she have returned home to Acadia and helped set up her homeworld's documents system?

Wake up, Kilian. She pushed the thoughts aside, buried them deep, and continued on her way. Hallway traffic had lessened, as it always did as one neared the storage facilities.

Then she spotted the warning signs. A little farther along came the portable gates, the splatter tape that would decorate anyone foolish enough to brush against it. And beyond that, the red and white crosshatched barrier that closed off the hallway like a cork.

Shit. She thought back to their approach to the docks, the warning buoys and repair crews. *The collision.* The document she needed was located in the damage zone, behind three meters of reinforced safety buffer.

"Excuse me."

"Sorry." Jani moved to one side, continued to study the barrier, hunted foraccess ports of any kind.

"Excuse me."

Jani turned, and found a different young woman, just as starkly clothed, just as stern, flanked by two much larger male security guards.

"Come with us, please."

Chapter Sixteen

The security guards bracketed Jani as they followed the young woman through the maze of corridors, which grew progressively wider as the offices that lined them grew larger and more impressively furnished. Single-panel doors expanded to double. The carpets thickened, muffling already-soft footsteps to silence.

They picked up Meck's ID signal, ran a check because Meck had just keyed out. Jani gave herself a mental kick. The problem with getting used to areas with spotty monitoring is that you got tripped up when you entered the ones that actually followed the procedures.

They passed the hallway that led to the entrance without slowing down. *So they're not throwing me out.* At least, not yet. Jani wasn't sure if that was good or bad. Granted, if they did toss her out on her ear, she'd have a hell of a time talking her way back in again. But posh offices meant Authority, which in turn meant Rules, which in turn meant...nothing good. If they treated her as human, she would be accused of impersonating the vendor and possibly arrested. If they figured out she was hybrid, then it became an Incident, requiring diplomacy, which meant Feyó.

You knew this could happen. Jani followed her escort into an office furnished in early Up and Coming, good stock furniture cast from high quality poly and a wall-spanning window overlooking the station's central gardens. The desk, a free-form arch dyed to mimic hardwood, held only a stylus set, a combination comport-workstation, and a nameplate. *Amari Chauvin. Senior Examiner.*

"Sit." Amari took her seat behind the desk.

Jani lowered into the visitor's chair, heard the office door close behind her. Crossed her legs. Sat back. Waited.

Amari watched her, face set in grim lines, no doubt expecting a gabble of excuse and explanation.

Good luck. Jani folded her hands in her lap, looked past the woman to the view through the window.

"What's your name?" Amari's voice held the slightest hint of uncertainty. "We know you're not Ilsa Meck."

Jani smiled. "I'm new."

"We know all our agricultural vendors. If anyone new is to be sent, they let us know and provide details. Like names."

They keep track of ag vendors at the executive level. Interesting. Jani could think of no reason why anyone at that level would be involved with a Purchasing function since the latter had their own documents staff, but she filed the information away for possible future use. *I wonder where Lucien is.* Had they connected him with her? *I still have the comlink he gave me.* What were the odds he wore his? Could she warn him? She glanced at her interrogator, who shifted in her seat as though she were the one being questioned. *Not a practiced hand.* Maybe it would buy her some time.

"Give me the ID you stole." Amari held out her hand.

"I didn't steal it." Jani dragged her duffel onto her lap. "Mère Meck dropped it. I planned to give it to someone here so it could be returned to her, and I got lost."

"You could've left it at the front desk."

"I got turned around. I have a bad sense of direction." Jani dug into the front pocket of her bag. Nothing. Opened the main compartment, hunted through the clothes and other items, came up empty again. *Too damned much stuff.* If she got herself out of this mess, she would need to get hold of a bigger Noah bag. She pushed her holstered scanpack out of the way and continued her search.

"What is that?" Amari shot out of her chair and circled the desk to stand beside Jani.

Dammit. Jani liberated the ID and closed her duffel. "I found it." She tried to hand the card to Amari, but the young woman brushed her hand aside and pointed to the duffel.

"You have a scanpack. I want to see it."

"What's a scanpack?"

"Please open your bag."

Jani started to say that wouldn't be happening anytime soon, but then she watched Amari shift her weight from one foot to the other, hands raised and fingers curled, as though she would tear the bag from Jani's lap unless she could see what was inside. No longer demanding, but pleading.

Twenty years of bullshitting her way out of situations like the one in which she now found herself had given Jani the sense to know when to set a plan aside and change course. She opened her duffel, removed her scanpack, and handed it over.

Amari took it gingerly and held it with her fingertips, as through she feared damaging it. "Where did you get this?"

"It's my scanpack."

Amari cradled the device as though it were made of blown glass. "This is a very special scanpack. Very few were made, and they're not made anymore. Not for years and years." Her expression hardened. "Did you steal it, too?"

"What good would it do for me to steal it? I wouldn't be able to use it."

Amari said nothing. She just held out the device.

Okay. Jani took it back, slipped it out of its holster. *Please you little bastard don't let me down now.* She wiped her hand repeatedly on the leg of her jumpsuit, then pressed it to the activation pads. Felt a sick tremor in the pit of her stomach as the scanpack remained cold, dull black.

Then, after a few seconds, it stuttered to life and executed its start-up sequence, all indicators showing lovely, lovely green. Jani swallowed a sigh of relief as she held up the scanpack so Amari could see it, and found the young woman staring at her wide-eyed.

"Who are you?" Her voice wavered.

Jani looked toward the window. The exterior lighting struck it in such a way that she could see her reflection as through she sat before a mirror. She studied that face that wasn't her own, the eyes with their glittery whites. Then she set the scanpack on the desk, worked her thumbnails under the eyefilms, and flicked out.

Amari clapped her hand over her mouth. Then she hurried back around her desk, picked up her comlink, stuck it in her ear, tapped it a few times to activate the connection. "Editha? You need to get down here." She fixed on Jani, and swallowed hard. "Now."

———

Editha's last name, according to her ID badge, was Bensimon. She proved to be the frozen-faced door dragon who had given Jani the brush-off earlier. The horror at realizing she had ordered Two of Six to cool her heels at the non-Reg jobs board informed her face with goggle-eyed fear that made her look even younger than she no doubt was judging from her dewy skin and the shiny tortoiseshell scanpack that hung from her belt.

My duffel is older than she is. Jani counted backwards. *Well, no, not really.* Looking from Editha to the even younger Amari just made her feel that way.

"Is this a security check?" Editha's voice held the tired resignation of someone who knew they had failed the test and just wanted to get the punishment over with.

For a fleeting moment, Jani felt the temptation to push that point. A blown security evaluation, which could be set aside if they could meet the challenge of finding a certain manifest. She could set a time limit, demand they search round-the-clock if necessary.

Except that there were all these images still fresh in her mind. How Amari had cradled the battered black scanpack like a sleeping infant, and the look on Editha's face just now as it sank in who the woman in the gray jumpsuit actually was. Because they were her kin, weren't they? Colony kids in a Commonwealth universe, who had heard since they were old enough to understand that *they would never be.* That they weren't smart enough, rich enough, connected enough to go anywhere worthwhile or do anything worth a damn.

You're going soft in your old age, Kilian. Jani had gained an advantage she could push to the breaking point, and now all she wanted to do was play fair. Be kind. "No." She sat forward, hands clasped, the supplicant making her pitch. "Actually, I need your help."

————

Jani set out the bare bones of her situation. Niall's disappearance. The need for certain documents to aid in his recovery. She didn't use the word *kidnapping,* nor did she mention the scavenger hunt missives with their mocking tone. She simply gave Editha and Amari the facts they needed. After spending half her life lying just to get from one place to another, telling even part of the truth felt daring, if not dangerous.

Editha had taken the seat at her subordinate's desk. She pressed her fingers to her mouth, then lowered them and shook her head. "I assume you saw the warning buoys when you arrived. The work being done." She gestured towards her colleague. "Amari found you at the safety buffer zone. You know what that means. That storage area is located in the vulnerable area of the station and is therefore closed off until all structural repairs can be completed."

Jani felt each successive fact drive into her like nails. "I understand the situation. But I do need that document, and no one else can find it for me."

Amari pulled up another chair and leaned close to her boss. "We have been evaluating robotics."

"But not with much success, I am afraid." Editha fluttered her fingers. "I understand that Registry Main Archive in Chicago has arrays that can physically sort through files, scan, identify, and extract, but those systems have yet to be transferred to the colonial annexes." Her smile came tight, the awareness of yet another slight, another sign that they were second tier.

Jani read between the lines, for all it didn't require much decoding. *Relations in the doc world sound a little tense.* "Chicago hasn't asked you to transfer any paper?"

"We have heard rumblings, but we haven't yet been advised to make transfer since we are considered to operate at a higher level of security." Editha paused. "That said, two weeks ago, a ship bearing a load of our documents for destruction was hijacked. We assumed at the time that the ship was the thing wanted, but from what you say, it sounds as though the hijackers wanted the paper."

Jani nodded. "Transport-related documents showing ownership of merchandise?"

"Among other things, yes." Editha pulled out her handheld and a stylus and began taking notes. "Why all the interest?"

Jani closed her eyes, sorted once more through the growing mess of details. *Less than two days since we left Thalassa.* Yet it felt like a month. A year. "I've gotten the sense that a number of file cabinets are being sorted. Inventories are being taken. I think. I've been out of the loop for a while now. This is all guesswork on my part."

"But you would be the one to sort it out, would you not?" Editha managed a smile. "I would love to match the dates of documents revisions and case studies with your path through the underbelly of the Commonwealth over the years. There would be a great deal of overlap, I believe."

Jani felt the heat rise up her neck, flood her cheeks. Discussing her former life of crime with a dexxie on the legal side of a highly-placed desk made her feel exposed. Soiled. "I think you overstate."

"I think you were Registry's one-person field test system for the last twenty years."

"Speaking of Registry. You understand that since I've been deregistered, you are taking a chance with your own status by helping me?"

Editha waved her hand. "The paper you seek is not classified. Your Thalassa would see the same sorts of documents over the course of standard trade, and you are the designated dexxie for such. Nothing about this suggests security risk."

Jani shook her head. "You will get pushback."

"I think we can deal with Chicago."

While Editha and Jani talked, Amari sat at her workstation and pecked at her touchboard. "Paper in that section was scheduled for destruction, Ditha. If we can somehow extract it, couldn't we simply label it as destroyed and give it to Mère Kilian?"

"Bypass a formal release request entirely?" Editha nodded. "It's a thought, Mari." Her smile at Jani held more than mere willingness to help. It held kindness. Pride. "Whatever we can do to assist one of our first."

Jani nodded thanks, then looked down at her hands. After years of getting slapped down every time she turned around, it felt odd to be admired for all the trouble she had caused. Hell, it felt odd to be admired, period. *Careful, Kilian. You might get used to this.* She wondered how long it could possibly last. "So. Who do I need to talk to about getting hold of that paper?"

Chapter Seventeen

Head of Station Ian Matrishi inhabited the upper reaches of the station's office complex, with half the floor belonging to him and his immediate staff. The furnishings had the look of real wood and leather, and the carpeting made that of the documents center seem threadbare. In addition to commanding views of the station gardens, occupants of these offices enjoyed terraced balconies furnished with tables and benches along with the odd fountain splashing merrily. Highly placed at New Indies Station looked like a good place to be.

Even the voices sounded different. Hushed, as though their owners labored in a sacred space. *The station could be interesting,* Jani's friend, Major General Frances Hals, used to say, her own New Indies lilt dulled by her years at Fort Sheridan. *Always afraid the Families will overhear.* "Tell me about Père Matrishi."

"Well, he's younger than you, so if you call him that, he'll ask you to call him 'Ian.'" Editha's smile thinned. "He can be...oh, how can I say this." She sighed. "He tries."

"That sounds discouraging." Jani ran through her mental checklist of the hierarchy of Family relationships. "His family's an Abascal affiliate."

"Yes."

"But the Nawars and Neumanns control this segment of the Pearl Way."

"...yes."

"I'd have expected to find him on Earth, or one of the Inner Circle worlds."

Editha started to speak, but quieted when a staffer emerged from one of the offices.

"Going to see the great man?" The woman clucked her tongue. "Lucky you."

"*Riva.*" Before Editha could say more, the woman swept into another office. "As I said, he tries. He means well. But some people aren't willing to look past his name." She leaned close and dropped her voice to a whisper. "He doesn't like to talk about his family, so don't bring that up. It's important to him that he blend in."

Jani felt the sudden sharpening of Editha's gaze like a physical punch. *It's important to you, too, apparently.* She followed the woman to an immense set of double doors at the end of the corridor, waited as Editha glanced through the window that framed one side before knocking softly. *Everyone is so careful around you, Ian.* Even Editha, who possessed a glare that could frost a flame.

"Let me talk first." Editha opened the door, then stuck her head in. "Ian—"

"*Editha.*" A cultured baritone boomed loud enough to cause a passing staffer to flinch and spatter coffee down the front of his shirt —he swore under his breath and shot a murderous look at Matrishi's door before hurrying back down the corridor and into a restroom.

Editha opened the door wider, then stood straight, hands clasped in front of her, like a child preparing to recite. "I've brought a visitor. She needs to speak with you urgently."

"Then speak with her urgently, I will." The voice came softer, but hit all the wrong beats, rendering the distinctive New Indies accent more a sing-song sway than a soft lilt. "Does she have a name?"

Editha licked her lips. "It's Jani Kilian, Ian." She beckoned to Jani to join her. "Mère Kilian, allow me to introduce Ian Matrishi, our head of station."

Ian rose from his seat and started towards them. His gaze settled on Jani, and his smile faded. "That's not Jani Kilian."

"She's—" Editha drew a circle in the air around her own face. "She has altered her features in the interest of anonymity. We know her by her eyes, and her scanpack, and—" She glanced at Jani, and her earlier confidence reasserted itself. "We just know."

"You just know." By the time he reached them, Ian's bonhomie had been replaced by a more formal wariness. "All right." He looked Jani up and down. "I will hear what she has to say."

Editha nodded, then shot Jani a smile that might have been encouraging or commiserating as she took her leave.

Ian ushered Jani into his office, gestured towards one of the chairs on the visitor's side of his desk, then sat. Even compared to the usual Family template, he cut an imposing figure. Mid-thirties, tall and broad-shouldered, dark gray daysuit of the same severe style as those John Shroud wore, impeccably tailored and murderously expensive. He had bound his black shoulder-length braids with a dark silver cord; metal studs of the same color trimmed one earlobe.

Jani tried to brush the rumples from the front of her jumpsuit as she sat, then gave up because what was the point? Instead, she took in the expansive views and museum-quality paintings and statuary. When she finally faced Ian, she found him regarding her levelly, waiting for her to fill the silence.

It's like something from the management playbook. Intimidation for Beginners. Jani folded her hands in her lap and regarded him in return. *He's tired.* His brown skin looked greyed, with smudges of purple beneath his eyes. *His hair is bumpy.* She tried to study the rows of tight braiding without seeming to. *Beads.* They were hard to pick out at first, black against his black hair, noticeable only by their sheen.

Ian made a point of staring at his timepiece before sighing loudly. "You've come here at an inconvenient time, Mère Kilian. Amari called me while you were on your way. She told me a little of what brought you here, but I would like to hear it from you."

Jani nodded. *And so it begins.* "I need a document. To help a friend."

"You're Jani Kilian. You can order it through Registry."

"No, I can't. Not anymore."

Ian's eyes widened. He sank back in his chair, sending the ergoworks into humming hissing overdrive. "They kicked you out?"

"Yes."

"Because you're not considered human anymore."

"Correct."

"As such, you are considered a security risk."

"That is my understanding."

"So what do you do? You sneak into my station under a false name, with a false face, and into my documents center using an ID not your own."

"If you say so."

"So what we have here is a diplomatic incident of grim proportions."

"Possibly."

"With added overtones of espionage."

"If you insist."

"You're awfully sanguine for someone who's in a shitload of trouble."

"Shitload of trouble is my middle name."

Ian met Jani's fixed gaze with his own. Then he smiled. "I lost count of the number of times I overheard my parents take your name in vain. A couple of years ago, when you were in Chicago. That mess with van Reuter. During the last idomeni civil war and the hospital cover-up. What did they wind up calling it? Illegal technology exchange?"

"That is one way of referring to it." *Human experimentation* was another.

"He blew up the transport carrying the survivors."

Jani nodded, eventually. "Yes."

"Then there was that thing with Tsecha. The documents forgery. You made some highly placed enemies." He flicked a finger in the direction of the door. "Editha is usually very level-headed, but I can tell that she is, what is the term, star-struck?" He shrugged. "I, however, well, given that I am not a documents person, let us just say I am immune."

Whatever I ask, he's going to say no. Jani let the silence stretch until Ian shifted in his seat. "If I might make a suggestion—"

"I really don't have time to listen—"

"—you're trying too hard."

Ian stalled in mid-sentence, mouth agape. Then he shook his head as though emerging from a daze. "What?"

"Your accent is too broad—it sounds like you're making fun of them. You're a Matrishi. Your family is an Abascal affiliate." Jani gestured toward his hair. "The beads were gold. The Abascal family color. You could've removed them, but instead you painted over them. I gather you were trying to make a point."

"I gather you are as well."

"You think you're displaying your rejection of your family. But colonial me, I see the beads are still there, which makes me think you haven't walked away entirely. All you have to do is remove the black paint, and you're an affiliated scion again." Jani pointed towards the door, the world beyond. "They think you're dabbling."

"So. You've been here five minutes, and you've already diagnosed the reason for my personnel issues." Ian drummed his fingers on the edge of his desk and a little too close to the security buzzer. "Some people here do like me."

"Ed—." Jani bit back Editha's name as she fought the idomeni tendency to blurt, which always intensified as her temper rose. *Not now, dammit.* She inhaled, then exhaled, once, then again. "It may sound trite, but be yourself. Earthbound accent. Lower volume. They're never going to not know who you are, so stop trying to be who you're not. Some will come around. But others will never accept you no matter what you do."

"Fuck. You." Ian pushed back his chair and clapped his hands on his knees. "Damn. This is how you ask for help?"

Jani checked the wall clock, and counted the hours that had passed since her arrival. *Three hours down, ninety-three to go.* "Call it payment in advance." Bargaining—she'd always been crap at it. Her way had always been to bull forward and pick up the pieces later, to count on forgiveness rather than ask for permission. But now Niall's life depended on her controlling her hybrid temper long enough to convince a powerful man whom she had already pissed off to break rules for her. "I need to get into your archive. I need a document. An old manifest."

Ian stood, paced. His anger showed in his stiff walk, the throb in his temple as he worked his jaw.

He wants to throw me out on my ass. Jani gripped the arms of her chair, then released, repetitive movement that helped her focus. *But something is stopping him.* Her job? Figure out what that something was in the next, oh, ten to fifteen seconds, and use it to get what she needed.

Ian paused in front of a window, one hand behind his back, the other pressed to the pane. He tapped it, one finger at a time, the scratchy click of his nails on glass the only sound.

Then the tapping ceased. "I'm sure you saw the damage as you made your approach—"

"I have less than four Common days to offer proof of possession or my friend may die."

Ian stiffened. "Pierce was kidnapped?" He turned to face her. "You may as well say his name—the word is out. I assumed he just bolted."

"He'd never do that."

"You seem sure. I know others who believe differently." Ian continued his slow pacing. "If you'd come here three days ago, we could've helped you." His accent had already mellowed into something less theatrical. "A transport missed its slip and rammed the storage sector adjacent to the archives. Structural informed me that the entire section of the station is unsafe. I can't let any of my people in there until repairs are completed and validated."

"When will that be?"

"Four to six weeks." Ian worked his jaw some more. "If you provide the code strings, I can see if someone pulled it prior to the accident, but I'm afraid that's the best I can do."

Jani squeezed the arms of her chair until the pain stopped her. "I don't have that information. All I know is the date and the station."

"I am sorry, but as I said, I can't allow any of my people in there."

"I'm not one of your people. Let me go."

Ian stilled, stared. "Assuming I would even consider allowing you to do so, damage was extensive. At minimum, you'd have to wear a suit."

Jani swallowed hard. She hated suits as much as she hated weightless flight. "All right."

"When was the last time you worked in one?"

"It's been a while."

"Uh-huh. Unless you can provide proof of recent safety training, I cannot even consider letting you in there."

"I'll sign a release absolving you."

"No. You'd need training and certification."

"I don't have time." Jani released her grip and held out her hands palms-up, the idomeni gesture of supplication. "Please. Just look the other way for a few hours."

"And risk having your injury or death on my conscience and my record? Not to mention the danger to everyone here if you should trigger some catastrophe." Ian shook his head so hard that his neck crackled. "I don't work that way." He stilled for a time, then turned back to the window.

Still not throwing me out. Jani took a deep breath and waded in. "This is part of something bigger, I'm sure of it. Registry is calling in low-level paper from colonial archives. Editha told me that one of your ships bearing documents for destruction was hijacked—I'm betting there have been more. You and I both know that the Families have to be involved. I don't know what they're planning, but whatever it is, you know it won't be good for the colonies."

Ian remained facing the window. "You don't stop, do you? You just slam into reverse, back up, try another angle."

"As I said, I don't have time." Jani counted one beat. Another. *Slow down.* Give each word a chance to settle. "You're out here instead of in the Inner Circle or Chicago. I assume it's because you know what's gone on out here and you're trying to help. I think we can help each other."

Ian looked back at her. The station lighting carved grooves and lines in his face, accentuating his fatigue, aging him. He studied her for a few moments, then resumed gazing out the window.

Jani stood, straightened, counted to three, then joined him. "New Indies is lucky. It has seas that humans can swim in without their skin peeling off. But the Neumanns and Nawars have their fingers in everything and their grip is strong. Every time a small private tries to start something, they get driven out of business. Or worse."

Ian eyed her sidelong. "What the hell do you know?"

"I'm Acadia-born, remember?"

Ian started to speak, stopped, ran a hand over his face. "If you knew all the shit I've been put through since I came here. They don't give up, they don't give in, and they don't let go." He laughed, a single, short huff. "And you think we can break them with a few lousy pieces of paper?"

"It has to start somewhere." Jani looked down at the activity in the concourse below, the tourists spending money little of which would remain on New Indies. "If we're ever going to keep what we make for ourselves, to buy and sell amongst ourselves, we need to find those first cracks and pry them wide."

"You say 'we.'" Ian hung his head. "To you, I'm one of them. An outsider."

Jani shrugged. "Welcome to the club. I'm an outsider wherever I go. Except for a small settlement of a few thousand that hugs a cliff face on a world that isn't ours." She paused. By this time, the sun would have risen over Thalassa. The kitchen staff would be setting out breakfast in the Main House courtyard, and Dieter would be relaying her the day's first set of intelligence reports. "We need a place where we can settle and feel safe. I don't believe we'll be safe on Elyas for much longer."

"That sounds ominous." Ian's voice came soft, the forced accent now faded to something approaching normal.

"It feels ominous." Jani decided to give a little push. "Amari said that you keep a special eye on the ag vendors. I can understand that. You're not allowed to manufacture your own foodstuffs. It's written into all your contracts with Family businesses—you need to purchase from them." She sensed Ian shifting his feet. "I know this because that's how it is on Acadia. Even small plots of dirt-grown vegetables are banned. Fruit trees you'd keep on your terrace for decoration." She waited a beat. "But yet ag vendors are visiting. You're setting up your own sheds."

Ian turned on her, finger pointed at her face. "If you tell—"

"I'm not going to say anything." Jani raised her hands in surrender and backed away. "Why the hell would I?"

"If they find evidence that we're manufacturing food of any kind, they'll shut down the hotels and close access to the beaches." Ian pressed his hands to the sides of his head, then let them fall. "Technically, they can, of course. It's their property." He looked out at the gardens, the cloud-wrapped blue ball beyond, and gripped the railing as though he would tumble into the void if he let go. "I love this place. I've loved it since I came here—" He rocked his head one way, then the other. "—twelve years ago. Spent uni break with Ina Nawar at their compound downstairs." He looked at Jani, eyes glistening. "Have you ever been down there?"

"No." Jani relaxed a little as she watched Ian's expression lighten.

He cut the air with one hand. "The sea air holds this sharpness that—it's like it rinses out your head, leaves you feeling alive. And at dusk, there are these insects, they call them skitters, they make this pinging sound like notes up and down a scale. Night music." He shook his fist. "And the people here are so, I don't know, relentless. Cheerful, but unyielding. Like, we will get through this together. One hundred eighty degrees from what I grew up with." He grew somber. "My father told me I'd last a year. It will be ten months tomorrow."

"So on top of the usual Family pressures, you're also getting the more personal touch."

"And then you come here and tell me that no matter what I do, I will always be on the outside looking in."

Jani held back an apology that she knew would ring hollow. She hoped Ian would eventually realize that she had done him a favor, but she understood how her assessment must have stung. "It will get better with some. Not with all. I'm sorry, but that's just the way it is. Too much history."

Ian nodded, eventually. "I want this world to be all it can be. All the possibilities turned into realities." He laughed with only a touch of humor. "How crazy is that, right? Acadia girl?"

Jani felt his gaze, the air of expectancy, that now it was her turn to repay in kind. "Like I said before, ominous. I get scared." She looked up into the bright station lights, felt their heat, and imagined the Elyan sun on her face. "Hybrid numbers are growing. Slowly, but, growing. Illnesses are the cause, mostly. Those strange diseases that crop up in the colonies. They try all sorts of treatments, but the only one that sticks is gene therapy. Doctors think they've silenced, for want of a better term, the other areas of whatever idomeni gene they infuse into humans. But something about the presence of even one fragment triggers a cascade, and the next thing you know, someone shows up at Thalassa because their family disowned them. Their spouse threw them out. Company fired them because they're not human anymore, are they? So they can't be trusted."

"We have orders here not to hire hybrids." Ian shrugged. "The edict comes from Chicago. We disobey, they clean out this station and repopulate it with loyal affiliates."

Jani examined her hands, on the lookout for the gold tinge that she knew would eventually show itself as the dye wore away. "For the idomeni who opts to be treated, it's even worse. The choice runs counter to one of their primary religious tenets, that the condition of one's body should not be altered to any degree. That all must progress naturally. Some of their priests fear that hybridization is equivalent to introducing a disease, that it's a disease state in and of itself. That means a life spent as a hybrid is a prolonged death, which means fragmentation of soul, the pieces irretrievable. And that means the way to the First Star is lost to any idomeni who hybridizes. And given the interrelatedness of skeins, their decision affects their offspring, whoever they mated with, and that idomeni's skein. They don't just alter themselves when they hybridize, they leave a lot of shattered crockery behind."

"So there aren't as many idomeni hybrids as human?"

"Not at all, but there are a few, and they have well and truly walked away from everything they've ever known. Thalassa is the only place that they can go." Jani tried not to think of the upheaval that was likely taking place as Feyó sought information concerning her renegade suborn's whereabouts. The turmoil felt by those who needed peace. *I'll make it up to all of you—I promise.* "They need a place where they can belong, as they are, as they evolve into whatever they become. A place where they can be safe. And I want to work with people who will help us build that place." She turned to Ian to find him regarding her less warily. "Are we really that different? Isn't it the same, this thing we want for those we've come to love? The chance for them to live their own lives?"

Ian studied her for a long moment. Then came a harsh laugh. "You're a witch."

Jani smiled. "I'll take witch. I've been called so much worse." She sensed her chance, and took it. "How long does the safety training take?"

Ian managed a smile. "Bare bones? One week."

"That's your standard class, six hours daily with breaks and lunch. How long if I go through it in one go?"

"That's too much." Ian lay back his head, closed his eyes. After a moment, he opened them, then counted on his fingers. "Two days."

"One and a half."

"What about sleep?"

"I'll sleep when I have that piece of parchment in my hand." Jani sensed Ian's underlying irritation, knew how far she had pushed him. "I suppose I should apologize for being a bother."

Another smile, weaker this time. "I think your hybrids are lucky to have you." His handheld chimed—he pulled it from his pocket and flipped on the display. "I'm not too sure about the rest of us." He read for a moment, brow arching. "Your security man is out in the waiting area with a couple of my people. Apparently he was lurking around the entrance long enough to attract their attention."

"I have been here longer than he expected." Jani checked her timepiece, counted the minutes since the last time. "When can I get started on the training?"

"I need to contact Facilities and make arrangements. They won't be happy."

"It's not my idea of how to spend the day. But it has to be done." Jani collected her bag and headed for the door, then paused. "Thank you."

"So who's the puppet master?"

Jani stopped short, almost stumbling over the thick carpet. She turned to find Ian seated at his desk, hands folded atop the polished wood.

"Who took Pierce? Who's jerking you around?"

"I don't know." Jani once again ran through a mental checklist that got longer by the hour. "All I do know is that it feels personal."

"Oh, that doesn't surprise me one little bit." Ian's New Indiesian accent lay by the wayside now, replaced by flat Chicago. "I will do what I can for you. But you must understand that if it comes down to a choice between you and my station, it's no choice."

And if comes down to a choice between your station and Niall— Jani nodded, and left to find Lucien.

Chapter Eighteen

By his best reckoning, Niall figured he had been held for three days. *More or less.* His captors didn't make it easy for him to determine time's passage.

The inability to see was disorienting enough. Every station he had ever lived on had possessed its own beat, subtle changes in light and noise levels that worked both consciously and subconsciously to assist in tracking the hours, and the inability to see meant he missed important cues.

To complicate matters further, they threw him curves. They switched what they fed him—sometimes he had two breakfasts in a row, other times, a string of lunches or dinners. Artur and the other two men who guarded him juggled shifts, so that he was never sure who sat outside his door until they spoke. He also wondered if they drugged him. He sometimes fell asleep immediately after a meal, and awoke with a dull headache and a dry mouth.

Of his three guards, Artur had so far proved the easiest to get along with. He liked to talk about football, and he made enough offhand comments about what went on at the station for Niall to piece together when Morwenna and her crew had arrived. Whiskey, it seems, had arrived separately some time later and immediately made known his displeasure with his accommodations, a detail which supported Niall's conviction that he was indeed Evan van Reuter. Only a Family member would act like an asshole during such a sensitive operation.

Unfortunately, it meant there was no Service base in the immediate vicinity. By this time, word must have gotten out that van Reuter was no longer on Earth. Since one of the crimes he had been convicted of was the murder of active duty Spacers, the Service had helped determine his punishment and were responsible in part for his incarceration. News of his disappearance would have been relayed to all bases—they would be on the lookout for him. All ships would be tracked. All stations, large or small, would have received a visit from a SIB team. *I mean, they have to be looking for van Reuter, don't they? They have to know he's missing.*

If van Reuter were indeed missing. If the scenario that had sunk its fangs into Niall's brain were in any way possible and not just the rattled imaginings of a disoriented old relic battling his own demons.

As they say, when the age is in, the wit is out. Words of a man belittling others though an idiot himself. *Get a grip, Pierce. You got yourself into this mess to do a job, so do it. Figure it out so that when you get back—*

Niall paused, and wondered if any SIB teams were out looking for him, as well. *Of course they are. Roshi would make sure as soon as he heard I was missing.*

Assuming he had heard.

Niall tensed at the sound of voices in the corridor. One of his other guards, who had yet to say one word to him, argued in a mix of Josephani Dutch and Hortensian German with one of his compatriots about the quality of the food. *Or maybe the quality of the plumbing.* Niall knew little of either language and the odd word or phrase that he could pick out made no sense. He rose from his cot, edged closer to the cell door, and determined that the two were far enough away that wouldn't hear him move around.

He sat at the desk, and resumed a task that he had started soon after he arrived. The pull-down sheet metal deck moved on three hinges instead of a flex zone, and like most every hinge Niall had ever seen, they were held together with pins. It had taken him the better part of a day to wring enough soap from a number of dispo towels to serve as lubricant. After he worked the slippery muck into one of the hinges, he had pushed the pin out one end with the aid of a tine he had broken off a plastic fork.

Now came the moment of truth. He had finally pushed the pin a centimeter or so out of place—he grabbed hold of the end and pulled. It took some force, but he was able to turn it one way, then the other, and work it out bit by bit. When he heard a sound in the corridor, he would sit up, grab the rim of the stool, and execute a few reverse push-ups. He cycled through that pattern a half-dozen times until he finally freed the pin. He grasped it like the prize it was and hurried back to his cot.

Ten centimeters, give or take. He measured it a few times with his thumb, just to be sure. Then he dug beneath his pillow for the wad of wetted dispo towel that he had tucked there earlier and twisted it onto one end. It would make a decent enough handle once it dried.

He held the hinge pin like a knife, practiced a few quick stabs, massaged the handle into a better shape. He would have preferred a real blade, of course, but he knew from experience that one could do a lot of nasty with a thin length of metal. Jam it in an eye or ear, or even stab someone in the neck if you rammed it hard enough. Hit the right spot in an alarm panel and you could disable it or set it screaming. Wreck an environmental board and you could suffocate an entire wing of a station.

However, his plan was less ambitious in scope but more immediate in import. He wanted to shank a guard and get hold of the blindspec key. He had tried to work out any number of escape scenarios, but the simple fact was that he would be nothing more than target practice if he couldn't see. To this point, all three of his overseers exercised the usual caution. They never entered his cell alone, and made sure he was immobilized before they removed or reset the blindspecs. *I need to lure one of them in here.* Unfortunately, the likeliest possibility was Artur.

Niall felt a twinge of regret. The Manxman had proved better than most, and had gone out of his way to give his prisoner a break here and there. *Sorry, friend. You picked the wrong side.* Whether the next shift change or the one after, Artur would be on duty.

Niall tucked the shank inside his waistband. *And I will make my move.*

———

Niall heard the food hatch slam open and edged toward the cell door, one arm extended. He tottered every other step, and swore under his breath. *Balance, old man.* Hard to maintain when one couldn't see, but dammit, he should have been more sure-footed than this. *No more booze.* If he lived through this, that was a promise he needed to keep.

Then he stopped, laughed silently at his own bullshit. *Maybe I'll cut back.* Baby steps, like the ones he took now. *Yeah. Sure.* Why did he even bother lying to himself when he knew he would crack a bottle the first chance he got.

Niall reached the door and grabbed for whatever had been left there. *Metal canister.* He felt both ends, found a dispenser tube. "What the hell is this?" He heard someone move close to the door. Artur, judging from the singular goaty stink that followed. *Doesn't anybody wash around here?* He did the best he could with dispo towels and his little sink, and he still felt overripe.

"Depilatory." Artur chuckled. "You need to neaten yourself up. You get to see the boss again today?"

"Morwenna?"

Artur let loose a howl, then laughed until he coughed. "Oh, man, you better not let him hear you say anything like that."

Niall suppressed a groan. More than anything, he wanted to be wrong about the suspected identity of his captor, but every time he convinced himself that he was mistaken, that there could be no way in hell that Evan van Reuter had wormed his way off Earth, some other damned detail would pop up that pointed straight to that misbegotten piece of shit. "Sensitive, is he?"

"Just a little. Word is that he does have a thing for our lady, but she won't take him on a plate." Artur waggled his eyebrows. "Leaves the path clear for you, Victoria. She seems, um, interested."

"Eh, she's past my pay grade." Niall almost added that he preferred women he could afford to turn his back on. But from what he could tell, Artur seemed to like her well enough, so that was one step too far for the moment. Instead, he shook the can of depilatory, squirted a puff onto his hand, and rubbed it over his stubble-rough face even as he winced at the sour milk smell. "How long you been working for her?"

"Rookie job. They said they're testing me. Next job won't be guard duty."

Niall felt a cold hand grab his gut. "Is everyone else here new, too? First-timers?"

"Mostly, yeah." Artur shrugged. "But we've all worked elsewhere. We're all experienced."

Sure you are. "Mind a little free advice?"

"Always worth the price paid, that is."

"Yeah." Niall started to speak, then hesitated. *Stick to your plan, Pierce.* Except that years of experience told him what was coming, and the thought made him sick to his stomach. "Don't wait for this to wrap up. Don't wait to get paid. Get out now while you still can."

"What the fuck—"

"They paid you what? One quarter down? One third? And the rest at the end of the job."

"That's standard."

"And this is Morwenna. This is shit no one will want to talk about and that means the fewer who are left to do so, the better." Memories returned, of triggers pulled and bodies shoved into airlocks. Oh, he had been such an ambitious young bastard. "The only thing you're going to get at the end of this job is a shooter blast in the head. Do yourself a favor and leave now."

Silence followed. Then Artur snorted. "You're full of shit." Metal rang as he slammed the food hatch closed. "Clean up yer fuck-ugly face before I do it for you."

Niall listened to the man's footsteps recede. *What about your great escape plan, shithead? You just drove off your prime target.* He walked to the sink, the point of his oh so carefully-assembled shank poking him with every stride. He finished de-bearding, washed his face, then stood dripping over the bowl, clutching the rim.

You've gone soft, boyo. And one lesson he had learned during those early years was that soft had a lousy life expectancy.

His trek to what he had come to think of as his royal audience proceeded as had the first. Immobilization field. Cuffing. Blind shuffle down the corridor. He still felt the shank, held in place by his waistband. *Couldn't leave it in the cell.* He assumed someone searched it while he was out. As for himself, Artur and his partner frisked him as they had previously. They checked his pockets, the insides of his shoes, patted down his arms and legs, but once again managed to miss the small of his back. *Yeah, you're experienced, Artur.* He just hoped like hell the damned thing wouldn't work loose and skitter down his trouser leg.

That would be embarrassing. Niall wobbled when Artur pulled him to a stop, then he stood rocking from one foot to the other as the other guard tapped on the door.

"Knock it off—you're making me seasick." Artur's growl indicated that their previous conversation still rankled.

"Sorry." Niall stilled. He didn't want to piss off the man more than he had already. Now was time to be the obedient prisoner.

Just as Artur's buddy started his third round of knocking, the door swept open. *Mechanism squeaks a bit.* Niall filed the item away, yet another indication that the station was not in the best shape.

"Hello, Colonel." The mocking voice maintained its disguise, that machine tinniness. "Please, come in. I've saved you your favorite seat."

Niall braced for another painful bout with the back of his chair as his guards steered him inside and pushed him into it. But instead of the brutal cuffing he had suffered the first time, they simply positioned themselves on either side. He sensed their presence mostly by smell, but also by that human sixth sense that indicated that others were close by. Just enough contact to serve as a warning.

He lay his cuffed hands on his thighs, took a deep breath. Waited.

"That's right, Colonel. Keep your hands where I can see them." The inevitable clink of ice and sound of pouring. "I can't say I agree with my partner's assessment of your docility. I think she overestimates her effect on the average male."

So, our redhead did turn you down. Niall heard Artur cough, and sucked in his lower lip to keep from smiling.

"Did I say something amusing, Colonel?"

"Holding back a sneeze." Niall sniffled for emphasis. "Dry station air."

"I hadn't noticed." The voice had gone flat. The king was definitely not amused. "How much do you remember about the war?"

Niall had been working his shoulders and shuffling his feet in order to find a more comfortable position in the stiff-backed chair, but now he stilled. "I try not to dwell on it."

"But you can't help yourself, can you?" The filtered voice grew deeper, colder. "I've had a lot of time to think these last few years. About the past, and the part various persons played in it." A pause to refill, ice cubes clattering like dice in a cup. "Roshi and I had a deal, you see. I keep my mouth shut about actions of certain of his underlings at the time—well, one underling in particular—and he'd keep me in the mix. Nothing unreasonable. A few advisory committees. The odd consultant job. But as soon as he was able, he broke that promise. Left me to twist in the wind while said underling flitted about the Commonwealth like a bloody ambassador."

Niall listened, heart thudding. He had settled on the surmise that he had been taken in order to lure Jani, but now he realized that his captor had more personal reasons as well. *Van Reuter's hearing.* It seemed a lifetime ago. Niall had been in and out of hospital, so much of that period a blur. He first met Jani during that time—that, he remembered. Still in the Service, so sharp in her uniform, but so ill. *She almost died.* And bought Fort Sheridan to a standstill in the bargain. *The more things change...*

"Colonel."

"I hear you." Niall dragged himself back to his current situation, which appeared to have deteriorated markedly over the last few minutes. "I fail to see what any of that has to do with me."

"You fail to see. Perhaps that's part of your problem." The voice had gone flat dead now. "Take it off."

Niall heard his guards shuffle their feet, his chair squeaking as they shifted their weight.

"Sir?" Artur, his voice pitched higher than normal, a combination of tension and question.

"Take off the blindspecs. I want to see the look in his eyes when I tell him how it's going to play out."

"But sir, Morwenna—"

"Just do what you're fucking told."

Niall listened to Artur and his fellow guard bicker in a mix of three different Channel World tongues. The other guard, whose name was Dola, proved to be the keeper of the blindspec key, but he didn't want to use it without Morwenna's okay. Artur, meanwhile, just kept repeating over and over that theirs was not to reason why, theirs was just to do or die, or words to that effect, until finally Dola handed him the key with a mumble of Guernsey French-English mishmash that it was his fucking funeral.

Niall almost moaned with relief as Artur unlocked the 'specs and slipped them off, but squelched it in case his captor took that as a challenge and ordered the damned thing back on. His eyes swam as they adjusted to the light, and he struggled to focus on the figure seated across the room from him. It was blurry at first, then sharpened with every blink. "It really is you."

"Yes, it really is me." Evan van Reuter sat with one leg slung over the arm of a throne-like chair, half-filled glass in hand. Jani once mentioned that on the day she met him he had just been voted the handsomest man in the Commonwealth, but a decade or more as a maintenance alcoholic had extracted a steep toll. Thin, high-boned face, the skin slack and pale but for cheeks reddened as though rouged, the eyes bloodshot and fever-bright. Black hair lank and in need of a good trim. He wore a black tunic and trousers that mimicked the uniform he had once worn as Interior Minister, but the clothing hung and bagged as though tailored for a man ten kilos heavier and the color drained the life out of him. "You don't seem surprised."

"All the questions and comments about Jani made me think." Niall quieted, breathed, forced himself to slow down. Learning he'd been right about van Reuter and being able to see set his mind racing. *Opportunity.* He had already been here several days and whatever Evan and Morwenna planned would have to take place soon. He didn't have much time to toss a spanner in the works. "I have no idea how in hell you got off Earth, but I am betting heads are rolling as we speak."

"Are you a betting man, Colonel?" Evan smiled, sipped his drink. "Because I will take that wager." He studied Niall over the top of his glass. "You know, it was sad how easy it was for us to sweep you up. I would almost call it pathetic. Makes me wonder why Roshi expended so much capital covering up for someone so incompetent."

Niall held back a groan. *So, it's going to be name-calling, is it?* Well, at least it was better than getting punched in the face.

"He was so eager to reform the bad old Service. Best thing he could've done was leave you to the firing squad."

Niall responded, eventually. "I shot escaping prisoners."

"Officers. In the back."

"Okay, so it's a contest now? Who did the worst?" Niall examined the room while he kept the back and forth going. "They all had sidearms when we rounded them up. Not my fault they didn't use them." It was furnished like a regular cabin sitting room with a couch and a couple of lounge chairs, but the larger size indicated that it would've been reserved for VIPs. "At least I did my dirty myself. I didn't order someone else to blast a squad of Spacers out of the sky." That drew quick intakes of breath from his guards—they stared across the room at Evan, who met their contempt with a glare of his own.

Niall took those few moments of shared hostility to glance to the side, the area near the entry. *Yes.* VIP cabins on stations came equipped with alarm panels that were connected to the closest Commonwealth Police facility. *And if there's no ComPol in the area, it goes to the nearest Service Port Security office.* The station was old and preventive maintenance likely nonexistent, but it was the best shot he had at attracting attention of someone who could get him the hell out of here and keep Jani out of it.

He just needed to trigger it.

He pressed against the back of his chair, and felt the shank dig into his spine. Rocked to and fro, and felt it edge down to his hip. All he had to do was stand up, and it would slide down his pants leg.

"I know the sound of forced bravado when I hear it." Evan had unhooked his leg from the chair arm and now sat forward, elbows on knees, glass cradled in his hands. "You're worried, Colonel. You're not sure whether anyone is even looking for you. You're wondering if Roshi is leaving you to twist, too."

"Not really." Niall decided for the moment that keeping Evan talking served a purpose. Dola had already stifled a yawn, and Artur seemed preoccupied with with the state of his fingernails. "I can understand why you might think that, though, given that loyalty and friendship aren't qualities you're familiar with."

Evan's smile thinned. "The only human being—well, make that *being*, period—who cares whether you live or die is currently collecting the information we need to set the Commonwealth on its ear. We will take it from her when she arrives, and then we will decide what to do with you both."

Niall heard the unspoken threat. *I'm not just a lure.* And he wasn't just a captive pastime for van Reuter to torture. No, they would hurt him, possibly even kill him, if Jani failed to perform whatever task had been set for her. *Or maybe just for the hell of it.* "So what you're telling me, in your overly dramatic third-rate traveling company way, is that odds are good that I will not leave this station alive." He shrugged, and felt that his guards were no longer as close as they had been. "Oh well. I always figured I would wind up in a situation like this some day. Pissed off one too many assholes. Bound to happen." *So, nothing left to lose, boyo.*

Evan raised his glass. "Good to see you're taking it so well. My partner was concerned that you might put up a fight once you realized what was going on."

"And you must keep your partner happy." Niall thought back to his own encounter with Morwenna. *Between the perfume and the cleavage, she must have you jumping through hoops.*

Evan stilled. "She and I get along quite well."

"But you're worried about Jani. I can tell because you haven't said her name once during this conversation." Niall met Evan's eye, caught the bare flicker of unease. "You don't want to talk about her because I can see your face now. Hear your real voice. See your reactions. You want to rub my nose in the fact that you're here, that you escaped your prison, that my life is on the line. But you really don't want me to know just how scared you are of her." He paused, made a show of thinking. "The thing I don't understand—"

"That's enough, Colonel."

"—is what makes you think you'll beat her this time?" Niall stretched out his legs and shifted in his seat, felt the shank slip down to his knee. "I mean, if we're talking about track records. You murdered her, the only woman who ever really loved you, on orders of your psychopathic father. And when you learned years later that you screwed that up, you offered her everything in exchange for her silence, all of which she threw back in your face for the shit you are. And now you think you have a better chance if you make her angry? After all you've been through with her, you still have no idea who you're dealing with."

The rest of Evan's face reddened to match his cheeks. For all he was an alcohol-soaked wreck, he was tall and as past incident showed, he did pack a punch.

Get ready, boyo. "But that's always been your problem, hasn't it, *Evan?* It's like a reverse magic wand—everything you touch turns to shit." Niall tried to fight his rising anger, keep his head, then decided *fuck it.* If he died now, they'd lose the hold they had on Jani. *And when she finds out what you did, you waste of skin, I wouldn't want to be in your shoes.* "That's what used to piss off dear ol' Dad, wasn't it? Acton the Old Hawk? That his only son and heir, the future V in NUVA-SCAN, had turned out to be such a fucking screw-up."

With a yell, Evan propelled out of his chair.

Niall waited until Evan was almost on him. Then he shot up and rammed his head into the man's nose, felt a jolt of glee when he heard the satisfying crunch of cartilage. Then he brought up his cuffed hands and whacked Evan under the chin as he stumbled back, slicing skin and spraying blood.

A beat too late, Niall's guards woke up and closed in. He kicked back and down, sent Dola screaming to the floor, hands clutching his knee. Turned and swung and slammed Artur in the side of the face with the cuffs.

Felt something slide down his leg, heard a clatter, and looked down in time to see the shank roll across the floor.

"What the hell is going on?"

Niall looked back to find Morwenna standing in the entry. A beat later, she barreled in, her focus on the shank. He beat her to it by half a step, shoved her to the floor, kicked Dola in the side when the man tried to grab him, and punched the sharp spike into the alarm box. Status lights flared, stuttered, winked out. Then came sound so loud it slammed like a physical weight, raging machine howl. Artur grabbed his arms and wrestled him away from the panel, kicked his legs out from under him and drove him to the floor. Shoved a knee between his shoulder blades and leaned hard enough to push the air from his lungs.

"Don't be a fuck, Victoria." Rough voice not quite drowned out by the alarm screech. "Keep it up and the only way outta this is dead."

Niall struggled against the weight pressing down on him, bit back a yell as someone wrenched the shank from his grip.

Then came darkness as someone jammed the 'specs back on his head, locked them, then tightened the tension until he thought his skull would burst.

Then came the pain. Like a hot spike driving into his right eye. He yelled, banged his forehead against the floor until the 'spec alarm bleated and Artur stopped him with a headlock.

Shouting, Morwenna and Evan.

"You damned fool."

"No one talks to me that way."

Niall's breathing slowed as the pain eased, replaced by numbness that rattled him even more. He fought Artur's hold and gripped the 'specs, tried to twist them off his head even as the alarm sounded, shook off the hands that grabbed hold of his and tried to pull them off the device.

"Don't touch them, Colonel." Morwenna tightened her hold. "Artur? Keep him down."

Niall fought Morwenna's grip, but she knew how to grab and where to apply pressure—small jolts shot up his arms and kept him from closing his hands. He felt the pound of running footsteps shudder through the floor, the sharp pain as someone jammed an injector into his upper arm and the rapid descent into the dark—

Chapter Nineteen

Niall awoke with a throbbing head courtesy of the sedative and sore ears courtesy of the tight 'spec band. He tried to sit up, then slumped back as saliva flooded his mouth and the acid rose to the back of his throat. *Breathe. Slow.* In. Out.

After a few minutes, he tried again. This time, he managed to sit up, and found he could steady himself if he leaned forward.

Memory returned in bits and pieces. Van Reuter's hatred. The screech of the alarm. Artur's knee in his back.

He gripped the edge of his cot when he heard the door open, braced to move, prepared to fight off any further attempt to drug or restrain him. If they killed him, so be it. At least he would go out swinging.

Footsteps. He tensed, ready to spring.

Then he sagged back as familiar stink filled his nose. "Art."

Artur huffed. "How's yer eye?"

Niall shrugged. "Don't feel anything, really. I think all the nerves get fried. Or maybe it'll hurt later. I don't know. I've never been blinded before." He heard Artur shuffle his feet, mutter something in

Manx English that could've been a curse or something else entirely. "Face okay?"

"Had worse. Part of the job. You paid a helluva price just to make a little noise, though." Artur shuffled his feet. "What van Reuter said, is it true? You did in officers?"

Niall hesitated. His crimes had been secret for so long. To talk about them now with a virtual stranger lessened them somehow, made them seem like just one of those things. "Yeah."

"Too many officers out there. He killed Spacers, van Reuter did. Kids. Figures. His sort thinks we're all garbage." Artur drew closer, lowered his voice. "They can fix your eye, right? Service medicos?"

"Yeah." Niall thought about Jani, who was without a doubt the most rebuilt person he had ever known. *Shroud grew her new eyes. He grew damned near everything.* You couldn't even tell. "I think they can pretty much build you from scratch these days. Brain's the only thing that gives 'em fits." He held onto the edge of the cot again, this time to steady himself as the adrenaline jolt faded.

"I was in for a while." The soles of Artur's boots squeaked as he walked about the cell. "The Service."

"Judicial reprieve?"

"Ha, thanks. Signed up after I graduated prep. Anything to get off of Man, man." Artur snorted, a rough laugh at his own bad joke. "Got through Basic like who cares—those ponces don't know what tough is. Made Spacer First Class. Assigned to the *General Cao.*"

"Nice billet." Niall tried to sound like he gave a damn, even as he continued to test his eye for any type of sensation.

"Jumped ship at Mars Station. Just couldn't see the point. Ten years ago. Still hear my Drill barking every morning when I open my eyes." The footsteps stopped. "Twenty-two years for you." Wonder in Artur's voice, seasoned with mockery. "And still just a colonel?"

"Full colonel." Niall thought for a moment, then shrugged. "I've turned down promotions—" He tapped a count on his fingers. "—four times."

"You don't like the sound of General Pierce?"

"I wouldn't want the job of General Pierce. Peacetime paper-shuffling personalities political bullshit. Roshi told me I was as diplomatic as a ham sandwich, and he was not wrong."

"You like being his dog?"

Niall thought for a moment, then shrugged. "Yeah. I do." Silence settled. He tried to lie down, but something trickled down the back of throat and made him cough, and while he hoped it was simply stuffed sinuses from the bad air, he feared his eye had begun to leak. *Is that even possible?* Would he even know? *Why should I care?* Damned thing didn't work anymore anyway. Still, the sensation drove him to sit up and tip back his head every so often to stop the flow.

Then he heard muffled conversation outside his cell, Artur and the gruff woman who had taken care of his busted mouth. More footsteps.

"Sit still, Victoria." Artur's accent made his rough whisper barely intelligible.

Niall placed his hands on his knees and held his breath as the locking mechanism clicked, then exhaled with a groan as the specs were removed. He hesitated, then opened his left eye, and found himself looking into a gaze of bloodshot blue.

"I'm Sharon." The woman pressed her lips together in the sort of smile you gave someone with minutes to live.

"I'll be outside." Artur touched her shoulder. Then he glanced at Niall, and shook his head.

Sharon waited until the cell door closed. "They don't know about this visit, the redhead and her friend, so don't mention it to anyone else." She sat next to him on the bed, set a medkit on the floor at her feet, then took hold of his shoulders and turned him until he faced her. "Open the right one."

Niall did so, slowly. Felt his gut clench when his field of vision didn't get any bigger. "He that is strucken blind cannot forget the precious treasure of his eyesight lost."

"Romeo and Juliet." Sharon took a scanner from her pocket and held it to the damaged eye. "Been a while since I saw that one. Just the uni troupe at Hortensia Combined, but I thought they were pretty good."

Niall caught the flickering light on the edge of his good eye's field. Closed that eye for a moment, and saw nothing but black. "I saw it at the Capitol in Chicago. Must be five years ago. Ellisandre played Juliet." His heart stuttered. The fact that Service Medical could give him a new eye didn't settle him as much as he thought it would. *Assuming I live long enough for them to do the job.*

"The Capitol. Fancy." Sharon winked at him. Then that hint of good humor faded. "Art told me what you said about, you know, getting out while we could. We go back a ways, he and I." She pulled the medkit onto her lap, opened it and dug out cleanser, pads, and creams. "A few of us did some checking. All the evac pods are missing."

"All of them?" That would have complicated any escape Niall might have attempt. *Of course, it's all hypothetical now.*

"Rescue grapples are gone, too. The guys who work around the airlocks aren't happy about that at all." Sharon cleaned and treated his facial wounds. "All the safety equipment." She shrugged. "Not a surprise, really. Place is a pit. Most of the rooms were stripped clean when we got here. Maintenance bays were a joke. We know the air isn't filtered properly. Smells more like a dirty bathroom with each passing day."

Niall looked toward the door, caught a glimpse of Artur's shadow in the glass. "You're a new hire, too?"

"Yup. Like I said, me and Artur." Sharon rolled her eyes. "Nothing, you know, going on. We just get along." She gathered up the med supplies and stuffed them back in the case. "Sometimes that's the best you can hope for."

"Yeah." Niall pointed to his eye. "So what's the verdict?"

"It's nonfunctional." Sharon patted his hand. "I'm sorry. Didn't mean to get your hopes up. Sometimes the spec pulse doesn't burn out everything, but His Highness must have zapped you to the maximum."

"Lucky me." Niall looked at the sink mirror and wondered if he dare survey the damage. "What does it look like?"

"It just looks cloudy. Milky. Someone giving you a quick glance might not even notice it. Any pain?"

"I don't feel anything."

"Maybe that's a good thing. Sometimes when the damage is limited, well, that means the eye is wounded, and you know what that can feel like."

"Are you telling me there's a bright side?"

"Take it where you can get it." Sharon stood, offered another sad smile. "I'm sorry, but I need to put that damned thing back on you."

"Yeah, I know." Niall braced for the weight, the squeeze, the click of the lock. "I had better be a good boy from now on, or I'll lose the other one." He flinched as he felt the woman's hand squeeze his shoulder.

"I know it does no good to apologize for things you didn't do, but I am sorry about this. There just aren't a lot of nice people in this business, you know?"

Niall listened to receding footsteps, and felt a scarred-over crack in his soul reopen. Flashed again on the life he had once led, where simple kindness was the exception, something to mock and take advantage of. He knew that some of what he felt was the tailing-off of the stress of the last few hours, the uncertainty of what would come next and the fear of what that might entail. He knew he wasn't thinking straight. *I just need to sleep.* Then he would consider next steps. *I could ask Artur to check out the other ships at the docks.* There had to be at least two assuming Morwenna and Evan arrived separately. He had done some emergency piloting in the past. Amazing the things you could do if your life depended on it.

"Still think that punch was worth it?" Artur's voice drifted in from the corridor.

Niall didn't reply. He just rocked his hand back and forth.

"Didn't think you had it in you. His Highness's nose looks like a melon. Talk about throwing it all against the wall."

"What can I say? Give it your all, something might stick."

"So does shit." Artur snorted. "You need anything?"

"The door code and an hour's head start."

"Heh—maybe later." Artur rapped on the door. "Sweet dreams, Victoria. If you plan some surprise for tomorrow, warn me first."

Niall listened to the man's footsteps die away. He lay still, afraid to move his head in case the motion shook loose some tenuous connection that would lead to further damage. Every so often, he blinked, tried to gauge any difference. Tried to avoid berating himself because really, what was the point, but did so anyway.

He fell asleep after a time, only to be awakened by sounds of banging. "Who's there?" He heard movement, men's voices, more banging, like a hammer on sheet metal.

They're removing the desk. They had figured out where he had gotten the shank and so closed off that route for good. He remained still on the cot, hands where they could see them. No sense adding a date with the immobilization field to all the other crap he'd had thrown at him that day.

The men left, and for a time it was quiet. Then Niall heard the soft footfalls, sensed someone standing over him. Smelled the perfume.

"A hinge pin with some toweling for a handle. I suppose you deserve some credit for inventiveness." Morwenna sighed. "You poor idiot. I thought you had better self-control."

"And I thought you had better taste." Niall knew words were routing from hindbrain to mouth without filtering through thought centers, but he'd gone well beyond his limits and was too exhausted to care. "That's one limp little star you hitched your ship to."

"Says the half-blind man locked in a cell."

"Are you aware of his history with Jani Kilian?" Niall managed a laugh. "It doesn't bode well for whatever venture you and he have cooked up."

"Really?" Morwenna's voice sharpened. "Evan has her on a

string, the other end of which is tied to you. She'll come when she's called and she'll do as she's told."

Not for the first time, Niall damned the inability to see someone as they spoke. Did the light in Morwenna's turquoise eyes flicker in uncertainty or shine hard and steady? Did she fidget? Avoid looking him in the face even though she knew it didn't matter? Was she as sure as she seemed, or was it all an act? *You know the answer to that, boyo. This is fuckin' Morwenna who just threatened you.*

"Oh, and Colonel?" Her voice came even softer now, as though she spoke in church. "I was asked a few upsetting questions earlier today. Heard some nasty rumors. Seems they all started with you, offering opinions about matters that are none of your concern."

Niall opened his mouth to protest, then decided it would do no good. He should've known that if Artur told Sharon, he likely told others, and that word would get back to the boss.

"Your lack of restraint cost you one eye today. If you don't learn to be more circumspect, it will cost you more than that." Morwenna started towards the door, then stopped. "I should let you know that you'll have a new guard from now on. His name is Saul, and he's not a football fan."

Niall tried to swallow with a mouth gone dry. "What happened to Artur?"

"He's no longer here." A pause. "Neither is Sharon."

Sharon's words ran through Niall's head like a recording on a loop. That the pods had been removed. The rescue grapples. No way to retrieve anyone who exited an airlock, accidentally or otherwise. "What the hell did you do?"

"It's what you did, Colonel." The voice hardened. "I will offer a friendly warning—don't try to worm your way into anyone else's good graces. You're the one who talked Artur and Sharon into poking their noses where they didn't belong. Therefore, the blame falls on you. No one here is particularly fond of you at the moment."

Niall struggled to speak. His voice rasped. "You were going to kill them anyway."

"But they wouldn't have known what was coming. Small mercies for jobs well done." Soft footfalls, followed by the door closing with a click and a hiss. Then came quiet.

Niall lay rigid, his breathing quick and shallow as the rage flowed. He fought the urge to yell even as his chest ached, struck his thigh with his fist again and again as his good eye stung and the tears spilled. For the first time since his arrival, he truly longed for a drink, if only to help drown out the images that tumbled through his head. Two bodies in space, one hulking and the other so much smaller, drifting farther into the void.

Chapter Twenty

Jani found Lucien sitting in the lobby outside the station offices, chatting amiably with the uniformed security guards bracketing him. English, for the most part, with forays into various forms of French. But as with her Acadian dialect, enough differences existed between New Indies and Earthbound Provincial to gum up the works, so the conversation was sometimes interrupted by laughter and head shakes.

"All's good here?" Jani slipped into Acadian, which drew smiles.

"Everything's great." Lucien gave her a look that indicated that things were less great earlier, but matters had been resolved to everyone's satisfaction. "I was walking up and down the breezeway, waiting for you, when Marcus and Selene—" He indicated the relaxed-looking guards seated on either side. "—showed up and advised me to accompany them."

Jani waited as Selene chatted on her comlink, then beckoned to Marcus that it was time to go. As soon as they were out of earshot, she sat next to Lucien and let out a weighty sigh. "They know who we are."

Lucien slumped, braced his elbow on the arm of the chair, and cradled his chin in his hand. "You told them?"

"Doc Center pulled me in for questioning. My scanpack gave me away." Jani patted the device, which she had returned to its usual place in her belt holster. "I should've thought of that sooner. The original models are pretty distinctive. Anyway, we're in. Sort of."

"I've told you before that you should use your star power more often."

"Have you? I must've missed that."

"Uh huh. What does 'sort of' mean?"

"It means that the documents chief is in my corner. The station chief, however, won't let me enter the archive proper without training." Jani explained the concern over possible lack of structural integrity and watched Lucien's expression alter to that unreadable blankness that meant he was hearing things he didn't want to hear.

After a few moment's silence, he slumped even farther down in his seat. "Have you ever worn a suit?"

Jani braced for the argument she knew was coming. "I was in the Service. Remember?"

"You were a land-bound sideline paper pusher. You had basic safety training. Evac drills. You never crewed a ship."

"I survived mostly on stations for almost twenty years. You'd be surprised what I'm capable of."

"In one respect, no, nothing you do could ever surprise me." Lucien pushed upright, gripped the arms of his chair, looked out over the breezeway and the busy concourse below. "This is different. A section of the hull blows out, you're dead, and you'll likely take a chunk of the station with you so yes, I understand his reluctance." He lay back his head and stared at the concourse ceiling, which displayed a bright panorama of blue sky complete with puffy clouds and swooping seabirds. "Why does it have to be you?"

"Because I don't have the code strings someone else would need to ID it. I do know what the paper of that era looks like."

"You'll know it when you see it? Seriously?"

"It was early days. We didn't have the filing systems in place that they have now." Jani nodded, as much to encourage herself as to assure Lucien. "It'll be okay."

Lucien didn't reply. He just massaged his cheek, which had regained some of its definition.

"You look more yourself." Jani pointed to his face. "Chin's a little bumpy, though."

"The stuff's already breaking down." Lucien poked his chin gently to avoid dislodging any material. "I knew it was degraded, but it should've lasted more than a few days." He glanced at Jani. "You look like you slept on one side of your face for too long."

"Great." Jani's handheld pinged, and she checked the display. "We have been summoned."

They reentered the station offices to find Ian waiting for them. With him was the facilities chief, who conveyed even less enthusiasm about the prospect of Jani entering the damaged section of the station than had Lucien. Only Jani's heartfelt pledge to work through all the training materials and undergo a dry run practical exam appeared to comfort the woman, and even then, she reserved the right to cancel the search for any reason she deemed sufficient.

"Fine." Jani agreed to everything, while Lucien's stare drilled a hole through the back of her head. A few minutes later, they were taken to an unused office equipped with a workstation and all the requisite manuals.

I'm in. Jani settled in at the desk. If they believed they could get rid of her before she had found what she came for, well, they could try.

Jani sat at the workstation and studied the archive layout that arrived a few minutes earlier courtesy of Amari. "This place is laid out according to Family and origin world of the document. Unfortunately, that puts Phillipan paper closest to the damaged part of the station." She looked up to find Lucien sitting elbow on the desk, chin propped up in one hand. "What?"

"Could you please focus?" Lucien set the course workbook in front of her. "We've only been at this for two hours and you've already gone walkabout."

"Ask me something."

"How long is your air—"

"Model TR-85 specs. Two hours in main supply. Fifteen minutes in emergency back-up. Switches on automatically when suit senses reduction in air quality or decreased oxygen level."

"In case of sudden reduction in air pressure—"

"If I am too far away from an exit, immediately hook suit harness to nearest inset attachment port and activate safety enclosure. Remain inside enclosure until retrieval by station rescue or all clear signal has been given."

"What do you know. You're taking it somewhat seriously."

"I am taking it very seriously. As soon as the quizzes are all checked and logged in and I get through the practical, I can suit up and get to work." Jani returned to the archive layout and began planning her route through the bob and weave of aisles, shelving, carrels, and compartments, the tappings of her workstation touchboard not quite blocking Lucien's occasional grumbles. "If you have something to say."

"You know what I'm going to say, so why bother?" Lucien scrolled through screens on his handheld, his frown deepening. He had gotten hold of information about the latest and greatest in security systems from his new friends Marcus and Selene, and the realization of how much work Thalassa needed to do to meet current standards had made him cranky. "I still can't believe you talked them into this."

"Ian called me a witch."

"That's one word for it."

"How many times do I have to repeat? No one else here would know what to look for. I remember what paper from that location and time looks like. I still have chips loaded in my 'pack that can scan it." Jani paused to massage the back of her neck, which had developed a burning ache. She felt on-edge and Lucien's foul mood wasn't helping. "In the early years, every dexxie could read everything. Now, there's so much out there that they've had to specialize. Could Amari or Editha or one of their other forensic dexxies dig out what's needed? Yes, eventually. We don't have eventually."

"Assuming your 'pack works."

"If it doesn't, I can identify it by visual. Feel of the parchment. Like I said."

"Which means you have to break the seal of your suit and remove your gloves."

"I don't need to break the seal of a model TL-85 to remove gloves. The suit is designed for certain types of operations that require bare hands. It's not optimal and in case of decreases in pressure I could experience some swelling. See? Paying attention." Jani flexed her left hand, which she sometimes forgot was animandroid. *Left leg, too.* But she wouldn't be pulling off the lower half of her suit, just the gloves. "I'm not sure what happens to semi-synthetic tissues under vacuum. I didn't see any references in the manual."

"I think you should postpone until you can consult with their medical unit about possible ill effects."

"Or maybe I'll just remove my right glove only." Jani mimed pulling off said glove. "Problem solved."

"The entire paper system is archaic and overly complicated." Lucien rose and paced from one side of the small office to the other, swinging his arms and pausing to twist his back. "It makes no sense."

"It does to the Families. Makes it more difficult for folks like me to find what we're looking for." Jani stared at the map with its random layout and utter lack of order. "This isn't a true archive in the sense that there's searchable history. It's a personal file cabinet as far as they're concerned, not meant for prying eyes like mine." She pressed her hands to her brow to combat an incipient headache.

"You really hate them, don't you?" Lucien had returned to his seat and resumed glaring at his handheld.

Jani recalled the expression on Ian's face when he talked about New Indies. She hadn't always made the best or wisest choices, but she had come to know true caring when she saw it. "Not all of them." She set aside the archive plan and opened another of the study guides. "Did you get anything back from your contact in Chicago?"

"It's too soon." Lucien met Jani's gaze, swore, and checked his messages. "No." He held up the device so she could peruse the list. "If Evan van Reuter's somehow involved, he had help. Help that wasn't available when Anais et al took away everything he owned. Help we don't know of yet." He shook his head. "Do you honestly see him working with any of the other Families?"

Jani paused to consider the question as unwelcome memories of her first visit to Chicago returned. The fear of discovery. The realization that Evan van Reuter could lie like he breathed, to himself as well as to her. "I think he would do anything to get even a fragment of his old life back. He lost his children. His fortune. His birthright, as he saw it. He has nothing left to lose."

Lucien tapped his handheld and stared at it as though willing a message to appear. "How the hell did you ever get together with him in the first place?"

"When we met, he gave the impression that he was like Ian. A rebel committed to the colonies." Jani felt the heat rise up her neck, flood her face. *Because sometimes it wasn't bad.* No, not bad at all. "I admit I was swept off my feet, at least at first."

"How long did it last?"

"It burned hot for about six months. After that, his father yanked the chain hard. There were occasional flares for a year or so after. Then the war started." Jani looked across the desk into dark brown eyes alight with bemusement. "Don't look at me like that."

"I just can't see you two together." Lucien flipped through a paper manual so quickly that the breeze from the pages ruffled his hair. "Or that you possessed the patience to put up with his shit."

"He was different then." Jani focused on her workstation display. "Plus he was handsome and a little wild. After the pressure of the Academy and then adjusting to the Service...there were times when I needed to blow off steam. Evan was good at that." She shrugged. "And occasionally, it just felt...right."

"Did you really think the 'V' in NUVA-SCAN would marry you?"

Jani stared at nothing for a time. Considered a lie, then decided it wouldn't work as Lucien had a knack for sniffing those out. "I thought 'maybe,' for a little while." She looked across the desk to find him rapt as a child listening to a bedtime tale. "One evening, he invited me to dinner. Private room at the Consulate. Very posh. He said there was something he needed to tell me."

"Had the war started?"

"Not yet. Tensions between the Laumrau and the Vynshà were peaking. The formal declaration was only days away. The general atmosphere was tense. I thought he was going to tell me that he had been recalled to Chicago."

Lucien snorted. "Daddy yanking the chain again."

"Pretty much." Jani didn't even have to close her eyes to recall the scene. The candlelight. The soft music. *Evan downing wine like water.* "He told me that he was being pressured to marry Alyssa. The engagement had been dragging on for a couple of years, and the Scriabin family was threatening to break it off for good." His eyes had actually welled as he spoke. "He said he would buy out my commission and I could return with him to Earth, to Chicago, officially as part of his staff. He'd set me up in a house or a flat, whatever I wanted. Arrange a position with one of the ministries." Her voice cracked. More than two decades on, the memory still gnawed. "Do I need to go on?"

Lucien smiled his "I wish I could've been a fly on that wall" smile. "I want to know how big the plate was that you threw at his head."

"I didn't—" Jani scrubbed her hands through her hair as the

headache intensified. "It all flooded back at that moment. As I sat there in this—" She waved around her shoulders. "—this ridiculous dress that I'd bought just for that night. Every prep school teacher who told me I would never be anything and the hell of the idomeni Academy and every Service instructor who told me that I didn't belong. Every slight. Insult. Kick in the teeth. And none of it hurt as much as being told 'good enough to fuck but not good enough to marry.'"

"Did you tell him that?"

"What good would it have done to argue? I was what I was and I would never be accepted no matter what I did. I got up and left. I never saw him again. Not until he tracked me down on Whalen." Jani sat back, pondered her reactions as though they belonged to a stranger. "The wonder was that I never grew to hate him. Even after everything. I blamed his father for what he'd become. I let him off the hook."

"What about now?" Lucien waved hand in the air, too impatient to wait for an answer. "Take it from someone who knows. You would've made the worst political wife in the history of marriage. And he'd have cheated on you and lied to you just as he cheated on and lied to Alyssa. You'd have been miserable. He did you a favor." He dug through his pockets, freed a packet of crackers, and wolfed them down. "And now look where you are, and where he is."

"Because I put him there."

"Because of what he did to you. For chrissakes, Jani, he did try to kill you."

"I know." Jani pushed back from the desk and sat, arms folded and hands tucked under her arms to warm them. "And he killed people I cared about. People I should've been able to save." She shivered, and told herself it was the temperature of the room, too cold for her hybrid self. "And the few good moments were just that. Moments." She stopped to breathe slowly, in, then out, to stop her voice from shaking. "And now he apparently has something planned for me, and it involves one of my best friends, and I am scared."

Lucien had grown somber, crumpling the cracker wrapper and flattening it again and again. "Because it's personal."

Jani nodded. "I wish it wasn't. I wish it were business, because then I'd have room to maneuver, to bargain. Something I did wrong years ago filling out a damned insurance form that cost somebody a lot of money, and now they're coming for me. Someone who wants to blackmail me because they think that now I'm someone worth black-mailing. I've seen what happens when it's personal. It can go off the rails so fast." Old images replayed in her head, some heartbreaking, others streaked with blood. "I've seen what hate can do."

All was quiet for a time. Then Lucien broke the silence, his voice soft. "Anais used to say that it was all personal."

Jani looked into the face that helped break the Ulanovs' grip on the Outer Circle worlds and cost his former patroness her ministry. "Probably something to keep in mind." She sat huddled, head down. Heard Lucien's chair creak, then flinched when she felt his arms envelop her. "What are you doing?"

"Figuring out what to do when it's personal." Lucien had pushed his chair next to hers. Now he pulled her close, so she could rest against his chest. "You don't know for sure it's him." He gave her a squeeze, rested his chin on the top her head. "If it is, well, you can beat him. You're smarter than he is."

"But am I more desperate?" Jani felt herself relax even as she thought to pull away, fear of what she faced warring with confusion as to what was happening. She trusted Lucien with her life, but love was another matter. He had been engineered not to feel the gentler emotions, but lately that appeared to be fraying around the edges. *With appeared being the operative word.* She wasn't sure she believed it, but at that particular moment, she wasn't sure she cared. All she knew was that, at least for that short while, it felt good to be held.

———

After ten hours of studying the effects of vacuum on a human body, the construction of spacesuits of various types, and the proper way to attach a safety line to an improvised hook, Jani sent Lucien away to get some sleep when his yawning became too distracting. She continued to read and fill out the quizzes, stopping every so often to rise, walk around the small office, bend and stretch. *It's like exam week all over again.* The brain overflow. The punchiness. The undercurrent of fear that one wrong answer meant utter failure.

Or in this case, death. She submitted the last quiz, then sat for a few minutes with her head between her knees to stretch her lower back. Then, with altogether too many color images of swollen body parts and radiation-burnt skin flitting through her head, she stood and hopped in slow motion around the room, arms held out to her sides, a weightless figure bobbing across a ship's outer hull or the surface of a low-g world.

"Feeling a bit silly, are we?"

Jani's shoes caught on the carpet as she stopped and spun towards the door—she stumble-fell into a chair, which rolled across the floor and bounced off the wall, all to the amusement of Ian, who stood leaning against the door jamb, grinning.

"It's been a long day." She forced a smile and shrugged agreement.

"I can imagine." Ian walked to the desk, flipped through a few pages of one of the paper texts, then perched on the edge. "Your man's in the infirmary, napping. We offered to put him up in one of our hostels, but he said he wanted to stick close in case you decided to, how did he put it?"

"Did the phrase 'pain in the ass' come up at any point?"

That earned a laugh. "Possibly. Editha found him sleeping under a desk in one of the vacant offices. She escorted him to the infirmary and said within a minute after he laid down his head." Ian closed his eyes for a moment and let his head tilt to one side. "There are times I would sacrifice a body part to be able to fall asleep like that."

"It's a gift. I think he learned it in the Service. Eat when you can.

Sleep when you can." The thought of sleep triggered a bout of yawning, which soon dragged Ian along for the ride. "I've lost track of whether it's night or day."

"We use planet time here. It's half six. Early evening." Ian paused to rub his eyes. "Second shift has settled in. I wait for the manager updates, then take off around eight. I am, however, on 'round the clock call."

"That sounds exhausting." Jani hung her head. "Thank you. I know you're not comfortable about this."

"I'm not." Ian's handheld chimed, and he took it from his pocket and checked it. "And your last exam has been approved. I should be shocked that you're pushing through the course so quickly, but then again, perhaps I shouldn't be. You'll take a dry run in the training module tomorrow during first shift, and then you will be ready to go."

"Is there any way I could take the dry run tonight?" Jani forced another smile in the hope that it would work to soften the irritation behind the sharp look that Ian shot her way.

"According to your timeline, you have more than two common days' breathing room. Don't you think you should get some sleep?"

"I'm not sure I could."

"You should try. Exhausted people make mistakes." Ian rubbed a hand over his face. "I'll see what I can do, but this is for the practice run only. You will get some rest before the real thing."

"Yes. I will. Thank you." Jani took a deep breath. "Could I ask—" She paused while Ian muttered under his breath. "It's only if you still have contacts in Chicago."

Ian eyed her in question.. "A few."

"Ask if anyone has seen Evan van Reuter in the last few weeks. Recent official visits, things like that."

"That's a name I haven't heard in a while. But he's old news—why do you want to know?"

"Ask if they've heard anything...odd."

"Odd as in...?"

"Escaped. Missing."

"I think that all stations would've been alerted if that were the case."

"You'd think so, wouldn't you?" Jani watched Ian stare off to the side for a time, and she knew his speculations as if they were her own. That for all Evan van Reuter was, he was also still Family, and that there must be at least a few sympathizers willing to break laws for him. Laws they themselves had written, to be enforced or ignored as needs required.

"I'll see what I can find out." Ian looked at her, and shook his head. "The commissary's open. Eat something. I'll ask Editha to find you crash space."

"Eat something. Get some sleep." Jani recalled another image. Another face, dour and pale. *My erstwhile doctor.* In point of fact, her erstwhile everything. "I've heard that before."

"I'm sure you have. Hostel or infirmary?"

"Infirmary. Lucien doesn't like it when I wander off."

"Can't imagine why." Ian gave her one last hard look, then left.

Jani sat for a few minutes and tried to concentrate on happier thoughts to settle her restless mind. Thalassan sunsets. The impromptu football matches that sometimes broke out in the corridor outside her Main House office. The scent of the courtyard flowers. Then she wandered down to the commissary, hunted for the spiciest item available, settled on a bean and kettle beef stew that she doused with something called fire sauce to make hybrid-palatable. By the time she finished, Ian contacted her to let her know the dry run was a go.

Chapter Twenty-One

For all Jani had spent the bulk of her lost years on stations of various sizes and classifications, she had never grown used to living offworld. A dirt girl at heart, she felt more secure with a planet under her feet, breathing air that didn't come in a can. So, even though she had watched the vids, passed the tests, and completed the dry run to the instructor's satisfaction, her hands shook as she snapped and zipped herself into the spacesuit. Gauges beeped and warning lights flickered as they dealt with the moisture caused by the sweat trickling down her back, her tripping heart and quickened breathing.

"You're nervous." Lucien worked through the steps as her checker, confirming that all the mechanics functioned properly. "It's messing up your baseline reads."

"I belong in a cave. Surrounded by solid rock." Jani shifted from one foot to the other as Lucien recorded readings and checked fasteners. "I'll be fine." She felt once again for her holstered scanpack, which was attached outside her suit to her harness. "I'll go straight to the Phillipan section. Editha said that everything is sorted by date, so I should be able to narrow things down pretty quickly."

"She asked me to tell you that she loaded a map into the suit database." Lucien glanced at the group milling on the other side of the set of double doors that separated the business section of the documents center from the archive entryway, which included Ian, the facilities chief and assorted engineers and technicians. "Tuck this into an exterior pocket." He stood so as to block their view and handed Jani her shooter.

Jani looked from Lucien to the weapon. "What do you know that I don't?"

"Not a thing. But given what happened at Padishah, I feel it's advisable."

"If anyone else was out there, we'd know. That area has been under constant monitoring since the accident."

"Says the female who educated me about station no-scan zones." Lucien clipped a small device to the outside of Jani's suit. "An alarm connected directly to me. If necessary, I would need one minute to suit up and come after you if no one tries to stop me."

"And if someone tries to stop you?"

"One and a quarter. If I'm being nice." Lucien tapped more entries into his handheld. "For the record, I told them that I'm not happy that the old rule about always working in pairs seems to have fallen off the edge."

Jani worked her neck and shoulders as best she could, the crunching made louder by the confined space. *Crepitus. Usually caused by air bubbles in the tissues.* She tried not to think about what would happen to those bubbles in a vacuum. "You know, I wasn't all that worried about going out there until right this moment."

"That's why you're sweating."

"That's just standard suit hatred. Getting shot didn't enter into the picture." Jani tucked the weapon into one of the suit's many exterior pockets.

"I'll be right here." Lucien gave one of the indicators a final tap, then backed away. "And you'll be in and out, no worries."

"Lord Ganesh, give me strength." Jani took a deep breath, stifled a yawn, then walked toward the second set of double doors, which opened into the archive proper. As she had feared, she hadn't slept well. Instead, she spent the restless hours planning her route through the archive and excavating documents details from the depths of memory. She had the dock request tucked in another exterior pocket, ready to pull out for comparison purposes. *Look for something linking the two.* A mark of some kind. A notation. *A bloody coffee spatter.*

Lock mechanisms whirred and clicked. The doors slid open.

Not particularly busy places, archives. In Jani's experience, tomb-like had usually proved the case. *Where old paper goes to die.* She stepped into the immense, high-ceilinged space, a central area filled by row after row of stacked shelves and ringed by carrels, cubbyhole offices, and supply closets.

She paused as the doors closed behind her, and placed a hand on her shooter. Every so often when she entered an area she'd never been in before, a remnant of her Service training would come up for air. Add to that the memory of dire experiences over the last two decades, a few of which she'd been lucky to survive, and the result was an unsettled sense that something wasn't right. That this place would be a nightmare to search and secure. That even now, someone could be observing her from any of a dozen hiding places, weapon drawn, waiting...

You should've gotten more sleep, Kilian. Fatigue always made her edgy. She activated the visor view screen and called up the archive map, checked directions she had gone over a dozen times or more, and headed for the section containing the documents from the colony of Phillipa.

Crown jewel of the J-Loop. The Commonwealth world closest to the idomeni homeward of Shèrá, where Service and diplomatic personnel who dealt with the challenging race on a regular basis fled to decompress. She had visited its main settlement, Ville Louis-Philippe, only once, and that had been enough. *You could call it wild.* And a superb training ground if one needed to acquire experience with forged and altered documents.

Those were the days. Jani listened to the soft buzz and click of her suit mechanisms, as though insects had burrowed within. The archive itself remained silent, any distant sounds of repair crews muffled by the protective barrier.

"So?"

Jani flinched as Lucien's voice sounded in her ear. "I'm just on my way to the Phillipan section." She trudged down the corridor, told herself all would be fine. "I think I overtrained for this."

"Better that than the opposite."

"Where's your sense of adventure?" Jani's imagination, which as a rule stayed in the reality lane, wandered onto weirder trails. When young, one of her favorite vid series featured a group of friends who explored abandoned stations. Being a kid's show, the scares involved the odd squatter who turned out to be a lost heir or a visitor from an alternate universe who just wanted to get back home. *The kids helped them, and no one got shot.*

"It's a search and patrol nightmare, isn't it? All those twists and turns."

"Feel free to shut up at any time." Jani looked up at the ceiling. "The lights aren't going on as I approach."

"Probably damaged as a result of the collision."

"They're self-contained units. They should go on." Jani listened to the muffled conversation as Lucien discussed the matter with the rest of the group.

"They should be going on. One of the engineers has gone to check."

"I can still see. Suit lights and safety lighting in the floor." Jani looked down one of the aisles, and saw that two file bins had been opened, the contents scattered across the floor. "Someone left a mess in here." She looked up at the signage. "It's the first row of the Phillipan section."

"Where you need to search?"

"No—it's too recent." Jani glanced down the next aisle, and saw another scatter of paper. "Is Editha there?"

"No."

"Have someone find her and ask her if there were any recent searches in this section that someone didn't bother cleaning up." Jani heard a couple of her vital sign indicators click and stutter. *Heart rate and respiration.* Didn't the designers of these suits realize that informing a person that they were nervous just made them more nervous?

She backed up past the Phillipan section to one that contained Serran documents. *Another J-Loop world, so?* No messes in the aisles that she could see. *Doesn't mean much—I'd have to check every aisle to be sure.* No time for that. Besides, she already knew what had happened. At some point, someone else had searched for the same document she hunted for now.

Question the first. Did they find it?

Question the second. Where were they now?

Why can't it ever be simple? As Jani approached the aisle containing the earliest Phillipan paper, she drew her shooter and disengaged the safety. The archive map scrolled along the interior of her faceplate, narrowing scope to show the dating and general contents of individual bins.

Her holstered scanpack bumped against her thigh with every step. *Fast and simple...simple and fast.* She studied the ID coding on the fronts of the bins, compared them to the rolling register she had memorized twenty years before. *How the hell do you remember that shit,* one or another of her Academy classmates had asked on more than one occasion.

"The sequences just make sense to me." Jani walked the aisle almost to the end, the earliest paper on file, then stopped in front of the bin that would've contained the dock request. *Mixed paper.* Which meant the documents here hadn't been sorted according to Family. No guarantee that the linked document she needed was contained within that particular bin. If there had been a delay of weeks or months in processing, it could be in one of the other locker-size poly containers that rested like coffins on the story-high racks.

But this was Family business. It would've been handled quickly, with a minimum of traceable documentation.

Jani placed her shooter on a shelf within easy reach, popped the lid off a likely bin. Pulled out an armful of documents, some as crisp and clean as the day they had been initialized, others, tatty and ragged-edged, folds and creases ground in as though they had been run over by large vehicles. She backed into the shadows and flipped through the stack, pulling out the messy sheets and slips and setting them aside. *Nondescript. Easily overlooked. Belongs in a trash bin.* In her experience, the three qualities usually found in really important paper that various and sundry individuals wished to slip through unnoticed.

Once she had finished sorting, she pulled out the dock request and placed it on an empty section of shelf. Took the top document from the stack, and compared.

Wrong date code. Next.

Wrong Family. Next.

Before long, she had worked through the entire set. *Didn't think it would be that easy, did you, Kilian?* Another stack, another round of sorting and comparing. A third. A fourth. Every so often, she stopped to listen for any sounds, and checked down the aisle for a shadow or any other sign that she wasn't alone.

"So?"

Jani's heart stuttered. "I wish you'd hum or tap the link or something before you say anything."

"Feeling jittery, are we?" Lucien lowered his voice. "I'm getting questions about your progress. As if I can read your mind."

"I thought you could."

"Only some things."

Jani pushed away thoughts about what those things might be. "Any news about the lighting?"

"Still checking."

"How about Editha?"

"Not yet—wait—" A gabble of voices followed. "No work

involving those documents prior to the collision, and no one on her staff would dare leave them scattered about on pain of pain."

"That's what I thought." Jani felt an all-too-familiar prickle along the back of her neck. "Someone else has been hunting for this paper."

"If van Reuter or whoever needs you to find it, what would this other searcher have to do with it?"

"Competing interests?" Jani paged through another armful of documents.

"Or that mess you found is unrelated. Someone got sloppy and didn't tell anyone because they knew they'd get into trouble."

"You really believe that?"

"If you want me to join you, I can push the point."

"Not yet." Jani finished sorting through the last paper in the bin. "Other than the paper, I haven't heard or seen anything unusual. If someone was back here, they cleared out when they realized they had company." She waited for a response. Waited a little longer. "Lucien?"

"Fine. I'll wait. But I'm suiting up so I'm ready to go."

Jani stuffed documents back in their bin and moved on to the next. The lid jammed when she tried to open it—when she pulled harder, a sharp plastic crack sounded.

"What was that noise?"

"Target practice." Jani set the lid pieces aside. "Kidding. I just broke a bin cover."

"That's not funny."

"When did you become such a worrywart?"

"After we were ambushed at Padi."

"Touché." Jani had sorted through an armful of paper when she realized that Lucien had yet to sign off. "I thought you were going to suit up."

"The engineers are running numbers." Lucien paused to respond to a question. "Their safety margins are ridiculous. I asked them to figure out a way to get me out there."

"You do keep pushing, don't you?"

"I learned it from someone I know."

No need to ask to whom Lucien might be referring. "Well, good. They took out the portable lifts because of the weight. You can boost me up to the higher shelves."

"Jesus, don't climb anything until I get there."

"Whatever happened to that devil-may-care boy I used to know?"

"A year and a half with you."

"Time flies." Jani stopped in mid-sort to flex her neck, and wished she felt as calm as she sounded. "Leave me alone—I'm working."

"I'm keeping this channel open."

Jani didn't reply. Instead, she crept to the end of the aisle and looked one way, then the other. Saw nothing but the rows of towering shelving, rendered menacing by the shadows cast by the safety lighting.

Get a move on, Kilian. She returned to her workspace and continued her search. Most all the parchment was light blue in color, the same as the dock request, with little in the way of decoration or special formatting to set it apart. Every time she finished examining a stack, she fought the urge to go through it again in case she missed something. *I can do it. I have the time.* The hours didn't pass with a sound like Niall's death knell as they had previously—she still had a solid two days by her last count. *Make that one and a half.* She fought to forget her surroundings—the darkness, the silence, the undercurrent of fear—and concentrate on her task.

Even so, she almost flipped past the slip of parchment that at first glance appeared just as unpromising as all the others. She stared at the creases, as though it had been crumpled, then flattened. Compared it to the dock request. *No crumpling.* Returned to the other document. It was an invoice, line after alphanumeric line identifying the cargo, the seller and buyer, the taxes and other fees. The value.

Jani slipped off her right glove, whispered yet another prayer to Lord Ganesh, and initiated her scanpack. Indicators fluttered green, then yellow, then flashed off. *Damn.* She hunted through her pockets for wipes, cleaned her hand as best she could, and tried again. Suit sensors chittered as they catalogued her stress level—she told them to shut the hell up despite that being a waste of breath.

It took three tries before green lights shone across the surface of the 'pack. She passed the device over the invoice once, then again. Read the output that stuttered across the display. *Patent transfer coding.* On an invoice? *Okay.* Like writing a will on a dispo napkin, technically legal but not the usual practice.

Jani continued scanning. *A patent ownership transfer.* From Elias Scriabin to Acton van Reuter, Evan's father. *Elias was Alyssa's father.* Alyssa van Reuter, whose death under mysterious circumstances had led to Jani's first visit to the Commonwealth capital of Chicago and, in the end, the ruination of Alyssa's husband, disgraced former Interior Minister Evan van Reuter.

So what is this doing here? Transfers at this level were worked out in lawyers' offices as hot-and-cold-running accountants determined the best ways to avoid capital gains and windfall profits taxes.

More than one patent. At least half a dozen, if her 'pack's balky readout could be trusted. *Slipped in under the radar at a dirty dock.* She had no idea how the new ownership of this steaming mess of intellectual property would be explained to various governing bodies. "I have a feeling that the issue never came up." Maybe one or both men changed their minds. Maybe Evan and Alyssa had broken up yet again, throwing a spanner into the dynastic works. All Jani knew was that control of patents meant ownership of licenses, which was how the Families extracted much of their income from the colonies.

There's no time limit mentioned. No conditions. If this transfer was never cancelled, it's still technically valid. Depending on what these patents covered, Jani currently held the equivalent of the lost will that led to murder and mayhem in any number of mystery tales.

She set aside her scanpack, laid the dock transfer and invoice side by side. Once again, her suit clicked and warbled as her vital signs kicked into overdrive. She compared the two documents, one old but relatively smooth, the other so battered that the parchment had lost its characteristic stiffness, leaving it limp as a cloth rag. *Nothing... nothing...*

Then she spotted them. A trio of near-invisible nicks near the lower right corner of each document, which overlaid perfectly. Too regular to be accidental. A way for someone without a scanpack to identify them and link them together.

Jani unfastened the front of her suit, tucked the documents inside, redid the closures. Turned, and found the end of the aisle blocked by a suited figure, their face hidden behind their helmet visor's reflective coating.

"Why didn't you tell me you were on your way?" Jani tapped her comlink. "Lucien?"

"Yes?"

Jani watched the visitor, who had yet to move a muscle. "Where are you?"

"In the passageway, getting ready to enter the archive."

"So you're not the person currently standing at the end of the aisle?"

In answer to the question, the newcomer extracted a weapon and pointed it at her.

Long narrow muzzle. Projectile shooter. Jani's weapon was a standard pulse device—it would garble suit systems and the wearer as well. *But bullets make holes.* In her suit. In her.

"The documents." The figure's voice emerged tinny and flat, all identifiable characteristics filtered. "Step forward three paces, place them on the floor, then back away."

At which time, you'll shoot me. Jani undid the front of her suit. Paused. Grabbed her shooter off the shelf.

The invader raised their weapon. Then they turned in the direction of the entry and fired. One beat later, a shooter blast hit them in the chest and flared like an aura over their suit, which sent off sparks as components shorted and cooked. They stumbled in the opposite direction, then regained their footing and ran, trailing smoke.

A beat later, another suited figure appeared, his visor clear, his face a pale oval in the dark. "Stay here." Lucien paused only long enough to glance her way. "And where's your goddamn safety attach?" He gestured toward her harness. "Hook up and stay put."

Jani watched him hurry after the fleeing intruder. Then came the crackle and hiss of shooter fire, the more explosive shatter of bullets striking metal and hard poly. She took hold of the safety line attached to her harness, extended it to snap it to the hook embedded in the wall—

—then released it. It retracted with a jerk, whacking her thigh hard enough to hurt. The pain drove her forward. She holstered her scanpack, secured the fasteners of the pockets containing the documents, and set out after Lucien.

Old habits resurfaced. She crabwalked sideways down the corridor, back bumping against the shelving, both hands gripping her weapon. She led with her animandroid left limbs, the arm slightly elevated to shield her chest, so they could bear the brunt of any hit. Up ahead, she spotted Lucien, crouched in a doorway on the other side of the corridor, reloading with a fresh power pack as a bullet struck the wall near his head. She tracked the direction of the shot. Raised her weapon. Fired.

Silence for one heartbeat. Two. Then came multiple shots, bullets driving into the shelving above her head, punching holes in bins.

"What the fuck did I tell you." Lucien's voice blasted inside her helmet. "Get out of here."

Jani ducked out of sight, then scuttled along the floor into an open area furnished with a scatter of carrels. She pulled one over on its side, glanced over the top, caught sight of the intruder hidden behind a waist-high binder case. When the top of their helmet bobbed above the edge, she sighted.

When it bobbed up again, she fired.

More bullets aimed at her, striking the sheltering table, splintering poly and sending it flying. Sharp-edged fragments bounced off her helmet and embedded in her suit, which bleated damage alerts and sent red warning lights skittering across her visor viewing area. She yanked out the shards, which activated the repair cells that pumped sealant through the suit's surface webbing. When the alarms went silent, she popped her head up and caught a glimpse of her attacker lurching across the open area towards the barrier. *Except there's a hole in it.* "Should there be an opening there?"

Lucien had exited his shelter and joined Jani by the carrels. "Are you seeing this?"

Jani heard a muddle of voices respond, and realized Lucien was talking to people back at the documents center. "What's going on?"

"Station security is heading to the location to intercept." Lucien holstered his weapon, then took it out and exchanged the power pack with a fresh one. "They want us to come in."

"They won't get there in time." Jani headed towards the gap.

"No. You are not going—" Lucien grabbed for her arm, and missed. "Dammit, it's a passageway. You walk into it, you might as well paint a target on your suit."

"So cover me."

"Cold fucking day when I let you go in ahead of me—"

They both stopped when a deep rumble sounded, like distant thunder. The floor rippled—Jani felt a tremor vibrate up her legs.

Then the wall at the end of the corridor fissured. With a sound like a high-pitched whine, the structure flexed, then gave way. The air rushed out, taking Jani and Lucien with it.

Jani tumbled across the floor, slamming against shelf supports, furniture. Her head struck something rigid and immovable—lights flashed and strobed inside her helmet before blacking completely. Blind and battered, she reached out, grabbed for anything she could hold onto. Her hands found something weighty and rigid and she wrapped her arms and legs around it as the gale buffeted her and her suit bleated and her heart pounded and something squeezed her chest like a vise and breathing grew harder and harder and harder—

Chapter Twenty-Two

Jani opened her eyes, then squinched them shut as light stabbed.

Her next attempt was more gradual, squint to halfway to, eventually, fully open.

She lay on a bed. *Room.* Four light-colored walls. Some framed prints of what looked like flowers through mist. An infusion pack nestled in the crook of her right arm. *Clothes.* They weren't hers. A loose wrap shirt and pull-on pants in shades of blue, dressier than the T-shirt and shorts she usually wore as pajamas.

She looked to one side and saw a figure seated in a chair set against the far wall. It was fuzzy—she needed to blink to bring it into focus. Tall. Slim. Pale blond hair. Dressed in white.

Jani struggled to speak as every drawn breath stabbed like a knife between her ribs. She tried to sit up, failed, surrendered to lying back, staring at the ceiling and inhaling in slow, shallow puffs. "Am I dead?"

"Not for lack of trying." An oh so familiar bass, dark as its owner was pale. "Three cracked ribs. Fair bit of bruising. Mild concussion." Footsteps followed. Then, John Shroud's austere face moved into her sightline. Oà coloring. Crystal blue eyes. Cream gold skin. The palest of humans and the palest of idomeni combined. "What in the actual hell were you doing in a suit in a damaged section of the station?"

"I needed something stored there." Jani found the adjustment pad on the side of the bed, and raised the head in small increments. "Lucien?"

"He's fine. He stopped you from getting sucked out into space. You barreled into him and you both crashed into shelving and brought it down on top of you. He's a bit better off than you. Ribs. Twisted knee. Dislocated shoulder."

"The person we were after—"

"Pieces. She had been trying to pilot an escape pod when she apparently lost control and crashed into the one of the construction jetties. Her craft disintegrated." John lowered to the edge of the bed. "Some of the wreckage collided with and ruptured the safety barrier, which resulted in—" He gestured vaguely in Jani's direction.

"She?" Jani thought back to her confrontation with the intruder. "I couldn't tell—the suit was bulky, and she kept her visor's reflective filter on and disguised her voice."

"Female, yes. Judging from what we could find." John crossed his legs, linked his hands around one knee, tried for relaxed and casual and, as usual, missed. "Mind telling me what's going on?"

Jani started to speak. Tears sprang as her ribs took exception. "What—are you doing here?"

John frowned and started fiddling with the infuser control, which was attached to the side of the bed. "Planning a clinic downstairs. I was just leaving a lab specifications meeting when the alarm sounded for a medico with hybrid experience. Imagine my surprise when I learned the name of the hybrid in question." The device's input pad beeped. "Is that better? You're apparently resistant to some of the first-round hybrid painkillers."

Jani sagged against the pillow as numb warmth settled. "Much." She struggled to track what had happened, what was happening now.

John continued to fuss with the infuser. "Any chance of my getting any answers before I die?"

"It's better if we keep this need-to-know for the time being. Sorry." Jani tried to sit up, stopped in mid-rise as pain broke through. Her ribcage seared and every muscle in her back cramped. She fell back into her pillows, breathed in short, sharp gasps of air.

"Those are the cracked ribs talking. They will have quite a bit to say for some time to come." John adjusted the infuser again before at last setting it aside. "I would advise limited movement for the next few days. You have some recovery ahead of you."

"I don't have a few days." Jani checked her wrist for her timepiece, scanned the room for a clock. "Date and time. I need the date and time. How long was I out?"

"You were unconscious for a short while after the accident—we're not sure for how long. Telemetry was spotty and your suit's memory was damaged, so we decided to play it safe. You were sedated because idomeni occasionally become combative after brain trauma and we sought to minimize chances of that given your other injuries. You were only out a couple of hours." John shifted back and forth, hands extended, trying to limit her movement without touching her. "What's going on?"

Jani counted backwards, forwards, her brain fighting her each time she tried to focus. "The documents I had in my suit when everything blew. Where are they?"

"Jani. You need to rest and avoid stress."

"The documents I had—"

"Are in a secure place. A young woman named Editha took charge of them and asked me to inform her when you came around." John gave up trying to keep his distance—he took hold of her hands and pressed them between his own. "Jesus, Jan, what the hell is going on?"

"It's not your problem." Jani tried to pull away, but her ribs sent out warning twinges. "I need to see Editha now."

"You're not going anywhere."

"Then bring her here."

"Not now."

"John—"

"Did you hear me say 'concussion.' I distinctly remember uttering that word."

"I can tell you this much—"

"I don't care what you tell me, you're not—"

"Niall was kidnapped."

John's mouth snapped shut. He let go of her hands, then stood and walked across the room to the window, which overlooked a lush tropical garden lit by a pretend sun. "Well, that certainly explains a lot." He glanced back at Jani. "That said, and with the understanding that he is your friend, you're not Commonwealth anymore. What does it have to do with you?"

"Why does everyone ask me that?" Jani knew that however he felt about her, John would keep pushing, and she debated how much to tell him. *But he knows people.* And despite his own hybrid state, he may have maintained connections with Chicago. *And he knew Evan.* He had even treated him after his incarceration.

And remember what Rudo said about first moves. "Okay." She compressed the events of the past several days into as few words as fatigue from the painkillers and a developing headache allowed. "Given the documents in question, I think Evan is involved. But someone else tried to prevent me from finding them and then tried to take them. They seem to know every move we're making, which forces me to wonder how in hell they're tracking us." She spent some time edging into a more comfortable position, wondered at the silence, and looked over at John to find him still by the window, head down, hands clasped behind his back.

"Boy, this brings back memories. Rauta Shèràa. Chicago." He hesitated. "Thalassa." He leaned against the window, arms folded. "I've been inside the house where they've stashed Evan. It is very much a prison."

"Still waiting for confirmation that remains the case."

"All right. So. I spoke with Ian. The best his engineers can tell, the collision was truly an accident."

Jani felt every muscle in her face move as she started to speak, and paused to flex her jaw. "She got into the archive via a passage in the safety barrier, which I doubt was supposed to be there. She had either been in the archive for some time—I found evidence of previous searches—or she had been in and out. Given that the area was supposed to be under constant surveillance, I think Ian needs to talk to his engineers again."

"He will as soon as they finish their recon of the damaged area." Ian slipped in through the open door and closed it behind him. "Forgive me for overhearing, but your voices do carry." He dragged one of the visitor chairs closer to Jani's bed and sat. He looked exhausted and a little ill, his skin ashen and his eyes dull. "According to what you saw and what Lucien relayed back, yes, you're correct. Whoever you ran into had been searching back there for quite some time. Security is checking with all the contractors connected to the project to find out who carved out that passage."

Jani hugged herself and tried to convince tense muscles to cut her a little slack. "What's above and below the barrier. What's nearby?"

"Such as?"

"Domiciles. Cafés. Bars."

"Are you saying that the workers carved a shortcut for the sake of convenience?"

"And disabled surveillance to hide the fact. The intruder took advantage." Jani shrugged, and immediately regretted having done so. "No one will admit anything. They'll sacrifice their jobs first."

"We'll find out who."

"No, you won't." Jani glanced at John, who looked down at his shoes. "No one will tell you because they would be found out and then it's the silent treatment and seeing their safety equipment get wrecked and their pay chits lost for the rest of their working lives. No one likes a snitch, especially in the case of expensive damage that leads to insurance claims."

"Then they'll never work again."

"Sure they will. There are a lot of stations out here and most of them aren't picky." Jani worked her neck as old memories returned and brought the resulting tension with them. "Just about every bit of bullshit I've ever encountered has boiled down to people taking short-cuts and other people capitalizing on them." She almost shrugged again, but stopped herself in time. "You can dig. See if you can ID the remains. But if she worked for one of the gangs, she'll have at least three aliases and so many gaps in between that you'll never link them up and if she worked for Family, you'll never find out anything no matter how many friends you tap for favors."

Ian slumped back. "I can't understand how that's even possible."

"Ian." Jani crossed her hands over her chest. "I hid for almost twenty years. John and Val Parini knew what I looked like and what sort of medical trail to follow, and they couldn't find me. The person who did had the force of an entire ministry behind him as well as Family resources."

"Evan van Reuter."

Jani nodded, eventually. "It's the outer worlds. Smuggler econ-omy. Even the little pockets of order have holes."

They all quieted, victims to various degrees of pain, fatigue, or memory.

Jani broke the silence first. "Given the people I believe are behind this, I don't understand why they didn't dispatch a Family-connected dexxie. All that person would have had to do was show up here with a Registry-authorized writ to collect their property."

Ian stood, pushed his chair back against the wall. "Given current conditions, we wouldn't have let them in."

"Yes, you would've." Jani sensed John's watchful eye as she sat up straighter. "They'd have persuaded you."

"Threats?" Ian sneered. "I don't respond to threats."

"Not to you. To someone else." Jani met the man's eyes, saw their warm, tired light flicker. "Caring. It's a weakness. That's how they get you. Every time." She watched him leave, his step heavier, and felt a twinge of sympathy. Learning about life outside the sheltered confines of Family compounds and corporations at his age couldn't be easy. Still, better to do so before someone close to him paid the price for his ignorance.

She breathed slowly. Told herself that she was fine, that John was just using her injuries as an excuse to pry. Glanced at the bedside table, bare but for a pitcher of water and a glass. Opened the single drawer, and found it empty. Patted the bed. Looked under her pillow.

John stepped away from his place by the window. "What are you looking for?"

"My scanpack. It must still be with the suit." Jani watched John stop, then look at the floor, the wall above her head, everywhere but at her. "What haven't you told me?"

———

John commandeered the clinic's single patient's chair, which had wheels instead of a skim unit and a tendency to pull to the left. He maneuvered it through a series of lifts and corridors in silence while Jani sat huddled under a blanket, heart pounding. Editha, eyes red and expression grim, met them at the entrance to the documents center and led them to her office.

Jani tried to get out of the chair when she spotted the refrigerated box of the type used to transport damaged 'packs resting atop the desk, but John gripped her shoulders and held her back.

"You hit the shelving so very hard." Editha glanced at John, then picked up the box as though it were made of sugar glass and set it on Jani's lap. "Your holster tore and the 'pack flew out. The damage crew recovered it within the hour, but the case had shattered and the dura mater tore and the core tissue was exposed for too long. Feed and waste cells ruptured. I am so sorry." She sniffled. "I didn't know if there was anything you wanted to try to save." Her eyes welled. A tear fell.

"The holster's reinforced. It's protected it in the past." Jani cracked the seals and lifted the lid. "It's not the first time I rattled around in a can." The smell hit her first, the ammonia stink of the cellular waste filter. The sight of the shattered case followed, the loose pieces tucked into a clear plastic bag, the exposed remnants of brain tissue visible through a cover of protective film.

"When Editha says you hit the shelving hard, she means hard enough to smash the hell out of your suit and wreck your helmet." John's voice emerged a soft rumble. "No holster could've withstood the impact."

Jani tried to sort through the pieces. "Some of the chips could be salvageable. I'd like to pull those." Her hands shook so that she could manage only some clumsy poking. "And the documents?"

"Yes. Doctor Shroud gave them to me for safekeeping." Editha removed a slipcase from one of the file cabinets and gave it to Jani, then sat at her desk and activated her work station. "I can set you up in the lab. If you're able to work today—?"

John grumbled. "I would rather you spent the time resting, but I know trying to convince you of that is an exercise in futility." He tilted his chin at Editha. "You'll assist, inform me if she passes out?"

Editha looked at Jani, eyes widening. "Of course."

"If I'm going to salvage the chips, I need to get to work as soon as possible." Jani closed the box and folded her hands across the top. Sat still for a few moments. "Did it know?"

John circled the chair and bent low to look her in the face. "What?"

"It is—it was a part of my brain. A part of me." Jani touched the back of her neck, the scar left by the sampling cannula. "Did it know what was happening? Was it scared? Did it hurt?"

Editha's breath caught. She wiped her eyes with her jacket sleeve, an action that made her look even younger than she was. "I think that mine hears me when I talk to it, but the technicians all tell me that it can't communicate in that way."

John looked from Jani to Editha, then back to Jani. "I know documents examiners feel a closeness to their scanpacks. It makes sense.

They're made from you, and without them you can't function. And I've heard the stories about...communication." His face reddened as a blush rose. Uncertainty stripped away the years, so that he once more seemed the young man who had pulled Jani's burnt remains from the transport wreckage all those years before, unsure of everything but his determination to save her. "I don't know. There's still a lot we don't know about bio-based devices. To this point, it hasn't been the focus of any work." He straightened. "The brain itself doesn't feel pain. The dura mater that covers the scanpack brain doesn't contain the type of receptor that would transmit the sensation."

"But could it sense danger?" Jani relived that short, terrifying tumble through the archive. The confusion. The blindness. "Could it know on some level what was going on?"

"We don't know." John pressed his hands to the sides of his head, then slid them down to the back of his neck. Worked his shoulders. "There is no reason to believe that it could."

Jani looked into his eyes, and tried to determine how much of what he told her was true and how much was a lie to spare her feelings. The latter had proved the case more and more towards the end of their relationship, the lies growing bigger and bigger until they formed a barrier that kept her from doing what needed to be done. For now, well, she didn't believe him. She didn't disbelieve him. She just wasn't sure.

And now, as then, it wasn't enough.

Chapter Twenty-Three

Jani worked out a deal with John on the way back to the clinic. If she agreed to rest until the time came for her appointment at the documents lab, he would refrain from locking her in her room.

"I'm kidding about that, by the way. Mostly." John showed her how to adjust the chair in case he wasn't available to ferry her back to the documents center. "I'm sure the Service is looking for him." He studied her face, read it as he always had. "Christ, Jan, he's Mako's right hand. They're not going to abandon him."

Jani boosted out of the chair onto the bed, waving off John's outreached hands along the way. "He and I talk sometimes about the old days. The old Service. How it was amazing we both survived it, albeit for different reasons." She paused in the middle of patting a pillow into suitable shape. "Well, I guess technically, I didn't survive it." She lay back and felt her body sag into the mattress, which responded by warming her, easing the constant cold she felt in human environments. "Anyway, he always says how much things improved under Mako. How different it is now." She pretended to stifle a yawn. "I just listen."

John straightened the bedspread, then tapped an entry into the patient record in the footboard. "Get some sleep. Please?" He started to leave, then paused. "Did you really think seeing me meant you'd died?"

Jani measured her words. "It's been a rough last few days."

"Uh-huh." A sigh. "Sleep."

"Promise." Jani watched John leave, listened to his footsteps recede, then counted ten minutes' worth of seconds. Wondered if the bed sent a message to the nurses' station if it sensed her get up, then decided the hell with it and boosted back into the chair. Her stomach grumbled, so she excavated her bag from the storage cabinet, dug out a few packets of Jaki Pax, and stuffed them in the pocket of her robe.

It took some maneuvering to wrangle the door and the chair at the same time, but she managed, steering herself down the corridor, checking each room as she passed until she came to Lucien's. She found him fiddling with the bed controls, wincing each time the mattress moved.

"What the hell is Shroud doing here?" He dragged a pillow onto his lap and punched it for emphasis. "You know, it's no fun being examined by someone who hates your guts."

Jani gestured for him to lower his voice. "He's opening a clinic downstairs."

"He should've stayed there."

"They didn't know how to treat me here, so they put out a call—"

"Oh, you mean he heard you were here."

"If you recall, we're not exactly friends anymore."

"Perhaps you should remind him."

Jani closed the door, then rolled over to Lucien's bedside. "What happened?"

"I followed you in." Lucien resumed rearranging his bedding, stacking pillows behind his head and pushing the bedspread with his feet until it hung over the footboard like a turquoise-striped tongue. He wore pajamas similar to Jani's, but in dark grey, a color that matched the bruises on his arms and the shiner beneath one eye.

"Matrishi pitched a fit because no training records, but I waved my ex-Spacer cred in his face and he stopped threatening to lock me up." He paused to press a hand to his side, closed his eyes, and slowed his breathing.

Jani felt her own ribs twinge in sympathy. "How bad is it?"

"I've had worse." Lucien opened his eyes and sagged against his pillows. "They had to give my augie a kick to activate it. It's still lagging behind. Shroud said we both hit the shelving pretty hard."

"Thanks to our intruder. Her pod slammed into the construction site."

"Her? Did she survive?"

"Unfortunately, no."

"So we'll never know who she was or who she worked for."

"Probably Family. The Scriabins or the Ulanovs." Jani explained the contents of the invoice in non-documents examiner terms. "I didn't find anything that set time limits on the transaction. It's still open, which would explain why they would try to keep me from making delivery if they couldn't recover it themselves."

"Could also explain the attack on Padi." Lucien shook his head. "Whoever the hell it is, they've been tracking us this entire time."

"That's what I think." Jani gave a quick rundown about the importance of the invoice. "Scriabin and van Reuter. It was a Family wedding, which meant it was a business merger more than anything." Decades-old memories replayed. Evan's foul moods after speaking with his father, and the fights that followed. "Evan kept squirming out from under, so the offerings would have to have been generous. I'm guessing some very broad patents, agriculture or water production. Building materials. Things that spanned multiple systems. Major supply lines."

"Enough to replenish the van Reuter coffers."

"And then some."

"He gives it to Anais in the neck for driving his arrest and imprisonment, and sets it up so you, the one who started it all in the first place, are the one who hands him the knife." Lucien nodded his approval. "Assuming he is in fact involved in all this, it is pretty neat."

"He always had a gift for certain types of maneuvering." Jani waited for Lucien to respond. But when the silence continued, she looked over to find him sitting arms folded, eyes fixed straight ahead. "What?" She watched him work his jaw, start to speak, then stop. "If you have something to say, just say it."

"What good would it do?" Lucien exhaled with a growl. "Okay." He shifted to face her. "When I tell you to do something, you do it. If I tell you to run, you run. If I tell you to stay put, you stay put. If I tell you that I will take care of it, that means you butt out."

"She had you trapped in the doorway." Jani dug out one of the snack packets and yanked it open, scattering half the contents across her lap. "I drew fire so you could get into a better position."

Lucien lay back his head and groaned at the ceiling. "You really don't give me credit for knowing how to do my job, do you?"

"I'm allowed to defend myself. You gave me the damned shooter."

"My showing up was your cue to leave it be." Lucien held up one finger. "She had only one weapon. Projectile. Eight-round magazine, which meant she needed to pause and change clips every eight shots, which was when I moved in closer. I had already whacked her suit three times—it was essentially nonfunctional. One more pulse and she'd have been stunned unconscious, at which point I would've gathered her up and brought her in for questioning."

Jani plucked sour fruit drops from various folds and pockets. "I told you who she likely worked for."

"And I used to work for those same people, which means I could've learned a helluva lot about their current movements out here now that Anais is getting back in the game."

"Not sure that would've helped us with the present situation. Besides, she was likely a grunt who wouldn't have known anything anyway." Jani rolled a candy between her fingers. The yellow coating reminded her of Teddy and the altercation in the Padishah Station basement. "I didn't listen to you on Padi and you said I saved your life."

Lucien muttered something foul about blind pigs and acorns. "Niall warned me. If I recall correctly, the term he used was 'fuckin' bullhead.'"

Jani started to object, then quieted as the chill settled. The same sensation she had felt during the attack at Padishah Station, that frozen rage that could only be dissipated by a quick, focused burst of violence. *The idomeni in me.* She took one deep breath, then another, conscious all the while of Lucien's sharp examination. "I'm not without experience, either." Her voice came raspy, words forced through a tightened throat.

"It's not your job." Lucien spoke more slowly, more quietly, sensing her mood, her state of mind, as he always did. "Ideally, I wouldn't be alone here. I'd be heading a security team with an advance crew and a rear guard, but we don't have those basics because Feyó's a bloody idiot." He drummed his fingers atop the mattress. "I have a question. How are you going to get those documents to them?"

Jani shrugged, and immediately regretted it. "They haven't told me."

"Think they'll send somebody here to pick them up? They'll bring Niall along and you'll meet at one of the docks and make your trade?"

"It doesn't feel like that."

"No, it doesn't, does it?" Lucien winced, then slowly straightened. "It feels like they're going to take you to wherever they're holding Niall. What do you think the odds are that you survive that?"

"Evan will consider the humiliation sufficient punishment."

"What if he doesn't? What if he isn't even involved?"

"Niall has been in situations like this too, you know. If you think he's sitting in a cell twiddling his thumbs, you'd be mistaken."

"You're depending on Niall to set things up? Really? What if he's drugged or injured? What if he's dead?"

"Niall's there. His captors, whoever they are, are there. That means there will be spacecraft in docks." Jani extracted a candy from a cushion fold, then looked up to find Lucien staring, mouth agape.

"Tell me you're kidding."

"I've piloted a shuttle before."

"Have you? A shuttle? What classification? How many hours do you have on record? Do you have a GateWay rating?"

"Do I possess every qualification and license necessary to pilot a small craft bearing passengers? No. Can I muddle my way through a basic breakaway and coast until some larger craft can tow me in? Yes."

"You've been holding out on me. I would absolutely love to hear that story."

"I'm here. How much more do you need to know?" Jani concentrated on the snack bag, folding it closed, then opening it. "I'll leave copies of the documents with you. My notes. In case...in case, take them to Dieter. He and I have talked about circumstances like this."

"Like what?" Lucien glared around the room, then pressed a hand to his ribs and swore. "Are you listening to yourself?"

"You said it before, if someone really wants to get me, they will."

"Why make it easy for them?"

"So you risk your life instead?" Jani crunched sour lemon, then held back a sneeze as astringent acidity rattled her sinuses. "I don't like sending someone to do something I wouldn't do myself."

"Get used to it. Or someday you'll get us both killed because I'll be too busy taking care of you to take care of myself." Lucien plucked at his pajama bottoms, then smoothed the creases. "I have been thinking about it. What to do if they pick you up. As soon as I can walk around, I will be resuming talks with interested parties."

"You're going to pull in station security. Ian won't like it."

"Fuck Ian. I sent out feelers as soon as we settled in. I get the sense that for the most part, it gets rather boring around here. Some folks are interested in a change of pace."

Jani sat back. Waited for some of the smoke to clear. "Now I have a question for you. Do you really believe that during all my time in hiding I never once had to convince someone not to kill me?"

Lucien hesitated, then managed a shoulder twitch. "You always claimed to have stayed out of the line of fire."

"I was a bottom feeder. That doesn't mean I was always safe." Jani struggled to find the right words, wondered if they even existed. "Sometimes the only way to learn the depth of the water is to jump. But there's a difference between going in blind versus knowing the risks and being willing to take them. Give *me* some credit." She started to say more, but her head ached and her ribs stabbed her every time she shifted in the chair, so she settled for a vague wave of her hand and set about crunching through yet another of the snack packets. This one was labeled *Hotter Than Hot Pepper* and proved to be the first thing she had eaten in years that made her eyes water. She wiped them with the sleeve of her robe, then looked up to find Lucien studying her with one hand over his mouth. "What now?"

"If you're going to keep eating that stuff, you will have to find some mouthwash or neutralizer or something or certain activities are going to become rather difficult." He lowered his head and eyed her from beneath his lashes.

"It's not that bad—" Jani choked as the spice burn brought on a coughing spell, which hurt only slightly less than the laughter induced by the various scenes that flashed through her mind. "Please don't." She struggled for breath and hugged herself to keep her ribs from flexing.

"Serves you right." Lucien did his own share of grimacing as he scooted farther down the bed so he could lie back. "You don't have a scanpack anymore, so what are you going to do?" He cocked his head in the direction of the corridor. "I overheard Shroud talking to Editha before he went in to your room to keep vigil. I couldn't catch everything they said, but that I heard." He paused. "They talked for a while."

Jani checked the wall clock and wondered if Editha had been able to secure the lab. "Well, she is his type."

"You're not even a little bit jealous?"

Jani pondered for a bit. "No. Those days are gone."

"Hmm. She's too young for him." Lucien shook hs finger when Jani shot him a look. "We're different. I'm much older than my years."

"You're the oldest person on this station." Jani shoved the half-full snack packet into the pocket of her robe. "Scanpack-wise, not sure yet what I'll do. I'll think of something."

"It's no great loss, though, right? It wasn't working properly anyway."

"No great loss." Jani's voice cracked. She covered it with a cough, then looked over at Lucien to find him watching her with narrowed eyes.

"Did you let our string-pullers know that you have what they wanted?" He spoke more softly this time.

"Not yet. I still have almost two days, and I have a feeling that as soon as I contact them, they're going to want me to come in and it sounds like there are some things we both need to do first to prepare."

Lucien lay back. "I'm making an equipment wish list." He closed his eyes. "Things are going to change after we get back to Thalassa. Assuming we both live through this." He quieted. His breathing slowed.

Jani waited for the sounds of gentle snoring. She maneuvered her chair out into the corridor and found Editha standing by the nurses' station.

"I didn't want to disturb." Editha stared down at her shoes for a moment, then looked up with a shy smile and handed Jani a set of lab scrubs. "They're ready for you."

Chapter Twenty-Four

Jani spent the rest of the station day with scalpel and tweezers in hand, teasing chips out of her scanpack remains. She paused every so often to wipe her eyes or look away until the ache in her chest eased. Occasionally, she would pick up a fragment of the case and rub it between her fingers. Study a chip, and recall what she had done in order to obtain it, the conditions under which she had installed it. Unwelcome images, some of them, more nightmare than memory. She wondered how she lived through it all, and whether she still had the strength to face situations like that again.

Guess you'll find out, won't you? The thought made her chest hurt even more.

After a time, she looked up to find people watching her through the windows surrounding the work area. Most were younger, but there were a few who were closer to Jani's age. Some took notes on their handhelds, holding up the devices every so often to image the scene, while the hardcore purists recorded the old-fashioned way via stylus on parchment pads.

"I hope it's all right." Editha sat at her elbow and handed her instruments, applied suction, and adjusted the sterile field as needed. "This is one of our teaching labs, and when word got out that you were operating..."

"It's fine." Jani shrugged. "I'm not sure how helpful it will be. It's not the sort of situation they're likely to encounter."

"Accidents happen." Editha offered a wan smile. Then she bent close, and lowered her voice. "It's the chance to watch you work, too. I had a lot of requests as soon as they learned you were here. There's even a shuttle from the offices downstairs."

"You're kidding?" Jani looked out again at the rapt faces, and gave a little wave. While she had adjusted over the last few years to what Lucien referred to as her "star power," and had on occasion even used it to her advantage, there were still times when it took her by surprise. She inhaled as deeply as her sore ribs allowed, and slipped into the teaching voice she hadn't used since her Service days. "The chips need to be cleaned and sterilized. After that, they can be tucked into vacuum bags. The pieces of poly case just need standard cleaning and disinfecting." Her voice caught. "Burn the tissue."

As she finished, she took questions, and made a promise to teach a seminar at some future date that she actually hoped to keep. Then Editha took over, ushering out the spectators and settling the staffers whose shift had been upended by the unplanned influx.

Jani remained at the worktable, staring at the neatly boxed and bagged remnants and wondering if she had miscalculated. *It's called second guessing and that way lies indecision, hesitation, and mistakes.* She felt sure that if either the Scriabin or Ulanov Families knew of the existence of the patent transfer, they would have cut to the chase and dispatched a dexxie to collect it. Simple, neat, and most of all, legal.

But what if they don't know about it? What if, against all odds, Evan had actually gotten the jump on his jailers? *He would have to have allies.* He wouldn't have been able to arrange Niall's kidnapping without them.

Consider every possibility. Including the fact that she hadn't, and that Evan's desperate gamble to regain what he had lost stood a chance of paying off. She sat back and pondered. The first seeds of a plan formed.

She heard a soft knocking, and looked up to find Editha standing in the lab entry.

"I can take you into the tank room. That is where we keep the—" She fixed on a point above Jani's head, her eyes filling.

"The incinerator." Jani stood and gathered the various packets and set them on a rolling cart. "Do you have any organoids in storage?"

Editha's brow arched. "In-process extras?"

"Or discards slated for destruction. It doesn't need to be responsive, but that would be a bonus."

"What are you thinking?" Editha walked to the loaded cart and drummed her fingers atop the packet containing the salvaged chips. "You want...to build a fake 'pack?"

Jani nodded. "They'll expect me to have one. The case will be the tricky part. The person I suspect planned all this has seen it before, but I don't know how much he remembers." Evan may have been a maintenance alcoholic for years, but he had always possessed a good memory and she couldn't assume it had deteriorated completely. "Plus, I've been assuming there won't be another dexxie involved, but if there is, whatever I cobble together will have to appear to function like the real thing. I'll need touch switches, illumin arrays, all the standard controls, but they will have to be fully controllable by me."

"They wouldn't test you?" Editha's chin jutted. "They wouldn't have the nerve."

"The one I believe is responsible for all this doesn't trust me. And at this point, I think he's capable of anything." Jani activated the cart and followed Editha, looking into the various labs as they made their way down the corridor to the tank farm. "You do a lot of research in this facility." She paused in front of one of the windows and watched a trio of white coats flipping through 3-D data visualizations that flickered in the air like reflections in water.

"We have to take care of ourselves out here." Editha keyed in through a set of double doors at the end of the corridor. "Fortunately, we do that rather well."

Jani swallowed hard as she entered the tank farm and a host of familiar smells washed over her that no filter ever seemed to remove completely. The cooked meat aroma of nerve solder. The ammonia stink of cellular waste products. The plastic undercurrent of cases, chips, solvents. If she had been working in the farm consistently, she would have grown used to the stomach-flipping mélange. But it had been a while.

There are some things I haven't missed. She breathed through her mouth as she maneuvered the cart through a series of sliding gates and into a workroom that looked like an autoclaved stainless steel version of the archive, floor-to-ceiling shelves packed with black poly bins.

"We keep all development stages in here." Editha stood fists on hips and surveyed the scene, eyes alight with pride and purpose.

"They're small." Jani motioned vaguely, arms spread, to indicate one of the large tanks she had encountered in most every documents center she had ever visited. "I'm used to the big metal vats."

"You've visited only planet-based labs, I assume? We don't have that kind of space. Floors can't take the weight." Editha mounted a kick stool and patted the side of a bin marked with a red X. "These are the experimentals scheduled for destruction."

Jani reached up and grabbed the bin's front handle, but stopped when Editha took hold of her arm.

"It weighs over seventy kilos." Editha took out her handheld. "I'll call a couple of techs."

"No, it's fine." Jani pulled the bin off the shelf and carried it to a table, and had just begun to pry off the lid when she realized Editha had yet to join her. She turned and found the woman still standing atop the stool, eyes wide.

"Oh, my. You're so strong." Editha stepped down to the floor, started towards the table, then hesitated. "Is it the change?"

Jani looked down at the human woman, younger and so much smaller. "I guess." She looked down at her hands, compared the real right to the animandroid left. *Time for another new arm.* Mere months since the last switch-out, and already the fingers of her right hand had grown longer, spindlier—she pressed her palms together and eyeballed the difference in length, slight but detectable. *Bird bones,* Niall called her. Muscles like rope. "I spend most all my time at Thalassa. There, I'm not unusual. I don't even think about it." One more thing to remember. One more thing that set her apart.

Editha gathered equipment and parts, and they set about assembling a scanpack. Jani extracted a dormant organoid from its container, then rinsed the fist-sized mound of gray and white brain tissue with saline. Set it beneath the sterile field generator and attached various leads and monitors. While the organoid itself was likely nonfunctional, she still wanted to maintain the proper environment for her chips. So she kept track of the temperature and oxygen level, just as though she worked on a living 'pack.

"I don't need to install all the chips. Just enough so that it looks like it's seen a few changes over time." Jani took up a scalpel and sliced through the vessel-laced dura mater. The tough sheath fought the blade before giving way with a sound like ripping parchment. She retracted the edges with clips and, with speed born of years of practice under less than optimal conditions, inserted an array of chips while Editha once again assisted.

"Now the problem becomes the case. We were only able to recover fragments. Not enough for a rebuild." Editha hunted through a carton of standard issues and cast-offs. "Also the fact that the style was reserved for the first six." She set down a case that, while black, was much too shiny, too narrow, and a few centimeters too long. "This is the closest I can find to yours."

Jani picked up the case and examined it. "Do you have a hand torch?" She searched through the tool kit. "And a hammer?" Editha provided both in short order—Jani used the hammer to smash the ends of the case, trimming several centimeters in the process. Then she used the torch to meld together broken fragments, smooth the seams, and blunt the curvature. Finally, after allowing the poly to cool and harden, she scuffed away the shine with a fine gauge buff pad.

"You've done this before." Editha's voice held a touch of disappointment.

"A few times. As favors to, well, idiots who should've known better." Jani shrugged. "They lied to the wrong people about their qualifications and were in so far over their heads that they couldn't see a way out." Memories so long set aside returned. A fear-pale face here. A shaky voice there. Panicked tears all around. *Please help.*

"Pretend documents examiners? What good is it to do such a thing? So many pitfalls. Any halfway-decent tech would be able to suss them out in minutes." Editha handed off instruments as Jani installed the organoid in the redesigned case. "What happened to them?"

"I never did find out." Not for sure, anyway, though Jani had heard rumors that had borne out her worst fears. "It's always easier to hide what you do know than fake what you don't." She heated nerve solder in a small crucible, then set up a vent box to absorb the aroma. "Some were passable. They'd had some training, but had to drop out for whatever reason. And you know there are bootleg 'pack suppliers?"

"Garbage they make." Editha clicked her tongue. "Unworthy of the name."

"A few are pretty good. Damned expensive, though." Jani spot-welded the organoid in place, waited for the solder to set up, then turned the case upside down and jiggled it to test the stick. "Thing is, their 'packs aren't registered in the big book in Chicago, so they can't format or confirm anything official. Systems kick them out. You can only lie about it for so long before your secret's discovered. Even crooks need legal paper from time to time."

Editha's expression alternated between wincing sympathy and rapt wonder. "How did you do it? Survive it all?"

Jani sat back and worked her shoulders. From tension this time, not injury. Memories, however old, left marks that never healed. "I kept my head down. Avoided all the headquarters and hot spots. Small companies and fly by nights only, where you didn't need anyone higher up the chain to vouch for you. Never tried to move up the ranks. The more routine and boring the job, the better. Inventory. File room. Docks. All places where questions are discouraged because most everyone has something to hide. There are a lot of places like that out here."

"It would've been easier if you'd just stepped away from paper."

"I had to stay close to supplies. Only way I could maintain my 'pack." Jani shrugged. "You do what you do."

Before Editha could respond, her handheld buzzed. She flipped through messages, and swore softly. "And I need to leave for a dinner meeting."

"Okay, I have the innards set. Now I need the hardware." Jani got up, stretched as best she could, yawned, then walked to the shelves and poked through a parts bin. "I could use some coffee."

"You'll have to go to the commissary or one of the break rooms. No food or drink allowed in here." Editha brushed off and straightened her fitted jacket, then checked her reflection in one of the polished steel doors. "I'm not the best person to help with the hardware, anyway, but I know someone who is." She beckoned towards the entry. "Come in."

Jani turned to find a lab-coated young man standing tentatively just inside the room.

"This is Doctor Aremu Ishola. He is our top design engineer." Editha gave the poor man a look that indicated that he had better live up to billing or else. "He is definitely the person to help with scanpack controls." With that, she slipped past him and out the door.

"Honor." Aremu offered a quick bow, then rubbed his hands together and joined Jani at the parts bin. "When was the last time you rebuilt a scanpack?"

"It's been a while. I don't recognize some of these components." Jani set out a few that looked correct.

"Close." Aremu returned a couple of them to the bin and chose a few others. "Some functions have been combined over the years. Lots of streamlining, and more than a few enhancements." He nodded towards the cart bearing Jani's deconstructed scanpack. "It is a shame, the damage. It would have been good to analyze the changes in tissue to see if it tried to adjust to your...condition."

"If it did, it wasn't doing a very good job." Jani tapped the side of her head. "How could it? It's isolated in its case."

"It's not completely outside the realm of reason." Aremu slipped into lecture mode with a tilt of his head, gaze shifting from Jani to the middle distance. "The scanpack brain senses its environment and adjusts in the best way it can, just like the one in our skulls. And I am convinced that yours adjusted to you in ways you are not aware of. You have been hybridizing for twenty years, after all, your progression constantly varying in rate and degree. An ever-moving target, as it were. How could you have used it for all that time without it having adapted to you?"

"You seem to know a lot about me." Jani hoped her irritation didn't show. The problem with having attained a level of notoriety was that total strangers laid claim to your life.

Aremu's gaze sharpened, his mouth working soundlessly for a moment. "Your...history is well known to those of us in the trade." He fixed his attention on the cart. "I understand that the remains have been gravely damaged, but I would greatly appreciate if you would allow me to examine them." He hesitated. "For posterity. And knowledge."

Despite her annoyance, Jani had to admit that the thought of turning over her scanpack to Aremu could serve a purpose. The chance to learn more about the device piqued the researcher in her and besides, the thought of burning it like a piece of trash made her sick.

And yet...

She pretended to stifle a yawn. "Before we get to work, I could use a boost." She tugged at the front of her shirt. "And I'm too whiffy to set foot in a commissary—I'd put everyone off their dinner."

"Coffee?" Aremu brightened. "We have a supply up here. I'll be right back."

Damn. Jani had hoped he would need to go to the commissary, but apparently these labs followed the unwritten rule of every lab in which she'd ever worked. *Just don't get caught.* As soon as Aremu hied off, she hurried to the discards bin and extracted another organoid. Then she scrabbled through cabinets and drawers until she found a refrigerated storage container. She slapped the organoid inside and tore open the dura mater with a scalpel.

Now I need a sonicator to break it up. After a short, fruitless search, she gave up and shook the hell out of the container in the hope that the delicate tissue would break up sufficiently, then switched it with the one that held the remains of her scanpack brain. She also grabbed the bag containing the rest of the chips, then grudgingly left the pieces of the case behind because she only had so much room on her person to stash stuff.

As the pound of running sounded from the far end of the corridor, Jani patted her pants legs. *No bloody pockets.* She grabbed a lab coat someone had left draped over a chair, pulled it on, shoved the chip bag into a pocket, then tucked the container beneath and into the waistband of her pants just as Aremu bustled through the door.

"Is everything all right?" He stopped just inside the entry, a vacuum flask in each hand.

"I'm just cold is all." Jani fastened the front of the lab coat and prayed that the box wouldn't slide down her pants leg.

"It's always a bit chilly in here." Aremu handed one of the flasks to Jani, then pressed a finger to his lips. "Don't tell Editha." He took hold of the cart. "I'll be right back.

Jani watched him wheel the cart out of the workroom. Then she readjusted the container so it rested at the small of her back and tightened the drawstring of her pants to hold it in place. Only then did she reward herself with a long draught of coffee, which tasted surprisingly potent for human-grade brew. By the time Aremu returned, she had seated herself at the bench, and together they worked on constructing her dummy scanpack.

The hours passed as they inserted touch switches and sensors along with various sound chips to emit the appropriate beeps and buzzes. When the time came for final adjustments, Jani took over completely while Aremu sketched diagrams on his handheld and wrote screen after screen of notes. By the time they finished, they had drunk so much coffee that Aremu's hands trembled and even Jani felt mildly jittery.

"Find me something to test." She looked around the workroom for any sort of paper. "A shipping invoice. Anything." She waited while Aremu dug through drawers and cabinets before finally excavating a warranty certificate for one of the bins.

Jani flattened the document on the bench top, smoothing bent edges and brushing off whatever flecks of dust or debris that could have adhered. Said a prayer over the dummy 'pack, then passed it over the paper, concentrating on the area where she knew the inset chips and threads containing the information about the bin were located. The data scrolled across the scanpack display, with the odd flash or skipped symbol as the dodgy brain glitched. "It's pretty responsive. This is better than I hoped."

"It will do everything but encode your personal biometric signatures." Aremu sat at Jani's elbow, chin cradled in hand. "So you can read, but you can't approve or confirm."

Before he could finish, Jani tapped the controls on the device's underside, bare twitches of her fingertips that would, she hoped, prove undetected by witnesses however eagle-eyed. Green lights flickered across the 'pack's surface in perfect imitation of an actual sign-off. "I can pretend to do that. If someone wanted to be really snotty, they could have another dexxie confirm my confirmations, but I've seldom seen that done. At some point, you have to accept that the thing is the thing, or otherwise what is the point?" She sat back, rubbed her eyes. Knew that even if she did her best to account for all possibilities, she would likely miss something, and that it was just the sort of upper stratum smugglers' alley bullshit that she had always sought to avoid. *You're in it now, Kilian. Up to your neck.* "I suppose it's possible, given who I think is involved."

"You know them." Aremu struggled to suppress a yawn. Apparently even his energy had its limits.

"One of them, at least." Jani hefted the dummy scanpack with both hands. "It won't detect fakes, either, so if they try to test mc I'll need to go by physical appearance. Sharp edges or deckled, the color and feel of the parchment itself. The fonts. General info based on the appearance of the paper at the time period in question."

Watery eyes widened, this time in head-shaking wonder. "How do you remember all that?"

"Well, I was there from the beginning. I was involved in a lot of the decision making concerning the requirements of the ministries and commercial entities." Jani shrugged. "It's always made sense. There's a map in my head with patterns and sequences and I connect the dots. Then you add in experience and, frankly, other peoples' willingness to go along with whatever I say because I'm me." She took a deep breath and found the pain from her ribs had subsided to mild twinges. "Paper's always been the one place where I feel completely at home."

Aremu sighed. "I would love to scan your brain."

Why, Doctor Ishola—you old charmer, you. "Maybe after all this is over." Jani eased to her feet, taking care to keep the container holding her 'pack remains from shifting. "I actually think we're done here."

"You're damned right."

Jani started, then turned to find John standing in the doorway.

"What are you doing?" He made a show of checking his time-piece. He wore a lab coat over dark blue scrubs, which meant he had also labored the night away.

He was working up here. Jani's mind shifted from document

details to a question she hadn't asked herself in a while, namely *what the hell is John up to now?*

"Dr. Shroud." Aremu held onto the edge of the workbench as though he needed the support.

"Dr. Ishola." John's smile, such as it was, barely made it to his mouth, much less his eyes. He glanced at the dummy scanpack, and his brow furrowed. "You constructed a 'pack?"

"Yes, and without Doctor Ishola's help, I'd still be digging into drawers for parts. And before you ask, I feel fine." Jani paused to consider. "Actually, I do feel pretty good. A little buzzed from caffeine, but other than that." She tucked the dummy scanpack into an already bulging pocket of her lab coat and headed for the door, but when she tried to skirt around John, he moved to block her path.

"You sustained a concussion."

"I had a headache earlier. It's gone now. Like I said, I feel fine. Not just lying to make you go away."

"Come with me to the clinic. I want to run some scans."

"John—"

"Now."

"I don't have time."

"Make time." John shot a look at Aremu that held promise of a long talk later in the day, then took hold of Jani's arm and steered her out of the workroom.

Chapter Twenty-Five

"Keep still when I give the word. That means no talking." John tapped on an instrument panel. "All is silence, starting...now."

Jani's heart stuttered as a scanner helmet lowered around her head. Utter darkness fell, like that moment when her head struck the archive shelving and it all went black. She squeezed the arms of her chair, the cushioning of which had been designed to expand, then press from all sides and immobilize her. "What does this thing do?" *Besides hug me to death.*

"What did I just say about—?" John paused. "It just visualizes your brain. It won't be drilling any holes in the back of your head."

Jani managed a smile, which earned another grumble. "No sampling?"

"Quiet."

Jani held back additional commentary as a series of hums and clicks filled her ears and memories returned. The jolt of fear as the stereotaxic restraint gripped her head. The sharp stab of an injector. Numb warmth, spreading down the back of her neck and across her shoulders.

Pinpoint pressure just above the base of her skull as the cannula pierced skin. The sudden jolt of pain that followed, because they never waited long enough for the local anesthetic to fully take effect.

Then came the machine hum as the cannula drilled into her brain, a beep as the device signaled that sufficient sample had been drawn. Withdrawal, followed by the restraint release, the blinding room light as the mechanism was raised.

The headache arrived later, and every one she had suffered since never came close.

Jani opened her eyes. It took her a few beats to register the silence. She unclenched her fists as the helmet was raised.

John looked down at her. "Are you all right?"

Jani turned her head to the right, then the left. Flexed and stretched as the cushioning retracted. "Just remembering."

"Barbarism. Any stem cells would've done."

"The Service wanted to impress upon us the value of what we were receiving."

"No. They just liked to hurt." John tapped the scanner touchpad, then made entries into his handheld. "Back to the present. There's a neurometabolic cascade that follows injury to the brain. I'm looking for neuronal activity and cellular damage."

Jani held back the questions that bubbled on the tip of her tongue like a carbonated drink. John had slipped into stiff, formal *business only* mode, which in the past meant that something had rattled or angered him. Best to go with the flow, at least for the moment. "An injury like bruising?"

"More granular than that." John glanced her way again. Back in his fully-human days, he had always filmed his eyes to complement his clothing, but now that he had developed Oà coloring, he left them alone. They shone like metal in the bright exam room lighting, the blue altered to silvery grey. "You said you had a headache."

Jani nodded. "That's gone."

"Any visual disturbances?"

"No."

"Confusion?"

"Story of my life."

"Jani, please answer the question."

Jani felt a chill that had nothing to do with the temperature of the room. The last time she had seen John this fixed, this grim, was on the day of Tsecha's assassination. "What are you not telling me?" The unspoken words *this time* hung in the air. "John, I was wearing a helmet designed to protect me from those sorts of injuries."

John set his handheld on a workbench and left the lab. He returned a few moments later carrying an open-topped box, which he upended onto a nearby table. A helmet—more correctly, helmet pieces—clattered across the polystone surface.

Jani rose and walked to the table. Picked up a section of helmet, inner protective layers bulging along the edges, the exterior surface crazed with cracks. "My helmet failed."

"Your helmet performed exactly as it was engineered to do. You hit a coated composite steel beam at speed. A slightly different angle and you'd have been decapitated." John looked her up and down. "And yet here you are, as ever you were." He gathered pieces and returned them to the box. "You should be many things right now. Conscious, communicating, and walking aren't among them, much less working in a laboratory for hours at a stretch. Yet your brain is showing no indication of trauma." He held up one of the fragments, studied it, then tossed it into the box with the rest.

"That's a good thing. Isn't it?" Jani forced a smile even as she tried to assess her balance, her hearing, whether her eyes focused properly. "Insert a joke about hard heads and move on?" When John failed to respond, she tried another tack. "People come to you to be hybridized because they're dying, because something about combination with idomeni genetics makes them whole again. Is this really so different?"

John turned back to the console. He flipped back and forth between the image holos, as though he searched for something. "Disease is one thing. Trauma is something else. This is the sort of issue that the Service developed augmentation to address, to prevent. But even the cutting-age experimental versions are nothing compared to what I am apparently seeing."

"I sense a paper. Evaluation of a post-concussive hybrid brain." Jani flexed her fingers as Editha's soft voice replayed. *You're so strong.* "Will you use my name, or am I still Patient S-1?"

John hefted the box of helmet remains and shoved it on a shelf. "I would never use your name. This isn't for publication. It's simply an addition to your file, the paper version of which takes up one entire shelf at my main facility on..." His voice trailed.

"On New Indies Station." Jani caught the hitch in John's step as he walked back to the scanner console. The barest hesitation. "I tend to distrust coincidence. You weren't planning a clinic downstairs. I'm guessing you've been in business here for quite some time." She paused, counted to three. "How long have you been working on a hybrid scanpack?" She watched him as she had learned to long ago, caught the throb in his jaw as he tensed, the shadow of a twitch that only someone who knew John Shroud well would detect.

After a few long moments, he buried his face in his hands and paced. "I told Editha to find someone else to help you, but she insisted you needed the best. Aremu—"

"Gets excited and babbles." Jani boosted up onto a counter. "In his defense, he didn't admit anything. But it was fairly easy to read between the lines. I assume things aren't going well. If they were, I doubt he could've restrained himself." She swung her legs out, then back, taking care not to bang her heels against the metal cabinetry. *Arguing with John in a lab.* The more things changed... "He wanted to scan my brain. You just did. I assume that it will be used to help you figure out where you went wrong." She stilled. "I want a copy."

John lowered his hands and leaned against a bench. "It's part of your medical file, so of course you can request—"

"Now, John. All the information. All the data. Every hand-scrawled note. Every image."

"That can be arranged—"

"You're not listening. I'm leaving this exam room with it. I'm not giving you time to filter and edit."

"*Why would I do that?*"

"Force of habit."

Their eyes met, years replaying in an instant. Before Jani could say more, John walked to the scanner and fingered entries into the console. After a minute or so, during which he kept his back turned, a data wafer emerged followed by a print-out of the testing and analysis. He gathered it all together, initialed each page, then tucked everything into a file envelope, which he handed to Jani without a word.

Jani ran a finger along the beige folder's blue trim. *Standard station issue—nothing special.* She had expected a logo and imprint bearing the name of John's clinic—he would've used it if he had one, just to rub it in. But he apparently had no official affiliation with New Indies Station. *Yet here he is.* She slid off the counter, taking care to land gently so as not to dislodge the case containing her 'pack remains. Tucked the folder under her arm and walked to the door as though the floor were made of glass liable to crack with any misstep, gauging every movement, alert for any wobble. *Stop it, Kilian.* She felt fine, the helmet malfunctioned, and John was just upset because he didn't have a hybrid scanpack to shove in her face. *Oh, Rudo—I don't think this is working the way you would've liked.* She paused in the doorway. "Theo told me that you tried to hire him away."

"I did." John kept his gaze fixed on the console. "Although technically, he is my employee. I simply offered him a transfer."

"That's what Rudo said you'd say."

"How is Rudo? I haven't seen him since Thalassa days, when the two of you stabbed me in the back."

"He's one of us now—did you know?" Jani saw John's eyes widen before he turned away. *Apparently not.* "Chicago would've stripped you to the bone no matter what you offered them. They might have even imprisoned you. Rudo salvaged as much as he could and you know it." She examined her hands, the yellow tone of her skin muted in the station light. "The ones you hire away, they work here? At other facilities?"

John looked back at her, face slack, his anger derailed by the change in subject. "Both."

"Are they all as open as you about their hybrid state?"

"Some are, yes."

"How are they doing out in the human world?" Jani held up the folder containing her records. "For that matter, how are you doing?" She didn't wait for the answer. She didn't have to. "You have no clinic here, per se. No official commercial presence. So that means Ian is harboring you in exchange for what? The hybrid scanpack?"

John drew in a deep breath and stuffed his hands in the pockets of his lab coat, eyes fixed on the wall opposite. The never-ending debate showed in his narrowing eyes, the tense line of his mouth. How much to say. What to hold back. "New Indies wants to break away from the Commonwealth. They're not the only colony that wants to do so. They want to put some financial stability in place before they make the attempt and before Chicago figures out what's going on. They would of course prefer to avoid a shooting war. A hybrid 'pack would give them an advantage and allow them to expand trade with the Haárin."

"What about Thalassa?"

"You'd have every opportunity to negotiate a deal once we have a functional device."

"We'd be just another customer." Jani nodded. "And not exactly in the top tier. John Joseph Shroud's revenge." John opened his mouth to protest, but stilled when she held up her hand. "The fact that continues to escape your notice is that all of this began with you. Val and Eamon got dragged along for the ride, and yeah, eventually they picked up some slack, but you were always the driver behind hybridization. You did the first research. You tested it on me, but if I hadn't come along, you'd have found someone else. Then Eamon went off on his own to prove he could do it better than you, and you pushed back, and now the tech is out there and people who would otherwise die are getting another shot at life. But it's life that doesn't fit in the human or idomeni boxes, our numbers are increasing, and we upset everybody."

"So now everything that's happened over the last two years is all my fault?" John's voice rose. "If not for my work—"

"None of us would exist without your work. I would be bleached bone strewn across desert sand without your work." Jani hugged the folder to her chest, and pushed away memories that never remained submerged for long. "But your work does not exist in a vacuum. It has repercussions. You're experiencing them yourself and you still don't see it or you won't admit it. You blame me for your losing Neoclona. You lost it the day you self-administered that first treatment." She stopped to slow her quickening breath and straighten the curve of her shoulders. Glanced at John to find him, even in his anger, staring, gauging, analyzing.

And the eternal experiment continues. Jani touched the door control—the panel whispered aside. "It's not about you or me or us. Not anymore. It's about a group of people. Our people. They need a home, and security, and whatever sort of society we can manage to piece together. Think of them." She sidestepped into the corridor, then paused. "I never wanted you to change for me. If you'd told me what you planned before you started the treatments, I'd have tried to talk you out of it." She met his eye one last time, and wondered if he felt as old as he looked. "I'm sorry it didn't work out the way you thought it would." She pressed the door pad, then stood still for a time after the panel swept closed.

Sorry, Rudo—I don't think that was the kind of discussion you had in mind. She pulled the storage case out of her waistband, tucked it inside the folder, and wondered how Theo and crew were doing with their own hybrid scanpack efforts. *This isn't a competition.* Except it had turned into one, hadn't it?

Jani eyed a row of wall clocks as she headed down the corridor to the lift bank, and picked up her pace. She had spent too long in the lab and hadn't figured in any medical time, much less confrontations with a former lover. Too much to do, and little more than a Common day in which to do it.

She pressed all the call keys on the lift control pad, headed towards the first sliding door, and collided with Lucien as he exited the car.

"I've hiked through half this station looking for you." He slumped against the wall and worked his sore shoulder. He had found a set of grey scrubs to replace his pajamas, and had borrowed someone's access ID in the process—the plastic card flashed reflected light with every movement. "I ran into Editha, and she said you were still at the lab. So I go to the lab—" He wrinkled his nose in odoriferous memory. "—and they said Shroud dragged you out."

"He wanted to scan my brain." Jani looked down the corridor she had just exited, on the lookout for departing doctors. "He showed me what happened to my helmet and he was concerned that I didn't seem to be injured."

"But that's a good thing." Lucien paused his self-ministrations. "Isn't it?"

"Apparently I should be comatose or something." Jani gave a quick rundown of the encounter with John. "So Ian is sheltering him. I don't believe it affects our current situation in any way, but once we get back, we need to—"

"—tell Theo to move his ass." Lucien straightened, hit a call key, then ushered Jani into a car. "What else?"

"Nothing. John was in exam mode, watching every move I made."

"Editha told me about the bin you carried. I think she was a little rattled."

"She made me feel like an ogre." Jani stepped out of the lift as soon as the door opened, then turned and pressed a hand to Lucien's chest to make him stop. "I'm not that bad." She tried to read those unreadable eyes. "Am I?"

"You can be a little disconcerting at times." Lucien rubbed his forearm, then looked down at the floor "Sometimes...you leave bruises."

"You always said you got them in the gym. Our hand-to-hand practice. Why didn't you tell me?"

"Because when anyone remarks about how you're changing, you get upset."

"*I don't get upset.*"

"You get upset." Lucien hunched his shoulders. "Then you curl in on yourself and your voice changes and then it's just back off and wait until you realize what's happening and undo the knots."

Several of the lift cars opened at once, disgorging station workers who swept Jani and Lucien down the corridor. "I remember when it used to only happen once in a while." Jani lowered her voice. "Now it's all the time."

"What did Shroud have to say about that?"

"We didn't get the chance to discuss it." Jani took Lucien's hand and pulled him after her into an alcove. "He thought he could hybridize and everything would go on just like before. He didn't think Chicago would push back. He thought he had power. That he could still control everything."

Lucien slid down the alcove wall to the floor and massaged his injured knee. "You still worry about him?"

"I feel...a little responsible. I just wish he'd asked me first. I'd have talked him out of it."

"If I told you I wanted to change, would you talk me out of it?"

"I'd try to."

"If I were more like you, perhaps some of your reactions wouldn't seem so..."

"Threatening?" Jani lowered to the floor next to Lucien and sat close enough to press against him. A touch of physical warmth to counter her never-ending chill. "When you tell me that I should step aside and let you do your job, what I hear is that you're afraid I'm going to kill somebody in front of witnesses. And so I keep pushing to prove I haven't changed, and maybe that just makes things worse."

Lucien rested his head against the wall. "That's not the only reason I tell you to back off. And I'm not going to stop telling you to back off."

"I don't want you to stop. I depend on you to tell me when I don't act human."

Lucien smiled for the first time. "If you're looking to me to be your conscience, you're in trouble."

"Maybe conscience is the wrong word." Jani held up a finger in an *ah-hah* gesture. "Guardrail?"

Before Lucien could reply, Ian appeared in the alcove entry.

"That question you asked." He fixed on Jani. "I have news."

Chapter Twenty-Six

They adjourned to a small conference room adjoining Ian's office, stopping along the way so Ian could order coffee. Judging by his rumpled daysuit and bleary eyes, he had pulled his own all-nighter.

"To be clear, the news about Evan is more along the lines of what people won't tell me." Ian dragged a chair to a round table to join Jani and Lucien. "I felt like one of those vacuum 'bots that keeps bumping into furniture. Back up, head off in a different direction, crash bang." He took a swallow of coffee, then regarded Jani across the top of the steaming cup. "It wasn't quite at the level of *Evan who?*, but it was close. Whether they're covering up the fact that they left the door unlocked and looked the other way, or they're scrambling because he slipped his leash with the aide of parties unknown, I couldn't determine."

Jani gripped her own cup with both hands, more for the warmth than any need for additional caffeine. "But you have a sense of which it is."

Ian nodded, eventually. "I think they're scrambling. Those with whom I spoke sounded more genuinely alarmed than anxious. A subtle difference, I know, but more than sufficient to point to what happened." He motioned towards Jani's file folder. "Have you let whoever's running this scheme know that you have what they want?"

"No. I need to lay some groundwork first." Jani sat back. "I wish we could figure out where the messages I receive are coming from. Lucien tried tracing them before, and wasn't able to break through the noise."

"I would need access to station secure systems." Lucien somehow managed an expression of innocent hopefulness. "I would guess that's not possible."

"You would guess correctly." Ian's smile flickered and died like the last ember.

Jani gestured towards Lucien. "We've been working on the assumption that they're close by, given the timing of Niall's abduction and the speed with which I've received their messages after I notified them about an earlier find." She assumed her own hope-filled expression. "Any information you could provide would be greatly appreciated."

Ian stared into his coffee, then set it aside and took out his handheld. "As it happens, one of my aides spotted something in a status update. Odds are it's nothing." He flipped through displays, then flicked one to Lucien's device. "Docks picked up something strange a day or so ago during a routine scan. They apparently didn't bother to notify security because they see strange things all the time and security barks at them if they send over too many false alarms."

Jani scooted her chair closer to Lucien's so she could read his handheld display. "An incident at a wildcat station."

Ian pressed a hand to his mouth to cover a yawn. "They orbit a few of the uninhabited planets in this system. They're nothing fancy, mostly rest and refurb stops for scavenger crews and other low-end traffic. Some of them aren't even staffed—they're fully automated. Docks detected an all-systems alarm, likely an indication of some major failure."

Lucien opened the report log so he could read the event coding and the observer's notes. "It happens. I doubt those stations are in the best of repair."

"Well, that's the thing. The alarm signal cut out within seconds." Ian reached inside his jacket and removed a meds tin. Headache tabs, according to the label. "Docks contacted the station using the last known tenant designations and received no response. A little while later, they received a message stating that the station was undergoing inspection and someone hit the wrong switch." He shook out three tablets, tossed them back, washed them down with coffee.

Jani's heart tripped, and she forced herself to breathe. "I've laid over at more than one wildcat. They're never inspected."

"Exactly. They're usually so decrepit that if they were, they'd be shut down." Ian massaged the med tin between his fingers like a charm. "It's just the sort of reply you receive when whoever is at the other end wants to cut off any further communication."

Jani tried to tilt Lucien's handheld to a better reading angle, but he pushed her hand away. "Which station was it?"

"It doesn't even have a name." Ian checked his handheld. "The planet's an airless rock, designation NI74A."

Lucien flicked back and forth across multiple screens. "How far away is it?"

"New Indies B-Gateway takes you fairly close. Once you're through, courier-class ship, it's a day, day and a half, Common time."

Lucien glanced at Jani. "You think it's Pierce."

Jani nodded. "It would be like shooting up a flare."

"Or, it really was an accident." Lucien suppressed his own yawn. "That said, the general location makes sense. We left Elyas not long after Pierce was taken. Whoever has him wouldn't have had time to travel much farther." He paused, eyes clouding with some memory. "And then there's Survival Training 101. Escape if you can. Disrupt if you can't. Sounds like Pierce had to settle for option two." After pushing away Jani's hands again, he gave up and turned over his handheld.

Jani fought back memories of her own as she studied the report.

Wildcat stations were not good places. "Is there any way to find out what traffic entered that area recently?"

"It's a region frequented by...let's call them vessels with flexible registration." Ian tapped out a message on his device. "Docks has the usual connections. I will ask them to dig." He paused and fixed Jani with the look of a man who really didn't have time for the crises of others because he juggled enough of his own. "You truly believe your friend is being held there?"

"It's definitely worth investigating."

"If it bears out, I will need some help." Lucien counted out on his fingers. "I will need a group to go in ahead of her. One to follow her in. Point teams along the way."

Jani shook her head. "No one's going in ahead of me or following me in. You do that, the first thing I'll see through my viewport when we approach the dock is Niall's body drifting past."

Ian tapped the tin on the table, then shoved it back in his pocket. "I know what you're asking and why. You want Cabinet-level stealth security. I don't have that capability here."

"I'll take whatever you have." Lucien again nodded towards Jani. "You owe her."

"For what? The new hole in my station?" As the silence settled, Ian slumped back. "John messaged me after you left him. He said you weren't happy."

"I wasn't happy with him." Jani gave Lucien back his handheld and tried to relax. *Time to switch gears, Kilian—we're in negotiating mode.* That meant slowing down in the face of fear and tension, which was definitely not one of her talents. "I can understand, given your goals, why you decided to work with him."

"You're working on a hybrid 'pack as well." Ian smiled calm assurance. "You'd have to be."

Jani shrugged. "Our resources are limited." Not a lie, technically. She ignored Lucien's under the table foot-tap. "It would be a valuable asset. I would be extremely surprised if Service and Registry labs weren't already working on their own designs." A way forward presented itself, the first steps down a winding path. She hoped it made as much sense when she had time to consider the details. "The next best thing is having a friendly working relationship with Haárin documents examiners who happen to live in your settlement."

Ian stilled, his gaze sharpening. "I'm listening."

And so it begins. "Thalassa can help you with ag. We have shed designs and media formulae to share. In-house component designs and the materials to fabricate them. Strains that do well at higher temperatures and humidities."

"The shipping paperwork would need to be carefully written and coded."

"We ship via Haárin craft, using Haárin docks and paperwork. Shipments originate in Thalassa and are sent to, say, John? Much of the material could be coded as for medical research."

"Audits."

"No Commonwealth entity has the right to audit Thalassan transactions. Ní Tsecha Egri obtained that agreement before he died." Jani paused as one hitch in the plan blared in her mind's ear. "I know we need to trust the Haárin to keep it all to themselves, something which they seem genetically incapable of doing at times. But if we work quickly, you can have the new tech in place before your Family suppliers cancel your licenses."

Ian sat forward, elbows on the table, hands clenched. He looked like a starving man who sat at a laden table yet feared to eat. "It's a helluva risk."

"No greater than the risk you're taking now working with Commonwealth companies that also work with Family firms." Jani paused. *You have spies on the brain, Kilian.* That didn't mean she was wrong. "Then there's the likelihood that you've been infiltrated by Family ops keeping tabs on a rebellious affiliate."

Ian winced in agreement, stared into the middle distance for time, then turned to her. "I'm not sure what John will do when he hears he's been pulled into this."

Did he just say yes? Did it actually work? "If you break it to him, I doubt he'll yell too much." Jani looked past Ian to the station morning, the bright filtered sunlight and palm fronds waving in the fake breeze. "If he's to continue to be based here, he will want you to be on solid footing."

Ian nodded eventually. Then his handheld dinged, and he exhaled with a sigh. "First meeting of the day." He ran a hand over a stubbly cheek. "Better if I don't go in looking like an unmade bed." He stood and gestured to Lucien. "Talk to Security. But there are limits. We don't know who we're dealing with here and I don't want to give whoever it is any reason to fall on us."

Lucien stood and offered a smile that announced to the world that discretion was his middle name. "Thank you, sir." He turned so Ian couldn't see his face and arched a brow at Jani, then pelted off to visit his new friends.

Jani grabbed her coffee, added her thanks, and was halfway to the door when Ian called her back.

"So, the paper you found." He walked to a built-in cabinet and extracted a crisp jacket, which he switched out for his rumpled one. "Was it worth all the fuss?"

"Yes." Jani looked around the room. All the framed images were New Indies scenes. The fabled beaches. Rainforests. Cityscapes. No images of his parents or other family members or friends. "It's an ownership transfer of licenses from the Scriabins to the van Reuters. I don't have the subcoding, but I'm guessing agricultural products and building materials for the J-Loop. Maybe the Outer Circle. Dated just before the war."

"Part of Alyssa Scriabin's dowry. Pretty much a bribe to encourage van Reuter to go through with the wedding." Ian laughed silently. "I remember my parents talking about it." He ducked into a side room. "I can't believe the Scriabins lost track of that. I also can't believe Evan thinks for one minute that he could hold onto the assets involved. The courts would never allow that transfer to go through—the licenses would simply revert to the Scriabins."

"I'm not a financial law expert." Jani caught sight of Ian in a mirror running a depilatory cloth over his face. "If it goes to court, the Scriabins would have to open their books so the exact worth of the licenses could be calculated. No Family wants to do that."

"So they'd try to settle out of court? Evan would have them where he wanted them then. He has a very large ax to grind." Ian emerged looking neater if not exactly bouncy. "Stripping him of his assets really wasn't required. The holdings should've been held in trust for a time in case some errant offspring or long lost relative turned up." He checked his timepiece, then grabbed his coffee. "The crime he committed, murdering Service members? It splattered the other Families as well. Colonies started grumbling about secession again. Affiliated families wondered what the hell they'd signed up for." He stopped in mid-stride. "My God. You were on that transport."

"John Shroud was first on the scene at the crash site." Jani pointed to her eyes. "That's how all this started."

"That snowballed, didn't it?" Ian led Jani into his office proper. "I know you two had a falling out. John never talks about it. If you come up in conversation, he changes the subject." He extracted a brief bag from behind the desk, then made an entry into his handheld. "He's done a lot of good work here. Last year, we had a measles epidemic downstairs. Measles, I mean, come on, right? Turns out the Nawars had dumped a substandard batch of vax depots on us years ago. It only took a spark. One exposed kid. John's group didn't just come up with a vaccine. They treated patients. They saved lives." He slowed on his way out into the vestibule and lowered his voice. "Not to mention the seasonal tourist influx, which may sound brutal but it's our economy."

"I never said he wasn't a good doctor." Jani quieted as a gaggle of support staff exited a nearby office and waited for Ian by the lift bank.

"Your silence was deafening." Ian stopped, bent closer, and lowered his voice. "Evan could make Family lives miserable. Demand a settlement or go public. And as you said, open the books time. It's a mess any way you look at it." He checked his timepiece once again. "I really have to leave now. Budget meeting." He glanced back at his underlings. "I've been taking your advice about easing off on...things. It seems to be working with some."

"Revolution's the easy part. It's the day to day afterwards that's hard. Take your time." That earned Jani a smile and a nod. She waited until the lift door closed. Then she ducked into a stairwell and headed back down to the documents center.

Chapter Twenty-Seven

Niall awoke to the sound of voices in the corridor outside his cell. He couldn't understand the mangle nor did he recognize the speakers. For all he knew, what they talked about didn't even concern him. Most everyone seemed to have forgotten he existed.

He estimated that two days had passed since his attempt to trigger the station alarm. Since then, his only human interaction had been with the medical technician who came in every so often to check his eye and other injuries, a cowed, middle-aged man who paled every time Niall tried to engage him in conversation.

They're all afraid of me now. That realization gnawed like an ache. He sat up, swung his legs over the side of the cot and stood, then took the slow walk to the toilet. The weight of the blindspecs caused him to lean forward, which messed with his balance. He lifted his head, pulled in his chin, and stood ramrod straight, which took the pressure off his neck and reduced his risk of stumbling. *Getting used to being blind.* The skill might come in handy if van Reuter decided to have a go at his other eye.

He pissed, washed his face as best he could, and was about to clean his teeth when he heard the cell door locks disengage.

Then came a rough male voice. "Bed."

That voice, Niall recognized. Saul, his taciturn head guard. He returned to his cot, lay down, struggled to relax as the immobilization field held him fast. Choked back a groan of relief as the someone unlocked the 'specs and slipped them off. He didn't recognize the blurry face that hovered over his for a moment before vanishing. He heard Saul say something to them, caught a few words that sounded like *clothes* and *soap*. Blinked rapidly as the overhead light stabbed and tears flowed from his working eye.

"Taking you to the shower." Saul stood in the open doorway, cuffs in one hand and a shock stick in the other. "Gonna go visiting this morning.

———

Over the years, Niall had endured all manner of deprivation and dire conditions. A youth spent in abandoned buildings with no water or power licenses, his only food whatever he managed to steal. Smuggling weapons through the Wodonga rainforests during the seasonal monsoons. Service survival training in the steppe deserts of Phillipa. He'd lived through all of it, came out the other side ready to fuck, fight, and drink the entire damned Commonwealth under the table.

But never had a shower felt so good as the one he took now. He scrubbed his skin sunburn red with the body brush and cranked up the water until the jets stung like needles and Saul banged on the door to tell him he'd blown through his allotment. They had provided a thick towel instead of a dryer wand and a toiletry kit containing proper shaving and dental cleaning gear and skin lotion to counter the dry station air. *Jani must be on her way.* Why else would he need to clean up?

He felt almost human until he emerged from the shower and found his new clothing hanging on a hook by the sink. Pants and short-sleeve pullover in dingy grey. No underwear. No belt. No socks, just slip-on shoes of the sort he received when he checked himself into the Psychotherapeutics ward at Sheridan, stretchy poly cloth with thin soles that squeaked like mice on the lyno floor.

Nothing I can use to kill myself. Or anyone else. *Well, not easily.* So who was he being taken to see? Morwenna was just the type to give with one hand after having taken with the other, but she had taken way too much this last time and Niall doubted she had any interest in further parley. *That leaves van Reuter. Shit.* What could that bastard possibly have to say to him?

Niall forced himself to look in the mirror, and tried not to think of Sharon as he recalled her description of his damaged eye. *Not too cloudy, she said.* Well, either she'd decided to be kind or matters had degraded over the last few days. *Hard-boiled egg.* Milky opaque white centered with the barest hint of darkness, the lids reddened and swollen as though he had been punched. He cupped cold water in his hand and flushed the area. The irritated skin stung from the chill. The eye itself felt...nothing.

He focused on the sink bowl as he finished cleaning up. Dug into the kit as needed without raising his head. Pulled out the toothbrush, and found it tangled with something else. An elastic band attached to a small piece of black cloth.

Niall unwound the band, flattened the cloth, and stared. Clenched his jaw as blood heat crawled up his neck. An eye patch, cut from scrap cloth and hand-sewn from the look of it. *Somebody's idea of a joke?* One guess who that somebody was.

You fried it, you son of a bitch. Now you don't want to look at it? He crumpled the thing in his fist, walked to the toilet, but stopped just short of dumping it in. *They'd probably knock me around a little for acting up, then take me back to my cell.* Clap the 'specs back on and leave him to stew in his own juice until Jani arrived. Just a lump on the bed. Useless.

Niall worked his neck, listened to the bones crunch. Van Reuter had asked for him for a reason and he had a duty to learn what it was.

It would also give him a chance to probe the ex-minister-slash-escaped convict for information. How did he get off Earth? Who helped him and why? Evan would resist, no doubt, and his political life had trained him in the fine art of answering questions while saying absolutely nothing.

But I'm a drunk questioning another drunk. They shared sore spots. *I just have to poke the right one.* And hopefully not get blinded or beaten in the process. *Stick your pride in your back pocket for now, boyo. You can't afford it.* He took a couple of deep breaths, then dragged on the eyepatch. Walked back to the mirror, adjusting as he went, and took in the finished product.

Huh. Niall turned one way, then the other. *Not...horrible.* He managed a smile, which his scarred and scabby lip twisted into a tooth-baring sneer. Every space pirate adventure he'd seen as a kid featured one character with an eye patch. Usually the villain, who confessed to their misdeeds with howls of maniacal laughter before meeting their doom.

Let's hope life doesn't imitate art. Niall gave the patch one final tweak, then gathered his gear and called out to Saul that he was ready to go.

———

"Good morning, Colonel." Evan van Reuter remained seated as Niall entered. He sat at a small round table arrayed with place settings for two and a number of covered dishes, a carafe serving as the centerpiece. He had opted for casual dress instead of the formal daywear he had worn during Niall's earlier summonses, a light blue open-necked shirt and dark blue trousers.

Niall hesitated in the entry until Saul prodded him in the back. Despite everything, his mouth watered as he inhaled the aromas of fresh coffee, toasted bread. *And bacon?* Judging from the better quality of the furnishings—well-stuffed upholstery, touches of real wood—he stood in the dining room of Evan's suite. Not quite Cabinet-class, but better than the metal frame and poly that filled most of the other rooms he had seen. *No way it was here when they arrived. It would've been stripped years ago.* That meant that either Evan had brought it with him or Morwenna arranged for him to have it.

Caring for her ex-Minister. Niall could see her taking the trouble...until she got what she needed. *Which is what, exactly?* No matter what angle he examined, he couldn't figure out why someone like Morwenna would attach herself to a loser like van Reuter. *A lure for Jani.* No, that's what he was for.

He walked to the table, Saul's hand clamped on his shoulder, steer mech and warning both. His chair had not only been bolted to the floor but outfitted with ankle brackets and a waist restraint. Once locked in, he wasn't going anywhere.

Niall sat, but before he could decide whether kneeing Saul in the face when he bent to secure him was worth the beating he'd receive in repayment, Evan broke in.

"Don't bother with those." Evan motioned towards the door. "You can go."

Saul shot him a look that would have gotten him fired for insubordination in any Cabinet Row office. "The lady said—"

"I'm sure the colonel will be on his best behavior. Now run along." Evan's smile was a curve of lip, nothing more. He sat back, hands clasped across his stomach, and stared down Saul until the guard turned and clumped out of the room.

Niall remained silent until the receding footsteps faded to nothing. "You sure that was wise?"

Evan filled two mugs from the carafe, then pushed one across the table. "You made your play the other day, and you paid with an eye. You know what life is like in blindspecs and, given your present circumstances, I don't believe you're particularly anxious to render them redundant." He raised his mug towards one of the serving dishes as though toasting its existence. "Do try the bacon. I've no idea where they got hold of real meat here in the back of beyond, but it is lovely."

Niall lifted covers one by one and swept various delicacies onto his plate. Coddled eggs. Freshly baked breads and pastries. Fried potatoes. And, finally, the bacon. He paused before digging in, pangs of guilt warring with those of hunger. *Jani would just sit and watch Evan eat.* Goad and irritate the man into telling her whatever she wanted to know. *Fuck.* He hesitated, then comforted himself with the fact that it would've been an easy call for her given that human food tasted like unsalted oatmeal. Besides, he needed to appear defeated, grateful for any scrap of kindness. Perceived vulnerability brought out the chatterbox in a certain type of bully. "I'm guessing our hostess is capable of accessing all manner of luxuries." He plucked a rasher from his pile and bit off half, savored warm fat and salt and smoky char. *Oh, you weak old man.* He washed it down with coffee, then went to work on his eggs.

"So I've noticed." Evan dipped a piece of toast in egg yolk, then grimaced and tossed it back on his plate. "This jaunt has proved most educational." He took up his coffee mug in both hands, sat back, and stared past Niall at something only he could see.

Niall took in Evan's slack, ashen skin, dull black hair streaked with gray, bloodshot eyes. *Oh, how the mighty have fallen.* Whatever damage the punch had done had healed for the most part. Only a bit of swelling remained, some bruising under one eye, a line of scabs under the chin, all of which unfortunately accentuated Evan's rolled-in-an-alley appearance.

Then he looked closer, and caught the slight tremor of Evan's hand as he reached for the container of cream. The tension around his eyes as though he suffered a headache. *He's drying out.* He wanted to be sober when Jani arrived. *Good luck, boyo.* Niall usually needed at least two weeks to get over the shakes and the urge to bust heads with the merest provocation, to look tired instead of sick, and he wasn't anywhere close to Evan's rate of decline. *Not yet, anyway.*

Evan met his gaze, then looked away. "Do I look that bad?"

"I've looked worse some mornings." Niall pushed away his plate as the thought of how much he wanted a drink kicked his appetite to the side of the road. He sat back, patted his pockets, then sighed when he remembered that he had left his remaining nicstick behind in his cell. "It doesn't hurt, by the way." He pointed to the patch. "On the off chance you give a shit." He caught the flicker in his host's bleary eyes and knew that, surprise breakfasts aside, loss of his remaining orb was still within the realm of probability. *You'll never learn, will you, Pierce?* His own fatal flaw. Despite his planning, no matter how careful he swore he would be, the smart ass always broke through.

Then Evan's glare softened. He even managed a smile. "A minor inconvenience, surely. Service Medical will have you fixed up in no time." He set down his mug, using both hands to keep it steady. Then he folded his arms and cocked his head like a critic assessing a painting. "Besides, it lends a rakishness to your overall air of dissolution. You fit right in with the rest of these sterling examples of colonial humanity." A pause. A snort of laughter. "This was your life once, wasn't it? Before Roshi dragged you out of the muck and hosed you down."

Niall took up his mug, stared into the inky brew for a few moments, then drank. Bit back every sharp rejoinder that bubbled up from decades of reserves. This was the bargaining phase—he had noticed Evan's weakness, which cleared Evan to mock his background. Humiliations balanced out—now they were even. "I'm sure you read all the Commonwealth Intelligence background investigations. The annual follow-ups." *Or had someone read them to you.* He congratulated himself for holding back that last remark.

Evan worked his neck. Flexed his hands, Drummed his fingers on the tabletop. Then he rapped the wooden surface with his fist so hard that ripples shuddered across the surface of his coffee. "So. What is she planning?"

"Jani?" Niall shrugged. "Your guess is as good—"

"Our flame-haired lady." Evan dug a sugar cube from the bowl and popped it into his mouth. "I'm sure you realize that I invited you to breakfast for a reason. Saul assumed another interrogation with added brutality, not this—" He gestured towards the food. "—and he no doubt messaged Morwenna with the news the moment he oozed out the door." A second sugar cube followed the first. "So many balls in the air our lady has. She's currently at what I guess you would call an off-site. Very fancy corsair docked on the opposite side of this hunk of rock we currently orbit. I'm sure she needed some time to extract herself without appearing panicked, but she should be on her way back here now. I am guessing we have fifteen minutes. Twenty at most."

Niall glanced towards the door, listened for any sound of approaching henchmen. "That being the case, I'm surprised Saul didn't intervene more forcefully."

"She and I are supposed to be equal partners. A flunky rousting you out of here would indicate a level of distrust that would give even an old drunk like me pause." Evan plucked several more sugar cubes from the bowl, but instead of eating them, he stacked them, then knocked them over. "I know she made you an offer. You'd be a free man now if you'd taken it. You may have even gotten the chance to learn if she's a real redhead." Another stack, another tumble. "What was her request? Inside man at Supreme Command? What did she offer in exchange?"

"We never got around to discussing benefits." Niall touched one of the lines of scabs that still dotted his jawline. "She ministered to my wounds and hinted a lot."

"She's good at distraction, isn't she?" Evan toppled the cubes one last time, then swept them aside. "But you turned her down." He glanced toward the door, then at his timepiece. "What offer could she have made that would've captured your interest?"

Niall thought back to that station night, the details that replayed again and again. *Two people dead because of me.* Two people whose only crime had been kindness. *Bring them back. That's the offer.* "Why should I waste my time considering? That bird has flown."

"But hypothetically. Just to kill the time before she arrives." As Evan spoke, the tension left his face and a hint of the old van Reuter confidence returned, the easy self-assurance that had won elections and spurred talks of the prime ministry. "Humor me."

"What are you driving at?"

"I simply want to know what could compel your cooperation."

"The only reason you would ask me that is if you felt you had something compelling to offer." Niall topped off his coffee, added sugar, then stirred, banging the spoon against the inside of the mug to prevent further conversation. To give him time to think. This was always the point when he stepped aside and let Roshi take the lead. *I'm no goddamn negotiator.* He lacked patience, always preferred the hard right cross to the soft word. "You have information."

"When I said this journey had proved educational, I wasn't simply referring to the food."

"If you have information about Morwenna's illegal dealings, you should be contacting External Revenue or Commerce."

"Colonel, if all I knew were the details of an Outer Circle smuggling operation, do you honestly believe I would be wasting my time talking to you?" Evan stared up at the ceiling for a few beats, then fixed on Niall. "But to kidnap the Admiral-General's right hand man? That requires more than a couple of insiders in a warehouse." A grim smile. "Surely you've wondered why your Service hasn't rescued you by now? We're only a couple of GateWays from Elyas, and you know that this sort of unmanned station is the first place any decent investigator would check."

Niall's gut tightened, as if a cold hand had taken hold of his stomach and squeezed. *Everything we've talked about, Roshi.* Criminal and Service hands down one another's trousers. The creeping return of the rot they had worked so hard to eradicate. "If you're going to tell me that smuggling rings have infiltrated Outer Circle bases, that's not exactly news."

"Oh, Colonel." Evan shook his head in mock sympathy. "For a man of your educational attainments, you sometimes display a startling lack of imagination. You need to think much, much bigger." He mimed zipping his lips closed. "No more free information. Hiroshi

Mako is the only person who gets to hear my piece. But now we need a plan, because once the chaos agent arrives, things will happen quickly."

Despite everything, Niall had to smile. "You mean Jani?"

"I mean Jani." Evan tented his fingers and sat back, his chair ergoworks clicking like nails on glass. "I've given it a great deal of thought these past few days. Jani is bringing something that will give me back my life, but Morwenna intends to take hold of it herself. I want you to get it instead."

Niall replayed in his head what Evan had said, just to make sure that was what he had heard. *Flying fuck.* "Wait a minute." He held up his hands, wrists pressed together as though bound. "Assuming I'm in the same room, I'm going to be cuffed."

Evan took a rasher from his plate. "You're not cuffed now." He bit into the slice, chewed thoughtfully. "As I said, pains have been taken to earn my trust. They need me to verify what Jani brings. I will tell them to refrain from cuffing you, that surely your burly guards should prove sufficient."

"And why would they agree to that?"

"I will say that seeing you uncuffed will file off some of Jani's edges, make her easier to deal with."

They won't listen, you dumb shit. Niall pressed his fingers to his temples as his scalp tightened like shrink wrap. "We would need an insider to pull this off, more likely two."

"You have me."

"You're not—"

"You just need to grab some paper, Colonel. Two sheets of parchment that were stashed in Pearl Way documents archives after the war. I'd forgotten they existed. Then I received a message with an offer—"

Niall held up his hand. "The guards that will be there will be the most experienced. Even assuming I am in the room, there will be at minimum two on me and one at the door. I can't take them all by myself."

"Jani will be there."

"Jani's a scrapper." *With a death wish.* "A trained fighter, she is not." Niall propped his elbows on the table and cradled his head in his hands as numerous ways in which a half-assed plot could blow up flashed through his mind like shatterboxes pounding a city. "Besides, she will likely be escorted by at least two guards. This isn't an adventure holoVee. A plucky attitude won't cut it."

"Colonel—"

"We could all die."

Evan hung his head for a few moments, then raised it slowly until he met Niall's eye. "I didn't think you'd make the same mistake Morwenna is making. She read Jani's files, her ServRec. She knows the words, but she misses the music." His flippant air dissipated, replaced by remembrance that aged him like an illness. "Jani doesn't stop. Offer her bribes. Threaten her. Poison her. Shoot her. It doesn't matter. Morwenna thinks she has her cornered. You don't corner Jani Kilian."

Niall pointed at Evan's timepiece. "Speaking of cornered, we better wrap this up before—"

Evan continued as though he hadn't heard. "She was dying, an allergic reaction to some drug. But she still came for me. She figured out that I had given the order to bomb her transport. Durian tried to stop her. He shot her." He glanced at Niall. "Durian Ridgeway. My Documents chief. Best fixer I ever had."

Niall listened for any sounds from the corridor. Voices. Approaching footsteps. He knew from his own experience that Evan would just keep talking no matter what. Because sometimes, without the alcohol to keep it down, the pressure grew too great. The past needed release.

"She broke his neck." Every shred of confidence had drained from Evan's manner. He stared straight ahead, mind and body focused on the memory of his last moments as a free man. "Then she came for me. The last thing she told me before the cavalry arrived. 'I want you around for a long time. I want someone to share my ghosts with.' She hates me too much to kill me or let me die. She's sitting in some cubbyhole even as we speak, making her lists and working it all out and if you think for one second that it will go as our red-haired lady plans, you're a bigger idiot than she is." He shook his head. "I'm not going back there. To that hole. This is my chance, and Jani's going to seal it for me." He raised a hand, index finger extended, as though imparting a lesson. "She owes me."

You piece of shit. Niall clenched his fists, beat down the urge to reach across the table and pummel van Reuter bloody. He had pondered some attempt to feel out Saul or one of his other guards, but now he had no choice but to push. *Because this sonofabitch will do something to get us all killed if I don't.* No pressure, nope. Not a bit.

Evan lowered his hand, then drew up straighter. "Do my ears deceive me, or are we soon to have a visitor?" He pulled a small flask from his trouser pocket. "Must maintain the fiction." He pulled the top off the flask and took a swig of whiskey, but instead of swallowing it, he swished it around like mouthwash, then spit it into his coffee and set the flask on the table.

Niall's heart thumped as footsteps sounded from both ends of the corridor, one set rapid and clipped, the other slower, heavier. He glanced at Evan, who smirked, then leaned back and clasped his hands behind his head, Family arrogance returned en force.

The footsteps grew louder, then stopped in front of the entry. Low voices followed, light female and dull male, a rapid back-and-forth in Hortensian German.

"She's pissed," Evan whispered. "She wants to know why Saul brought you to me in the first place." A silent laugh, followed by a sing-song. "Somebody is in trouble."

The door slid open and Morwenna stepped inside. She had dressed for battle in form-fitting white that covered everything yet left more than enough room for the imagination to play. *Damn her.* Niall despised her for the cold-blooded killer that she was and yet he felt the pull—

"Gentlemen, for shame. You had a party and you didn't invite me." Her smile held all the warmth of a Chicago January. She shot Evan a look of disgust, then waved a hand in Niall's direction. "Take the colonel back to his cell." She stepped to one side as Saul entered, cuffs in hand. "And this time, leave him there."

Evan threw his arms wide. "But you've been so busy these last few days." His voice filled the room, all spoiled brat petulance heavy with inebriation. "And I do hate to breakfast alone."

Niall stared at nothing as Saul secured his hands, then pulled him to his feet and strong-armed him out of the room. He felt Morwenna's glare rake the side of his face and ignored Evan's jovial "Later, Colonel." He stumbled as the soles of his shoes grabbed on the lyno and would have fallen if Saul hadn't grabbed him by the back of his shirt and dragged him like a sack of potatoes. Just as he staggered around the corner, he heard the raised voices emanating from the dining room and caught Saul's grimace and repeated glances back over his shoulder as the volume ramped up.

Niall held back grim laughter. *Ah, the good ol' days.* When the stink of panic filled the air and survival was the only rule. *Somebody's been double-dealing.* "What did van Reuter offer you in exchange for setting up our little meeting? Money he doesn't have? A posh job on his nonexistent security staff?" He paid for those remarks by getting tossed atop his cot and slammed with a extra strong jolt of the immobilization field before Saul clamped on the blindspecs. "What do you think—she'll do when she realizes you—went behind her back?"

"You keep your mouth shut." Saul yanked off the cuffs. "Or you're going to find yourself floating out there with Art and Sharon."

After the field cut out, Niall worked into a sitting position and massaged his aching wrists. "So will you after she blows this place. She's reached the point where everyone's expendable." In reply, he heard only Saul's breathing. Heavy. Shaky. Like someone who was very, very scared. *Christ, van Reuter—you were actually right about something.* "She's having problems. Losing control. What was that meeting of hers about? Trying to salvage a deal?" He jerked a thumb in the direction of the dining room. "She didn't look too happy back there. Something tells me the dress didn't work."

"Your mutt friend better be on her way here pretty damn soon." The odd squeak of boot soles on lyno sounded as Saul paced. "I mean, where the hell is she? Kilian. At first we get messages every day or so—yeah, she got what the lady wanted. Now, three days and nothing." A snort of disgust. "Maybe she ain't such a friend after all."

"Jani will be here." Niall crossed his fingers as he spoke, an old superstition long buried. "Not sure if that helps you, though. Morwenna's all about survival at this point." He paused, listened, heard Saul's step slow, then stop. "Gives a man a lot to think about. Watching business dry up. Bonuses get smaller and smaller. Holed up in shit stations that don't even have a decent bar." Another pause. Time to add butter to the bread. "You're a smart guy, Saul. Been around. You know when a job starts to smell as bad as this recycled air."

Long moments of silence. Then Niall heard Saul draw closer, and he braced for a punch. Instead, he heard the buzz and click of the blindspec locks, and felt blessed relief as the weight lifted and light poured in. He looked up to find his guard looming over him.

"What's your mutt friend got?"

I've no fucking clue. Niall tried to form an answer as all the scenarios he had pondered over the last few days flashed through his mind. Had Jani left Elyas alone, or had Pascal hitched along? Had Feyó sent her security suborns after her? Had she already been recaptured, imprisoned in Thalassa, to be let out only on holidays and for the odd glimpse of the sun? *Well, here goes.* "She'll have what Morwenna wants. It's worth a lot, according to van Reuter. Documents of some kind that are worth a lot of money to some very important people." He made a conscious effort to speak slowly, softly. He could not under any circumstances let his nerves show. "My crew would be interested, as well."

"Service?"

"All the shit that went on during the war—this is part of it. Hiroshi Mako is still digging deep. Tying off loose ends."

Saul stared down at the floor. "Lady says by the time we're through here, she'll own the Outer Circle."

Niall shook his head. Nothing wrecked a gang faster than a boss with delusions of grandeur. "That would mean she's getting between Family and what's theirs. Outer Circle, that means the Ulanovs. The Scriabins. The ones who torpedoed van Reuter. One of their own, and they slit his throat. How long do you think your lady will last?"

Saul shrugged. "So what's the deal?"

"We rescue Jani Kilian and get hold of whatever she brought."

Another shrug. "And then what?"

"Then things get tense." Niall ticked off items on his fingers. "It would help if I were in the room. If my hands were free. And if we had a clear path to a ship."

"Hmm. And what do I get?"

Niall hesitated, then decided the hell with it. Surely being the A-G's Colonel allowed him some bargaining power. "New name. New face."

"Money?"

"Sure. Whatever you need to make a new life."

Saul stood still and silent, turning the blindspecs over and over as though seeing them for the first time. "Let me think about it."

Niall felt a quiver of apprehension. Had he agreed too readily? Promised too much? "We could get a head start on prep if you let me know now."

"You'll know when you know." Saul motioned for Niall to sit on his hands, then clapped the blindspecs back on. Then came his heavy steps. The opening and closing of the cell door.

Quiet.

———

Niall lay on his cot and struggled to think calmly even as every sound outside his cell door made his heart race. Morwenna's patience with him had worn thin—if Saul told her of the offer to flip, he had no doubt he'd be hustled out an airlock with no chance of reprieve.

Leave it to a Family jack-off to dump a half-baked pile of shit in his lap and call it a plan. *Too many moving parts.* A patchwork held together with spit, hope, and trust in the wrong people. *I should've kept my damned mouth shut.* Let the deal go down between Jani and Morwenna and leave van Reuter to twist in the wind. Nothing that idiot knew could possibly be of use to Roshi—

His breath caught as one thing Evan had said spooled through his head. *She read Jani's files. Her ServRec.*

Niall sat up. *Not possible.* Access to Jani Kilian's Service record had always been closely controlled; after her discharge, it had been buried.

A smuggler broke into our files? How? Electronic records had been obliterated. Someone would've had to go to Earth, to Fort Sheridan, and gain access to the paper archives. *Sign-off from Roshi. The PM.* Not just unlikely. Impossible. Jani's records would be sealed until the principles, their children, and their children's children were nothing but scattered ash. Knevçet Shèràa may have been the most momentous event delineated therein, but there had been so many others. Investigations Jani had led while in 1ˢᵗ D&D, the Documents and Documentation Division, the results of which touched every NUVA-SCAN Family, scandals involving the types of financial manipulation that made Niall's head ache. No one wanted the details of Jani Kilian's ServRec to ever again see the bright light of day.

So how the hell did Morwenna MacCallan get hold of it?

Niall leaned forward, his weighted head cradled in his hands, and struggled to beat back rising panic. *God, I need a drink.* He used to be better at this. He tried not to think about the fact that he stood a good chance of dying in the next few days—if he dwelled on that, he'd freeze when it came time to act. Assuming that time ever came.

Jani, where the hell are you?

Chapter Twenty-Eight

Jani stood in front of the documents center outgoing mail bin, holding her carefully-sealed parcel close to her chest. Said parcel, wrapped in padded sheathing devoid of any documents center-specific identification, contained copies of the docking slip and manifest, her brain scans, the refrigerated box with her scanpack remains, and a coded message to Dieter Brondt care of Elyas Station. The addressee location was coded as well, one of the thousands of rentable lockboxes of the type used as mail drops by frequent travelers.

She placed the parcel in the bin opening, then pulled it out just before it slid down the chute. Checked the wall clock. Fifteen minutes until pickup. After that, hours until the next collection, by which time she would likely be en route to Niall and his captors.

Once again, she placed the parcel in the bin opening. Once again, she caught hold of it just as it was about to fall.

"Figured it out yet?"

Jani flinched, then turned just as Lucien grabbed a stool from a nearby carrel and dragged it beside the bin. "Figured what out?"

"What the hell's going on?" He set a binder atop the bin,

followed by a small, clear-sided sample carton containing devices of various types, bugs and observer fleas, the fruits of his meeting with station security. "I figured you'd sequestered yourself in an empty office and broken out the notepad."

"I don't have time."

"Colored styluses for drawing arrows every which way." Lucien sketched curlicues in the air with his index fingers. "A straight edge for underlining everything just so."

"I didn't do any of that." Once again, Jani started to put the package in the bin, then set it on top instead. Ignoring Lucien's self-congratulatory chuckle, she reached into the waistband of her pants and pulled out a folded sheet of parchment that looked as though it had been crumpled into a ball, flattened out, then crumpled again. Repeatedly. "I just made a few notes." She unfolded it and set it atop the bin, ironing out the crinkles with the edge of her hand.

"I knew it." Lucien leaned forward and looked over the document, tugging one corner to shift its position so he could read it more easily.

"It didn't help." Jani worked her neck. "Ships carrying paper for destruction being hijacked? Could have nothing to do with the paper —someone just wanted the ship. We're attacked at Padi, why? A competing interest trying to intercept us? Somebody spotted us on the concourse and thought we looked like an easy mark?"

"Teddy fucked us over?" Lucien pushed the paper away, then sat back, arms folded. "Don't give me that look. You trust him. I don't."

Jani leaned against the bin. "Say he did. Just for the sake of argument." She held up a finger to silence Lucien. "What was the point? The docking slip isn't worth much on its own."

"Depends what whoever sent in that crew already had." Lucien ticked off points on one hand. "None of them carried any identification. Their clothing was clean—no badges or patches. Their weapons were top of the line and devoid of any markings. They were pros."

"That means Family or one of the bigger gangs, which we already knew. It doesn't get me any closer to figuring out what connects everything." Jani straightened, then folded the worksheet once again and shoved it back in her pocket. "I'll be going in blind. I don't like going in blind."

"So you've sent the message that you have the paper."

Jani pushed away from the bin, paced to the wall opposite and back again. "Not yet." She toed the carpet, then looked over at Lucien to find eyeing her with arched brow. "What?"

"I know what you're doing."

"No, you—"

"I've watched you work at close quarters for over a year." Lucien lowered his voice as a pair of staffers walked past. "You think that whatever happens will affect Thalassa, and you're trying to figure out how. And you feel guilty because Niall isn't first in your thoughts, but he can't be now, can he?"

Jani's denial died on her lips. *Niall.* He had talked more than once about sitting in on the negotiations that had led to Evan's imprisonment. *They despised one another.* She could only hope that he hadn't had too rough a time up to that point, and that her delay hadn't made things worse for him. But after days of rushing through stations, her forced downtime had allowed her a chance to think, and those thoughts always led her to the same conclusion. "I can't shake the feeling that Anais is part of this. Yevgeny Scriabin kept her on a short lead. But since his death she's become more visible. The Outer Circle is her familial territory and you know as well as I do that she'd have the people capable of snatching someone like Niall."

Lucien hesitated before nodding, no doubt recalling the years when he had been one of those people. "But you still think Evan's involved?"

"Oh yes. He wouldn't care who made the offer—he would crawl over broken glass to get his old life back. Throw in access to the level of technology stated in those transfers, to all that money? He'd have enough to come after me. Make things rough for hybrids. We're so vulnerable, and everybody wants us gone."

"Not everybody. You've made a friend in Ian."

"He has his limits." Jani gripped the edge of the bin and executed a few modified push-ups, upper back muscles fighting every movement. "I'm not first in his thoughts, either." She glanced at the wall clock. *Five minutes to pick-up.*

Troubled silence fell. Lucien poked at the contents of the sample carton, then plucked one of the devices from the pile and eyed it like a jeweler evaluating a dodgy stone. "Ani could've sent the Padi team even though the Pearl Way is not her familial territory. She's done things like that before." He tucked the object in his pocket, then continued rummaging. "For what it's worth, I think she hates us both enough that she wouldn't hide. Her emotions get the better of her—you know that. She'd want us to know it was her."

"Well, that is a comfort." Jani nodded towards the binder and the devices. "How did you do?"

Lucien pocketed another device, then pushed the carton aside. "My new friends in Security didn't know as much as I hoped about that errant emergency signal or the station itself. I was hoping that they'd have recon in the area, but all their ships are on the small side and not well-armed, so they get challenged by larger craft that don't want to be observed. They don't even have scans of the place because records are sparse and when they try to get close enough to glean useful detail, like I said, challenged. Service is also supposed to patrol regularly, but according to everything my friends didn't say, that seldom happens."

Jani shrugged. "Colony-born Spacers turning a blind eye to colony-born smugglers."

"Or being paid off."

"Or not wanting to confront them directly." Jani checked the time. One minute. She heard a distant *ding* that announced the arrival of a lift, and her heart thumped. She picked up her parcel, set it on the edge of the chute, then stopped. "Get any volunteers for your team?"

"A few. Ex-Service, which is helpful. They're prepping a ship now."

"Progress."

"So what are you going to do?"

"I'm going to let whomever know that I have what they want and—"

"No." Lucien nodded towards the parcel in her hands. "What are you going to do with that."

Jani shrugged. "Ship it out."

"Uh-huh." Lucien braced one foot against the bin and tipped back his stool a hair's breadth short of a backward tumble. "Since I've been here, you've put it in the outgoing bin three times, and removed it three times. You're worried that someone will intercept it on its way to Elyas Station." He lowered his seat to a more stable position and leaned forward. "So?"

Jani stepped aside as a clerk pulling a skim cart stopped in front of the bin and looked at her. "No, I'm—" She swept up the parcel and stood aside as he unlocked the bin, emptied the contents into a secure mailbag, then reset various locks and went on his way. *Okay, now we're committed.* An idea had formed hours before. She had batted it away repeatedly, but it kept coming back. *And now it's my only option.* "I have to go somewhere."

Lucien nodded. "Uh-huh. And I'm going with you."

"I'd be better off alone."

"Not happening."

Jani paced, mind racing. The deadline for contacting Niall's kidnappers was fast approaching—she had no time to argue. "Are you up to a walk?"

Lucien stood. "I am. Augie's doing its job." He worked his shoulder, then pressed a hand to his ribs. "Just a little cramping." He paused to bend his injured knee, which strained the seams of his scrub pants. "Still a little puffy. Got it wrapped with a cold pack. You?"

"Fine." Jani poked her ribs, and felt the barest of twinges. Then she looked from her rumpled scrubs to Lucien's. "We can't go like this." She beckoned to her self-appointed shadow. "Follow me."

A staging site for some of the materials and light equipment needed to repair the damage to the documents archive had been set up in the corridor near the archive entry. Jani walked through the area as though she belonged, grabbing gear as she went: two sets of coveralls, a couple of helmets equipped with tinted visors, a pair of tool bags. She then met Lucien at the doorway of an empty office—they ducked inside, emerging soon after in full worker kit. They continued down the corridor and through a door leading to a stairwell, where they encountered workers clumping up and down the stairs, entering from or exiting onto every floor, footsteps and voices bouncing off the hard surfaces so that the noise pressed like weight from every angle.

Jani joined a line heading up the stairs, then stepped to one side and motioned for Lucien to follow her to a side door coated in brilliant red.

Lucien tugged her to a halt. "That's an alarmed exit."

"Wanna bet?" Jani pushed open the door and stepped out onto the main concourse of the station, the hard light of the artificial sun blasting her in the face so that her eyes watered despite the filtering provided by the visor. "Look around." She pointed to the food stalls and bars that ran along both sides of the concourse. "The floors above and below are mostly expensive shops and offices. Those alarms are active. I bet this one was accidentally broken the day work began." She scanned the overhead signs until she found the one pointing the way to the nearest tram stop, and headed out.

Lucien drew alongside, then flipped up his visor. "We look like ourselves again, walking with these visors down could attract attention of a security 'bot, and Feyó's feelers should've latched onto something by now. Someone's bound to ID us if they haven't already."

"You're no doubt correct." Jani raised her visor, but only halfway. "Let's just say I'm not in the mood to make anyone's job easier today."

"Does that mean there are days when you do feel like making someone's job easier?" Lucien pressed a hand to his heart. "Could you let me know when that happens? I'd like to be there to catch the lucky bastard when they faint from shock."

"Okay, smartass." Jani cut through the crowds, dodging travelers and crew members, luggage skims, and the odd two-wheeled passenger cart pulled by robotic horses. The concourse mirrored the main walking street of Thomasine, the capital, the storefronts a patchwork of multicolored stucco, the air so heavy with flower fragrance that it tasted sweet, the sunshine holding enough heat to warm even a hybrid's eternal chill. Just enough similarity to Thalassa to cause her to slow and savor a little, and let go of a fragment of the tension that had held her for days in its muscle-clenching grip.

They boarded a tram that afforded sweeping views of the multi-level concourses and the holographic flora and fauna that shimmered to life, then vanished, as the angle of approach changed. They drew the barest glances from the other riders, who flicked through hand-held screens, ate out of dispo cartons, chatted, or dozed. After they settled in, Lucien slipped off his helmet, then draped his arm across the seat back so that his hand rested on Jani's shoulder.

Assuming we've been identified, there's no reason for him to keep acting out of character. And yet, Jani found she didn't mind. She dragged off her helmet, pressed the back of her neck against Lucien's arm, and tried to clear her head even as every thought and action scrolled through in a never-ending reel. She concentrated on the view, and managed a smile as a holographic monkey kept pace with the tram, swinging along the railings and lighting fixtures and chattering all the while.

"I often wondered what it would be like to work with you." Lucien looked around as though he, too, relished the opportunity to sit and watch the scenery flit past. "So far it's been quite the educational experience."

Jani shook her head. "I doubt I could teach you anything."

"Most of my missions were pretty well planned. I had a schedule. Designated stops. Places where I could lie low." Lucien eyed her. "I think it's more a matter of style. You're an improvisor. And you never look furtive—you just keep moving. Forget getting hold of these." He tugged at the front of his coverall. "Look how easily you got into the documents center in the first place."

"They caught me, didn't they?"

"Not until you got as far as a secured area related to a suspicious incident with nothing but someone else's ID and some quick foot-work." Lucien lowered his voice. "You do realize the levels of security you bypassed to get as far as you did? Someone in doc center security is going to find sitting rather uncomfortable for at least a week." He reached into the tool bag on his lap and shook the box of devices. "I think I'm going to use you as the tester after I get Thalassa's systems upgraded. Whenever the hell that happens. We are so behind the curve, it's terrifying."

"Niall never complained about equipment."

"He finagled Service resources. When they pulled him back, that all went with him."

Jani winced, then looked down at her hands to find she had tugged at a hangnail so hard that it bled. "Idomeni aren't used to thinking about security the way humans do. Even Tsecha's assassination hasn't been enough to wake them up."

"Don't make excuses for Feyó." Lucien shifted until he straightened his injured knee. "Sometimes I think she's trying to set you up."

"She wouldn't go that far." *I hope.* Jani looked around the car at the other riders in search of anything she had seen before. Clothing. Shoes. A distinctive bag. She used to look at faces, a burned-in habit from her days on the run. *So much for that.* Something apparently so definite, so fixed, could no longer be trusted. "You think she'd let me get killed, and yet you don't think it possible that some of the new hybrids are plants?"

"Possible, sure. Likely?" Lucien pondered for a time, then shook his head. "You need to have faith in an agent, and conversely, that agent needs to have faith as well."

"Trust. I get that."

"It's more than that. They need to believe that whatever risks they're taking are worth it." Lucien pulled Jani close, then whispered in her ear. "Hybridization is a huge risk. It isn't reversible—that agent is committed to that outcome even after the job is done. It's a life sentence. They'd have to feel some sort of connection, a willingness to become, in order to make that commitment, and if they possessed that feeling, why would they want to hurt Thalassa?" He leaned back, his brown eyes unreadable.

The one question Jani had never asked him bubbled up before she could stop it. "You've never considered it, have you?"

A flicker in the dark stone. "Perhaps you don't remember your time in Chicago, but I do." Lucien looked past her, eyes narrowing. Whatever he saw, cute holographic animals played no part. "At Sheridan. How many times did I find you on the bathroom floor? Service Medical utterly clueless. Shroud and Parini scrambling, throwing everything at the wall and praying something stuck." He touched his forehead. "I already have one thing that could bite me. I don't need anything else at present."

At first, Jani thought he referred to his Service augmentation. Then she realized he meant the behavior mod that Eamon DeVries had installed on Anais Ulanova's order that boosted his inherent sociopathy. "We've both been experimented upon."

"At least Shroud cared about you. In his own possessive, overbearing way." Lucien hunched and hugged himself. "To Ani, I was just another knife in the drawer. Someone else to order around."

"I order you around."

"You tell me what you need. You leave it up me to decide how to get it. With Ani, in the Service, I had to follow orders. Which I did, because I felt that in the long run...." Lucien's voice trailed as the memory of his unceremonious discharge grated, as it always did. "Anais paid my freight, so she considered me hers. And I went along until, well." He met Jani's eye, looked away, then sat up straighter as the tram eased to a stop. "End of the line. Everyone's getting off."

"There's still one more stop." Jani pressed a pad on the arm of her seat, then tapped in a code she had found on the tramline information site. The doors closed, and the tram exited the main concourse and entered a transparent tunnel that ran along the outside of the station. The viewports filled with the blinking lights of docked spacecraft and cargo rafts, the flicker of buoys and guide beacons. Sprays of stars, and the faint reflected light of New Indies' moon.

Then, as the tram continued along its arc, another concourse came into view.

Lucien stilled. "Are we going where I think we're going?"

Jani nodded, eventually. "Yeah."

"Well." Lucien blew out a breath. "This should be interesting."

Chapter Twenty-Nine

Humans who wished to ship goods on Haárin craft worked with official liaison offices overseen by multiple ministries tasked with ensuring that no militarily or commercially sensitive materials or information were involved. Those offices made the actual shipping arrangements, eliminating the need for direct human-idomeni contact between shippers and ships' crews.

However, at Commonwealth stations like Padishah and Elyas, where the Haárin docks were located in separate wings easily reachable on foot, simple curiosity drove humans and Haárin to venture into one another's territories. Most interactions consisted of mispronounced greetings and halting attempts at conversation, translators at the ready, which often ended in confusion on both sides. But, every so often, an acquaintanceship would bloom. Gifts of food, clothing, or artwork would be exchanged, and with every such connection the interface blurred just a little more.

But hard boundaries existed at some stations, usually for structural reasons. New Indies Station, as one of the oldest and largest, had long ago reached the limit of the number of docks that could safely be serviced via the main concourse, so when the Haárin trade associations petitioned for slots, they needed to settle for the overflow shipping annex on the opposite end of the station. No problem when it came to loading cargo—that's what the rafts were for—but it made those myriad incidental interactions much less likely. Jani had seen no Haárin wandering along the human walkways to gape at the sensory overload of video advertisements and hologram displays, the bustle and yammer of the crowds. As the tram approached the first of the platforms in the annex, she could see no humans jammed in a gymnasium entry to watch the balletic fencing of an à lérine training bout, or standing in a games room pondering in silence as they tried to decode the myriad rules and subtle strategies of advanced pattern stone matches.

So quiet. She stepped off the tram and entered a cathedral-like expanse decorated in the Pathenrau style, abstract shapes in shades of green and blue. She felt odd, displaced, as though she had entered the main concourse at Rauta Shèràa station and not an add-on to a human facility.

That feeling intensified when she entered an environment calibrated for idomeni comfort. It washed over her like the breeze off the Bay of Siros, brushed her face like a caress. She took one deep breath, another—her shoulders relaxed and clenched fingers uncurled as the chill that had gripped her since she left Thalassa eased its hold.

"I'm glad these things have cooling cells." Lucien drew alongside, helmet tucked under his arm, and undid the neck of his coverall. "I suppose you're in heaven now." He hesitated as a trio of Haárin, a female and two males, strode past, their steps slowing as they examined the new arrivals. "I believe you've been ID'd."

Jani took in the Haárins' shorter stature and darker skin tones. "Pathenrau." She swore under her breath. "My Pathenrau Haárin stinks." She headed towards them, left hand at waist level, palm-up, a gesture she hoped indicated a need for help, as she struggled to recall that language's versions of common phrases. "Glories of this day and time. I most seek Departures."

One of the group, a female dressed in billowy purple and yellow, stepped forward. "For which station?" She had taken a style direction opposite most Haárin females, cropping her black hair into a feathery skullcap rather than leaving it long and loose or lightly bound.

"Elyas."

"You wish passage?"

Out of habit, Jani made a quick slashing motion with her left hand. A mild negative in Vynshà Haárin; she hoped like hell it meant the same in Pathenrau Haárin. "I have something I most wish to send."

"Ná Kièrshia." One of the males, the tallest and most traditionally attired of the three, spoke in lightly accented Vynshà Haárin. "You speak to ná Dila Serai. I am ní Jero Bes—" He nodded towards the second male. "—and he is ní Zal Karon." He pointed down the concourse. "You will accompany." He wore a shirt and trousers in soft shades of green, and had braided his hair in a traditional breeder's fringe. In contrast, ní Zal wore black, an unusual choice for any idomeni regardless of age or sect, and had shaved one side of his head and bound the hair on the other side in a shoulder-length ponytail.

Ná Dila led the way. "The time of Vynshà is past." She glanced over her shoulder at Jani, meeting her eye for the barest instant before facing front. "You must learn Pathenrau now."

Jani looked back at Lucien, who sucked in his lips and fell in behind her.

"You know Feyó sent out a call to all Haárin to be on the lookout." He whispered in rapid-fire French. "She has informers here. One of them will spot you eventually."

"By the time any message reaches her, I'll be on my way to Niall."

"What if she ordered them to detain you."

"Whether they would obey depends on how much influence she has beyond Elyas. If it happens, I'll deal with it." Jani felt a subtle shift in the air as they entered the concourse proper and came into view of more Haárin. Most paused to watch them pass, then returned to whatever they had been doing. But a few followed, crowding close enough to force Lucien to pick up his pace.

"Here we go." Lucien swung his helmet like a bucket to keep from being jostled. "I'm having flashbacks to our trip to Shèrá. No sermons this time, okay?"

"It wasn't a bloody sermon." Jani lowered her voice when Dila shot her another hard glance. "I told stories about Tsecha."

They passed the entry to a gymnasium just as several Haárin emerged, blade rolls tucked under their arms. One of them, a female whose bare arms bore à lérine scars crosshatching from wrists to past her elbows, called out "ná Kièrshia!" and broke into a trot until she caught up to the growing throng. Her cry carried—a beat later, Haárin appeared in doorways of other gymnasiums, games rooms, message centers. Most remained in place, but individuals and small groups broke away and joined what had become a fair-sized crowd.

Jani glanced up towards the ceiling and saw observer bugs flit overhead, blinking like fireflies in the night. Recording. Transmitting.

"Bet Wuntoi sees this within hours." Lucien banged his helmet against his thigh for emphasis. "It should thrill him no end."

"I doubt he cares." Jani shook her head. "He has too many other things to worry about."

"Don't think for a minute that you're not one of them."

Before Jani could reply, they rounded a corner and came to an immense walkway lined on both sides with corridors; at the head of each turn-off, a lightboard displayed scrolling idomeni script. Vessel designations. Enclave registries. Departure times.

"Those who travel to the Elyan station are docked at these gates." Dila waved a hand towards the corridors on their right.

This time, Jani stuck with a simple human nod of thanks, then headed for the nearest lightboard and read the first few entries. *Pathenrau.* But she knew enough of the written language to pick out sect designations and departure times, and had spotted a likely candidate when she sensed movement at her shoulder and turned to find Dila studying her.

"It is Pathenrau." Dila tilted her head in question. "The language you cannot speak."

"Yes. I read it well enough that I can understand these schedules." Jani edged closer to the board, and hoped she had managed to keep the irritation out of her voice. When dealing with idomeni of any status, one had to accept the constant poking, the possible challenge of every word and action. But in the female's tone, she detected something else, the same inflections she had heard during her time at the Academy. That as humanish or even part humanish, she lacked. She was deficient. She could not possibly understand. "I can recognize some of the Vynshà ships."

"Those who are anathema." Dila's shoulders rounded slightly, a posture that conveyed determination to push the point rather than outright anger.

But Jani also saw the set of the female's jaw, the more direct gaze, which combined indicated intensity of feeling that so often led to challenge, the declaration of esteemed enemies followed by an à lérine bout to seal the deal. She struggled to keep her own back straight, felt her heart pound, hard and slow as the thump of a fist. "I do not consider them such."

"Even though they killed ní Tsecha?"

Jani sensed movement behind her, heard the odd footfall, and looked back. The crowd had moved closer, those in back pushing towards the front while those in front struggled to hold their places. But all so quietly, the only sound the soft slide of boot soles across the floor. "One killed ní Tsecha. Another gave the order to do so. I killed them both. It is done."

Dila bared her teeth. "Such is not for you to decide."

"Nor is it for you to decide for me." Jani's voice rasped, deepened. "The Samvasta Vynshà are and always will be most as Haárin." She quieted, continued to meet Dila's eye, the Haárin as still as a frieze, the only sounds the machine noise of rolling walkways.

Finally, after a few long moments, Dila's companions detached from the crowd. Jero beckoned to Dila, then looked towards Jani and inclined his head. Dila backed away for several steps before turning, shoulders still rounded. Black-clad Zal lagged behind, meeting Jani's eye, expression unreadable, before following the pair across the corridor and into one of the message rooms. The rest of the Haárin remained where they were, watching Jani as she tried to concentrate on the departures board, blood pounding in her ears, hands clenching and unclenching.

"Just one time, I would like to see you not go out of your way to make it harder." Lucien moved in next to her, a wall between her and the unmoving crowd. "Just one time."

"I can't deny the Samvasta Vynshà and you know it." Jani replied in rapid Acadian French, which earned her the usual plea to slow down. "It isn't just because there are eyes and ears everywhere and word would get out and how could I face any of them after that?" The soft tones of her native language calmed her, like her mother's comforting touch. "I'm responsible for their existence."

"You had plenty of help. Wuntoi could've told you to go to hell when you made your pitch to let them live, but he understood enough about humans to know how the mass slaughter of an entire sect might look on our vid displays." Lucien glanced back at the Haárin, who had yet to disperse. "You're not the alpha and omega, you know. Everything that happens isn't your fault."

"I never said it was." Jani watched the curves and whorls of Pathenrau script flow past, waiting for the departure she had spotted before Dila's interruption. "That one." She trotted down the corridor, leaving Lucien to hurry after her, grousing all the while.

By the time they reached the ship in question, a Sìah freighter bearing supplies for the Elyan Haárin enclave, the crew had made their final flight check and begun boarding. That didn't leave much time for discussion, but luckily, Jani and the engineering dominant had a mutual friend.

"Ná Kièrshia." The female, garbed in every shade of yellow imaginable, bared her teeth. "I am ná Bein Diné, and I bear word from ní Dathim. He said that if I should encounter you, I should offer you his glories of the day and tell you that he is most hopeful of your return."

Jani gestured thanks, tried and failed to shake a pang of guilt.

Feyó must be giving him hell. She would assume that he knew what her hybrid suborn planned and had failed to pass that information along, which would be treated as serious dereliction of duty. "If you see him, you must convey my offering of the same." She dug the package out of her bag and started to hand it over, then hesitated as it hit her that this would be the first time since her Service years that she traveled without her scanpack.

She stood still and quiet until Lucien's nudge brought her back to the present. She gave ná Bein the package, then dug through her bag for something to close the transaction. Payment wasn't the issue since there was no official Shèráin currency. Over time, dealings between humans and idomeni had evolved into complex manipulations of comdollars and "resource equivalents," but those between idomeni did not involve money or any other form of legal tender. Small tokens, however, were considered appropriate. After some searching, Jani freed the last of her Jaki Pax, which were accepted eagerly and with profuse thanks. Moments later, the crew headed down the gangplank, the hatch sealing with a hiss.

By the time Jani and Lucien reentered the main concourse, the crowd had thinned to a cluster of stragglers. Mostly Vynshà, judging by their medium coloring and height, their dress the usual blinding mash of hues.

But what struck Jani most was the way they watched her, their fixed gazes following her as one. Not threatening, no. But rapt. Expectant. When she and Lucien walked down the concourse, they followed at a distance, pausing, then resuming walking as they did, like distant shadows.

"Now what?" Lucien squinted at an idomeni wall chron, then shook his head and checked his handheld. "You have six hours remaining on your deadline. You're cutting it close and there are still some things I have to do."

"Yes." Jani stilled, hands in pockets. "Automated stations are open to anyone with a shipping license, human or Haárin. And they're cheap. No docking fees."

Lucien nodded. "That does not follow anything I just said, but I am guessing you have your reasons for saying it."

"They would be the way stations of choice for chronically under-resourced shippers." Jani nodded in the direction of the tagalong group.

"Samvasta Vynshà. Who just heard you stick up for them." Lucien rolled his eyes. "Fine. You made your point. I will never criticize your picking fights with members of the worldskein's ruling sect ever again."

"I didn't pick a fight." Jani turned to the attentive cluster and slipped into the gesture and flow of Vynshà Haárin. "The automated station off New Indies' secondary GateWay. Does anyone know of it?"

Silence for a time. Then one of the males raised his hand. It took Jani a few moments to recognize the action for what it was, imitation of the common human gesture.

"I do not, ná Kièrshia." He straightened as he spoke and pitched his voice higher, both indicators of the greatest regard. "But I know those who do."

Chapter Thirty

Jani and Lucien followed their guide to the Vynshà Haárin's assigned wing. It proved even quieter than the main concourse, and not as well-appointed or equipped. One message room. One games room. No gymnasium. Fewer light-boards with more blank space between the listings of arrivals and departures, which meant not as much business. In its way, it reminded Jani of every low-end dock in which she had ever tried to scrounge a job.

But here and there, she took note of the differences. The schedules and other signage displayed in Vynshà instead of Pathenrau. Traditional artwork, leaves and flowers in pale shades of green and creamy white, framed doorways, while in one short hallway, the lyno flooring had been removed and replaced with mosaic tile that portrayed a flowing stream complete with grassy banks and a grove of flowering vrel trees. In ways large and small, the Vynshà had turned their isolation into a journey back to the recent past, when ní Tsecha Egri still lived and their sect had ruled the worldskein.

Jani listened as the soft tones that flowed 'round her. The first idomeni tongues she learned had been the Laum variants, but she had always felt more at ease with the rhythm and sounds of the Vynshà. A language she spoke daily in Thalassa. Occasionally, the language of her dreams. She felt a sense of place, of belonging, like a calming touch, and drew in a long breath as the weight she had felt since Niall's disappearance and the arrival of that first taunting message eased just a little.

"No observer bugs." Lucien drew alongside. "I'm surprised they can get away with that."

"No one cares enough to check." Jani glanced overhead at the clear airspace. "Another advantage to dropping by this end of the Haárin docks."

"You knew?" Lucien frowned. "You never told me."

"Whenever I try to tell you what Dieter tells me, you roll your eyes and walk away."

"He kidnapped you."

"And you were twice sent to kill me. Now you're both working for me. Life's funny, isn't it?" Jani turned to Lucien in time to catch his scowl, then detected movement out of the corner of her eye. Her Vynshà guide, hands raised with palms turned in, fingers curved. A beckoning gesture.

"Ná Aicha Egri knows of the station." He pointed to a female who stood at the opening to one of the gangway access corridors, a still figure clad in orange and blue, shoulder-length brown hair trimmed in a face-framing bob.

Jani drew closer, right hand held waist-high and curved in question. "Egri? You shared skein with ní Tsecha?"

The female nodded. "Through our house fathers." She met Jani's eye, a steady amber gaze. "I spoke with him only once, so many seasons ago. His braiding ceremony, in celebration of his first breeding." She pointed to one of the display screens. "I watched here as you released his soul at Knevçet Shèràa, then honored the souls of the Laum you killed." She eyed Jani's clothing. "You are no longer a priest?"

I never was. Jani gestured agreement. "I am that which I am."

"Ná Kièrshia." Aicha bared her teeth, then turned and headed down the corridor. "Come."

Jani followed, Lucien at her heels and their escort bringing up the rear. As they neared the gangway leading into the Haárin ship, she caught a cinnamon-like whiff that reminded her of one of the warm spiced tisanes that Vynshà often served with meals. That memory was confirmed when she crossed the threshold into the craft and a male with a shaved head handed her one from a tray filled with steaming cups.

Lucien accepted his own drink with a fairly accurate Vynshà gesture of thanks. "What is this?" He mumbled in French. "This never happened at any of the enclaves."

"I think it's a 'welcome aboard' treat. Like an hors d'oeuvre or a glass of champagne." Jani sipped and held back a cough as the sensation of peppery heat bloomed, then intensified. Bearable, even pleasant. *To me.*

Lucien took a tentative sampling, then stilled before swallowing hard. "Did I just poison myself?"

"No." Jani followed Aicha down a short tunnel-like walkway that led to the nav deck, where one male set out low seats while two females activated a visualization table. "You may feel a little heartburn later."

"Will I feel a burn anywhere else?" Lucien shook his head before Jani could answer. "They like to test. Is this a test?"

"Possibly."

"Great. Can I test back?"

"No."

"Hardly seems fair." Lucien swirled his cup, tossed down the rest of the brew, then vented a long, slow exhale. "Did I pass?"

Jani tried to read his expression, but saw only his watering eyes and heat-reddened mouth. "What are you doing?"

"Just trying to get through this day." As the tray-bearing male walked past, Lucien grabbed a second filled cup, then stepped over to the visualization table and studied the 3-D views of the station as they rotated and spun.

Jani edged closer and listened to his questioning of the two females. *Correct verb forms.* His postures and gestures could have used some adjusting, but he erred on the side of more formal and respectful and judging from the females' reception, they didn't take offense. "Do you need me to translate anything?"

"No. I'm good." Lucien embellished his reply with a submissive head tilt that under different circumstances would have earned him an elbow in the ribs.

"Okay." Jani stepped away and wandered about the deck as Vynshà Haárin scurried in and out. Some had changed clothes, exchanging ship coveralls or typically clashing color combinations for more formal trousers, tunics, and overrobes in quiet shades of sand and brown. One of the males entered bearing yet another tray of tisanes, and the spicy aromas that filled the air, combined with the ebb and flow of the language and the faint sweet hint of idomeni body odor, triggered memories of those first months at the Academy, when every new experience had filled her with uncertainty and fear of making some dreadful cross-cultural error.

School's over. I'll be fine. Jani watched as Lucien accepted a third cup, then said something to one of the females that earned a bark of laughter that held more appreciation than typical idomeni derision over a humanish attempting to speak their language. He seemed at ease, as though he didn't need to remember what to do or say because the responses came automatically, as though he stood on a Family ship and conversed in his native language with a Family crew member. *I shouldn't be surprised. I see him speak with Thalassan Haárin all the time.* But this was an idomeni ship, and Lucien was doing more than communicating. *He's fitting in.* It was admirable. Sweet, in an odd way, but also unexpected. Disconcerting.

He's planning something. And Jani felt she knew what it was. She rejoined him, nudged him in the side, and leaned close. "No."

Lucien's eyes widened—he looked the very image of innocence. "I don't know what—"

"You are not getting them involved in this."

"They already are."

Jani pulled him away from the table. "I'm a hybrid—Feyó has the authority to kick my ass and she no doubt will, but when it comes to Commonwealth-idomeni relations, I'm a nonentity. All hybrids are nonentities. We're not included in any treaties or agreements." She pointed towards the Haárin. "You get them involved in something the ramifications of which they may not understand, it's a political incident that rattles all the way up to Cabinet Row and the Oligarchy. They're already struggling. You want to make it worse?"

"So why are we even here?"

"We're here because I'd like to see where I'm going. What else is in that station." Jani glanced at the females at the table, who were making a bad job of pretending not to eavesdrop, and lowered her voice. "Once I make sure Niall is safe, I'll return with my tail between my legs and throw myself on Feyó's mercy. She'll sentence me to spend the rest of my life sorting seeds in the ag sheds, and I'll go back to working under her detection limits like I've been doing for the past year." She became aware of stillness, and looked around to find Haárin ringing the deck in straight-backed silence, watching her. "But with more information." She walked to one of the chairs. "Time to sit."

"I'd prefer to stay here." Lucien remained by the visualization table.

Jani slipped into Acadian French. "It's an honor to be offered a seat."

"But the honor is for you." Lucien replied in Vynshà Haárin as he drew up straight as a buck Spacer in his first inspection. "That means I should stand, too." He approached one of the females and held his hands palms facing up in gratitude as she stepped aside to allow him room.

Jani stared at the back of Lucien's head, willing him to turn and face her so she could ask what the hell he was up to. But before her exercise in mind control could take effect, Ná Aicha entered with an older male.

"This is ní Sha Qoi, my...co-pilot." Aicha bared her teeth as she uttered the humanish term for navigation suborn. "He performed repairs on this vessel at the station three sun cycles ago."

"New Indies sun cycles?" When Aicha nodded affirmation, Jani did a quick conversion of New Indiesian day length to Common hours. *Two and a half Common days, more or less. Niall would've been there.* She glanced at the deck timeform, converted to the numbers of hours she had left before she needed to contact Niall's captors, bit back the questions that tumbled from all directions. How many humanish craft in the docks? How many humanish did Qoi see? Was one of them a male with a facial scar? Their hosts had allowed her and Lucien over a line seldom if ever crossed by those outside the worldskein. They needed to tell their tale in their own way, at their own pace.

Ní Qoi took his place beside the table. He proved short for a Vynshà, the top of his shorn head barely reaching Aicha's shoulder. "We call this station, how do you say?" His accent and rhythm rendered the common English sentence into a single word barbed with hard Vynshà consonants. He tugged at the loop of cloth he wore like a scarf, a humanish neckpiece in lime green that stood out like an illumin against his dull brown tunic. "Rat. Hole."

"'Agash déla.'" Lucien hit all the correct tones, so that his response sounded like a question instead of a correction.

"Infested place. Yes." Qoi looked from Lucien to Jani, that at Aicha, who shrugged. "It is a humanish facility," he continued in Vynshà Haárin. "Thus our access is limited." He paused, looked once again at Jani and Lucien in turn, then bared his teeth before continuing. "They allow us a section of the completely automated side." He called up a 3-D rendering of the station. "There are hard barriers here, here, and here—" He pointed to areas shaded in solid colors. "—designed to cut us off from the rest of the facility." He stood back, then once again bared his teeth, milking the moment. "They have failed to do so."

Jani hid a smile. While by idomeni standards the Haárin were "most as disordered," humans found them nearly as rigid as their bornsect dominants. *Except they found a way around the barriers.* Because they needed parts. Because they wanted to see what was on the other side. *Because they were pissed.*

As if on cue, Qoi pointed to the middle barrier, which was conveniently located at the end of a corridor. "There is an opening here. It is one we made. Humanish have not yet found it, for we have inserted that which would notify us of such."

Lucien gestured in question. "They could have found a monitoring device and left it in place to catch you in the act."

Qoi gave a negating flick of the hand. "We were of the military skein. We have—" He hesitated, then offered a humanish shrug. "We have."

Lucien turned to Jani, brow arched. "A military grade com code?" he asked in English.

Jani caught the first rounding of Qoi's upper back. "I most believe, and truly, that we should respect that." She shot Lucien a warning glance. Once they had come out the other side of the task at hand, he could fiddle with any code he wanted, but for now they both needed to defer to their hosts. She waited until the Haárin's shoulders straightened. "You have explored the station when no humanish were present. Which rooms could hold more than half a dozen?"

"Humanish or idomeni?" Qoi held up his hand to the middle of his chest. "Many humanish are smaller. More would fit." He counted on his fingers. "Three such rooms. One must have a wall removed in order to serve as such."

Jani tried to match Qoi's descriptions to the 3-D visualizations, but being seated and on the opposite side of the room didn't make for the best view. She rose and walked nearer the table, circling and gauging even as she tried to maintain a respectful distance, until finally she admitted defeat and wedged in beside Lucien. So much for protocol. "Where are the rooms in relation to the airlocks?"

"Well away." Qoi pointed to one end of the station, where the thicker walls and safety barriers shown milky white slashed with yellow. "The airlocks are located in the same wing as the docks. The structure is stronger there."

"Could the same number fit in an airlock antechamber?"

Qoi paused, then shook his head. "Only one or two."

"Monitoring equipment was probably stripped ages ago. Assuming it was installed at all. I suppose they could stick a flea-cam in there with him." Jani saw the questioning looks and postures of the idomeni, then glanced sidelong at Lucien, who kept his gaze fixed on the station image. "I expect them to threaten my friend when I am there by putting him in an airlock." She felt the reflexive curving of her shoulders, the flash of anger like a welding arc. "They would do so to ensure I do that which they wish. They would want me to see such." But first, she could ask to see Niall in person to assess his condition, say whatever was necessary to get him in the same room. *Then we go from there.* They had both survived similar situations over the years, gotten by on wits, bullshit, and the occasional shooter blast. *Accept the fact that you'll bleed.* She just needed to ensure that her opponent bled more. "Do you store any supplies on the automated side?"

Qoi's eyes narrowed, gold slits against gold skin. "Supplies, ná Kiershia?"

Jani drew in a long breath. "Weapons." She felt the change in the air, the collective stillness, as the sound of the word settled and the ramifications of any response scrolled through minds that struggled to balance their desire to help her against the need to protect their secrets.

But of course they would stash weapons at the station. They transported cargo, and because of their status they didn't receive the protections that the other Haárin shipping groups did. The threats of piracy from human smuggler gangs and harassment from other Haárin were always present.

But if word got out that idomeni cached weapons in Commonwealth stations, reactionaries on both sides would twist every detail.

"I cannot carry my own weapons. I will be searched." Jani held out her hands, palms up, in pleading. "I have seen humanish with idomeni shooters and blades. I would say I found them. And since the kidnappers are criminals, they would not be believed if they denied knowing of them."

Aicha focused on a point over Jani's left shoulder. "If we hid such as you seek, we would store them as we did our monitors. But access is coded to us and would do you no good."

"Such codes can be disabled from a distance."

Everyone turned towards the deck entry, where a tall, black-clad figure stood within.

Jani felt a tremor of unease. *One of the Pathenrau Haárin.* Ní Zal, the young silent one, his attire even more startling in the bright confines of the ship than it had been out on the concourse.

No one spoke for a few moments. Then Aicha emitted a sigh that reminded Jani of all those times her mother had sat her down to *have a talk.*

"We have asked you not to disable our alarms before entering, ní Zal." Aicha placed a hand on Qoi's arm, and kept it there until the male straightened his rounded shoulders.

Zal held out his hands palms up in supplication, and waited for Aicha's nod before entering the deck. "The shielding of the automated stations is most inadequate, if not nonexistent. To establish controls over the extant systems is quite possible."

"Ní Zal." The heightened pitch of Qoi's voice brought to mind clenched teeth and a tightened throat. "We are most grateful for your attendance." A long pause, followed by finger drumming on the edge of the visualization table. "Ní Zal is most expert in communications systems."

Lucien studied the new arrival, who responded by looking him directly in the eye. "Idomeni systems." When Zal shrugged, his tone sharpened. "Humanish systems?" Another shrug. "Secure systems?"

Zal bared his teeth, then walked to the visualization table and circled it, stopping every few steps to wedge between bodies and touch one of the station's highlighted control panels. "I can type to you." He pointed to Jani. "You look as ido enough. I may not need to recode."

Jani met his stare until he resumed his circuit of the table. *So helpful.* And at just the right time, too. She had heard no rumors of Wuntoi setting agents among the Haárin, but there was always a first time and the Chief Oligarch was by all accounts a studier of humanish histories and a quick learner.

"If those who hold your friend have ships docked at this station, I can monitor their communications. All I must do is pull the ship code strings." Zal wiggled his fingers like a musician warming up. "Once I have entered those systems I can install trackers and continue to monitor."

Lucien took a step back from the table, arms folded. "You can merge and slipstream undetected?" He remained still and silent for a long beat after Zal's answering nod. "Can you exert control over transmissions? Override?"

Zal started to speak, then stopped. For the first time, his air of confidence faltered, the slightest of deflations. "I can monitor. Alteration is...different."

"Yes, it is." Lucien glanced at Jani, then at his timepiece. "Do you have what you need?"

Jani made one last pass over the station layout, sure in the knowledge that whatever she learned now, it wouldn't be enough. "As long as I know there are weapons and that I can get to them." She looked from Aicha to Zal, waited for their affirmative nods. "Do you need to scan or sample me?" Before she finished speaking, another of Aicha's crew approached her bearing a bioscanner—she held out her right hand, felt the warm tingle as nanodots withdrew microscopic samples of skin. The eyescan proved noninvasive—blinding flashes in both eyes. As she blinked away the afterimages, she felt a tug on her arm.

"Now I think you should head back. Sleep, if you can." Lucien took Jani by the elbow and steered her away from the table. "Change clothes."

Jani started to argue, then looked down at her rumpled coverall and realized that yes, appearance mattered. She needed to project confidence balanced with the realization that she needed to deal, and looking like she had just been rolled in an alley definitely did not hit those marks.

She extracted herself from Lucien's grip and turned back to the others. "I must leave now." She pitched her voice higher as a sign of respect. "I am most grateful, and truly, for your assistance." She stood up straight and raised her chin, adding an extra layer of gratitude. "Some of you know of Colonel Pierce. That he is my friend. We seek to save our friends." She struggled to find words as the realization that zero hour approached head-on at speed sent a shudder down her spine. "We do that which we do." She turned and walked to the entry, then waited for Lucien to catch her up.

"Your Vynshà Haárin is really good." She looked over his shoulder towards the vis table in time to catch Zal glance in their direction before fixing on the rotating station image.

"I had a lot of practice." Lucien sniffed. "That year you abandoned me in Chicago, I spent most of my off time at the enclave. I thought it might come in handy someday."

"Hmm." Jani paused as memories of that time flashed. She and John, together again. The heady sense of purpose as the enclave grew and grew. *Only a year and so much changed.* She forced herself back to the present and more immediate problems. "What are you up to?"

"Learning as much about that station as possible. Because I'm going to come in after you."

"I would really like to meet this group you've assembled."

Lucien took a step forward, nudging Jani ever so gently into the passageway. "Contact me before you notify Niall's hosts."

Jani planted herself so that her boot heels squeaked against the flooring when Lucien bumped her. "You're planning something."

"I'm gathering information. You're not the only one going into this blind. I'd at least like to get an idea whether it's day or night." Lucien leaned close and spoke in her ear. "You're thinking that you and Niall—who isn't in prime physical shape to begin with and who has likely not received the greatest of care—can somehow overpower a hardened gang that outnumbers you at least five to one and then beat it to the Haárin side of the station to wait for rescue." He straightened, gaze steady and jaw set.

That's because Niall will have prepared the way. Jani held the thought like a favorite prayer. "As I believe I've mentioned, I have been in similar situations in the past."

"I know. But as I keep trying to tell you, you can't be that person anymore." Lucien nodded towards the Haárin. "I'll finish up here and meet you on the human side."

"Remember what I told you about politics. Me going off half-cocked is a day ending in Y. You have the sort of background that triggers enquiries." In response, Jani received a sigh, a nod, and a second nudge into the passageway. Before she could say more, Lucien turned and reentered the deck. She edged back towards the entry in time to see him walk to the table and wedge in next to Zal, who caught sight of her and jogged his new neighbor with his elbow. Lucien looked up, but before he could react, Jani held up her hands in surrender and departed.

The return trip to the human end of the station proved less eventful than her arrival. A few head bows from passing Vynshà. Curious glances from those of other sects. The only other human she encountered, a staffer studded with com links and carrying a portable workstation, wound up sharing her tram car. The woman took a seat at the opposite end and regarded Jani with narrowed eyes in between rapid-fire conversations in a number of languages.

Jani hugged her bag, empty now but for her dummy scanpack. She waited for the staffer to depart before exiting the tram, and entered the human concourse to find Lucien's friends from station security waiting for her with the message that Ian needed to see her immediately.

Chapter Thirty-One

Jani expected her escort to ferry her upstairs to Ian's office. Instead, they led her down a narrow corridor off the main concourse and through a set of scratched and battered double doors that opened onto a nondescript hallway. White walls. Bare composite flooring. At the far end, another set of doors.

More memories from her years on the run returned. The sharp odor of battery hyperacid. The hum of skim dollies and lift mechs. *A loading dock.* She passed through the second set of doors and entered a hive world lit by glaring ceiling illumination and flashing safety lights. She immediately checked the floor for the painted path that those without proper gear needed to stick to, and barely avoided colliding with a doc tech who cut in front of her, recording board in hand, attention focused on the chatter streaming in through his comlink.

She found Ian standing by a stack of crates in deep conversation with John Shroud, who spotted her first and jerked his head in her direction. Ian's shoulders sagged—he turned and started towards her. John met her eye for the barest moment, then headed in the opposite direction, disappearing behind a wall of shipping containers.

"You okay?" Ian slowed his approach. "You look shaken."

"I spent whole chunks of my life in places like this." Jani scooted aside as a loader veered too close, a move that earned the operator a glare from Ian. "Even back in Thalassa, I'll be walking through one of the warehouses and it hits me. Not the best memories." She hugged herself. "What's up?"

Ian led her to a quiet corner. "Incoming is picking up coded chatter. They can't crack it. We don't know if it's Service, a ministry, or Family." The harsh lighting washed the life from his skin, leaving it greyed, dulled. "All they can tell is that there's more than one ship, and they'll be here in twelve hours."

Jani looked past him, and spotted her and Lucien's gear piled atop a skimdolly. "You need us gone."

Ian stared down at his hands. "We won't know exactly who they are until they arrive, and I can't take any chances. I truly am sorry."

Jani nodded. "I will need to access this side of the station when I hear from whoever's holding Niall."

"I know. But I assume it will be one of the gamier areas, in which case who will know? As I learned from someone recently, despite our best efforts monitoring is spotty in some parts of this station, if not totally nonexistent." Ian tried to smile, but the attempt soon faded. "You've been to the Haárin side."

"I needed to contact someone." Jani held out her hand. "You've helped me more than you realize. I do know the risks you've taken, and I thank you."

Ian clasped her hand in both of his and squeezed. "After the dust settles—"

"Certain discussions will continue." Jani waited until he departed the dock, then gathered the bags. She bid the toolbag farewell, stuffed it into an empty crate, and moved the dummy scanpack to her duffel. Then she slung one bag over each shoulder, but while neither was heavy their mismatched sizes made walking a challenge. She tried a few different options before settling for leaving Lucien's larger bag on one shoulder and carrying hers by hand. That matter settled, she headed into the depths of the staging area and scanned the crate-lined rows until she spotted the familiar pale head.

John kept his gaze fixed on the portable workstation held by a white-coated subordinate. "I assume you've been apprised of the state of things." He flicked through a series of pages and muttered under his breath, then shook his head and motioned for the staffer to leave.

Jani waited until the underling bustled off. "You're bugging out, too? Why?"

John met her eye for a moment, then looked away. "Ian's a good friend. And he's in a tight spot. He's getting pressured by his parents. And they're getting pressured by the Nawars. He gets caught acting out of line, they could lose everything."

"And he has been acting out of line." Jani let the bags slip to the floor and leaned against a crate that had been labeled *Cafeteria Supplies* and no doubt contained everything but. "What does that have to do with you? You're trying to develop a hybrid 'pack. Chicago would love nothing better."

John stared into the distance for a time. Then he shoved his hands in his pockets, strolled a crooked line to the other side of the aisle and slumped against some shelving. "You're not the only one who lost their license because they hybridized."

Oh. Jani hesitated, then shrugged. "You don't need it to do research." That earned her a hard look. "Okay, you treated me, but that shouldn't matter."

"And Pascal. And then there was the measles outbreak Ian said he told you about."

"That's ridiculous. Your record's impeccable."

"Was impeccable." John started to speak. Stopped. Then came a grim smile. "Let's just say I never realized how many people relished the thought of me twisting in the wind. If they can use me to harm Ian, so much the better."

Jani started to offer encouraging words, then paused. This was John, after all. The list of rivals and enemies probably filled both sides of several legal-size pages in very small font. "Can Val help?"

John huffed. "He's got his hands full hanging onto what's left of his cut of Neoclona. Chicago has him on tracker trace. He can't take a piss without them knowing where and how much. And Eamon is undercutting him every chance he gets. Dreaming of the day he finally owns it all." He grew quiet. Flexed one hand, then formed a fist. "I'm waiting."

"For what?"

"The 'I told you so's.'"

"What would be the point?" Jani worked her shoulders, tried yet again to loosen the knot that had set up permanent camp at the base of her neck. She had no time for the professional travails of erstwhile lovers, but Rudo's counsel rattled in the back of her mind along with the irritating fact that however much John Shroud had upended her life and infuriated her in general, she still cared about him. "So what will you do?"

"We've been through this drill before." John stifled a yawn, and rubbed his eyes with the balls of his hands. "Resident staff will move equipment downstairs and scatter it around various facilities. Work can continue to an extent. After the smoke clears, we'll move it back up here and reassemble."

"What will *you* do?"

John stilled, then looked off to the side. "I have places I can go."

Jani nodded, eventually. All this to avoid Thalassa. *To avoid me.* She straightened and hoisted the bags, then glanced at John to find him watching her.

"You're heading out."

"Yeah. Waiting for Lucien to do some prep work. We're assuming whoever's supposed to meet me is nearby. As soon as I let them know I have the docs, they'll contact me and I'll be gone." Jani waited for a reply, met lengthening silence instead. "What?"

John's gaze took on a familiar cast. Cool. Assessing. Medical. "When did you sleep last?"

"Yesterday. Last night." Jani checked one of the wall clocks, and counted backwards. "Day before?"

"Unconscious doesn't count." A grumbling sigh. "God knows what you're running on at this point." Another huff. "Sheer bloody-mindedness." John started to say more, then stopped and shook his head. "I'm not even going to ask." He beckoned for Jani to follow and headed down the narrow aisle. "These will probably taste like shredded parchment to you now—" He popped the lid off one of the smaller crates, rummaged, then pulled out a poly sack bearing the Neoclona caduceus and handed it to her. "—but at least it's calories."

Jani looked inside the sack and caught a whiff of chocolate. "Meal bars? I remember these. Thanks." She stuffed them into her bag, then glanced at the crate interior just as John reset the lid. "Wait a minute." She pushed the lid aside. "You're—" She reached in and pulled out several familiar-looking packets. "Hotter Than Hot Pepper.'" She looked at John to find him struggling to suppress a grin and failing. "You're Jaki? You hate being called Jack, Jacky, whatever—"

"I know—"

"—like, fistfight hate. I recall dragging you off Eamon once when he wouldn't stop."

"What better name?" John shrugged. "Who would associate it with me?"

Jani read one of the packets until she found the company information, including the location. "Based on Felix?"

"It's a shell company. I don't have anything going on there, so no reason to visit and risk some enterprising reporter making the connection." His smile faded. "Things seem to go more smoothly if I don't appear to be involved. Ian knows. A few others. I would appreciate—"

Before John could finish, Jani mimed locking her lips. "Your secret is safe." She added the packets to her bag, but as she started to leave she saw John raise his hand.

"Milk." He held up thumb and forefinger a few centimeters apart. "Just a small glass. Neutralizes the heat."

Jani felt her face warm. *Just his way of acknowledging Lucien.*

And letting her know that he had reason to look into a remedy himself. *It's been a year, John. I didn't think you'd joined a monastery.* "Good to know." She nodded thanks and headed back the way she had come, felt the pressure of a stare, and looked back to find John standing still as shadow.

"This is dangerous, isn't it?" His mouth moved soundlessly for a moment. Then he took a labeler from the top of a nearby crate, and turned it over and over. Something to look at that wasn't her. "You'll be careful."

Jani smiled apology. "No. The only way to learn anything worth a damn is to be the opposite of careful." She resumed walking. "If I live through this, maybe we should talk." She listened for a reply even though she knew John wouldn't respond. Felt his gaze follow her until she walked around the corner and out of his sight.

———

On the way to the station tram, Jani ducked into an empty vend alcove and scanned both bags, then checked for any new tears, nicks, or odd bumps, indications that they had been loaded with trackers or otherwise tampered with. She found, to her surprise, that Lucien had left behind a number of monitoring devices of various types, from simple scanners to systems infiltrators. *Probably didn't think they'd make a difference.* They'd have been worthless in the busier sections of New Indies—the facility's immunity network would've detected and destroyed them. But in the *gamier areas*, as Ian called them?

When it comes time for me to leave, Lucien will toss up a few to do recon. If her escort disabled them, he would send her out with something at her back that would try to scan faces or snatch any other information before said escort disabled them as well. *Or just got fed up and shot me.* For the first time in a long while, Jani felt the old fear like a cold finger tracing down her spine. How many times had she walked into a deteriorating situation without knowing how or even if she would land? Stood at the cliff's edge, looked down, saw only endless nothing, and yet had no choice but to take that final step?

The thought that she might not survive this adventure had risen to the surface more and more over the last few days, only to be beaten down by more immediate matters. But now it anchored into place with hooks like needles formed from ice. She should've died years before, after all, in a desert on an alien world. In some eternal exchange, a debt lingered, waiting to be paid.

She stuffed the scanner back into a side pocket of her bag, felt a hard lump, hooked it with a finger and pulled it out. It looked at first glance like a chunk of melted plastic — one had to study it for a few moments before the details became apparent. A human male with an elephant's head, seated upon a cushion, one hand raised in benediction. Her first Ganesh, a prize won in some grammar school contest, the cheap white poly yellowed from age, the surface scuffed and chipped from years of rattling around in pockets and sling bags. Her mother had found it in Jani's old bedroom and sent it to her along with a missive that she had been following the news on ChanNet and thought her daughter might need it.

Lord Ganesh. *God of Wisdom.* Remover of Obstacles. Jani had always prayed to him when she faced a challenge, but what faith she possessed ended there. Jamira Shah Kilian had often tried to impress her beliefs upon her only child, that the soul returned again and again until it reached its height of enlightenment and peace, and that there were other things besides immediate goals worth praying for. Jani wanted to believe it. But she had seen so many lives tossed aside like so much garbage for so long—

Stop it. She shook her head, tucked the figure back in its pocket. Then she stood, hoisted the bags, and headed for the tram.

———

Jani shared the ride to the Haárin docks with yet another human documents staffer, who eyed her as warily as had his colleague. She forced a smile and a nod, received a frown in return, and passed the rest of the trip with her eyes fixed on the passing view.

Not every dexxie loves me. Well, no news there. Despite the fact that the Commonwealth documents system had sprung from that of the idomeni, the two had diverged around the time Jani went into hiding with the similarities becoming fewer and fewer with each passing year. *Idomeni feel humanish broke their system.* Rendered it disordered, practically useless. Humans, meanwhile, considered the idomeni system an overcomplicated maze of useless repetition. *They're not completely wrong.* Thing was, however, the useless repetition made alterations like backdating, forgery, and other forms of chicanery that much more difficult.

Yes, for every Editha who admired her, there was a documents examiner who felt her at best a dinosaur. *And at worst?* A traitor to her profession, to the human race.

Wait until Theo's hybrid 'packs hit the system. They would damn her from one end of the Commonwealth to the other when all their human-based devices crashed into obsolescence overnight.

The tram passed from the lighted concourse through a darkened tunnel. She caught the glint of her jade green eyes in her reflection, and managed a smile.

———

Jani disembarked the tram and double-timed through the Haárin concourse to Aicha's ship. She entered the nav deck to find Lucien standing by the visualization table, deep in conversation with Zal and Aicha—he turned when they fixed on her, then headed towards her while the two Haárin continued their discussion.

"We've been booted." Jani gave Lucien a quick rundown of Ian's situation. "Think it's Service?"

"Or one of the ministries. The Nawars. Random inspection. Who knows?" He pointed to the bags. "Did you pack these?"

"No. They were waiting for me." Jani slipped Lucien's bag off her shoulder and handed it to him along with her own. "I ran a scan. Felt for any implants." In reply, she received a look of professional-grade disdain. "Fine. Do your worst." She watched as Lucien set the bags atop a console, opened all fasteners, and turned pockets inside out. "How are you going to scan them? Your gear isn't any better than mine."

"Let's just say that our new best friends are full of surprises." Lucien held up a device that looked like a stylus dotted with a line of blue pin dot illumins. "And for a change, they're surprises I like."

"They can detect human bugs?" Jani reached for the scanner, but Lucien brushed her hand away.

"Isn't it marvelous?" He inserted the scanner into one pocket of Jani's bag, shot her a cool smile when the device emitted a sharp squeal, and rooted around until he dug out a device that looked like a large grain of sand. "I wonder who left this?"

Damn. "Our gear was in our rooms, unattended. The bags were piled atop a dolly on the main loading dock. I don't know for how long. Anyone could've—"

"Ian."

"We were both unconscious for a while."

"Ian."

"Anyone—"

"He would definitely rat you out to buy himself room to maneuver." Lucien held up the bug to the light and rolled it between his fingertips, like a jeweler examining a gemstone. "You look new." He dug into his coverall pocket, pulled out a small container coated with a silvery scan-blocking material, dropped the bug inside, then tucked it into his own bag and continued scanning. After a few minutes of silence passed, he glanced over at Jani. "You're usually sharper than this. Are you all right? You look—"

"Thoughtful."

"Worried. Second thoughts? Just say so. I'll go along with whatever story you invent."

Jani leaned against an instrument console. "I need to keep going.

I don't know if anything I learn will be enough, but I have to try." She felt Lucien's examining gaze, and deflected it by pulling the gray jumpsuit out of her bag and giving it a shake. "This needs a run through the cleaner."

"It needs more than that." Lucien grimaced. "Is that blood on the sleeve?" His eyes widened. "You were not thinking of wearing that?"

"I can't go like this." Jani tugged at her coverall. "Stumbling in like I just woke up in a cargo hold." She eyed the deck chron. "I need to cross back over to the human side. Go to one of the shops and—"

"You don't have time."

"You said it yourself—I can't wear this."

"This is fact. You are the Kièrshia, and so you must appear."

Jani turned to find Aicha standing in the middle of the deck, arms folded. Another female crew member stood beside her bearing two stacks of folded clothing, multicolored piles that reached past her chin.

Aicha held out her hand to Jani. "You will come."

Jani eyed the array of clashing hues. "I don't—"

"You will come."

Jani glanced at Lucien, who pursed his lips and continued his scanning. Then she looked down at her coverall, nodded, and allowed herself to be ushered off the deck.

What followed took her back to her teenage years and every clothing wrestle with her mother, most of which she lost. She managed to veto a vivid pink shirt and a yellow vest so fierce she would've needed sunshields. That left a variety of greens and blues, which she winnowed down to comparatively sedate medium blue trousers topped with a grey-green wrapshirt threaded with silver. Aicha's assistant dresser sighed and muttered in Vynshà Haárin about boring humanish. That earned her a sharp reprimand from her dominant, who confined herself to a sad shake of her head.

Clothing settled. Time to deal with hair. The straightener Jani had applied had worn off days before—the females took turns tugging at her wavy curls, snapping them like elastic bands. Then Aicha added a comb studded with purple stones and as a final touch, inserted curves of silver wire through the holes in Jani's ears.

Jani winced as the metal rubbed against tender skin. She'd had her ears pierced as a child, but let the holes close when she learned earrings were considered a fair target during Service self-defense training. Her rebuilding and years in hiding followed, during which personal adornment had been the last thing on her mind. Then, earlier that month, on a whim, she'd had her ears repierced, only to remove the tiny posts a few weeks later. The urge to stay on defense, to stay hidden, never remained submerged for long.

"Now you look most as Haárin as you will allow." Aicha stood back while her assistant dragged in a reflective wall panel to serve as a mirror and propped it against a console.

Jani stared. *Not hiding now.* She had worn idomeni garb in the past, priestly overrobes and other items in bland shades of cream and brown that could have found a place in a human's closet. But the mash of color combined with the distinctive flow of idomeni cloth, though sedate by Haárin standards, set this outfit apart from anything she had worn since the holiday saris of her youth. The green of the shirt made her eyes seem brighter and brought out the gold in her skin. The stones in the comb glittered through her hair like stars.

As a finishing touch, Aicha added a slingbag, looping the strap over Jani's head and pulling her arm through like a mother dressing her child.

Jani stroked the bag, made of grey leather with the feel of silk. She had seen ones like it during her time in Rauta Shèràa, carried by propitiators and members of the Oligarch's staff. "Ní Tsecha used one such as this. I remember it."

Aicha gave a human nod. "He did so."

"Then now I am ready, and truly." Jani removed her handheld, the dummy scanpack, and documents from her duffel and tucked them inside, paused, then dug around for the Ganesh figurine, rubbing it and uttering a short prayer before stuffing it in an inner pocket. "Let's go."

Aicha and her aide escorted Jani back to the deck, where Lucien stood at the visualization table together with Zal and the other Haárin. They all turned as she entered.

A few of the Haárin bared their teeth. Zal stood with his hands stuffed in his trouser pockets, an indefinable posture.

Lucien simply stared.

"I'm ready to go." Jani walked up to him, fidgeting all the while. She rubbed her hands together, tugged at a sleeve, then looked up to find him still studying her. "What's wrong?"

Lucien met her eye for a few moments more, then fixed on something above her head. "Nothing." He straightened, nodded. "You look...official." He glanced at the deck chron. "It's time."

"I know." Jani withdrew her handheld from her bag, activated it, entered two words. *Got it.* Then she waited, her finger hovering over the transmit key. Counted backwards...three...two...one...tap, and sent the message that she had the paper.

The response arrived within seconds. A dock. A slip number. A departure time. "They're leaving in twenty minutes—I need to go." She heard voices behind her, and turned to find Aicha's crew had assembled along with ní Zal, whose garb looked like a column of shadow amid the brilliance.

"May Caith and Shiou guide you on your path, ná Kièrshia, so all that is chaos may return to order." Aicha raised her hands above her head, her sleeves sliding down her arms to reveal her à lérine scars. The other Haárin followed suit, sleeves along skin, whispers of cloth like sighs. Even Zal raised his hands to shoulder level. Eventually.

"My thanks to you all." Jani raised her hands above her head as well, which wasn't exactly proper, but made the point she wanted to make. Then she turned and left, her mind racing, Lucien at her heels.

———

They hurried down the concourse towards the tram stop, Jani checking the schedule on each display they passed.

"I'd lose the comb." Lucien plucked it from Jani's hair and made as if to fling it over the railing.

"It would make a good weapon." Jani grabbed it and tucked it back in place.

"And if whoever they've sent is worth a damn, it's the first thing they'll take when they search you."

"And if they're not? Let's not do their job for them, okay?"

"Jani, they're armed and you'd go up against them with a hair accessory?"

"Let them take it."

They arrived at the tram stop to find the platform deserted and a car approaching. Jani bounced on the balls of her feet as she watched it draw near, then pushed through the doors before they opened completely, which sent safety alarms squealing until Lucien backed off long enough to allow the doors to close and reopen on their own.

"You need to settle down." He slid into the seat next to her and leaned close, his voice a whisper even through they were alone. "I remember your stories. You've been in situations like this before."

"And this was how I felt." Jani wiped her sweaty palms on the seat to avoid staining her clothing. "Being Feyó's unwanted stepchild for almost a year wore away my edge. Different sort of pressure." Even her animandroid left hand felt damp. *The medicos thought this was an improvement why?* "I'll be fine." She waited for something to kick in. Chill idomeni focus. Residual augmentation. Anything but this sensation of the ground shifting beneath her feet.

"Still time to back out."

"I think you know my answer."

"Yes, I do."

Jani sat back. At first she watched the hologram monkeys pace the tram as they had on the way in. But this time their antics made her feel pursued, and she fixed on the car ceiling instead.

The dock slip was located in one of the secondary human concourses, a quiet, low-traffic area designated for smaller private and light commercial craft. No shops or restaurants, only vend alcoves, a bathroom, arrival and departure displays. Monitoring would be standard, but given the imminent arrival of whoever had sent Ian Matrishi into panic mode and driven John Shroud underground, Jani doubted security currently paid much attention. They had bigger things to worry about.

She disembarked the tram and headed towards the corridor, heard the carpet-muffled thump of Lucien's footsteps behind her, and stopped. "You should stay here. I'm supposed to come alone."

Lucien stared down the empty walkway. "Just promise me you won't try anything heroic."

"I'll do what I have to." As he drew near, Jani caught the sharp herbal scent of the hospital soap. "You've been in contact with your team? I don't know how you're going to be able to pull them away from their current crisis."

"I'll be meeting with them as soon as I see you off." Lucien quieted, hands clenching, then opening, again and again. "I have to tell you something." He sidestepped until he stood in front of her, blocking her path. "Look at me."

"I have to go—" Jani tried to scoot around Lucien, but he once again moved to stop her. He gripped her shoulders, then moved one hand up her neck until he set his thumb under her chin and tilted her face up and all she could see were eyes dark and shining like stones in a cold stream.

"I want you to understand. I don't give a fuck about Niall or Ian, Thalassa or ag deals." Lucien's voice came low and rough. "Van Reuter or whoever the hell's behind this, the documents, any of it. My only concern will be to get you out of there." He drew closer. "I'll do what I have to as well."

Jani didn't expect what happened next. Nothing Lucien Pascal had done to that point, not the hand-holding or hugging or casual touches, prepared her for him gathering her in his arms and kissing her in the middle of a public thoroughfare. She tried at first to untangle herself, to push him away, but sensation stopped her. The warmth of his skin and the deeper native scent that the harsh soap couldn't hide, his hands and his taste and all of it overlaid with the forever-strange realization that she wasn't going into this alone.

He released her too soon. "See you at the end of this." He backed away for a few strides, eyes locked with hers. Then he turned and trotted towards the main concourse.

Jani stood in place as the seconds ticked by. Felt her heartbeat slow. Then a tram arrived from the human side and disgorged a business-suited pack, spurring her to move. As she drew nearer the slip, she slowed, straightened, forced herself to display an ease she didn't feel.

They stood waiting for her just outside the gangway. Two men, the older tall, dark and bearded with a wrestler's build, the younger shorter and wiry with light hair. They wore black daysuits, the jackets fastened, whatever weapons they carried hidden beneath. The older man gave her a bored once-over, then reached inside his jacket and took out a scanning wand. The younger one looked her up and down once, then again, and licked his lips.

Oh great. A lover boy. Jani couldn't yet tell how the older man would react if his partner pushed the point. *Bored* could mean anything from *all-business-brook-no-bullshit* to *just-don't-kill-her.* Time would tell.

Older gestured for Jani to extend her arms to the sides. Then he passed the wand over her, starting at her head and working his way down. After that, he gestured for her to set her bag on the floor and back away.

"Shouldn't we pat her down?" Younger sidled up to his partner. "She could have something sheathed."

Older ignored him, continuing in silence. He crouched, grunting with the effort. Circled the wand around the inside of the bag as though stirring a pot, then set it aside and switched to manual inspection. Removed each item in turn—the scanpack, documents slipcase, the handheld—then returned the first two and pocketed the last. When he came upon the figurine, he examined it, glanced at Jani, then returned it to the bag. He stood, gestured for her to remove the hair comb, pocketed that as well. Finally he pointed to the bag, waited for her to shoulder it, then waved in the direction of the gangway.

Jani headed down the narrow corridor. Heard a commotion behind her, and turned in time to see Older elbow Younger in the gut and push him back. *He's keeping Lover Boy away from me.* An unexpected move. She hadn't often encountered any form of gallantry among the criminals she had known. Apparent kindness usually expected something in return. Over the course of the journey, she would no doubt find what that was.

The craft's passenger cabin proved utilitarian. The area nearest the entry contained sparse furnishings, seating arranged around a table littered with food cartons, cups, and a couple of decks of cards. Two pulldown racks were attached to the wall opposite, one still in the raised position, the other lowered, the bedding rumpled.

Jani looked towards the rear of the cabin, a curved wall cut by three doors.

Older pointed to the middle door. "In there." His voice emerged deep, ragged, a victim of dry, filtered air.

As Jani neared the door, it slid aside to reveal a compartment that proved even smaller than the one she and Lucien had shared on the Padishah-New Indies leg of their journey. Two pull-downs, a narrow rack and a table barely big enough to hold one of Niall's old books. A sink and toilet tucked behind a half-height divider. Buttons and pads dotted a small wall panel, their functions listed in three languages none of which she could read.

She stepped inside and heard the door close behind her. A few seconds later, the *whirr* and *click* of a lock followed. She pulled down the rack, unrolled the mattress pad and waited for it to inflate, dragged off her bag and set it aside. Then she boosted onto the bed and sat on the edge, legs swinging back and forth at the knees.

Eventually she stilled. Leaned back and rested her head against the bolster. Stifled a yawn.

I should sleep. John had been right—unconscious didn't count.

After days of relentless motion and mental and emotional overdrive, the sudden stillness, the quiet, overwhelmed. Her limbs felt heavy, her eyes as grainy as they had when filmed. She gripped her upper lashes and pulled her lids out and down in an effort to kick up the tear production—it helped a little. Then she bundled the sling bag to form a pillow, swung her legs up onto the rack, and lay back. Stared at the featureless ceiling.

After a few minutes, she heard a series of signal tones, then felt the subtle vibrations and changes in background noise as the craft broke away from the slip and headed out.

See you soon, Evan. The thought crossed her mind that she could be mistaken, that Ian's sources had erred and that Evan van Reuter remained safely confined in a house on the outskirts of Chicago. But here in the silence, memories surfaced that reinforced her instincts. Things he used to say when Tsecha summoned her, mocking her quick response. *Tsecha's calling. Better run!* Or how he would occasionally call her Two of Six instead of Jani. Sometimes affectionately. Other times...not so much.

Pretty thin soup, Jani-girl, her father would've said, and he wouldn't have been wrong.

Or maybe what Anais Ulanova had told Lucien was true. It really was all personal.

She yawned again. Pushed aside thoughts of what might await her at journey's end, and closed her eyes.

Chapter Thirty-Two

Niall flinched when he heard the fuzzy clatter of lock mechanisms, the soft hiss of the cell door opening. He had just sat up to go to the can and he really did not want to deal with a dose of immobilizing charge given its unfortunate effect on bladder control.

"She's on her way." Saul's voice came quiet, nearly a whisper.

Relief flooded through Niall like alcohol warmth, but he caught himself in time. "When?"

"Common day, day and a half. Depends on the route. They gotta sneak around wherever your lot set up checkpoints." A sharp snort. "Took her long enough. Pretty much down to the hour or so. Wondered for a while if she was leaving you to swing."

"She always has her reasons." Niall did his best to project confidence, but it pained him to admit that he had begun to worry. Jani's life had become one of hard decisions and if forced to choose between him and her home, well, he had a pretty good idea which she'd pick. "I knew she'd come through in the end."

A pause. A sniff. "You in love with her?"

Niall shook his head. "No. I just have a tremendous amount of respect for her."

"She's not human, though, is she?"

"Depends on your definition." That earned Niall a derisive chuckle, so he backtracked. "She's half-human. She's a hybrid. She will always be half-human."

"Saw her on one of the news vids. Looks weird. Too skinny. Those eyes would give me the creeps." Saul's voice deadened. "The lady will kill her if she tries any shit."

"Kilian's dominant of the Thalassan settlement, which is affiliated with the Shèráin worldskein. I'm sure your lady's backers wouldn't appreciate her involving them in what would essentially be an assassination." Niall paused. Time for the first gentle probing. "And they'd know you worked for her. That you were part of it." He listened, held back a curse as the silence lengthened.

Then he heard his cell door close, followed by heavy steps that stopped by his cot.

"I'm going to take off the 'specs without the field, so don't you try any shit."

"Wouldn't think of it." Niall remained still as Saul unlocked and removed the device. "Thanks." He worked his neck, felt as well as heard the crackles. Opened his good eye slowly but not slowly enough, and blinked back tears as the light stabbed.

Saul returned to the door, slid it open just enough so he could stick his head out and check the corridor, then closed it and leaned against the wall. "What could you do?"

"I told you. New face. New identity."

"Yeah, but they have people in every ministry. In the Service. They can find out what I look like. Where I am."

Niall remained silent for a time. How could he swear to impenetrable Service security given that Morwenna had somehow gotten hold of Jani's ServRec? *Lie, you dumb ass.* Except he couldn't stand the thought of more blood on his hands. "Well, you could take the deal I offer and accept the possibility that someday, maybe, they might find you." He paused and counted to three before continuing. "Or you could go it alone, and know they will."

Saul stood unmoving, arms folded, gaze fixed on the floor. Minutes passed. Then he checked the corridor again, returned to his spot by the door, twitched a finger at Niall. "So? What's the plan?"

"How many are here, total?" Niall held his breath. He had never seen more than three or four guards at one time in addition to Morwenna and van Reuter, and hoped like hell for a number less than ten.

Saul counted on his fingers. "Twenty-one."

Jesus. "How many of them do we need to worry about?"

"About half. The ones who are always with her. A couple of the ones on her ship."

"Find out where I'll be held before Jani comes. Stash weapons in there ahead of time—if you carry extra on your person, they're going to wonder why. Throw in any kind of spy devices—fleas, drones, 'scopes. A layout of the place." Niall's mind raced, details flicking past like pages of an old book in the wind. "If we're not in the same room with Jani and van Reuter, we need to get to where they are. That door will be guarded by the ones we need to worry about, and there will be more inside." Memories of past raids bobbed to the surface. "Once it starts, it's going to get ugly fast. Shoot to kill. It's the only way we get out alive."

Saul rocked his head back and forth, then shrugged. "Then what?"

"We need a clear path to a ship. And someone to pilot it." Niall shook his head. He had spent the time since Breakfast with Evan pondering how the hell he could make so many moving parts fit together when he knew only one of parties he needed to make it work and wasn't sure he could trust him. *Goddamn you, van Reuter.* "The ship needs to be armed because they will come after us."

"Only one ship like that. Hers." Saul stuffed his hands in his pockets and stared at the floor. "I know the pilot. She was one of you lot. Kicked out."

I'm not surprised. "It happens." Niall held back further commentary.

"I'll put out feelers." Saul pushed off the wall. "No promises." He walked back to Niall. "Time for lights out. Be a good boy."

"Always." Niall tensed as Saul slipped the 'specs over his head and the weight once more descended on his neck and shoulders. He listened to the receding footsteps, the closing and locking of the cell door. Imagined Saul talking to the wrong person or heading straight to Morwenna and spilling everything himself, and wondered if he had just signed his own death warrant.

Make not your thoughts your prisons. From "Antony and Cleopatra," that one. Far from his favorite work, but every so often that line emerged from his memory cave and gave him a stern look. So many things could go wrong, yes. But the other side would be forced back on their heels, at least for a few vital minutes. Sometimes that was all the time you needed.

He felt certain they would keep Jani alive long enough to deliver the documents. Van Reuter wouldn't want to miss his chance to gloat.

Van Reuter. No matter how many times Niall took apart all the pieces and fit them together, he always had that one left over. *Morwenna's partnering with him—it makes no sense.* Was she that desperate? Had her circumstances grown so dire? If so, who was squeezing her?

That person was the one they really needed to worry about.

The need to piss broke through his pondering. He trudged to the toilet, hoped as usual that his sense of aim proved true, then cleaned up. Ran a hand over his face, felt the rough growth, and resumed his mulling. They would want him shaved and showered. Depending on what he was given to wear and who guarded him, it would be a good time for him to secure a weapon.

Might might might. Niall paced, stretched, then dropped to the floor and managed twenty-two push-ups before his arms gave out. Then he turned over on his back to wait for his muscles to stop trembling and let his mind go walkabout.

Should've taken your suspicions to the SIB, boyo. Should've let the folks who were commissioned to investigate do their jobs while he wrote his report and returned to Chicago. *I'm going to die and get Jani killed in the bargain and it's my own fucking fault.* He waded into the pit for a time, imagined every shit thing that could happen, watched the bloody scenes that unfurled before his mind's eye and replayed them again and again. Got it all out of his system as he had since the ragged days of his youth, when he had convinced himself that if he worked through every way things could go wrong, he would trick the fates into thinking that they had already happened and in doing so thwart them and live to fight another day.

He returned to the present by reciting a verse from a Lewis Carroll poem because he found them so damned silly that they shook him out of whatever hole he'd imagined himself into. "His form is ungainly—his intellect small, so the Bellman would often remark. But his courage is perfect! And that, after all, is the thing that one needs with a Snark." Then he worked to his feet, paced some more, and resumed his planning.

Chapter Thirty-Three

J ani awoke to the faint sounds of scratching, like fingernails lightly scraping a wall. Her first thought involved mice. *Dammit, they're back.* Then she remembered that the mouse problem had been years before, during a two-month stint at the slow-motion dockside collision that was old Guernsey Station. *Wake up, Kilian.* She opened her eyes, and her past slipped back into memory as her present stepped up to take its place.

"Kitty, kitty, kitty." A whiny sing-song just outside her door. "How many lives you got left, kitty kitty?"

Jani rolled her eyes, which were the reason for the mockery. *The pupils aren't slitted, asshole.* She kept that comment to herself, hoped that if she remained silent Lover Boy would take the hint even though she knew from bitter experience that his kind never did.

"Hey, kitty." More scratching. "Kitty, kit—"

"Leave her alone."

Jani sat up, the last traces of sleep evaporated. Older, coming to her aid once more. Again, she didn't know whether to feel relief or concern.

"Aw, I'm just—"

"Yeah, I know you just." Sounds of jostling, like someone being manhandled away from a door. "Go check on our ETA. Then help Pope with those crates."

"Why do I have to—"

"Just go."

After a beat of silence, the locks hummed. The door slid aside to reveal Older, rumpled and jacketless, shoulder-holstered shooter now visible, bearing a tray that held a prepack meal and an insulated cup, both steaming. "You hungry?"

Jani swung her legs off the mattress. "Not really, but I should eat something." She reached out for the tray but took care not to lean too far, to avoid making it look like she might try to grab the weapon.

Older responded by waving her back. Then he lowered the table, set down the tray, and stepped back into the entry. "Tried earlier. Guess you were sleeping."

"It's been a long week." Jani glanced at the food, which proved to to be some type of kettle meat sandwich that she knew would taste flat as cardboard, and grabbed the coffee. "How long was I out?"

"Seven-eight hours?" Older shrugged. "We're through the Gate-Way. It's all cruising from here on. Eighteen hours, maybe less depending on the burn."

Jani nodded, then tried the coffee, which to her surprise tasted good. *Somebody cleaned the brewer.* She offered silent thanks to them. Such was her reverie that it took a while to realize that Older still stood watching her.

He nodded towards the meal. "I heard human food makes you sick."

Jani shook her head. "No. It just doesn't taste like much of anything." She wrinkled her nose. "Flat, like it needs seasoning." When the man made no move to leave, she sat back and waited.

"You didn't want to be like this, though?" He flicked his hand in her general direction. "You'd rather be all human again?"

Jani hesitated. In her experience, guards usually didn't make conversation. *He's not like Lover Boy, though.* He didn't give off assault stink. More the curiosity she sometimes encountered in Karistos, all wide eyes and *why how what-if.* "It's not possible to reverse it, so I don't see the point in thinking about it." She could tell from the way he nodded that he would construe that to mean *yes,* and she didn't care enough to push back. She had learned as a rebellious preteen that it didn't pay to argue with the one who held the code to your room.

Instead, she broke off a piece of the sandwich and gave it a try. *Yup. Mushy cardboard.* "It's fine. Thanks." She forced a shade of a smile. "I'm Jani, but I'm guessing you know that."

"Georg." He pronounced it *Gay-org,* and an accent that had to that point been well-buried fought its way up for air.

Jani nodded. "Hortensia. What part?"

"Das Tal. Twelfth Settlement. You been?"

"Long time ago. Unter den Linden. Easier to get lost."

Georg allowed a thin hint of a grin. "The Scheißestraße, I bet."

Shit Street. The low-end sector where the bottom feeders lived. "Pretty much." Jani gave up on the food and sat back, gripping the cup in both hands. "May I ask, how is he? Pierce?" Her stomach clenched when Georg hesitated, but she held back further questions. *He's just weighing his words.* Figuring out what was safe to tell her. *Don't stir up the mud,* an old hand she'd once worked with used to say. *Just sit tight and troll the line.*

"He's okay." Georg stared down at the floor. "Pain in the ass, though."

Jani had to smile. "He can be that, yes."

"You're friends with him." Georg gave a vague back-and-forth wave of the hand. "How did you two...?"

"Chicago, a few years ago."

"He was in the game. Deep."

"Yeah."

"So were you."

"In a small way. Pushing the paper."

"We've got one of you. Weird. Talks to that thing." Georg pressed his hands together fingertips to fingertips to form a scanpack oval. "Like it can hear him."

So they do have a dexxie. Which meant they intended to confirm the paper. *Oh well.* Not unexpected. "Some documents examiners do talk to their scanpacks." Jani decided against admitting that *some* included her. "They're a part of you." She tapped the side of her head. "Some believe they can understand."

"Hmm." Georg shrugged. Started to back out of the doorway, then stopped. "The kid. Björnson. Don't worry about him." He nodded, then turned and left.

Jani watched the panel slide closed, heard the hiss of locks. *Well, that was interesting.* She savored the coffee as details of her old life came to mind. Most outsiders thought smuggling an anarchic free-for-all, but she had found it as rigidly hierarchical as the Service. Gang members worked to move up the ranks and then guarded those gains like misers their treasure for one simple reason: higher rank meant bigger share of the take.

Guaranteed share. How many times had she been denied a promised payment because earnings had been less than expected that week and rank had its privilege? She'd just been a low-end paper pusher, readily replaceable. But someone like Georg, a trusted soldier, would always be paid. A gang leader who broke that trust might as well paint a target on their back and hand out the shooters.

Jani looked around her compartment. She'd had more experience in the lesser reaches of colonial transport than she cared to recall, and this was not a high-end ship. Not that she expected Cabinet-class transport, but her captors didn't seem to have it much better. *Pull-down racks. Cheap furnishings.*

Then there was Lover Boy getting stuck helping with cargo. Disciplinary action by an older hand? Or were they that short-handed?

One thing that occurred to her as she thought back over every-thing Georg had said was that he knew about her past. Knevçet Shèràa didn't count as it was public knowledge—even if the

Commonwealth wished to hide the details, the idomeni felt no such compunction. But her criminal exploits was less well-known. *He could've met someone who knew me when.* For all the life expectancy in the smuggling game was low, it wasn't zero. As her public presence grew, she had no doubt been a topic of conversation in some of the rougher regions of the Commonwealth.

Or had Niall been the source, feeding out just enough detail to make her seem approachable?

Groundwork. Making conversation. Dropping hints. Figuring out the beat of the place, then trying to work it to your advantage.

Jani stared into her coffee. Colonel Niall Pierce wasn't just very much alive. If her instincts were correct, he had also been busy. *Planning...what?* The only thing she could think of was escape. *He doesn't think they're going to release us after I turn over the docs.* That was... not totally unexpected.

She wondered how well Lucien was getting on with his team.

Then she pondered what she needed to do to hold up her end of Niall's plan. Whatever it was.

———

"That paper you got. It's important." Georg had taken his place in the entry, this time with his own coffee as well as a fresh refill for Jani.

Jani sipped, then wrapped her hands around the hot cup. Over time, the compartment had grown human-level chilly and her clothing didn't exactly qualify as cold weather gear. "It's important to somebody." She shrugged. "Can't figure it out myself." Sometimes playing dumb worked. For all sorts of reasons, people liked to show off what they knew.

"The la—" Georg pressed a fist to his mouth and coughed. "My boss says it's worth a lot. Gonna make us rich."

His boss is female. A list of names scrolled through Jani's mind. The problem was that few of them possessed the reach to extract a prisoner from an Earth-based location. "Guess that depends."

"On what?"

"If your boss is working with someone, who they are." Jani picked through her memory file. "From what I remember, alliances always got tested when a lot of money was involved. You'd think hey, enough here for everyone, but sometimes someone who should know better starts thinking like Family. What's mine is mine. What's yours is mine." Another pause. "They forget how to share."

"My boss doesn't share." Georg shook his head. "This one's all ours."

Jani rocked her head back and forth. "I don't know anything about what's going on here. Who you work for. All I do know is that if you're not at the top of the tree, then you're answering to someone, and that someone has power over you. And if your boss steps wrong, they won't be the only one who pays the price."

"My boss takes care of their own."

"You're no doubt correct. You know a lot more about what's going on than I do." Jani pressed fingertips to the spot between her eyebrows. Picking through words like grains of sand always led to a headache. "I just always think back to my days in the game. You finally find that job where you think, this is good. I can spend some time here, build some cred. Put something away for later." She paused as more than one long-forgotten incident replayed. Yet another small hope dashed. "And then things start fraying around the edges and the next thing you know, payday comes and goes and you're left with nothing and you have bills, right? Responsibilities."

Georg shrugged. "Sounds like you made some bad choices."

Jani nodded in agreement. "It always looks good until it doesn't." Another hunt through her mind files until she found another story. How had she lived through so many stories? "I knew a kid, always messing up. Came running up to me one day, said they made a great deal. Finding something for somebody important. Payout was half up front, then pick up the other half after delivery." Another heavy sigh. "Partial deals are always hard, you know. I mean, if you're higher up the ladder, they have to pay you because you're strong enough to make it rough for them. But if you're a grunt?" A tilt of her head, a studied wince. "This kid was a grunt."

Georg remained silent for a time. He didn't look at her, instead concentrating on his coffee. "What happened?"

"Went back for the second half of the payment, hired gun for the party in question was waiting. Knocked them out, was about to shoot them. Point blank. No way out." Jani hesitated until Georg's questioning look spurred her to continue. "Kid got lucky. A friend had followed, took care of the hired gun, got them out of there."

"Good friend."

"They exist."

Georg laughed, a short exhalation that sounded like a cough. Then he turned, head down. Started to close the door, then paused, mouth slightly agape as though about to say something. But after a few silent moments, he left. The door slid shut.

Jani heard the hum of the lock mech. A few beats passed before she heard his footfall. She lay back her head and listened to the soft background hum of the craft. *Just a few hours to go, Niall. Not sure what else I can do.* She couldn't tell if she had made any headway at all with Georg, if she could unsettle him enough to make him question his loyalty, weaken his link in the chain. That sort of seed needed time to take root and spread, and time was one thing she did not have. *He may not even know what's going on.* Just because he seemed to have some authority didn't mean he knew anything worthwhile.

Stop second-guessing yourself. She flexed her hands as the nerve bug bit and the venom spread.

His name was Sasha, the kid in her story. At least, that was the name he had used. He had gotten in too deep and she had taken it upon herself to pull him out. It hadn't been a good time for her. The shell she had built around herself had almost hardened to the point that nothing would crack it. Leaving Sasha to his fate would've sealed that last dehumanizing layer.

Deep down, she knew what must've become of him, because some people never learned. But she still hoped that maybe, somehow, he had figured out the way the game needed to be played, or better yet gotten out entirely.

Except you're never really out, are you? Jani thought back to the situation at Thalassa, how the never-ending struggle for supplies warred with the need to be careful from whom those supplies—

"Oh, damn." Jani knocked her head against the bolster. Of the handful of female gang leaders who could've possibly snatched Evan, one name should've risen immediately above them all. One with Family connections and a habit of betraying partners. One who had already sunk at least one hook into Thalassa.

Morwenna. And Evan may not have been her only target. *What if she grabbed Niall as well?* After days of trying to nail smoke to the wall, something had finally grown solid enough to stick. *If Roland is hers...?* That meant she had burrowed into Amsun, maybe other Outer Circle bases as well. Was that where the weapons currently stashed in the Thalassan warehouse had come from?

"What a mess?" Jani flexed her hands again, wished like hell she had packed parchment and a stylus in her bag. *Some ideas need a lot of columns and arrows.*

Think. She lay back her head, closed her eyes, and did just that.

———

A rap on her door shook Jani out of her thought maze.

"Docking in an hour." Georg's voice rumbled like a low note. "Be ready to go."

Jani slid off the rack, picked up her bag, then laughed when she realized she had been ready to go since she boarded. She set the bag back down, edged over to the cup-sized sink, and checked herself in the polished metal plate that served as the mirror. Wet her hands, then patted her hair. Hunted through various cubbyholes for any sort of dentifrice, and found a half-used packet that some previous occupant had folded and used to raise one corner of a shelf.

Survival tip number five-oh-three for life on the run—don't be picky. She shook out some of the powder onto her finger and cleaned her teeth, then washed her face. Wished she'd thought to bring make-up, at least something to hide the circles under her eyes. *Nobody cares what you look like, Kilian. They just want what you're carrying.* She braced her hands on the sides of the sink and stared into her eyes as parts of her life she had thought well-buried approached at speed.

Morwenna and Evan. Jani wondered if Evan realized with whom he dealt, or if Family arrogance clouded his thinking. *What do you think?* "If you're not at the top of the tree, then someone has power over you." And Evan hadn't been at the top of the tree for a very long time.

She remained at the sink, staring at nothing, until the series of tones sounded that signaled their approach to the dock. Felt the mildest of jostling as the ship settled into its berth and various connections initiated, then gave herself a final once-over. Heard the hum of the door lock, grabbed her bag, paused to wait for the panel to sweep aside—

—and found an unwelcome surprise awaiting her.

"Hey, kitty." Björnson stood before her. He looked all of twelve years old at first glance, all lopsided grin and shining eyes. "Your friend Georg had to see to some problem elsewhere, so I decided it was my turn." He wore either the black suit from the day previous or its identical twin, the stark color washing out his pale skin so he looked ill.

Jani tried to step around him, but he moved to block her. She sidestepped in the opposite direction, then pushed with her shoulder, knocking him aside. "I do not have time for you."

"You better make time." Björnson grabbed her left arm, the animandroid one. "Because you're going to need a friend after you make your delivery."

Jani looped her arm up and around, breaking his hold. "I'll take my chances." When he moved to the other side and grabbed her right arm, she shook him off again.

Then he grabbed her shoulders, spun her around, pushed her

face-first against the cabin wall and closed in, pressing his body against hers and slipping his hand between her legs.

Jani brought her booted foot down hard on his instep and and elbowed him in the stomach at the same time. He staggered back but recovered and closed in again.

Jani straight-armed him with her right arm, but instead of pushing him back, she gripped him by the throat. A lousy hold—she knew that. Lucien would've had her on the floor in a heartbeat, giving her elbow a good pop along the way.

But Björnson wasn't Lucien. First he grabbed her wrist and tried to yank her hand away; when that didn't work, he pulled at her fingers while kicking out at her legs. His eyes goggled as he struggled to breathe.

"Let him go."

Jani looked in the direction of the voice. Georg, standing in the cabin entry, still in shirtsleeves, one hand reaching for his shooter.

Jani released Björnson, who doubled over wheezing, one hand to his throat.

Then he looked up at Jani, eyes like ice, and made as if to spring. But before he could, Georg grabbed him by the hair and dragged him across the cabin and out the exit, yelling in Hortensian German all the while.

Jani recognized a few words. *Big mouth. Animal.* She listened as the shouting faded. Then Georg reentered alone.

"Apologies. I should not have left you with him. He's no good."

Jani nodded. "Not a problem." She flexed her right hand, stretching her fingers in a musician's warmup, then forming a fist and releasing it again and again. Looked at Georg to find him staring at her.

"You're strong."

"So I've been told." Jani shoved her restless hand in her trouser pocket, then took it out. "He said I'd need a friend after I handed over the documents."

Georg said nothing. After a few moments, he walked to one of the chairs, removed the jacket that had been draped across the back, reached into one of the pockets, and removed Jani's handheld and the hair comb. He handed them to her, waited for her to tuck them into her bag, then gestured for her to walk ahead of him. They exited the ship and headed down the gangway, where they were met by two new black-suited men along with a sullen Björnson.

The two men bracketed Jani and led her into the station. She glanced back to see if Georg was still there, but he and Björnson had already gone.

Chapter Thirty-Four

Niall wiped the last of the depilatory foam from his face and stared at his reflection. His right eye had grown milkier since his last visit to the showers. It reminded him of a horror vid he had seen years before, a tale of a haunted space station. The story had been predictably ludicrous, but one scene had disturbed him. An old man in a rocking chair who slowly raised his head to reveal an eye like his own, the same egg-white mass.

Get your head straight, boyo. Jani would be arriving at any moment, and he'd still had no word from Saul about weapons, the ship, or even if the man had agreed to his scheme. *Assume he has.* Just for shits and giggles. *We've got one person on the ship on our side—the pilot. Maybe one or two more, if I'm lucky.* Saul, plus whoever else he had brought into the mix. *About half the ones I would otherwise need to worry about.* The ones who could be counted on not to freeze. Who wouldn't think twice about mowing down people they had worked with for however long.

Niall held up his right hand, thumb up and index finger pointed at his reflection. Shooters weren't as touchy as projectile weapons— his messed-up sighting wouldn't affect his aim too much. *I hope.* Hell, given this was Morwenna's outfit, the weapons might even have target-lock. All he'd have to do is avoid blowing off his own dick.

He once more dug through the toiletry kit that Saul had left in the bathroom in the hope that he had missed something. *A weapon.* A message. He held his breath when he found a slip of paper tucked deep in one of the side pockets—he almost tore it in half in his hurry to unfold it.

So, Colonel, how goes the day?

"Just dandy, you sonofabitch." Niall crumpled the note and flushed it, then imagined their scramble to get to the ship. All of them giving and taking fire while Evan Fucking van Reuter strolled after them, calling out the occasional order and advising them to hurry themselves along. *Pray I don't leave you behind, you bastard.* Unfortunately, he couldn't toss him over the side given that the Service had been one of the parties charged with handling his imprisonment. Roshi would definitely want to know what the hell went wrong there.

Grab Jani next. That would likely get messy given the interest in the paper she carried. *Morwenna?* His first impulse was to leave her smoking corpse in the middle of a corridor, but given she had likely orchestrated Evan's jailbreak, they had to take her in for questioning. *That's when even more fun starts.* They would be pursued by her people. The ship would take fire.

One step at a time, boyo. Get to the damned ship first. Niall took a deep breath. Another. So immersed in thought was he that it took him some time to hear Saul's banging on the door.

"What the hell? You asleep or what?" Saul dragged the panel open. "They've docked."

Niall dug the eye patch out of his trouser pocket and slipped it on. They'd given him actual clothing this time, dark blue shirt and trousers and black trainers with soles that didn't squeak quite as much as the slippers he'd worn for Breakfast with Evan. "Where will we be in relation to Jani?"

"Later for that. We need to go somewhere else first." Saul waved

Niall to leave the bathroom and walk ahead of him, then drew a shooter from his belt holster. "Just keeping up appearances."

Or making ready to shoot me in the back. Niall edged to the side opposite Saul's gun hand so he could stop short and grab for the shooter if he heard the charge-through hum. Eyed every doorway and crossways corridor they passed for places to duck, for anything he could use as a weapon. As the number of doors decreased and alarm stations and emergency lighting increased, he knew they neared the airlocks and docking slips, a fact that didn't fill him with confidence as to his situation.

"Stop here," Saul said when they entered a narrow corridor that led to one of the slips. "Waiting for a friend."

After a few minutes, a door at the far end of the corridor slid aside and two men entered, one older and stocky, the other younger and skinny. The older man nodded a greeting to Saul; the younger remained silent and kept a narrow-eyed glare fixed on the floor.

Niall studied the newcomers without seeming to. The older man reminded him of so many he had known during his time in the smuggling trenches. Solid but a little slow, good enough to a point but lacking the drive and wit to make it into the upper reaches. The younger one, meanwhile, brought to mind every snitch he'd ever known, the effect heightened by signs that the kid had been roughed up recently. His hair stuck out every which way, and his neck bore reddened marks as though someone had tried to choke him.

"So?" Saul shrugged.

The older man looked down at his shoes for a few moments, then raised his head. "Ja."

Saul nodded. Then he pulled out his shooter, aimed at the younger man, and fired—the pulse packet hit him square in the chest, then exited through his right leg, igniting his trousers, sending charred bits of cloth and tissue spraying across the floor and the opposite wall.

"This is Georg." Saul pointed to the older man as he reholstered his weapon. "He rode in with your friend."

Niall nodded as he stared at the body, at the kid, splayed out on the floor, at the thin wisp of smoke that rose from his chest and the stench of burnt meat that drifted along with it, and the realization struck that if Georg had said *Nein*, he'd be laid out on the floor instead. "We need to get to her."

"She'll be all right." Georg thumped Saul on the shoulder. "Let's go."

Niall wondered what Georg knew that he didn't. Then he cast one final look at the body before falling in behind the two men. Whatever sin the youngster had committed, he had paid for it in the way of his kind. "Yeah. Let's go."

Chapter Thirty-Five

Jani followed her guards along corridor after corridor and struggled to match what she saw with the diagrams from Aicha's ship. *One door gone here...a new one installed there.* She shivered when they came upon a passageway closed off with strips of barrier tape, reliving her tumble through the archive as they waited for one of her escorts to reattach a fallen detour sign.

Finally, they came to the corridor that led to the room she had asked about back on Aicha's ship, the one that could hold more people. *Please let Niall be there.* Whatever his captors, her...hosts, planned for them, they stood a better chance if they met it together.

Two more black suits met them at the door. One took Jani's bag and searched it—he took the hair comb, but left the handheld. The other ran a wand over Jani from head to toe—when he finished, the other gave Jani back her bag, then rapped once on the door, which opened to reveal Evan van Reuter sitting in a lounge chair, legs crossed, a cup of what may have been coffee in hand. He wore black trousers and a blue dress shirt open at the neck, the elegant image of a former minister in repose if you ignored the drawn features, the mottled complexion.

"Hello, Jani." His cold smile wavered at first but he'd always had a knack for quick recoveries and he executed this one perfectly. "You don't seem surprised to see me."

"The messages I received had a certain familiar flavor. And the documents I needed to find had a very narrow focus." Jani stepped inside the room, which possessed the characteristic staleness of recycled station air laced with the ozone sharpness of recently cleaned clothing. "The Ulanovs and Scriabins could've kept this very low key. They have dexxies on staff they could've sent out to do the search. You no longer have dexxies on staff. You could've hired one, but you always had a preference for drama."

"Not to mention how much I relished the thought of you scrambling as the time ticked away." Evan set his cup on a nearby table, then sat back, hands folded in his lap. "How long has it been?"

Not long enough. Jani shrugged. "Four years, give or take."

"Oh, to enjoy the luxury of ignoring time's passage." Evan's smile vanished. "I remember every bloody hour."

"I hope you're not expecting sympathy." Jani took a step farther into the room. "I remember names."

"It isn't that I'm not enjoying this journey you're taking down memory lane, but we do have business to attend to."

Jani looked toward the speaker, who had just entered through a side door. A tall woman, slim, with shoulder-length hair the color of copper touched with tarnish. She wore an olive jumpsuit of the type worn by ship's crews. A utilitarian garment. Lots of pockets. *Am I looking at a legend?* She had heard Morwenna MacCallan was a redhead, but hair color meant little when it came to identification. However, like clothing, it could serve as a distraction.

"Ná Kièrshia?" The woman offered a questioning half-smile. "I believe that's your title?"

Jani continued to stare at the woman, who regarded her in turn. A week spent with altered features had heightened her awareness of how little adjustment was needed to change a face just enough. But as she had learned from Lucien, a true transformation took weeks and involved more than a few injections. The way one carried oneself. One's walk. One's voice. All would require retooling. If those weren't altered, chances were that just enough of the person beneath remained, a reflection in a clouded mirror.

And then there was the accent, the way one pronounced an alien word.

"Major Beech." Jani watched the woman's eyes widen, caught the slight jerk of her head. "You've changed your hair."

Chapter Thirty-Six

"Who the hell is Major Beech?" Evan's voice held the slight whine of a host who caught his guests making early escapes from his party.

Jani ignored him. "So what do I call you?"

The woman started to speak, then paused. Raised a hand, then let it fall as if to say *who cares*. "For purposes of this discussion, we may as well stay with Beech."

"As opposed to the legendary Morwenna." Jani nodded. "Doesn't quite have the same ring, though, does it?" That earned her a narrow-eyed glare, so she decided to back off, at least for a little while. Give the puzzle pieces tumbling into her brain a chance to slot into place.

"I believe you have something to deliver." Beech rolled up one sleeve to reveal a wide wristband and pressed one of the pads that dotted its surface. The door through which she had entered opened and a young man bustled through, the swing of a bulky slingbag knocking him off-balance, a familiar-looking object hanging from a belt holster.

"This is Porter." Beech eyed him like a dubious purchase as he dumped the bag atop a table and started rummaging. "He'll be confirming the documents—"

Jani smiled and held up her hand. "I would like to see Niall first."

"After we confirm that you brought the correct documents."

"At which point you'd tell me that if I want to see him I should look out a porthole?"

"In case you missed something, may I remind you that you're not dictating the terms here."

"And if you were, you wouldn't have to tell me that, would you?" Jani started to say more. But a sound like water being sucked down a drain interrupted her, and she turned to find Evan with his hand over his mouth, shoulders shaking.

"I told you she would do exactly what she's doing." He waved one hand, a lazy back-and-forth. "Just let her see him."

Beech shot Evan a look that should've killed him. Then she touched her wristband again. This time, two new black suits entered, shooters still holstered but the clasps undone.

Jani nodded and hugged her bag to her chest. "I will just say that if they shoot me when I'm near the paper, the charge can jump and wreck the document inset chips. Makes ID more difficult. Estate Court would get involved, and they would want Registry involved. Does whoever you're working for want that? I am assuming whatever dealings these documents will be involved in are intended to remain...informal?" She noted that the word *Registry* made Porter flinch. *You know what that means, don't you, kid?* Use of a scanpack in the commission or support of a crime meant loss of same, along with being deregistered with little if any hope of forgiveness.

She met his eye and he looked away and she could read his thoughts like her own. *They take away your 'pack before you even leave the hearing room. And you know where they're taking it.* To the labs, for destruction. *If the adjudication board is feeling particularly brutal, they make you watch.*

"Let her see him or we will all have turned to dust before she's so much as taken the damned docs out of her bag." Evan's face flushed and his voice cut the air, a fragment of ministerial authority returned.

Beech glared at Evan, then at Jani. Then she tapped the wristband again and a wall display activated. A trio of faces appeared, then just as quickly vanished.

"Saul?" Beech tapped the band once more, then again. "What's going on?"

"Sys—tem's been glit—ching, ma'am" came a rough voice made choppy by whatever interference affected the transmission. "I'll—ask a—tech to—" Before he could finish, the display lightened and the faces reappeared.

Jani took note of the smooth white wall in the background, the edge of a hatch barely visible. *They're in an airlock.* Because of course Beech would use a threat to Niall's life to keep her in line. *Georg's there?* She met his eye, but his expression remained blank. The second man, Saul, she didn't recognize.

At the sight of the third, a wave of relief. "Niall." Her heart tripped as she took in the cuts and bruises, the puffy lip, the eye patch. "What the hell happened to your eye?"

"Just a little accident, gel." Niall focused on some point over her shoulder. "Got caught acting out of bounds."

"Uh-huh." Jani followed his sightline to find Evan looking up at her, chin in full defensive jut. "Was he tied up when you did it or did someone hold him down?"

"He had just punched me in the face and tripped an alarm."

Good job, Colonel. "I'm guessing you deserved it."

"Okay, that's enough." Beech cut the com. The display blanked. "Now do what you were brought here to do." She pointed to Porter, then waved him towards Jani.

Jani met him halfway, smiled and offered her hand. He grasped it gently, as though afraid it might break, his rapt expression conveying the same sense of wonder that Editha and other dexxies had lavished on her at New Indies Station. He looked fresh out of school, his face unlined, light brown hair bound in a neat ponytail, grey shirt and trousers crisp.

But the eyes... The eyes always gave them away, the ones who were in over their heads. A little too bright. Opened a little too wide. In too deep and no way out. "Confirming a transfer from Two of Six. I'm not worthy." That comment drew a groan from Evan and an eye roll from Beech.

Jani set her bag next to Porter's, removed the dummy 'pack, then held her breath as she activated it. But the green illumins skittered across the surface in the proper order, and the processors Dr. Ishola had installed required only the barest touch to control.

She set the 'pack on standby and removed the documents slipcase from her bag. Their appearance drew the attention of both Evan and Beech; Beech drew closer while Evan stood and held out his hand.

"It's what I'm here for." He took the slipcase from Jani, removed the two sheets of parchment, and lay them side by side on the table. "See these marks?" He pointed to the nicks near the documents' lower right corners. "That was how our doc techs kept track of our important paper."

Jani glanced at Porter, who stared at Evan in knitted-brow confusion. "We still need to confirm the usual way."

"But the marks—"

"Indicate the docs may belong together. It tells nothing about what they are. You know better than that."

Now it was Evan's turn to look confused. "I was told—"

"By whom?" Jani shot a look at Beech, then turned back to Evan. "I know to look for marks." She pointed to Porter. "He knows to look for marks. We don't need you to point out the marks." She stared at the man, and questions that had troubled her since this venture began once more came up for air. "So why are you here, Evan?" She turned back to Beech. "I gathered from a conversation I had with one of my handlers that I'm not meant to survive this." She nodded towards Evan. "I'm guessing he isn't, either."

"That all depends." Beech nodded to her black suits, and they left their posts along the wall and took positions by her side. "Get on with it."

Chapter Thirty-Seven

Niall checked the charge level of the shooter Saul had handed him, then dug out extra power packs from the case that the man had stashed in the airlock. "We need to move. We can't hang around waiting for any technician."

"There's nothing wrong with it." Saul pointed to the visual relay. "I messed with it so she'd think there was. If she tries to contact us again and we don't answer, she'll figure glitch."

"Good thinking." Niall continued to hunt through the case as he considered what excitement they might encounter over the next several minutes. Found the mapping goggles with which he could view the station layout, tried them on, and activated them. *Goddam place is a maze.* So many doorways and empty rooms. So many corners. *And we just need to get from one end to the other at speed without dying.* "No sightbots?" He hunted through the case. "Drones? Fleas?"

"Only her personal guard has them." Saul shrugged. "They don't share."

Oh, lovely. "Okay. Have either of you ever taken part in a room-by-room search?" Niall watched the two men shake their heads, and flipped up the goggles so he could look them in the eyes. "You." He pointed to Georg. "You're the rear guard. You have two jobs. You're on the lookout for anyone approaching from behind and watching uncleared rooms. I'm in the middle at your back." Then he pointed to Saul. "You're lead. You're first around corners and into rooms. I'll be behind you going in while Georg stands guard outside, at your back the rest of the time."

Saul paused in the middle of working a bandolier over his bulky midriff. "You've done this before—why aren't you lead?"

"Because I have one eye and I don't know this hellhole as well as you do." Niall clapped a gun belt around his waist and loaded it with all the power packs it could hold. Set the goggles back in place, then flipped them back up because the imaging blocked too much of his vision span. *Goddamn you, van Reuter.* He had a feeling the man was in as much danger as Jani, but damned if he could muster the will to care. "Let's go."

They edged out into the corridor. Niall felt Georg's breath on his neck and poked Saul in the ribs. "Move."

"But you said—"

"You can actually walk. Just stay alert." Niall looked to the ceiling. *My kingdom for a searchbot.* Hell, at this point he'd even take the horse.

They edged around the first corner. One door on their side, the panel slightly agape. Two doors on the other side, both closed. When Saul stopped dead, Niall stepped around him, edged up to the gap, waved him to move to the other side, beckoned to Georg to keep an eye across the corridor, then pushed the panel open, activating the room lights. He waited for a beat, gestured for Saul to stay put but ready to fire, then leaned around the jamb to check the interior. A quick back and forth, weapon raised and activated. The space proved small, empty but for a couple of wrecked chairs.

"Okay, it's clear." Niall closed the door and fired a low-energy burst into the control board, sealing it shut. "Lock each door as we go. Lowest setting. Less noise." He pointed to the first door on the other side of the corridor. "Now we check that one. Then we zig-zag back. Every room behind us is one we've checked and locked."

Behind them, Georg muttered something foul. "Why do we have to check every room?"

"To make sure there's no one in there who will come out and shoot at us after we pass by." Niall's stomach flipped at the stink of burnt flesh even though he knew it was just his augmentation sending out feelers. "Saul shot that kid for whatever reason. I have a feeling there's a lot of that going on around here today."

"He was a fuckin' snitch. If he'd learned about this, he'd have gone straight to her." Georg shrugged. "Besides, he tried to hurt your friend."

Niall couldn't help but grin. "Is that where he got the marks on his throat?"

"Yeah." A pause. "She was okay for whatever she is. But the look on her face when she..." Georg's voice trailed. Then he shook his head and resumed his watch.

What kind of look? Niall held back the question. They weren't supposed to talk anyway.

After they cleared the rooms in the first corridor, Saul and Georg picked up the pace and Niall felt able to resume his middleman station. A second corridor secured. A third. He almost let himself hope that the worst was over and they'd have a clear shot to wherever Jani was being held when a shooter crack sounded from the adjoining corridor.

He waved the two men still and edged along the wall until he reached the corner, then peered around in time to see a man in a black suit exit one of the rooms and turn in their direction. He spotted Niall immediately and reached for his weapon.

Niall had already sighted down. He fired. A solid chest hit. The man dropped.

At the sound of the shot, Saul and Georg pushed past him and headed towards the fallen man, ignored his order to back off and take cover. He scanned the line of closed panels, hoped like hell the man had been alone.

Saul stopped beside the body, turned it over with his foot. "Kleist. One of her personal guard." He headed for the open door. "He came out of there." He entered before Niall could stop him, then pulled up short. "Elsie?" He walked to what at first looked like a pile of clothing on the floor—you had to look closely to pick out the small hand, the mass of grey hair. He bent to shake the woman's shoulder, then swore. *"Elsie."*

Niall watched from the doorway, torn between the desire to give the man a moment and the need to keep moving.

"Our doc tech." Georg edged in beside him. "She just did her job. Never hurt anybody."

"They're killing all the nonessentials." Niall scanned the opposite side of the corridor, alert to any sound. "That means they're planning on pulling out soon." He turned back to find Saul crouched beside the woman's body. "Saul, we need to go."

Saul straightened, then wiped a hand over his face. "We can't leave—" His voice cracked, and he pointed to the body and shook his head.

"You can't help her." Niall raised his weapon and sidestepped into the corridor. "We need to move." He waited for Saul to draw alongside, then pointed to him and Georg in turn. "And what you two just did? Don't ever do it again. If he'd had a partner, you'd both be laid out next to your friend." He waved Saul ahead of him, then fell in behind. "Love of Christ, how you two have managed to survive this long—"

Georg knocked him on the shoulder with the back of his hand. "Well? You so smart maybe you tell us what's going on, ja?"

Niall hesitated. How much could he say? *Oh hell.* He remembered how much he and other mid-levels had gossiped, scrabbling for bits of information that made them appear more inner-circle than they were. Saul and Georg probably knew most of it already. "Service bases in the Outer Circle have been bleeding weaponry over the last year or so. Some of it has been turning up in the hands of secessionist groups. Some, in gangs like this one. We know the scheme is being run from the inside. We're trying to find out who they are."

Georg nodded. "So they grabbed you why?"

"To make me an offer. Pull me in. I guess they figured once in the game, always in the game."

"What about your friend?"

Niall counted time's passage in his head. *Stall 'em, gel. You're one of the best at it I've ever seen.* "They needed her to find some documents. They used me as the bait." He rubbed his forehead. Trying to keep it all straight gave him a headache. "There are a couple of things going on here. But it all boils down to the same old shit. Money and power. Keeping things on edge and playing both sides." He nudged the men forward. "We need to move."

They had only gone a few steps when the sounds of a struggle reached them, muffled grunts and the squeak of shoe soles on flooring. Niall pushed ahead, weapon drawn. Pressed against the wall and peered around the corner to find a black suit scuffling with— *What the hell?* The green shirt and orange trousers screamed Haárin, but the man who wore them was the last person he expected to see engaged in hand-to-hand in the middle of this particular station corridor.

Lucien Pascal knocked away the black suit's attempted grab, then before the man could recover stepped forward, gripped his shoulder, buried a knife just under the ribs, then pulled it out halfway and shoved it upwards into the heart. The black suit collapsed against him —he stepped back, withdrew the knife, let the body fall.

Then he caught sight of Niall, and his face brightened in recognition. "Colonel." He stepped over the body without a backward glance and strode towards him as he wiped the blood from the knife blade with the tail of his shirt, which already bore a number of similar stains. "I heard shots."

"We're okay." Niall felt the shudder of revulsion that he sometimes did when dealing with Pascal even as he reminded himself that the man had been prized by the Service for exactly the behavior he currently displayed. "What—?" The days of isolation and blindness, of fear of death and the brain-churn of planning all fell on him at once, leaving his mind a blank but for the useless observation that not even Lucien Bloody Pascal could make acid green and pumpkin orange look good.

"Jani?" Pascal glanced at Saul and Georg before settling back on Niall.

"Saw her—" Niall rocked his head. "—maybe twenty minutes ago. Via vidlink. She thinks I'm holed up in an airlock with my guards." He gestured towards his co-conspirators, who offered vague greetings.

"We docked on the Haárin side." Pascal turned and looked back in the direction he had come as though he expected to see something.

"No." Georg shook his head. "Only Haárin ships can dock there. The mechanicals are—" His voice cut out and his eyes widened.

Niall followed his gaze, then stared as an Haárin rounded the corner and walked towards them. Then another. And another. Eight in all, dressed in the usual eye-bleeding color clashes except for one Pathenrau male garbed all in black.

He heard Saul and Georg grumble. Then came the soft hum of activated shooters. "Stand down—they're with him." He pointed to Pascal.

"Is he another *friend?*"

"He's not a hybrid. He's just dressed like an Haárin for whatever...reason." Niall struggled for words, torn between relief at the additional support and the chill realization that the idomeni were now neck-deep in the muck with the rest of them. He motioned to Pascal. "What did you do?"

"Same thing you always have to do when Jani's involved. Improvised." Pascal nodded to one of the Haárin, a female with short brown hair held back with a white headband bearing the team logo of the Acadia Central United football team. Then they slipped into Vynshà Haárin complete with truncated gestures and postures, a conversation that ended with head nods on both sides. "We've secured everything between here and the control room. Now it's just the corridor with the room where Jani's being held, but whoever's got her is probably figuring out by now that something's up. So we have to move." He paused. "To add to the fun, a ship's approaching and we cannot get a read." He turned to the Pathenrau male. "Anything?"

The male stared at a handheld display, fingers flicking across the inputs, then shook his head.

"Still don't know. We need to go. Come on." Pascal led the way, the Haárin hustling after him like children on an outing trying to keep up with their father while Niall and his team brought up the rear.

"We ignore them. We always do because they can't get—" Saul pushed a hand through his hair. "How did you get on this side?" He called out in an addled mix of English and Hortensian German. "No alarms. No one heard you."

Another of the females held up a long knife streaked with blood that still looked fresh. "Blades are quiet," she replied in the same garble, which rang down the curtain on further conversation.

"So who's the pretty?" Georg muttered in the irritated tone most men used when encountering Pascal for the first time.

"No one you want to mess with, boyo," Niall said as they rounded the corner to find four more black suits lying in puddles of blood. "I'm getting the sense that there were more than seven or eight people we needed to worry about."

Saul shrugged. "I'd heard a few more might be coming."

"That would've been nice to know ahead of time." Niall quickened his pace and wondered what the hell other surprises awaited them.

Chapter Thirty-Eight

Jani and Porter worked in silence, scanning, filling out forms, checking each other's work, the young man occasionally casting concerned looks in her direction.

Every so often, she glanced at the two black suits. One stuck by Beech, shooter in hand. But the other had moved closer to the wall and spent much of his time on his comlink, uttering rapid-fire questions and, judging from his frown and continuous fiddling with the device, not getting any answers.

Time to try a little distraction. "I gather you've never had reason to learn this particular meaning of the phrase 'working under the gun?'" She glanced at Porter, who managed a strained smile. Then she checked on Evan, who had fallen into thoughtful silence.

"I am guessing that you're thinking about the other names on these papers and who our host is probably working for, and then asking yourself why you're really here." Jani waited until Evan raised his gaze to meet hers. "Why you were extracted from your prison and dragged out here to a piece of shit station in the middle of nowhere."

Evan shrugged in question. "Why go through all the trouble? Why not simply send someone to visit me in the night?"

Jani thought back to the broadcast of a groundbreaking seen what felt like years ago. "That person is trying to rebuild their career. Earth really was not an option—Service shares responsibility for you and if anything happened they would find out who did it if only to save face. Outer Circle is out because it's that person's territory. It would be like shooting you in their house and burying you in the backyard."

"Pearl Way is the Nawar's base." Evan frowned. "I've no argument with them."

"Muddied waters."

"Seems awfully...complicated."

"Multiple layers between you and Anais Ulanova and no-one knows enough to make the connections." Jani felt the change in the air when she uttered Anais' name, and knew she'd guessed right. "It's the Family way. Surely you haven't forgotten." That earned her a look weighted with pain and the unspoken wish that she would just shut up, so she turned back to her work and caught Beech regarding her with clinical interest. "I'm guessing a murder-suicide set-up? Repayment for past sins. Doesn't matter who's one or the other. We both have reasons." Lucien's words returned to mind as they had a habit of doing lately. "Of course she would think that's how it would go. To her, it's all personal."

Evan exhaled with a grumble. "Why is our host letting us discuss it so openly?"

"Because one or both of us will soon be dead and if the former, the other will be in no position to say what's really going on because they would've been well and truly suborned."

Porter scanned the documents, then turned to Jani, face set with the grim determination to just do his job despite the topic of conversation. "No confirmation by you?"

Ah—time to bullshit. "Given that these docs could be used as evidence in a legal battle, it's better if the court-appointed examiners execute the formalities." Jani added a sigh for emphasis. "Plus we've already subjected them to quite a bit, and there's always a risk of damage with chips this old. That would complicate matters further."

"Yes, I definitely see your point." Porter continued his examination at a pace that would make a snail seem a sprinter.

It's my star power. Jani had to stop herself from laughing out loud, and caught Evan watching her out of the corner of her eye. *I'm fine.* She continued to manipulate her dummy 'pack through a series of finalization steps—the device performed so well and looked so familiar that she caught herself more than once treating it like her old 'pack. Stroking it like a pet . Whispering to it in whatever language came to mind at the moment. If she somehow made it through this ordeal alive, she owed Dr. Ishola a drink.

Focus. She still had questions and possibly little time remaining to get answers. Plus her black suit with the comlink had been tapping his device with increasing urgency, which meant...what? *Niall making trouble?* Or had Lucien's crew come through for him? *Just keep talking, Kilian.* "So what was it?"

Beech looked up from her over-the-shoulder monitoring of Porter's documents handling. "I'm sorry?"

"What led to...?" Jani gestured around the room. "Did you start out undercover and decide the benefits were too good to pass up? Or was it part of the baggage you brought along when you signed up?"

"Option two." Beech offered a hint of a smile. "Rather like our dear colonel, only he seems to have lost his nerve over the years."

You mean he rediscovered his soul. Jani shrugged. "You were stationed at Amsun before what I assume was your fairly recent transfer to Fort Karistos?"

Beech nodded, eventually. "Yes."

"Roland's yours." Jani waited for another nod. This one took longer. "Did you tell him hybridization's not reversible?"

Now Beech seemed restless. She glanced back at the black suit with the comlink, then stilled as though listening for some sound or other. "What makes you think he would wish it to be?"

"His edge. Everyone who comes to Thalassa, at first they're a little lost. They've been forced out of their life. Sometimes they arrive with nothing more than the clothes on their backs, and they're scared.

They tiptoe for a while. Get their medical needs sorted. Get a sense of the place." Jani's throat tightened—she tried to loosen it with a cough. "But Roland was different. He just muscled in and went for the warehouse straight away, and next thing I know we're stockpiling weapons." She set down her 'pack and flexed her hands. The joints ached, as though she had carried something heavy for a long time. "Some of my people, they're...worried. They think we need them."

Beech nodded. "It's a dangerous world out there."

"I think that was the point he was sent to push with the help of assorted outsiders." Jani flexed her neck as the tension took hold of her shoulders. "You're trying to set up a gunrunning operation. Maybe to supply secessionists. Or just whoever pays the most. And I want you to stop."

Beech smiled, a "what can I do?" expression. "It's a perfect location. A little piece of unaligned territory in the middle of the Outer Circle. The Commonwealth can't touch you and I know people who can ensure that it stays that way."

"And you have the perfect population to intimidate and control, medical dependents who have nowhere else to go."

"You're the little guy. As you said, your hybrids are worried. We would have your back, and we would pledge not to interfere—"

"Unless we gave you cause. And every so often, you'd yank our chain just to remind us who's who and what's what."

"Because you know us so well."

"I grew up in Ville Acadie. Then came the Old Service. Then years in places a lot like this. I've known you all my life." Jani paused, felt the rise in tension, Evan's stare fixed on the side of her head. "Does whoever you're working for know about this plan, or are you moonlighting?"

"I work for myself." Beech's reply came fast and harsh, drawing a sidelong look from the black suit at her side.

"No, you were always part of the joint operation. Assisting Families in matters of tax avoidance. Except something's happened that's driving you to go solo." Jani waved a finger at the woman. "You were the missing piece. I was waylaid at Padishah after I retrieved the first document and someone tried to take the second one from me at New Indies. There were signs they'd been looking for it for quite some time. They were yours. You were trying to undercut whoever runs you. I'm guessing they want to take all this away from you. Cash out, maybe? Or lay low for a time, leave you to take the fall? Well, sorry, but I have no interest in providing you with an exit route."

"You can deal with me." Beech took a step towards her, hands held waist-high and open but her tone cool, matter-of-fact. "Or else you'll have to deal with that someone, who I believe you know would be much less generous." She laughed, as though they discussed a silly disagreement, not the fates of three and a half thousand hybrids. "It can work." She tilted her head in Evan's direction. "Tie off a loose end. Go on from there."

Jani studied the woman's face and for the first time got a good look at her eyes. An unusual color, rich turquoise, likely fake but what did it matter? *Poor Niall—between those eyes and the red hair you must've really knocked him for a loop at first.* But she saw only desperation and a willingness to drag everyone else along for the ride. "Bright eyes. In too deep." She brushed off Beech's puzzled look. "When people start dying, the hybrids will be blamed. Then the idomeni would get involved. But you don't care if you start a war, do you?"

"Just means more customers." Beech exhaled with a huff. "Alright, playtime's over." One more tap of the wristband. "Saul? Display up. Open the airlock." She tapped again. "Saul?" She turned to the black suit with the comlink. "Contact Kleist and tell him to find out what's going on at the airlock."

The man held up the link and shook his head. "I've been trying— he's not answering."

Beech gestured towards the main door. "Call in Biedecker and we'll—"

Comlink shook his head. "He said he heard something and went with Viggo to check it out."

"*When?*"

"A minute or so—ago."

Jani glanced at Evan, who looked back at her, head tilted to one side, appearing altogether too calm for a man who had just been called "a loose end." *He did plan something.* With Niall. *It better shake out soon, don't you think, Ev?*

Beech stood hands on hips, then gestured to Porter. "Are you finished?"

Porter held up a stylus. "I just need to fill out—"

"Do that later. Pack up." Beech turned to Comlink. "Notify Tessa. Start final checks. We're pulling out." She squinted at her two prisoners. "Now, which of you is worth saving?" She nodded to Evan. "You're a bargaining chip." She barely looked at Jani. "You're about to die for nothing." She nodded to the black suit at her side, then took a step back.

He raised his shooter and pointed it at Jani.

Fired.

Chapter Thirty-Nine

Pascal and one of the Haárin males had just dispatched the two black suits who had been guarding the door to the room in which Jani was being held when a shot sounded from within, a high-power burst like a thunder crack.

Niall grabbed Pascal's wrist as he raised a shooter to blitz the control board. "No. Shooting the panel locks it." He looked around until he spotted Saul. "We need a cutter. A laser torch." But Saul just shook his head.

Then he caught a look pass between Pascal and the Pathenrau male, who reached into a belt bag and pulled out an all-in-one tool.

Niall paced a tight circle, hands pressed to the sides of his head. "He's going to take the door apart? We don't have time for that shit."

"As opposed to wasting time hunting down a device that may not even be available." Pascal's voice emerged too even by half. Robotic calm. Augmentation kicking in, maybe. Or just his nature.

The male popped off the panel, shone a penlight into the opening, then pulled another tool from his bag and began to probe.

Chapter Forty

Jani had been shot before. As soon as the black suit raised his weapon, she did what she had done previously and turned so her animandroid left side took the worst of it. The burst sent her staggering into the table, left arm flapping as though boneless, pink carrier spraying from the exit wound.

A sensation of heat. Not something she felt before.

Then came the pain, her arm in flames, nerves gone mad. She braced against the table, breathed in short gasps.

The black suit sighted down again.

"That's Two of Six—you can't kill her." Porter grabbed his slingbag and flung it at the man, who lost his balance and stumbled into Beech but recovered too quickly. He fired at Porter, who dropped, then lay still.

Jani felt the pain recede. Watched everything slow down, as though all action had frozen but for hers. Like with augie, but different. Heat instead of chill. Silence in her head instead of the constant yammer of that mad little implant urging her onward.

Red instead of icy clarity. So much red. It closed in around her sightline, tunneling, then filling in so all shone red. A world seen through blood.

She saw the black suit point his weapon at her again, his arm ratcheting into position, still images one after another. She moved towards him one step then two and she gripped the front of his shirt and dragged him across the floor and slammed him against the wall once twice again until he dropped the shooter and tried to pull her hand away until she slammed him one more time and then another and he slid down the wall to the floor trailing red in his wake.

"You're not—a bit human—anymore, are—you?" a voice in fits and starts.

Jani turned.

Beech raised her weapon. "We're not even going to ask—we're going to raze that shittin' home of yours to the ground—"

Voices sounded from out in the corridor. The door mech whined. Beech hesitated.

All the distraction Jani needed. She closed in. Hooked her right arm around Beech's extended forearm, then rammed her left hard into her elbow.

First the crack of the shooter as Beech squeezed off then her scream as bone snapped and jagged yellow edges broke through skin.

Jani released her and she crumpled to the floor.

Chapter Forty-One

A second shot sounded.

"Come on." Niall paced while Saul, Georg, and the other Haárin watched Pascal and the Pathenrau male work on the door, the former holding the penlight as the latter continued to probe the exposed controls.

Then came a third shot. A scream.

"Not Jani." Pascal's voice had gone from calm to dead.

Niall leaned close. "Whatever he's doing, could he do it faster?"

"He's almost finished," said the male. Another poke with the probe, and the door swept open.

Niall stormed in first, Pascal on his heels.

They both stopped.

Jani stood over Beech, who knelt on the floor cradling her right arm, eyes closed, breathing too rapid and shallow. Against the wall, a black suit sat slumped, eyes staring, blood smearing the wall behind him. Another black suit stood pressed into the far corner, hands raised, eyes wide and jaw working silently. Nearby, the body of another man, his shirtfront blackened by shooter scorch.

Niall caught sight of van Reuter crouched on the floor behind his chair.

"What did I tell you, Colonel?" He worked to his feet. "Chaos agent." He laughed, a little too loud and a little too long, then fell back into the chair and buried his head in his hands.

Niall looked back at Jani and saw Pascal had led her off to one side, talking to her in a low voice as he examined her damaged arm. She seemed dazed, her responses limited to nods and head shakes.

———

"Jani?" Lucien slipped his hand under her chin and raised her head. "Jani? Look at me."

Jani fixed on his voice first, so soft and slow, before finally meeting his eyes, framed in spatters of red as though he wore a torn face mask.

"Breathe when I tell you to. In, then out. Ready?" He inhaled through his mouth, then exhaled. "Breathe." A pause. "Breathe."

Jani breathed. After a few cycles, her vision began to clear. Voices and movements smoothed.

She looked around the room. At Evan, slumped, hand pressed to his mouth, staring at nothing. At Niall, standing inside the entry, gaze moving from Beech to the slumped black suit and then to her, fixed and focused, as though seeing her for the first time.

———

Morwenna had yet to move or make a sound. Niall crouched beside her—she raised her head but didn't look at him. He touched her hand, felt the icy chill. "Do you people have a medic?"

"Tessa knows some things." Georg had wrested the comlink from the other black suit and alternated between talking and tapping. "I can't raise her."

"Is that the pilot? Short blonde? Big mouth?" Lucien set his hand against Jani's back and guided her towards the door. "We locked her and her second in the storage room just off the dock in case we needed them. They're fine." He stopped to talk to the black-garbed Pathenrau, who never took his eyes off his handheld.

Niall tried to coax Morwenna into a more comfortable position. But she shook her head and hunched further over her broken arm, so he decided to leave her be until it came time to move out. He rose and walked over to Jani. "Are you all right?"

Jani remained still for a few moments, then nodded.

Niall waited for words, then gave up. "Your hand."

Jani looked down at her left hand. What was left of it. "It hurt before," she said in a hoarse whisper. "It's numb now." She worked what remained of her fingers over and over again.

Please—not two injured and sliding into shock. "I assume you'll be riding with them." Niall looked out into the corridor, where the Haárin milled. Most had drawn blades, although a few held shooters as well. No need for quiet anymore. "I'll be taking charge of Morwenna's ship and—"

"Beech." Some life returned to Jani's face, her voice emerging a touch stronger. "Major Beech. SIB transfer to Karistos from Amsun. She led the team that investigated your kidnapping."

"What?" Niall looked back at the woman, who raised her head long enough to fix on Jani with a look that managed to chill despite the pain haze.

"You wouldn't have recognized her. Different hair. Different face." Jani poked her cheeks and forehead in what looked like an attempt to simulate injections. "Let's just say this has all been very educational." She patted Niall's arm, then left him to stand by the door.

One last patient to see. Niall walked over to van Reuter just as the man raised his head and scrubbed his hands over his face.

"Colonel." He looked around the room. "Jesus, I need a drink."

That makes one of us. Niall swallowed hard. He'd have passed by an entire rack of bottles without a thought. *What I need is water.* In a glass filled with crushed ice. *Dehydrated.* He could tell from the low-level muscle ache, the muzzy head. *Concentrate.* "I'll be contacting Sheridan as soon as we move to the ship. Let them know what was lost has been found. You'll accompany me to Karistos for a debrief. Sorry, but then it's back to Earth." He waited for the man to meet his eye. "Promise me you won't try anything stupid."

Van Reuter traced an X over his heart. "And hope to die." He lay back his head and stared at the ceiling, his previous bravado a distant memory.

Niall turned back to Morwenna and spotted Saul heading towards her. "Saul? What are you do—" Before he could get the words out, the man closed in and pressed his shooter to the side of her head. "Saul? What the hell are you doing?" He left his weapon holstered, hoped like hell he wouldn't have to use it. "Back away now."

"She was going to leave us here to rot." Saul switched the shooter out of standby. The activation hum seemed to fill the room. "Kill us all and leave us like Elsie."

"I said back away now. She is my prisoner and I am taking her to the nearest Service base for initial processing and then on to Fort Karistos." Niall calculated how fast he needed to move and how hard he needed to hit. "This is where your path and mine diverge, boyo. Back away."

"I'll get him." Georg circled around Niall and placed one hand on Saul's shoulder while easing the weapon from his hand with the other. "Let them take care of her." He patted the man's shoulder as he steered him out of the room.

One crisis averted. With no doubt more to come. It occurred to Niall that the ship's crew might feel the same way towards their erstwhile boss and he wondered how in hell he would be able to maintain a guard on her that he could trust not to kill her. "Time to go." He took hold of her good arm, and caught a glimpse of bone poking through the skin of the broken one. "Can you stand?"

Morwenna nodded. She started to rise, leaning against him so heavily that he set one foot behind the other to brace himself.

Then she caught sight of Pascal and her eyes widened.

God—they can be half-dead... Niall supported her as she struggled to her feet, but as Pascal passed, she let go and stumbled against him, full speed ahead in damsel-in-distress mode. Looked up into his eyes, one hand pressed to his chest—

—and stilled, then backed away and watched him move on.

"Forget it, my lady." Niall leaned close to her ear. "You were going to kill the only living soul he has ever cared about. Pray you never run into him again."

Chapter Forty-Two

Jani walked to the door, then stopped and waited for Lucien to catch up. "Niall's watching me. He looks worried."

"Let's not care about the way Niall is looking at us." Lucien gestured for Zal to follow. "You did what you had to."

"Yeah." Jani watched Evan walk to the table, collect the documents, and tuck them inside his shirt. "I need my bag."

"I'll get it." Lucien collected her gear and stuffed it into the slingbag, which he hung off her right shoulder and adjusted as Aicha had.

As Lucien worked, Jani looked around the room, finally fixing on Porter's body. "He was the dexxie they brought in to confirm the documents. He saved my life."

Lucien gave the body the barest glance. "He took part in the kidnapping of a Service officer, then stood aside while you were held captive, forced to work under threat, and nearly killed. At least he did something right." He ushered her into the corridor. "I wish I knew who the hell was coming."

Niall followed on his heels, gripping a subdued Beech by the elbow of her good arm. "Given the identity of our host, I have a feeling I know who they are. They're porting over from a Service craft, corsair class or higher, crew of ten or twelve, out of Amsun."

Lucien looked back at Zal, who arched a brow as his fingers flicked over his handheld. "A patrol would come from one of the Pearl Way bases."

"It's not a patrol. It's a clean-up crew." Niall looked to the group of Haárin and shook his head. "This is going to get pretty damned interesting pretty damned fast."

They started down the corridor towards the docks. Haárin moved to the front and brought up the rear except for Zal, who tagged behind Lucien and called out the occasional one-word comment to him in Vynshà Haárin about whatever it was he tracked.

Jani focused on the Haárin front line, an array of colors that served to jar her brain and shake her out of her daze. "I see you didn't listen to me about the Haárin."

"Station security went dark. I needed help. They were willing, able, and equipped. Remember what I said when I saw you off." Lucien handed her a shooter. "We raided the stash on the way in. Can you manage?"

"*Yes.*" Jani watched him join Zal—together, they slipped to the back of the group to join the Haárin rear guard. Then she tucked the weapon into her trouser pocket and concentrated on putting one foot in front of the other. Her sight had cleared—no more red. But she felt drained, as though she had slept badly for weeks.

"So Anais really planned all this?"

Jani flinched as Evan drew alongside. She pressed her arm closer to her body to avoid brushing against him, wondered why he sought her out at all. "Most of it. Beech added a few moves of her own, but I don't believe they helped her very much."

"No, they didn't, did they?" Evan bent closer; either he knew it bothered her or he was so oblivious he didn't think about it. "I know why she came after me, but why you?" He looked back until he spotted the pale blond head. "All because of him?"

"There were a few business dealings I quashed during my time in

Chicago. And I was responsible for her involuntary retirement. I get in her way. She wants me gone." Jani remembered the stress and fear as those events unfolded, as she fought to save new friends and old from getting dragged under. *And history repeats.*

Evan lowered his voice. "I am guessing that dropping me off at the nearest station and forgetting you ever saw me is out of the question."

"That's not my call. You're Niall's prisoner now." Jani saw his jaw tense at the word, in their past the first indication of the fight to come, a jog of her memory that she could've done without. "You'll never have the life you had, but you could eventually have a life." She pointed towards the front of his shirt, where a corner of one of the documents peeked out from beneath the placket. "You've got your paper, so you can make Anais' life miserable for a while. You may be able to score a few points with the Service with what you learned here." She looked back at Niall, his expression grim, the black eyepatch like a wedge of shadow. "You'd have scored more if you hadn't half-blinded the Admiral-General's Colonel."

Evan huffed. "He's almost as much of a disruptor as you are." He glanced down at Jani's damaged hand, and winced. "I had a feeling it would end like this, but knowing it and seeing it are two very different things."

Jani managed a nod. *And this life's lesson will stick as long as all the others you've lived through.*

They had almost reached the final turn when voices sounded from an adjoining corridor.

"Here we go." Niall moved to the front of the group, Beech in tow. He positioned her to one side, where Georg stood ready to take over guard duty, then moved to the middle of the corridor and stood, still and straight, hands clasped behind his back.

The new arrivals rounded the corner in a tight pack, then slowed as one when they saw what awaited them. Nine Spacers, all fitted out in light armor. All wore sidearms. Three carried long shooters. Their craft no doubt came equipped with light and heavy ordnance. Pulse bombs. Particle beam cannons.

Jani watched them approach. *They could've wiped us out from a distance.* Blown the whole station to atoms. *But they need someone here.* She glanced at Evan, who had stuck a hand inside his shirt to adjust the documents. *Or something.*

"Colonel." The lead man nodded to Niall. "Scholt, SpecOps out of Amsun." Medium human height. Dark hair trimmed high and tight. An Outer Circle accent blunted by rapid delivery. He looked past Niall to Jani and the rest, gaze pausing on the Haárin before moving to Beech and settling.

Niall nodded. "Colonel." He took a step closer to the man and they started talking.

Jani watched the men behind Scholt scan them. Gazes settled mostly on the Haárin, but a few found Evan and locked. She tugged on his sleeve, pulling him back until they stood behind Saul. "The next few minutes are going to be very difficult for you. But you need to keep your mouth shut and your head down until we get off this station."

Evan glanced at the Spacers. "They're Service."

"They're out of Amsun." Jani pointed to Beech. "That's where she's from." She watched Scholt—could she read his mind if she stared long enough? "We don't know whose side they're on. Are they here to arrest her or rescue her?"

"How sweet—you're looking out for me." Evan laughed, a single, bitter exhalation. "Because I need to live."

"What the hell are you—?" Then Jani remembered the last words she had spoken to him that final night. ...*someone to share my ghosts with.* So many ghosts since then. Maybe it was time to lay a few to rest. "We all need to live, okay? This has nothing to do with us."

Evan started to speak, but before he could get the words out, the sounds of raised voices fixed everyone's attention.

"...our prisoner, Pierce."

"She was transferred to Karistos and is under our jurisdiction."

"Like bloody hell."

As the back-and-forth continued, Beech stood pressed against the wall, head down but occasionally snatching glimpses of the men behind Niall and Scholt.

She's afraid of them. As Jani watched her, she also tried to follow the argument, which had lowered in volume but judging from the expressions on the two men's faces had ramped up in intensity. "I'm going to move up a little." She waited for Evan to respond, but after a beat of silence she turned to find he had moved farther away and now stood behind the Haárin rear guard. "Evan?" She beckoned for him to move closer, but he either didn't see her or ignored her.

Then he broke into a run and headed for the corridor that led to the human docks. He had almost turned the corner when the shooter burst sounded. The pulse packet hit him square in the back and exited out his left side, scorching the floor before dissipating like a puff of smoke. He dropped like a puppet with its strings cut, the back of his shirt blackened and smoking.

A few twitches as the last of the electrical charge worked through his limbs. Then, stillness.

Time stopped, a frozen moment, shock and held breath.

Jani turned towards the Spacer group. All the men stood motionless. No indication of who fired the shot.

Scholt stepped around Niall. "I would advise everyone to remain in place." He looked around until he spotted Jani. "If you could inform your, uh, compatriots to refrain from wandering off."

Niall approached the men. "Who the hell fired that shot?" A few looked away. Scrapes of boot soles on flooring sounded as feet shifted. But no one spoke.

Scholt ignored him. He walked past Jani and the others to Evan's body and turned it onto its back with the toe of his boot. Then he pulled antistatic gloves from a belt bag, dragged them on, and patted down Evan's body until he found the documents and tucked them into a slipcase he just happened to be carrying with him.

Never realized they were part of standard issue. Jani looked back at Niall, who stood shaking his head. *They're running an errand for Anais.* Not even bothering to hide it.

"This station will be cordoned off and searched." Scholt returned to his spot at the head of his team. "Afterwards we will transport all of you to the nearest Service base for debriefing."

Jani closed her eyes. *We'd be spaced within minutes after break-away.* But how to avoid that outcome? Violence now would lead to disaster. It would play into their hands, allow them to shift blame, endanger the Haárin, her hybrids, the shaky relationship with the worldskein.

What would they fear the most? Not any authority, apparently. *Investigation. Exposure.* She took a deep breath and walked towards Scholt, stopping first by Niall and holding out her hands palms-up, requesting his permission to speak.

Niall's frustration showed in his reddened face. He knew what she knew, that to push back hard against Scholt meant shooting and they were badly outgunned. He started to speak, stopped, then nodded.

Jani set herself directly in front of Scholt. She stood half a head taller and that seemed to bother him—he took a step back so he didn't have to tilt his head quite so much. "What languages do you understand?" she asked in English.

"We have translator capability." Scholt's stab at the language held a harshness that pointed to Hortensian.

"It does fail at times. It misses nuance. And we need to be very precise here, do we not?"

Scholt's eyes narrowed. "Mostly Hortensian. Josephani. Some Elyan Greek."

Jani turned to the Haárin and asked in Vynshà Haárin. "Who can speak with them?"

No one moved at first. Then ní Zal stepped forward.

Jani struggled to keep from smiling. "How fortunate that you are with us, ní Zal." *Wuntoi's agent.* He had to be. *Appears out of nowhere. Gives us exactly what we need when we need it.* Time to show him what could mean. "I can speak Elyan Greek well enough," she continued in Vynshà, "but our chance of surviving this is better if the words come from you, Pathenrau."

Zal drew up next to her. He gave off the same air of matter-of-fact arrogance he had displayed since their first encounter, which would serve them well in this instance.

"I begin." Jani waited for Zal's nod. "We are here under the auspices of Aden nìRau Wuntoi, Chief Oligarch of the Shèráin worldskein." She detected the barest hesitation in Zal's flow of words, but he soon recovered. "We learned of interference with Haárin ships, and came here to investigate. We have learned that which we came here to learn." She motioned towards Evan's body. "What has occurred here is a matter for you and your dominants and no concern of ours." She waited for Zal's translation, her eyes on Scholt, whose glances at the Haárin had grown more frequent. *Tall, aren't they, Colonel?*

Zal nodded, and she continued. "We have been in constant communication with the offices of the Chief Oligarch and the local Trade Associations. They know why we are here and that which we do. We must report to them regularly or they will send additional personnel to assist and support." She detected little if any hesitation in Zal's speech now, which meant that he was either a better liar than ninety-nine percent of all idomeni or he had indeed been keeping someone informed of their activities.

A little bit of Scholt's bluster flaked off as it sank in that he wouldn't be able to misrepresent what happened here as easily as he first thought. "We...have no quarrel with the worldskein."

"Then we shall be on our way." Jani waited until Zal finished, then turned to leave.

Scholt raised a hand. "However—"

"*We shall be on our way.*" Jani spoke, switching to Elyan Greek without thinking, her voice deepening, shoulders rounding.

Scholt swallowed hard. Sucked his teeth repeatedly. Then he

looked down at her injured arm, brow furrowing. "I see you've been shot."

Jani nodded, then pointed to Beech with her damaged hand. "On her order. Such has already been reported as well."

———

Niall watched the transition, the curving of Jani's shoulders and change in her speech patterns, the barely-concealed disgust on Scholt's face that warred with the realization that he had stepped in a diplomatic shitpile and would soon be in over his head. Listened to the back and forth, fingers crossed behind his back.

Then came silence, the only sound the occasional *plip plip* of carrier dripping from Jani's arm to the floor.

He checked the Haárin. More rounded shoulders, but all weapons still sheathed and holstered. As for Pascal, he appeared... focused. Yes, they could do some damage, but they'd sustain a helluva lot more.

Georg nudged him. "What the hell is she doing?"

"She's informing them that it is definitely not in their best interest to kill us." Niall glanced down the corridor at van Reuter's body. "We just witnessed an execution, boyo. They were supposed to wait until they got him aboard the ship. I believe someone got a little overexcited."

Saul looked back at the Haárin. "Would they kill idomeni?"

"They would say they were provoked. But we have agreements in place and this is a commercial automated station, not a Service base or secured facility, and the rules of engagement—" Niall caught Saul's frown and ran a mental filter of all the rules and regs for a shorter answer. "They'd be in a lot of trouble if they shot anyone else."

"Will that stop them?"

Niall hesitated, then gave the only answer he could. "I hope so."

Jani nodded to Zal, started to leave, then paused. She met Scholt's eye, and slipped again into Elyan Greek. "The Admiral-General has a long reach. I would not want to be the one who deprived him of his colonel." She waited as Scholt started to speak, then stopped, as the thought settled that Sheridan knew about the situation as well. Then she motioned to Zal to return to the group while she stopped to talk to Niall.

"Hitting them between the eyes with the worldskein." Niall nodded. "Looks like it worked."

"Seemed pretty weak as I was laying it out. They were ordered to keep a low profile and killing Evan in front of witnesses bitched that all to hell. They're in trouble." Jani heard Scholt talking to his men—she thought she caught the words *fan out* and *search*, but she couldn't be sure. "They could always change their minds."

"Sometimes all you can do is slow them down for a step or two—you know that." Niall looked down the corridor at the crumpled figure. "I told him he'd be going back to Earth. That was the last thing he wanted to hear." He glanced at Beech, who was being examined by a medic. "Well. Best get on with it."

Jani lowered her voice. "Please come with us."

"You know I can't." Niall squeezed her good arm. "Thanks for coming after me and for getting me this far. I'll see you back in Karistos."

Jani watched as he joined a couple of non-coms setting up search drones. Caught Scholt's gaze one last time, and held it until she felt a hand on her elbow.

"We're moving now." Lucien pushed her into action and steered her down the corridor towards the Haárin docks.

Jani looked back as they turned the corner in time to see two Spacers muscle Evan's corpse into a body bag.

Chapter Forty-Three

Niall boarded the shuttle and headed for the seat farthest from the hatch, buckling in as the first breakaway alarm pinged. Sensed Scholt's glare, the sidelong glances of the others, and for the first time in his Service career felt in his bones that he couldn't trust his fellow Spacers. Even in the bad old days, before he had ever heard the name Hiroshi Mako, he had known that trust. It had been the one thing that chipped at the wall he had built around himself, that prepared him for the time when a certain captain would see past his problematic history and give him the chance to redeem himself.

Where would I have wound up without my captains? Mako. Jani. *Probably like Scholt.* Throughly corrupt, but not high enough in the food chain to avoid the inevitable fallout. *Always a hell of a wake-up call when you finally realize you're the one who takes the hit.* That you weren't nearly the operator you believed yourself to be.

He didn't look up until he heard some rough back-and-forth, and saw two of the Spacers maneuver Morwenna into the prisoner compartment at the front of the cabin. The medic had applied a cast to her forearm; the grey surface bedecked with illumin-studded monitors and infusers looked way too festive for a medical device, especially given the circumstances. Morwenna herself appeared drawn, shaky, shining sea-eyes rendered dull by pain, drugs, and circumstances in general.

Niall pretended to be asleep to blot out the view. Felt exhaustion settle like a lead blanket. Wondered if he dared risk falling asleep.

"Help a girl out?"

He opened his eye, turned towards the compartment.

"I still have some reach. I can make it worth your while." Her voice barely rose above a whisper. "We're not so different, you and I. Came from the same place." She looked off to the side, the compartment lighting carving hollows in her face. "I never knew my father. My mother abandoned me, too—"

"If you're just going to recite my ServRec, don't bother." Niall debated moving. Unfortunately, Scholt sat next to the only open seat left. *So much for that.*

Morwenna tried again. "Next place we dock, take me for a walk to stretch our legs, then turn your back." She smiled. "I'll even shoot you if you want. Some place that won't hobble you too much." As the silence stretched, the smile faded. "Why not?"

"You know why."

"They would've talked."

"They didn't know anything. They didn't want to know anything." Niall thought of Sharon and "Romeo and Juliet" and knew he'd replay that bit of conversation for the rest of his days. "They just wanted to get by."

Morwenna watched him for a time. Then she turned her face away. "You have gone soft."

"I'm good with that." Niall lay back his head and pretended to sleep.

Chapter Forty-Four

Much to Lucien's annoyance, Jani delayed their departure to help Saul and Georg free their pilot and her second from their storage room prison and bid them thanks and good luck. Then she followed him through the retrofitted passageway to the Haárin wing of the station and down the gangway to the Vynshà craft. Once aboard, she buckled into the jump seat next to his as best she could one-handed. "Where are we headed?"

"Away as quickly as possible in case they change their minds about letting us go." Lucien sat still for a few moments, then unbuckled and headed towards the front of the craft, where the pilot's cradle was located.

Jani watched him talk to the pilot. Zal and his ever-present handheld soon joined them—when breakaway commenced and the shudder of mechanicals and accelerated fuel burn radiated through the cabin, they continued to confer, Lucien and Zal braced against the cradle.

"It is a great thing, and truly, to be a trusted suborn of nìRau Wuntoi."

Jani gestured apology as Aicha lowered into the seat that Lucien had vacated. "I may have stretched the truth a little." The female's Acadia Central United headband caught her eye. "Where did you get white ones? I used to own every piece of fan gear I could find and I've only seen the red version."

"We have traveled to your homeworld. There we bought the red, then removed the color so we could wear them." Aicha slipped a finger under the edge of the headband and snapped it. Then she hesitated. "It is permissible?"

"Yes, it's fine. The players' uniforms have white in them—" Before Jani could finish, Lucien reentered the cabin and pointed to Aicha.

"Get her out of here." He gave Jani the barest glance, then returned to the pilot deck.

"Get who what out where?" Jani struggled as Aicha and an Haárin male unbuckled her and pulled her out of the seat. "What are you doing?"

"We must go, ná Kièrshia."

"Go where?" Jani tried to break Aicha's hold on her good arm, but the female's grip tightened like a manacle. She fought as the Vynshà muscled her out of the cabin and into the hatch containing the escape pod, then stuffed her inside the pod and crowded in after her. *"What the hell is going on?"*

Aicha wrapped her arms around her, immobilizing her like a straitjacket. "For your safety, ná Kièrshia."

"What about Lucien?" Jani elbowed the female in the stomach and broke away long enough to stumble to the door and grab the release. "What about everybody—" The male peeled her fingers loose and dragged her back to Aicha, and together they held her fast. "No— take me back. *Take me back right now that's an order goddamn you.*" She fought their ruthless holds and kicked and screamed as the airlock opened and the pod ejected and shot away from the ship and she twisted around until she could see out the porthole and watch it grow smaller and smaller until the curvature of the dead world blocked it from view.

———

Another ship awaited them on the other side of the planet. Jani didn't recognize any of the crew, who were all Vynshà from what she could see—they watched as she entered the main deck and buckled into a jump seat.

She closed her eyes and saw Niall's face but heard Lucien's voice. *Get her out of here.*

"You will see ní Lucien again."

Jani looked up to find Aicha standing over her. The female had removed her headband in order to make room for a command crew headset. Closer inspection revealed the beating she had taken at the station. Her face bore cuts, a bruised lip, and a developing shiner, and streaks of blood showed as black on her purple shirt. "I don't understand."

"He said as we planned that it might occur that we would need to separate you from him. That is all he said."

I still don't understand. Jani picked at her bandages, watched dried flecks of carrier drift to the floor. "You're going to be in trouble. He shouldn't have asked you—"

"He did not ask. We asked." Aicha sat in the seat next to her. "He told us of your fear. That there would be an incident and that we would be punished. But he said also you feared for your home. The place of the blending, where ní Tsecha died. I hope someday to see that place. To walk where he walked and see all that he saw. So I did that which I could do. As did we all."

Jani nodded. "You would be most welcome." She tried to think of more to say, but her mind had no room for anything but images. The ship vanishing behind the planet. A blood-spattered wall. Scholt turning over Evan's body with his foot as though he kicked a rock.

Then she felt a touch, Aicha's hand on her shoulder.

"I know your look. I saw it in some on the Night of Vynshàrau Ascension. The Night of the Blade. I asked them what had happened and they told me." Aicha's voice lowered to a whisper. "In that room where you fought, you were blessed. You saw the goddesses."

Jani tried not to laugh. The touch of the divine had absolutely nothing to do with how she felt at that moment. "Which ones?"

"You should know, you who studied with ní Tsecha."

"My studies." Jani managed a smile. "They did not go as planned."

Aicha leaned close. Her eyes were dark for a Vynshà, gold unto brown, like winter grass. "First, Caith came to you, and you felt—" She clenched her hands into fists, then shook them for emphasis. "The blessed red filled your sight until you saw all through red. Until all was red." She took Jani's hand and pressed it between hers. "All became as chaos for a time, and you did as Caith bade. But even as chaos spread, the seed of order formed within. Caith departed and Shiou came to you. The red faded for you had restored order. Such is the highest purpose of ido." She released Jani's hand and rested it on the arm of the jump seat. "Not all see them. You must be chosen. You are most as ní Tsecha wished you to be, for all your studies did not go as planned. He would laugh and be glad."

Jani gestured agreement she didn't yet feel. She would come around eventually. Maybe. She had no choice. She was that which she was, and there would never be any going back. *Only onward.* "How long will it take us to reach Elyas?"

"Ní Lucien bade us take a long way." Aicha counted on her fingers, an oddly humanizing gesture. "Ten ship-days."

Shèráin days are a little longer than Common. So, eleven, more or less. Not enough time to do what she needed to do, but she had no choice. "Is there a documents examiner on board?"

Aicha gestured in the affirmative. "Always."

"I need to compose a document, a formal report to trade dominants of Samvasta, Amsun, and Elyas." Jani hesitated as she plumbed for the right words, then gave up. This would be the wrong hammer for the nailing she needed to do, but again, she had no choice. "It is not the sort of document an idomeni examiner would ever compose."

"Ah." Aicha bared her teeth. "The blending."

"You could say that." Jani felt more of the mental haze lift and for that she sent a silent note of thanks to Shiou, then apologized to Lord Ganesh for spreading her already thin faith even thinner. She doubted she would ever be a true believer, but right now she would accept all the help, mortal or divine, that she could get.

———

Working with an idomeni documents examiner. How could she have forgotten the sheer unmitigated hell?

The thing was, idomeni as a whole did not possess much in the way of imagination. They didn't extrapolate well. There had been exceptions, yes, but for the most part their documents system had been designed to record facts. Numbers. Events verifiable by measurement and multiple reevaluations. They lacked experience in basing conclusions on senses and feelings. Their languages had no concept analogous to "gut instinct." Humanish messiness and hidden meaning. What Tsecha had christened "the world between the lines."

The report Jani needed to write was pretty much all between the lines.

"I do not understand." Ná Helet Melas, the ship's documents examiner, pressed her fingertips to her forehead and closed her eyes, which might have been either a posture of prayer or a sign of an incipient headache.

Must be going around. Jani worked her shoulders, rolled up the sleeves of the crew coverall she had scrounged from ship's stores, and tried again. "Ná Helet. These actions—the hostage-taking, the attempt to steal the documents after I found them—happened. They may have happened for one of several reasons. I discuss those reasons, and then I explain why I believe one is most likely."

"The documents were stolen because those who stole them wanted them."

"Yes. But why they stole them and for whom—it is important for all to know these things." Jani showed Helet her handheld. "I have copies of all ní Tsecha's treatises. All his work explaining 'between the lines.' I will reference them in footnotes and discuss."

For a moment, the female's expression lightened, and it looked as though Jani had finally gotten through. But then—

"What do you explain ní Tsecha's treatises when you are to write of stolen documents?"

And so it went.

During breaks, Jani adjourned to the games room, where the crew played pattern stones as they took their meals. This was the first time she had seen Haárin dine together since leaving Elyas, and the sights and sounds of their bickering over pattern switches as they ate and drank gave her a sense of home that settled nerves stretched to breaking by the stress of her task and fear for her friends.

At one point, a few of the crew actually managed to rope her into a game. She hadn't played since Academy and lost badly, which earned her a standard round of mockery. She tested her heat tolerance with some of their foods, and learned to her surprise that she still had a ways to go—she ate what she could and found herself longing for the meal bars she had left behind on Aicha's ship. More enjoyable were the herbal tisanes, some of which cleared her head as thoroughly as John's coffee. Every time she entered the room, she found a fresh kettle on the heat, and the similarity to the brewer in the break room down the hall from her office gave her another reason to smile.

By Ship-Day Seven, the headache that had toyed with various cranial locations finally settled for good behind Jani's eyes. She had completed the bulk of the discussion and conclusions, tabulated what hard data she had been able to track down via masked transmissions, and compiled the list of dominants who would receive the report. She added Dieter Brondt to the list because given all he had likely been put through after Feyó realized his dominant had vanished, he deserved to see the result. If he bounced said result back at her with the request that she fold it in three corners and stick it, well, she really wouldn't blame him.

Just as Ship-Day Nine passed into Ship-Day Ten, Jani scanned the completed document into the transmission web, keyed in the send codes, waited for the scatter of green illumins that confirmed transmission, then keyed in a deletion order to wipe the scan from the ship's network. Maybe a systems technician of ní Zal's caliber could extract the bones from various bioelectric nooks and crannies, but officially, on this ship, the document had ceased to be. Ná Helet had informed her that Shiou, the guardian of all ships, demanded order in all things, and since the document was not as ido, it therefore had no place in the memory core of an ido ship. Jani had agreed. When one executed a CYA maneuver, a divine justification definitely provided an extra layer of coverage.

Afterwards, Jani and her headache, which she had christened Meva in honor of a particularly irritating Haárin of her acquaintance, adjourned to the games room. Shift change had yet to occur, so she had the place to herself. She extracted the dregs of a tisane from the kettle and sat at a table near the wall. Sipped. Winced. Stared at nothing. Let her thoughts drift to the whereabouts of Lucien and Niall and the others and what sort of welcome awaited her back on Elyas until eventually she felt herself being watched. She looked around the room, and saw no one at first. Then a shadow in the passageway that led to the kitchens moved.

Jani waited. Eventually, a figure stepped out and crossed the room to stand by her table. An Haárin female, waist-length brown hair bound in a single braid, dressed in comparatively subdued mossy green and purple. She appeared the same age as Jani, which meant she could've been anywhere from forty to seventy in idomeni years. A scar cut across her forehead like a constant furrow. A bump in the bridge of her nose hinted at an old break. Her skin appeared pale brown in the room's light, a few shades darker than Vynshà, gold muted to the merest tinge. Her eyes shone darker also, brown topaz, with still enough difference in degree to differentiate between sclera and iris.

That coloring. How long had it been since Jani had seen it? She stared as the realization broke through her fatigue. A few Laum had survived the War of Vynshàrau Ascension, as did members of every losing sect in Shèrá's serial civil wars. Individuals relocated to remote regions of the homeworld or one of the colonies, forbidden to regroup with other sect sharers until granted permission.

She dredged her memory for words in a language she had once known as well as her own, but had not spoken for over twenty years. "Iuva Laum?"

The Laum female said nothing. She pulled out the chair opposite Jani and sat, all the while meeting her eye, her face a mask. After she had settled, she held out her hand.

Jani responded by holding out her right arm, the real one, the one she had cut into twenty-six times during a ceremony of atonement a little over a year before in the middle of a Shèráin desert called Knevçet Shèràa. The female pushed up the coverall sleeve past her elbow, revealing the crosshatches of scars, some pale and flat, others, darkened and raised. At first, she simply stared. Then she traced each in turn with the tip of her finger, picking them out from amid the numerous similar scars Jani had acquired before and since, lips moving all the while, until she had acknowledged each and every one. Afterwards, she paused for a time, gaze fixed on nothing, before tugging the sleeve back into place, releasing the arm, and leaving the way she had come.

One day later, they docked at Elyas Station. Aicha and the other Vynshà assembled on the main deck to bid Jani farewell. They gave her presents: a yellow shirt, a small framed mosaic of a shell, a white Acadia Central United headband. She looked for the Laum female there and then once more as she disembarked, but she didn't see her again.

————

Jani checked her handheld for messages as soon as she exited the gangway. As usual, the Vynshà ship had been assigned a dock well away from the main concourse of the Haárin wing, so for a time she walked alone, flipping through screens, thanking Ganesh and Shiou and whichever other gods happened to be listening when she came upon the message from Niall.

See you soon.

"Is that a quotation?" She smiled, then stopped in the middle of the corridor and breathed slowly, in and out, and felt some of the tension that had settled into her bones leach away.

Then she hunted for another name. Scrolled through her messages once, then again, and then a third time. *They would've told me. Aicha would've told me.* If something had happened, they wouldn't have held back.

She entered the main concourse at a trot, dodging around the increasing press of Haárin, looking out over the tops of brown heads for a glint of white-blond.

She spotted Lucien near the junction between the Haárin and human wings. He stood leaning against the wall, hands in pockets, but straightened as soon as he saw her. He had changed clothes, exchanging orange and green for his more usual uniform of tan and white, which meant he'd had time to check in at Thalassa.

But not enough time to send me a message. Jani slowed as she neared him, stopped when she came within reach. Then she struck him in the chest with her fists as though he were a door she sought to batter down, once, twice, again and again, until he took hold of her wrists and held them fast.

"They locked in on us thirty seconds after breakaway." He pulled her in closer, and lowered his voice. "I expected it. Aicha arranged for the second ship—it followed us in."

Jani tried to extract her hands from his grasp, but his grip tightened even more. "Why didn't you come with me?"

Lucien just stared at her. He had never been one to show physical signs of stress; the purplish smudges under bloodshot eyes looked as out of place as snow in Karistos. "I didn't know for sure if they could scan us, so I had to assume they could. Humans and idomeni have different heat signatures. Idomeni run hotter."

Jani stilled. "I scan as idomeni?"

"Close enough to be within margin of error." He finally let her go, then prodded her towards the human concourse. "They didn't know how many idomeni were aboard, but they knew of one human. If they didn't find me, they'd know we'd pulled something and they'd go looking because they'd assume we'd stick together. Aicha's ship was fast and had longer range, but it had inferior shielding and their weapons weren't up to the challenge of a combat ship. So she arranged for a second ship to follow us in. That was the one we transferred you to."

Jani shoved her hands in her pockets to still her left arm, which had finally shown signs of carrier shortage and tended to twitch uncontrollably. "You set yourselves up—"

"What did I tell you? That's the job. That's what you are now." Lucien shrugged. "We took precautions. We had an extra pod loaded. Gear in case we needed to eject." He picked at, then bit at a thumbnail, another nervous tic making a debut appearance. "I'm still surprised they let us get away. We were the only witnesses to van Reuter's murder that they couldn't control."

"Maybe Niall held them off."

"Why would he? Did you ever think about why the Service pulled him off your security?"

Jani remembered Niall's words to her when she asked him to return to Elyas with her instead of risking his life on the Amsun ship. *You know I can't.* "The Service is human and Commonwealth and I'm neither. Mako's position is shaky. I was something that his enemies could use against him. I do think about things like that, you know."

They walked in silence for a time. Then Lucien sighed. "God, it was marvelous while it lasted. Including yours, I had three different ships on three different routes, each one monitored at check points along the way."

Aicha's words rang in Jani's memory. *For your safety, ná Kièrshia.* Funny how the idea of multiple decoy ships deployed for the purpose of protecting her made her feel even more vulnerable. "All Vynshà Haárin?"

Lucien nodded, eyes fixed on some middle distance and soft with memory. "Ná Aicha sent out word and they organized."

They continued side by side down the concourse, the tension between them still present but on a downward trajectory. Jani filled the silence by talking about her report, her conclusions about Morwenna's efforts to funnel weapons from Amsun to Thalassa and set up the latter as a gunrunning hub. "Roland was hers. I'm sure there are more—we need to shut them down."

"They're gone." Lucien gave a farewell salute. "They took off soon after we departed the station, so someone must've reeled them in." His voice sounded a little lighter, as though the tension of his homeward journey had finally begun to ease. "Counterargument. About who's behind all this."

Jani braced. She'd had no one to discuss her report conclusions with, and she would have a hard time salvaging what relationships she had with the trade associations if she botched them. "Okay."

"I've known Anais for almost fifteen years. This is going to sound odd, but soliciting murder? Yes. Gunrunning? No." Lucien held up a hand and rubbed his thumb and fingers together as though feeling something sticky, dirty. "It's not her style. It's too—"

"Grubby? Low class? Colonial?" Jani smiled. She had this one. "How about quid pro quo? She's making her comeback out here in the old Family territory, but revelations of corruption and gunrunning would ruin her homecoming and possibly lead to suspicion that she's involved. So she agrees to...mitigate the fallout in exchange for selective eliminations?"

After a moment, Lucien nodded. "That, I could see. Evan is pure revenge. You are—" He eyed her sidelong. "—a multitude of things."

"Niall? Wrong place wrong time?"

"She'd even accuse him of complicity, bring up his past. She never liked Roshi—it would be a great way to sully him." Lucien's eyes widened. "Do you come right out and—?"

"I blame unnamed entities. Shadow groups. I don't mention her name once."

"But it's there between the lines?" Lucien pondered for a time. "So who did you send this report to?"

"The trade dominants on Amsun and Samvasta, and here. Feyó, for all the good it will do." Jani checked a wall clock and made a few rough calculations. "I doubt they've received it yet. Even if they did, it's kind of long and involved."

Lucien drew figures in the air. "Lots of graphs and tables?"

"Footnotes."

"Hmm. Guess it would depend on whether any transmissions from you were automatically classified as 'extremely urgent' and recoded accordingly."

"Why would they do that?"

"No idea."

"Did your new best friend tell you something I should know?"

"I don't have any friends."

As they drew near the secondary concourse that led to the shuttles, a trio of bornsect Pathenrau approached. A male and two females, arrayed in dark blue. They stopped some distance away, then one of the females stepped forward.

"Ná Kièrshia." A bandolier loaded with comlinks and charge packs for a shooter announced her as a member of a security skein. "You will come."

Chapter Forty-Five

Niall stood in the doorway of the cell and surveyed the scene. As if that would tell him anything. A standard brig cell in the high security wing. A bed. A toilet behind a half-height privacy screen. A sink with a mirror of polished poly bonded to the wall. A pull-down table and a stool bolted to the floor.

Looks bloody familiar, doesn't it? He relived the sensation of the blindspecs being fastened onto his head and shuddered.

"The security vid covering the time in question has been wiped." Captain Randal Pullman, Niall's newly-arrived aide, made entries into his handheld as he gave the rundown. He'd spent his first few days dashing between buildings wresting information from various departments and the Karistos sun had already done a number on his redhead-fair skin, which had gone from its usual baby pink to something approaching medium rare. "MilPol completed their scanning a few minutes ago, so we're clear to enter. Their site coordinator confessed to feeling a little jumpy about taking the lead on this. It's outside their usual range of duties."

"They share responsibility for this place and right now they've got the cleanest hands, so they can just suck it up." Niall felt the anger flare as it had repeatedly since he received the call early that morning. Early morning calls never meant good news.

Weapons flowing out like water. Investigators called in from Pearl Way and Inner Circle Regional Commands because every Outer Circle security organization had been neck-deep in the scandal. *How did I miss it for so long?* Well, he hadn't, really. In his bones, he knew. *I just didn't want to believe it.*

"Base SIB's not happy about being locked out." Pullman's voice held the irritation that resulted from being the one tasked with fielding the complaints. "They're claiming everything about her transfer and records came up clean. Nothing even hinting at a red flag."

"Yes, well, they're the ones who let the fox into the henhouse, so until they all pass high security background checks they can go whine to someone who gives a shit." Niall's gaze moved to the blanket-covered mound on the bed, and his chest tightened. "Total cleansing, from Regional Command on down. What a fucking disaster."

"Sir."

Niall approached the bed, then leaned over until he could see Morwenna's face. At first glance, she appeared to be sleeping. It was only when you pulled back the blanket that you saw the thin red line that ran across the front of her throat, the red-soaked bedding beneath. "Blades are quiet."

"Sir?"

"Nothing." Niall watched as the younger man looked from the cell door to the bed and shook his head. "You appear perplexed, Captain."

"I'm just—" Pullman pointed to the gaping entry. "She slept with her back to the door. Given all you told me, if I'd been her, I'd have been holed up in a dark corner behind the bed frame and the mattress with a filed-down anything."

Niall recalled a time when he would've said the same thing, back in his youth when he knew he could live forever if he just kept his wits about him. "You have to sleep sometime." He smoothed the blanket back into place. Tried to ignore the feel of the body beneath and couldn't quite manage it. "I think she knew it was coming. She just wanted to get it over with." He took one last look around the room. "Impound all the scans. Duty rosters. Visitor rosters. Incoming. Outgoing. You know the drill."

"Sir."

"Did you finish the check on Pascal? If anyone could circumvent everything, it's him."

"He was either upstairs—" Pullman pointed to the ceiling, which means Elyas Station. "—or at the Thalassan compound during the time period in question, sir."

"Hmm." Niall knew he shouldn't have bothered to ask. Pascal would've planned every step in order to avoid suspicion and, more importantly, he'd have shown patience. His type would wait weeks, months, years if necessary; this was a *hurry before she talks* hit. *Except they managed to wipe the scans.* Another fucking inside job.

Problem was, the entire damned mess was an inside job.

"Sir." Pullman pointed to his handheld display. "You wanted me to let you know when she'd been sighted. She was seen entering the Elyan Haárin workroom complex fifteen minutes ago."

"She has a name, Pull."

"I just don't—know what—" Pullman scrunched his shoulders. "Ms. Kilian? Ma'am? Ná Kièrshia? It's hard to keep track."

"Welcome to the club." Niall patted the pockets of his desert casual shirt to make sure he had his nicstick case, something he'd done repeatedly since his return. "See what else you can find out." He set his lid in place and turned to leave. "I'm going to take a walk."

Chapter Forty-Six

The anteroom leading to the workspaces set aside for visiting dominants had been decorated in a traditional Pathenrau manner. Cloth in all shades of green covered the walls and ceiling, while the floor had been carpeted with mats woven with patterns resembling grasses and flowering undergrowth. The overall effect brought to mind the depths of a forest, and Jani felt the weeks of stress and fear seep from her very bones.

I guess the Trade Association dominants received the report. She wondered why she hadn't been summoned to Feyó's workroom first for a debriefing-slash-reaming-out. To be honest, she wondered why she had been allowed to see the dominants at all. She hoped they wouldn't grill her for long.

I need a vacation. Maybe she could return to New Indies as a tourist, walk long stretches of beach and swim in waters that didn't blister the skin. *Or I could just, I don't know, sleep for a few days.* She yawned, lay back her head, closed her eyes...

...then jerked awake as pain radiated across her midsection and looked up to find a Pathenrau male, hand raised and index finger extended in mid-poke, staring at her wide-eyed before turning away as their gazes met.

"You will—" He motioned for her to stand, then again for her to follow him, all the while looking back in her general direction as though making sure she was still there. When they reached the entry to the first workroom they came to, he swept open the panel, then practically pushed her inside.

The door closed. Jani heard the whisper of locks. After the darkness of the anteroom, the brightness of the Elyan sun through the wall of windows blinded her—she blinked until the shape framed by the glass came into focus.

Aden nìRau Wuntoi, Chief Oligarch of the Shèráin worldskein, sat in a low seat framed by the central pane. The wash of sunlight brought forward the gold undertones of his bronze-black skin and the leaf-patterned edging of his green overrobe, but the angle proved such that his broad-boned face remained shadowed. On his lap, a bound document lay open, sun striking the pages so they shone as though bathed in lamplight.

I see a lot of footnote formatting. Jani felt a jolt. *Oh well—he would've heard about it eventually.* She had assumed, however, that whatever he saw would have been whittled down and predigested by suborns from diplomatic and priestly skeins into a précis suitable for updating a very busy individual. She'd wandered well into the weeds with respect to discussions of Earth-colony history, Family lineages, and Tsecha's treatises, at times getting herself in so deep she wondered if she would ever find her way out the other side.

Wuntoi looked in her direction—she caught the glint of his brown eyes, so dark that sclera and iris seemed as one. To this point, he had made no sound, but she sensed from his posture and the tilt of his head that he'd already had a rather long day.

Then he fixed on the remains of her left hand.

Jani pulled down her sleeve to hide the bandages, the mangled fingers. "It's my animandroid hand, nìRau ti nìRau. Not a true injury." She spoke Vynshà Haárin out of sheer reflex, then hoped like hell she hadn't just insulted the Pathenrau dominant of all dominants.

"Yet you felt pain." Wuntoi replied eventually in kind. "My security suborns spoke to those Vynshà who aided you." His voice, deep though it was, sounded wistful. "I myself have never seen the goddesses. Such is most as ido." His tone sharpened as his shoulders rounded. "Falling asleep while awaiting a meeting with me is not most as ido."

I didn't know I'd be meeting with you, did I almost slipped out, but Jani caught it in time. "Apologies, nìRau ti nìRau. The journey home—" She dug for an excuse, excavating the one that would have the ring of truth by virtue of being all too true. "Not since the Academy had I worked under direction of an idomeni documents examiner."

Wuntoi's head jerked. Then he bared his teeth so his face seemed to split. *"Hah.* For once you worked with paper as you were meant to." He pointed towards a high seat set against the wall. "Bring that out. Sit."

Jani dragged the chair to the center of the room, then moved it a little to one side to avoid facing Wuntoi directly. It proved to be more a stool than a chair and a tall one at that—she could lean against it but the seat pitched forward and actually sitting on it would require a greater sense of balance than she could manage at that moment.

As she adjusted the seat and positioned herself, Wuntoi turned to the report's table of contents and ran his finger along and down the page.

"This report was not composed in Middle Pathenrau as required."

"We did not trust our facility with the language, nìRau ti nìRau."

"You will need to learn."

"Yes, nìRau ti nìRau."

Wuntoi's finger stopped midpage. "Military weapons at Thalassa."

Jani winced. As bad as it read on paper, it sounded worse spoken out loud. "They will be removed, nìRau ti nìRau. My security suborn informed me that those hybrids who aided the dealers are no longer there."

"Where did they go?"

"Unknown. They will require certain types of medical care eventually and may surface at that time. Assuming they live long enough." Jani gestured an apology as Wuntoi raised a cupped hand in question. "It can be a complex process, nìRau ti nìRau. It must be closely monitored."

Wuntoi nodded. "Members of the military skein will assist with removal of weapons."

Good. "Their assistance is most gratefully accepted, nìRau ti nìRau." *I am sure the chance to examine Service ordnance never crossed your mind.* If the human part of Jani felt any guilt over this, she soon squelched it. *They threw us out.* A little basic decency at the outset and none of it would've happened.

Wuntoi closed the report and tapped the cover with his finger. "Deputy Exterior Minister Ulanova has somehow obtained a copy of this report. She has formally protested the conclusions. She has informed me that she is most insulted and demands from you a formal apology and a revision."

How the hell did she get it? "I did not mention Her Excellency's name anywhere, nìRau ti nìRau."

"Between the lines." Wuntoi pressed one hand to his forehead, then pulled it away. He may have suffered a headache, but a bornsect of his status could not acknowledge such a weakness in the presence of a suborn. "I most recall ní Tsecha's talks of such. If we wish to know of humanish, we must learn to read between the lines." He closed his eyes. "NìaRauta Ulanova felt that nìRau van Reuter was most involved with the death of a...niece. A body daughter of a house brother."

"And body mother of his youngish." Jani gestured agreement. "She does believe that, yes."

"Ownership of property also was involved."

"Yes, nìRau ti nìRau."

"How do humanish maintain order of such?"

"It is a challenge, nìRau ti nìRau."

"The Prime Minister has most assured me, and truly, that those you and the Vynshà Haárin killed were outside of all humanish law and therefore outside all humanish protection." He cupped his right hand in question. "So outside are they that they might not even have been humanish at all."

That means the scandal must extend to the PM's office. Could have been as simple as missed signs, or something more. "That is most...fortuitous, nìRau ti nìRau."

"You say differently in the report."

"I say only that I regret their deaths, nìRau ti—"

"NìRau is sufficient."

"NìRau. I would greatly prefer to avoid such."

"Such is often inevitable."

"Yes, nìRau."

Wuntoi started to speak. Stopped. Massaged the report as though he could absorb all meaning if he pressed hard enough. "You mention a Pathenrau Haárin who proved most as helpful but you do not state a name."

"Ní Zal Karon, nìRau. I wondered if he was of a military or diplomatic skein."

"He is not."

"Apologies, nìRau."

"He is...was...my house son."

Jani's mind blanked. Of all the possibilities, that was one that had never occurred. *You're losing your touch, Kilian.* "NìRau." Scramble scramble. "My security suborn esteems him greatly. He proved most helpful in monitoring the communications of those who sought to interfere with us." She didn't mention that his life had been at risk for possibly the entire journey to Elyas. It didn't seem the right time.

"He disdains all that is ido. He wishes to be humanish." Wuntoi's voice lowered to bare audibility. "He is now in Thalassa."

Might've mentioned it, Lucien. "NìRau. I did not know."

Some individuals said more with silence than great speakers managed with words. The Pathenrau gesture for sadness resembled that of the Vynshà, the right hand crossing the chest to grip the left shoulder, but Wuntoi also lowered his head so his chin touched his chest. He sat that way for some time, a study in dark and light.

Then he raised his head, picked up the report in both hands and slammed it atop his lap. "Why did I know none of this until now?"

"I did request information and assistance from your suborn offices several times, nìRau." Jani paused. "Through ná Feyó's offices."

"Such were not received." Wuntoi smoothed the report cover, then adjusted the binding, which he had loosened during his outburst. "I have spoken with ná Feyó. Communications from and about Thalassa were accidentally blocked. No one understands how such could possibly have occurred."

Oh Feyó. Another idomeni who has learned to lie. Jani nodded. "Such is indeed most unfortunate, nìRau."

"The blockage has been cleared—you may now communicate with my suborn offices as often as required."

"I hope to do so only when absolutely necessary, nìRau."

"You will have to do so most frequently as preparations are made for your journey to Shèrá." Wuntoi picked up Jani's report and riffled the pages. "I do not fully understand that which is between the lines here, and I must, must I not, in order to deal with humanish? Especially nìaRauta Ulanova, who demands you retract all you have written."

Jani replayed Wuntoi's words in her head, unsure if she had indeed heard what she thought she'd heard. "NìRau?"

"Yes or no?"

"Such knowledge would be most helpful to you, nìRau." Jani gestured affirmation. "Yes."

"So. You will be Speaker of Humanish to me. You will explain to me why they act as they do, and the priests who fought with ní

Tsecha will fight with you instead. My suborns will provide you with that which you need to know. Timing. Requirements." Wuntoi had been patting the report cover, but now his hand stilled. "You will not be the only one who serves me thus. I know I must receive opinions from many sources. But you were esteemed by ní Tsecha."

Jani's eyes stung, and she blinked back the tears before they fell. "I esteemed him as well, nìRau."

"I remember his death. I also remember a meeting amid crowds of Vynshà, when you wore clothing soaked with the blood of my predecessor, who ordered that death." Wuntoi cocked his head in question, a posture more humanish than idomeni. "Personal. Such is the correct word?" He clenched his left hand, a sign of disagreement. "I have read much of humanish histories. Too much is personal."

Jani debated keeping silent. *No.* Advisor she'd been named, so advisor she would be. "If I may, nìRau. NìRau Cèel's hatred of ní Tsecha, hatred so great he ordered him killed in secret and from a distance, was personal. His attempt to kill me because I was a favored humanish of ní Tsecha was personal." She gave a humanish hand-wave in Wuntoi's direction. "Your confronting me in the orbital station as I followed ní Tsecha's soul to its place of release was also personal, I most believe?"

"It was strategic."

"Ah. My mistake."

Wuntoi looked past Jani towards the door. "You will tell me of ní Zal?"

"I will do so as best I can, nìRau." Jani braced one foot on the floor, ready to slide off the godawful stool as soon as was seemly. "But I will not control him. He will do that which he will do."

"Yes. We all do that which we will do." Wuntoi stood. "We are finished. For now."

And on that note, which could have been anything from a simple statement of fact to a not-so-veiled threat, the newly-designated Speaker of Humanish took leave of her new boss. As she left the workroom, she encountered a different male standing in the corridor

—he handed her a slipcase packed with documents, then escorted her out.

Just as she passed though a corridor adjoining the wing containing the Elyan Haárin workrooms, one of the doors opened, and Anais Ulanova emerged. She wore a tunic and trousers in brown, her usual garb when meeting with idomeni. She froze when she saw Jani, her stare armed with a full complement of daggers.

Jani stilled as well, and met her eye until activity in the corridor interrupted and they went their separate ways. Gauntlets thrown down. Silent. Invisible. But thrown all the same.

———

Jani paused in the building entry until she spotted Lucien parked in the area reserved for humanish vehicles. But before she could cross the circle, he pointed at something behind her.

Jani turned, and sagged in relief. "You."

"Me." Niall fanned himself. "We can stand out in the damned sun or find a shady spot. Between proximity to the base and your security person, the place is covered. You're safe."

"I think Lucien overreacts, personally."

"I don't."

They found a cluster of shade trees with a bonus fountain, which brought them within shouting distance of another familiar figure disembarking from a Service standard issue sedan.

"*Pull!* It's been too long." Jani waved, then grabbed the ends of her collar. "Congratulations, Captain."

"Ma'am." Pullman beamed like the proverbial boy who had finally gotten the puppy for his birthday.

"Get back in that skimmer before you burst into flames." Niall shook his head as he watched Pullman wave to Jani, then pile back into the vehicle. "Jesus, was I ever that young?"

"No." Jani pointed to his eyepatch, the tan color of which matched his desert casual shirt. "How's the eye?"

"It's..." Niall formed a circle with his thumb and index finger, then curved them inwards to form a very small circle. "They have to grow a certain amount of tissue first and then they transfer it to this eyeball-shaped scaffold—" He flicked a dismissive wave of his hand, then adjusted the patch. "Actually, I'm thinking of keeping this. Lends a certain aspect."

"It does go well with the scar."

Niall plucked his nicstick case from his trouser pocket, then looked towards the Haárin building. "Too many bornsect around today." He tucked the case away. "Thank you for the, uh, parting shot you directed at Scholt. I don't believe they'd have killed me, though, for the reason you mentioned."

"Ejected you in a pod with a note?" Jani sat on a bench in the sun and savored the heat on her back. "'If found, return to H. Mako, Fort Sheridan, Earth?'"

Niall laughed, then wrinkled his nose. "Probably more like a basic drug-and-dump. I'd have awakened three days later in a happy house dressed in clothes not my own."

Jani nodded. "You apparently gave this a lot of thought."

"A boy can dream." Niall pointed a finger at her. "I have a proposal. I propose that if either one of us conjures the bright idea to jump into the deep end of the pool ever again, we immediately contact the other whose job it will be to talk them the fuck out of it."

Jani raised her hand. "I second that proposal."

"All in favor, say 'Aye.'" Niall clapped once. "Motion carried."

They both laughed. Jani turned to check on Lucien to find him leaning against the skimmer, arms folded, watching them and shaking his head. "I think my security chief will be relieved." She turned back to Niall, who strolled tight circle after tight circle before finally stilling and settling back on her.

"You okay?"

"Fine." Jani forced a smile. "You?"

"Still working on it." Niall scuffed at the ground, then bent to brush the resulting dirt off his tietops. "A corsair from Pearl Way

Regional Command intercepted us before we hit the GateWay. Arrested Scholt and the others. Took charge of Morwenna. Beech. Whatever. They put me up in the suite reserved for the Fleet Commander. I think I took the longest shower in Service history, then slept for thirty-six hours straight." He winced. "And there was a Misty waiting for me from Roshi—I'd messaged him right before Morwenna's crew grabbed me to let him know what I thought, what I planned."

Jani bit her lip to keep from laughing. "What did he say?"

"'Bout what you'd expect. 'You dumb son of a bitch, what the hell were you thinking?' Then I got an annotated follow-up that included sections of my SpecOps MilSpec with portions describing my duties underlined. 'Do you see any mention of "allow self to be kidnapped" here? Do you?'" He rolled his eye. "I think I'm in for a lecture when I get back."

"You've been recalled?"

"It's temporary. I think. Lots of planning to do."

"I'm guessing Morwenna will have a lot to tell you."

"Yeah." Niall looked away, hands in pockets.

Or she would, except she's dead. Jani knew that Niall would never admit it, that this was where the Service discussion would end. Except for the personal comments, he had said nothing that hadn't already been broadcast on OCNet or ServNet. *And I won't tell him about our infiltration or the weapons we need to dispose of.* Because he would have to inform Roshi and word would get around and before she knew it Thalassa would be on a watch list. *So we've added yet another brick to our wall.*

Niall looked around. The Haárin workrooms were located in the older section of Karistos, a town within a city, comprised of narrower streets and shorter buildings with multicolored roofs visible from across the bay. "I'm going to miss this. Well, maybe not the heat." He tugged at his shirtfront. "I guess I have to go back, but I shouldn't have to. I can do everything I need to right here."

And a few things you don't need to, which is what Roshi is worried about. Jani watched him pace. "Yours not to reason why."

Niall drew up short and looked to the clear blue glare of the sky for respite. "I always worry when you start with the quotations. Especially that one. God, I hate that poem." He checked his timepiece, and swore under his breath. "I need to get back and talk to the crew that's taking over."

Jani stood. "When do you leave?"

"Tomorrow afternoon." Niall held out his arms. "Take care of yourself."

"You do the same." Jani walked into his hug, smelled mild soap and the harsh remains of nicstick smoke.

Niall gave her a final squeeze, then released her and headed to his skimmer. "Plain ol' survival's the best revenge, Captain." He dug a nicstick out of his case and activated it just as he reached the vehicle. "Rub the bastards' noses in it." Pullman secured him within, waved farewell, then slipped into the driver's seat and sped away.

Chapter Forty-Seven

Jani fell into the skimmer passenger seat, then sagged into the cushions and felt them adjust to her position and apply warmth and light massage to her upper back. "Niall's been recalled," she said as Lucien piled in and steered out of the parking circle and into the Karistos afternoon bustle. "He assumes he'll be back, but he's not sure."

"I predict Roshi will sit on him for a good long while." Lucien paused to grumble at the traffic, then steered them down the road that led to the bay. "He hadn't been out in the field in over fifteen years. You lose your edge. Someone with some muscle would've sucked him dry and spit out the bones." He eyed Jani. "I can't decide if you're a bad influence on him or he's a bad influence on you."

Jani pushed her shoulders into the seat, which ramped up the massage intensity. "I don't think either of us needs any help, do you?"

"Probably not." Lucien eyed her expectantly. "Well?"

Jani dug the topmost sheet of parchment out of the slipcase and scanned it. *It's in Vynshà. How nice of them.* She read it, then buried her face in her hands and thought about how much she'd been looking forward to a few days of relative quiet. "I am to assemble a staff and depart for Shèrá within two weeks Common. The title is Speaker of Humanish. It's an advisory position. Providing background history and information about humanish behaviors." When Lucien failed to comment, she looked to find him grinning at her like the only man who got the joke. "Why are you looking at me like that?"

"Zal and I talked during our jaunt through the nether reaches. Wuntoi's security monitors all stations. Zal was pretty sure he saw your speech."

"I told you—"

"Yes and you told the Vynshà Haárin, too, and that told Wuntoi that you have how many millions at your back? Seventeen at last estimate?" Lucien's grin turned feral. "Given the Oà threat, he wants you on his side. And he wants to keep an eye on you."

Jani let him enjoy himself for a few moments before springing the rest of her news. "Your new best friend is Wuntoi's former house son."

"What?" Lucien turned so sharply that he steered the skimmer into some chop, splashing water over the windscreen. "So that means Wuntoi helped raise him."

"But no blood relation. Their families were closely related by skein, so Zal's body-parents must've been pretty highly placed in the military or upper strata of the administrative." Jani looked out over the water. The seasonal algae bloom had just begun, blue waters showing the first hints of purple. "He wants to be human. Wuntoi wants me to keep him informed. Okay, fine. But you have to sit on him when necessary. We don't need him trying to enrage Daddy and dragging us along for the ride."

"Wuntoi doesn't want you to have too much influence on him, either." Lucien's nasty grin had returned. "Think about where that could lead?"

"I'm a hybrid. I'm no threat to him. I have no standing in bornsect hierarchy." Jani fiddled with her bandages. "I have—" She shook her head, and fell silent.

Lucien glanced at her repeatedly as the quiet continued. "If this concerns the—"

"I saw the look on Niall's face when he entered the room. Evan's reaction. I felt like a spring-loaded trap releasing. Everything through a red haze, and everyone else moving so slow."

"Sounds like augmentation."

"It's different. There was no clear-headed chill this time. It's just the opposite. It's rage." Jani hunched further into her seat. "Aicha could tell from the look on my face. She'd seen it in other Vynshà during the Night of the Blade. She said I saw the goddesses. First Caith, who drove me to chaos, then Shiou, who calmed me after I restored order." Her favorite views, of the Bay, the cliffs, unfurled before her, but they may have been a blank field for all they touched her at that moment. "She said I was blessed. I guess that's one word for it." Silence settled. Then she slid against the door as the vehicle banked and came to rest on a secluded stretch of beach.

"Look at me."

Jani met Lucien's gaze eventually. *When brown eyes chilled, the cold came from within.* Her first thought at their first meeting, just a scant handful of years before. *Now who's the broken one?*

"I watch people. How they react. How they behave. I have to. I don't feel it, so I have to learn it." Lucien's brow knit, as though he tried to recall a fact for an exam. "The hybrids, they don't change in their essentials. If they're loud, they get louder. If they're nervy, they get jumpier. But that's around the edges—at their cores, their personalities, their drives, they're still the same." He pointed at her. "You are a killer. But there's more than one type. You're just basic. With you, it's survival. Self-defense. To save others."

"Nahin Sela was neither."

"Oh, you mean the assassin who murdered your beloved friend and mentor and would've killed you and laughed about it. Okay, fine, add a touch of vengeance if that makes you happy. But you're not—it could never be just a job. It could never be just something you do. Something you...need to do." Lucien massaged the steering wheel, knuckles whitening with every squeeze. "You'll never be like the ones at the station, or who ambushed us at Padi." He stilled, met her eye again, then looked away. "You'll never be like me."

Jani remained quiet. Eventually, she nodded.

"I'm going to upgrade our training exercises. I think you can handle a little more. I may get Dathim involved." Lucien switched the skimmer out of standby and steered back out over the water. "And I would like to add that I am really uncomfortable in the role of emotional counselor and I would like this to be the last time I have to function in that capacity."

"You're good at it, though." After a few minutes, Jani took out her handheld, flipped through page after page of messages, then stopped. "A note from Ian." She ignored Lucien's grumble, and laughed. "We've been immortalized in song." She turned her handheld so Lucien could see the replay of their kiss on the concourse. "I guess the security 'bots edged into Haárin jurisdiction."

Lucien groaned. "I knew that was a mistake as soon as I—" His voice dwindled to an undercurrent of rude French.

"The title is 'Chanson du Galant.' That means 'Song of the Gallant.'"

"I know what it means."

"It's one of the top three most requested songs on the station network. Ian predicts it will be number one by the end of the week." Jani rocked her head back and forth to the beat. "A journey into the unknown...her moonlight-haired guardian awaits—"

"Stop." Lucien hit the decelerator for emphasis, causing the skimmer to jerk.

"You always accuse me of lacking a sense of romance." Jani waited for the song to end, and tried to recall if there was any way to broadcast it throughout the Main House. *I bet Zal could figure it out.* She tucked the handheld back into her bag and dealt with the all-too-familiar sensation of her life approaching at speed. "I've just come back and I'm going to have to leave." She turned to Lucien. "You're coming?"

"Try and stop me." Lucien tapped a beat on the wheel. "Did you tell Niall?"

"No. That kind of news needs to come from Rauta Shèràa. It's not really my place to make that type of announcement."

"He'll be disappointed that you held out."

"He didn't tell me Morwenna is dead, so I think we're even."

"How do you know?"

"What he didn't say."

"You think he liked her. Redhead."

"Pretty sure it was more than that." Jani drummed her fingers on her thighs. "I saw Anais leaving Feyó's workrooms. Feyó leaked her a copy of the report."

"So we can look forward to interference in all manner of things." Lucien shrugged. "Except you have quite the back-up now, so perhaps it won't be as bad as you fear."

"Maybe." Jani lay her head back and stared through the sunroof at the brilliant sky until her eyes stung. "I left Acadia because of the gangs. I joined the Service because I believed it was different, and we all know how that turned out. You'd think somehow, somewhere, someone would try something new but it's always the same garbage every damn time." She heard Lucien snort. "Do not laugh."

"I'm not." Lucien raised his hand to cover his mouth, then lowered it. "Not at that. It's you and Pierce. You've been through more than any two people I've ever met and you're the ones who think that if you just look hard enough you'll find..."

"Find what? Just say it."

"Peace. Goodness. Light and love at the end of the rainbow. Who the hell knows—I sure don't." Lucien smacked the steering wheel as yet another aspect of the emotional world left him flummoxed. "I don't know why I bother."

Jani rested a hand on his shoulder. "Because you're my moonlight-haired guardian."

"Not even as a joke." After a moment, Lucien smiled. "Speaker of Humanish. Anais will shit herself."

As they followed the curve of the cliffs and the rainbow roofs of Thalassa came into view, Jani felt her heart lighten. Home with all too many complications was still home. "Maybe ní Lano is the spy for Wuntoi."

"You have spies on the brain." Lucien maneuvered the skimmer along the stone-strewn roads that led to the Main House. "If he is, I'll handle him the way I used to handle Anais. I'll feed him mostly junk, see where it winds up." He parked in the mural circle. Then they both gathered their gear and trudged up to the entry.

As the doors opened, the aromas hit Jani first. Lunch had wound down to a scatter of half-filled tables, and the rich scents of chai and coffee managed to slice through whatever spicy concoctions the kitchen had produced. She stood in the middle of the courtyard and soaked it all in, the chatter and the clatter. After a time, she tugged Lucien's sleeve. "Thank you."

Lucien met her eye. "For?"

"Everything." Jani watched his face, caught the look of...not surprise, exactly. Wonder, possibly. He had mentioned more than once that Anais has never thanked him for anything. He'd been a purchase and proper operation had been his function and duty.

He stood silent, as though pondering what she had said. Then some of the old Lucien found its way to the surface. "Feel free to show your appreciation later." He arched his brow as he ran his hand across her lower back, then maneuvered around tables until he reached a group that included Zal and Lano.

Jani watched the way the sunlight that shone through the glass roof made his hair seem to glow. Then she caught the attention of one of the staff. "Do we have milk?"

"Three different kinds." The young female pointed in the direction of the kitchen. "I can get—"

"Later. I'll...let you know." Jani walked around the courtyard, smelling flowers that filled the planters, pondering what awaited her over the next few months. That was when she spotted Theo and one of his techs standing at the far end, near the corridor that led to the labs.

———

"How does it feel?" Theo pushed the limb sealer back into its niche.

Jani worked her new arm, first by rolling her shoulder forwards and backwards, then bending her elbow while twisting her hand one way, then the other. "Feels okay." She pressed fingernails to fingertips, then did a pinch-and-twist of the skin on her forearm. "Still a little too sensitive, though."

"Pain is a warning, remember?" Theo concentrated on making an entry in Jani's medical file.. "It will take a while for it to match the strength of your right arm. Your self-defense sessions with Lucien have led to some pretty impressive muscling. I've programmed the adjustments into the next set of reserves."

"The next set?"

"We always make extras. Never know when you might take off without a word and then get yourself shot." Theo eyed her over the top of his recording board. "News about you spreads like the sand around here. It gets everywhere. We call it JaniNet."

"How reassuring." Jani pushed up her right sleeve and was comparing her forearms when the tech, a new arrival named Deirdre, steered a cart into the room.

"Have you told her yet?" She maneuvered it to a spot beside Theo, then hoisted herself atop a stool. She had a slight build and a cap of blond curls and radiated energy like a sparkler in contrast to her solemn, reserved dominant.

"I was just getting ready to." Theo set the board aside and headed for the cart. "We may have something. We ran preliminary response testing. Reactions to the usual stimuli. Light. Chip-level bioelectrical signal. Touch via the input array." He dragged a small bin off the cart's top shelf and carried it to one of the few areas of bench top that wasn't crammed with instruments or racks of sample cells. "It passed, so we held our collective breath and started piling on the challenges." He popped the bin lid, pulled out a small bundle wrapped in anti-static cloth, and handed it to Jani.

Jani's heart pounded as she felt the hard outlines of what lay within. Removed the cloth and stared down at the scuffed black oval, a nearly identical copy of her old scanpack.

"It is, according to all our results, the hybrid equivalent of the virgin 'pack you received from the Service." Theo bent towards her and tried to catch her eye, like a suitor fearing his gift would be rejected. "We did our best with the case."

"We left it out on the flat during a couple of windstorms to duplicate the scuffing." Deirdre pointed out some of the deeper scratches. "If that's not enough, we can go to Facilities and use one of the sand blasters."

Jani hesitated, recalling the numerous disappointments she had suffered in this room. Then she touched the input pad, and watched the familiar pattern of green activation illumins skitter across the surface. No skips. No delays. "Did the packet I sent help you?"

"We were in the middle of evaluating this one when it arrived." Theo shook a finger. "Not saying the info won't be valuable—I really want to study those brain scans."

"I forgot. We have chips." Deirdre pushed off the stool and dashed out the door.

"How did you get chips?" Jani waited for Theo to answer, but received only a blank look. "Human or idomeni?" More blank. "I've been a bad influence, haven't I?"

"The worst." Theo rubbed his hands together. "I'll leave you to it, then. Take good notes, and yell if you need anything." He started to leave, but stopped when Jani raised her hand.

"Who's the best person on your team to talk to about behavioral?" Jani caught his flicker of curiosity, and ignored it. She didn't want to talk about it now.

"Walid. Maybe Aki." Theo pulled out his handheld. "Should I set something up?"

"In a couple of days. After I get settled." Jani looked around the lab, the controlled chaos she had missed so much and needed to leave all too soon. "Things are going to get a little frantic around here. I'll make the announcement tomorrow."

"I can't wait." Theo walked to the door, shot her a backward glance loaded with questions, then left.

Jani stood still, her thoughts beans in a rattle, cradling her new scanpack like a kitten. Tomorrow would bring the organized tumble of preparations for a long-haul journey and whatever awaited them on Shèrá. But for a few hours, she could be a dexxie, her only concerns the state of her scanpack and what the next stack of documents would reveal.

Deirdre returned bearing a tray heaped with small antistatic chip bags. "Shall we to surgery?"

"We shall." Jani followed her out of the lab and down the hall to the sterile chamber. Time to have some fun.

Books by Kristine Smith

Code of Conduct

Rules of Conflict

Law of Survival

Contact Imminent

Endgame

Echoes of War

As Alex Gordon

Gideon

Jericho

Acknowledgments

Many thanks to my beta readers—Sherwood Smith, Rich Bynum, Dave Klecha, and Julie E. Czerneda—for their comments and encouraging words.

About the Author

KRISTINE SMITH is the author of the Jani Kilian series and other science fiction and fantasy novels and short stories under her own name. As Alex Gordon, she has written the supernatural thrillers Gideon and Jericho. Her fiction has been nominated for the Locus Award for First Novel, Philip K. Dick Memorial Award and the IAFA William L. Crawford Fantasy Award, and she was the 2001 winner of the *Astounding* Award (formerly known as the John W. Campbell Award) for Best New Writer. Prior to becoming a full-time writer, she spent 26 years working in pharmaceutical product R&D. She was born in the Northeast, grew up in the South, and currently lives in the Midwest.

Find out more at her website, www.kristine-smith.com, and sign up for her quarterly more or less newsletter.

Praise for the Jani Kilian Novels of Kristine Smith

"Remarkable...extraordinarily solid...complex and deftly shaded...with vivid, memorable characters—a universe of power politics, commercial and political espionage, and personal and interpersonal relationships."

-Elizabeth Moon

"Deep intrigue, richly diverse characters, and a plot entangled enough to delight—Kristine Smith supercedes herself with each new book."

-Janny Wurts

About Book View Café